Lady Avely's Guide to TRUTH and Magic

MATRONLY
MISADVENTURES
BOOK 1

ROSALIE OAKS

Contents

In which the sky darkens

The ear of a Truth Discernor can be trained to hear very subtle changes in a voice. A bald-faced lie will sound with a tinny echo, while a white lie will merely coat itself with a faint distortion, as if heard through a glass. An exaggeration sounds different again, almost as if it carries itself on a wave. However, simple uncertainty in the speaker can also give rise to these effects, so the Musor must be careful to not jump to any conclusions.
  - from Lady's Avely Guide to Truth and Magic

THE COACH RATTLED and swayed its way along the deplorable English country roads, and Mrs Judith Avely - no, *Lady* Judith Avely, as she must come to think of herself now - felt the toll taken on her weary bones. She was not as young as she used to be, and her body ached with the interminable jolt and clack of the vehicle. Still, there were some benefits to middle-age: a lenient attitude toward afternoon naps, for instance. Judith rather desperately wished to have a nap, though of course it was impossible on this cursed coach.

It was the stage, crowded with travellers, and not the carriage that she could have perhaps allowed herself with her new courtesy title. Yet it hadn't seemed right, to take on airs and graces for *this* particular journey.

Judith held herself erect despite the lurches, and her companions no longer cast her any curious glances. A matron in a plain gown of brown and blue was nothing to excite much interest, though the quality and cut of her clothes clearly marked her out as more well-bred than the usual stage traveller. She had been careful to wear a modest mobcap over her blonde hair and keep her gaze calm and expressionless.

Outside, the countryside bore the first etchings of autumn: trees with russet, primrose, and bronze standing out against the leaden grey of the sky. The coach bowled into the wind but she kept her posture upright, her mind inward. She had a delicate task ahead of her, one that she should have seen to a year ago - if not ten years ago. A familiar pang of guilt assailed her, tightening her lips as the carriage thudded over a particularly monstrous pothole.

The tedium of the journey was relieved when the coach stopped at Exeter to pick up new passengers. A large man who smelled strongly of tobacco squished next to Judith and began a tale generously spiced with exaggeration. She could hear his voice change with the liberty of it, though no one else was the wiser. She shook her head slightly, trying to close out the sound. There was no point employing her Gift now, when it would just tire her further, or worse, muddle her mind.

Briefly she touched the lapis lazuli pendant that hung over her bodice, hoping the talisman stone would keep her thoughts clear. Thankfully, her particular talent was only in Discerning lies. She would not be distracted by the presence of water or jewels or lost things; just the Banbury stories of her fellow travellers.

She must remain focused, she told herself, for she had three weeks only until she must return to Devon. Her task at Sargenet should only take a day or two, as the Duke of Sargen's estate should be on a caretaker staff - unless his sister had already repaired from London. Would the old butler, Fitzroy, still be there? Thank God, the duke himself was still exiled on the continent.

Then, as if echoing her thoughts of Sargen, a sentence caught her ear. It came from the tobacco-scented man next to her; except this time, his voice rang true.

"Have ye all heard about a ghost at Sargenet? I heard some strange talk of it at the tavern."

Judith stiffened and managed not to turn her head. He spoke the truth as he knew it, but she did not put too much store in that: hearsay was unreliable. People would believe all sorts of nonsense, especially in a tavern.

Fortunately, the thin lady, who had been travelling with them since Plymouth, asked the tobacco-scented man to cite his sources.

"A stable lad from Sargenet," he said, overturning the objection neatly and with satisfaction. "From the horse's mouth, as it were. He told me that a ghastly skull glooms round the library, weeping blood."

Judith frowned. Ghosts didn't exist. It must be something the stable-hand had invented to amuse himself, to compete with the tobacco man's own tall tales. Unless it was some *other* kind of apparition?

Then a farmer spoke, wedged between the thin lady and a cleric. "Ay, folks reckon it is the ghost of the old duke - trouble-maker that he was."

Judith creased her brow at this second confirmation of the story. Yet the old duke was long dead, cut down in his prime, like so many of the Sargens. It was unlikely his ghost would make such a delayed appearance, especially in the library, for he had reputably been a man of swords and horses. Furthermore, although there was a secret strain of magic throughout England's population, as far as she knew it did not extend to the existence of phantoms from beyond the veil.

Her companions, however, were eager to speculate. "Could it be the young Duke of Sargen returned to haunt us?" suggested the thin lady. "He was off in Spain, wasn't he? Maybe he died abroad by foul means and he wants to come home."

Something skewered in Judith's heart at the idea. Yet the current duke was too vain to appear as a skull, and moreover too wily - and powerful - to get himself killed.

She spoke at last. "Young duke? The current Duke of Sargen is older than I."

The thin lady gave her a pitying look. "It is different for men, isn't it, love?"

Judith acknowledged it with a small nod. She was a matron and a widow, with two grown children. The duke had yet to marry and was gallivanting about the continent: for all intents and purposes he was in his prime while she was on the downward slide to the grave.

These lowering reflections were cut short by the tobacco-scented man, who leant forward with an air of import. "Whichever duke it was, he's gone and killed someone."

This time Judith's head did snap round. "Whatever can you mean?"

"The skull bashed someone on the head." The large man drew his chin back into his jowls, then suddenly whacked his head forward in a sudden, vicious jab. "Like that. Brained 'em. Dead on the drawing room floor."

Judith narrowed her eyes as everyone gasped. There was a flat note of mendacity in his voice now: a lie, or his own particular spin on the story. She very much doubted that anyone had died at all, let alone by such a vulgar method.

"Do you know why the skull was enraged?" asked the thin lady, with bated breath.

"'Cos of a book, I heard."

There was general confoundment.

"Found next to the body," confirmed the farmer. "A big book. Mayhap the old duke didn't like it. He was never one for reading, I hear tell."

Judith politely did not roll her eyes. Still, it was a curious story. Perhaps the rumours were based on some fact, though she could scarcely credit the idea of a death in the ducal drawing room. The duke's sister, Lady Agatha, would not allow it.

"The young duke always had trouble following him," said the thin lady wisely. "Maybe the ghost is after him - think of all those men he has killed."

"Two men," said Judith. Two was more than enough.

"What were the names of his victims?" asked the cleric. "*I* heard that the skull goes by the name of Fred."

Judith sighed. It had been Lord Charles Garvey, more recently, and Sir Edwin Barnes, when the duke was twenty or so. No Freds. Regardless, the rest of the travellers began the arduous task of sifting through all possible local Fredericks who might have turned into a murderous skeleton. It was all arrant speculation, based in pure fancy.

Nonetheless, a trickle of unease crept across Judith's shoulders. What mischief was brewing at Sargenet? She only hoped that any skulls would not impede her own undertaking there. Who could be behind such foolery, and for what reason?

Outside, the wind battered at the trees, making the first scarlet leaves swirl downwards. Ignoring the other passengers, Judith turned her mind to her children, wondering how they fared at this moment. They must already be at sea, on the way to Sark, two blonde heads turned toward the horizon, their minds full of youthful dreams. Or, more likely, their heads were bent close together, plotting some devilry.

Still, she would not become overly concerned. Even if her daughter Elinor was to commit an indiscretion, she would be married within a month. It would be unkind to indulge in righteous judgement if life (or to be precise, Elinor's behaviour) unfolded differently to how one might think best. Judith might play the upright mother, guiding her children with conscientious advice, but she was old enough to know that young people would make their own errors, regardless of the wisdom one imparted. That was only right: it was the privilege and the burden of youth to make mistakes.

The carriage lurched, and Judith stiffened her spine. The problem arose when one had to redeem one's errors of judgement. You could only hope that no irrevocable damage had been done.

Her fingers ran over the unfamiliar absence where her wedding band used to be. She had given the ring to her daughter before she left. It felt strange to no longer have it on her finger now, though it had been twelve years since Nicholas had died. She had continued to wear it, for her children's sake, even though there had been a time when she had wrenched it off and thrown it across the room.

Despite her anger, old grief echoed through Judith, faint but intimate. She knew Nicholas would have loved to set sail with his children to Sark. She could just imagine his blue eyes alight with curiosity, his rich brown hair tousled by the wind…. He had not aged in her memories of him. Although her own face was now showing lines and shadows, she still envisioned Nick's as young and smooth.

Outside, the hedgerows and hills of Sargen county were achingly familiar. She had walked along these laneways with Nicholas in springtime twenty-three years ago, her hand tucked into his arm, the world alight with the pleasure of their courting.

They had both lived a few miles either side of Sargen, so they had found plenty of excuses to meet one another in the village or the woods between them.

Nicholas had also been teaching her all he knew of Discernment. They shared the same Gift, though she had known little of it compared to his family's secret legacy. She had been thirsty for the knowledge of it, just as her daughter Elinor was now. Nicholas had been a font of knowledge, his own quick mind matching hers as they discussed and practiced the subtleties of Discernment, even though his Gift ranged more broadly than her specific talent. He had been a charming teacher, his initial reserve giving way to warmth. They had laughed together, and she had trusted him implicitly.

Would Robert look like him? She felt certain that he would. A twist of shame and anger squirmed inside her belly.

LATE IN THE AFTERNOON, the coach pulled into an inn, an old stone building with lichened walls. It was her destination: the Gryffin, a respectable accommodation at the edge of Sargen village.

She squeezed past the tobacco-scented man and nodded at the others as she stepped down from the carriage. Wincing, she stretched her neck with a faint crack, and turned back to retrieve her valise. The inn was busy with arrivals and departures, but she managed to gain the attention of the innkeeper and bespeak a private room.

The innkeeper ran an eye over her plain gown and tired face, resting momentarily on the ornate gold setting for her lapis. "Whom do I have the pleasure of serving, my lady?"

Judith paused. "Lady Avely." She might as well take advantage of the courtesy title that had come with the pendant. Perhaps it would throw the locals off the scent, if they were to hear of her presence. They would only remember Miss Judith Horis, who became Mrs Nicholas Avely some twenty years ago. They would not expect 'Lady Avely' to be one and the same.

The form of address sounded strange on her lips and she lifted her chin. The innkeeper bowed, taking the valise and leading her upstairs. He pushed open the door, revealing a small but well-appointed room: a bed, cupboard, and armchair ranged along a wall, facing a window with an oak dresser. She crossed to the dresser, glad to see the view overlooked the fields beyond, rather than the noisy yard. A small river ran across the scene, thick with reeds.

Turning, she thanked the man and pressed a coin into his hand. He informed her that a supper tray would be brought up for her in an hour. She bethought herself of another important matter.

"Do you serve drinking chocolate?"

He named an exorbitant price. She sighed. It wasn't affordable on her widow's pension, despite the title, for she had yet to sort out the financial arrangements that accompanied it. It was only in the last month that Nicholas's services had been fully recognised, and she was yet to feel any of the advantages other than a new mode of address.

"Supper will be sufficient." She nodded.

With the innkeeper gone, she locked the door and turned to take a deep breath in the quiet of the room. What a relief to be alone. Not only was she away from those loquacious carriage-fellows and their ridiculous stories, but she was apart from her children, independent from them at last. She smiled to herself. Wasn't it usually the children who were keen to flee the nest? Yet it was a calming sensation to realise that here she had no one to worry about except herself; no household to oversee, no youthful dramas to untangle, no scandal to scotch. Until Elinor returned to

England, of course. Her brother Peregrine, too, would no doubt land himself in trouble somewhere along the line.

For now, Judith was all alone, and she revelled in a soothing sense of freedom, even as she knew an unpleasant task faced her on the morrow.

She sank into the armchair. Perhaps it was time for that nap. Ah, the freedoms and advantages of age.

Yet, as she settled back in the cushions, a faint noise made her pause.

It was a rhythmic whisper, as if someone was breathing in the room. Judith's first unfortunate thought was of a menacing skull, conjured by the coach tales, and she shivered. She pursed her lips and looked around, searching the room for any drafts. The window was shut tightly, the cupboard empty, and only a trunk squatted under the bed. No skull, thank goodness.

Yet the raspy breathing continued, close by. As she listened, it began to sound almost like ... snoring.

The snoring of a small person, perhaps. One with a tiny nose and quick, even breaths. A suspicion formed in her mind.

Judith crept toward the dresser. A gap lay between the wood and the wall, creating a dark alleyway protected from the rays of the setting sun. She peered into the shadowy gap.

Her surmise was correct. A small bat hung from a crevice, its brown wings folded neatly round its body. The faint snoring emanated from its little furry face.

Judith's eyes ran downwards, unsurprised to see a small pile of fabric on the floor. A gown, by the looks of it, yellow and crumpled.

Hmm. A vampiri resident. Or a passing visitor, like herself?

Whoever it was, they would not be rising until sunset.

Judith moved the armchair so she could view the vampiri's hidey-hole, and ate her supper of meat, potatoes, and gravied vegetables, then availed herself of hot water for bathing. Twilight fell, the sky briefly lacing itself with pink before darkening to black. Thoughtfully, she closed the curtains and lit some candles. Nothing stirred in the room, except for the faint snoring that still whispered from behind the dresser.

She took up her knitting, repressed a pang of wistfulness for chocolate, and kept half an eye on the dresser.

Not long after sunset, her patience was rewarded.

In which a duke thunders home

A Discernor is advised to practice her magic when well rested and in companionship with a vampiri. The inevitable Bemusement will be reduced by the blood bond alone, however, having one's vampiri companion in close vicinity will further improve one's mental clarity.
 - from *Lady Avely's Guide to Truth and Magic*

FROM BEHIND THE CUPBOARD, a tiny head peeped out, topped with curly hair.

Judith leaned forward with interest to see a piquant face, heart-shaped under a pile of curls, and bare little shoulders.

Brown eyes widened. The head and shoulders vanished.

Judith waited, then cleared her throat. Silence met her.

She coughed politely.

A small voice floated out. "You saw me, didn't you?"

"I'm afraid so."

"You didn't think I was a faery?" The little head popped out again, brown hair in a tangled mess.

"Uh, no."

"Usually, if someone sees me - if I disappear quickly enough - they put it down to the fair folk."

"I know better." Judith put down her knitting needles, examining the sweet face.

The little eyes narrowed. "How did you even know I was here? I've been sleeping quite unobserved for days."

"I heard snoring."

"No!"

"Very quietly, I assure you."

"Hmph." A reluctant pause, then the creature stepped out, now dressed in a yellow silk gown that was wrinkled, with a dirty hem. A faint smell of hay emanated from her. "I am Miss Marigold Cultor. Who are you, to have such acute hearing?"

"I am ... Lady Judith Avely." Judith stumbled once more on the title. "I am staying here for two nights. I thought I would make your acquaintance and enquire as to your situation. You ought to be resting in a safer place."

Miss Cultor subtly straightened her shoulders. "My situation is quite fine, though I thank you for your concern, my lady." Her voice was an odd mixture of accents: well-bred overtones with the occasional slip into something less cultured.

Judith leaned back into the armchair, considering. "May I ask, who is your blood companion? You can forgive my curiosity when you are alone in an inn."

"I am not alone," asserted Miss Cultor. "I have a Musor companion below."

Judith heard a faint distortion on the last word. "Below?" she queried.

Miss Cultor wrinkled her nose. "Very well, out in the stables."

That explained the pleasant odour of hay. "I wish you would tell me; I am only concerned for your safety and propriety. We Musors and vampiri must look out for each other, especially after the Edicts."

The brown eyes flashed with heightened interest, as well as relief. "So you *are* a Musor. I didn't know there was Ear Musing."

Judith laughed. "My particular strain of Discernment means I know how to listen carefully, that is all. Now, tell me who is looking after you."

"I look after myself," stated Miss Cultor. Then she unbent a little and continued. "I have befriended a young boy, by name of Jimmy. I sensed him casting magic when I was passing through. He is a stable-hand here, and we have a mutually beneficial arrangement. He uses his Gift to soothe the horses, so he is constantly Bemused, as I'm sure you can imagine. Until I came along, everyone thought he was quite the simpleton."

This was true enough; Jimmy no doubt had a clearer mind if he was feeding Miss Cultor every night. The vampiri bond did more than the talisman stones to soothe the effects of Bemusement. However, traditionally a Musor should also offer shelter to his vampiri companion, yet Miss Cultor remained upstairs behind a cupboard.

"Oh? And how do you benefit? It seems an unusual match."

Miss Cutlor's hands twitched, as if she wanted to fold her arms again. "I *like* Jimmy. If you *must* know, I was terribly bored with my last Musor."

"Bored? How so?"

She sniffed. "My last companion was a scholar, a Memor."

Ah. Those Gifted in Memory did tend to be insular, taken up with the vast tracts of knowledge they could store in their heads. "Memors are *occasionally* entertaining conversationalists," ventured Judith.

The vampiri sauntered forward, bare feet showing below the yellow hem. "Not this one. All he did was read books on Ancient Greece, or have scholarly discussions which I could not attend. You know how it is with the Edicts."

Judith nodded. Ever since the French Revolution, King

George had passed secret edicts among the Musor circles to keep the vampiri well hidden. It rather curtailed Musor-vampiri relations, at least in public. Miss Cultor must have been relegated to the bedroom while her scholar embarked on his learned dialogues and mental contortions.

Miss Cultor's lips twisted. "I wanted no part of his boring arguments anyway. I needed a change, so we parted a few days ago. I can tell you, Jimmy has been much more fun." The last was said with a hint of belligerence.

"Hm." Looking at Miss Cultor, Judith rather thought that the change had wrought some unfortunate effects as well. "What about your clothes? Can I assist you in washing them? I can request some more hot water."

Miss Cultor shrugged, coming to a halt a few feet away and sinking to sit cross legged on the green rug. "That is kind of you, but what is the point? My gown shall just become dirty again."

"You are determined to be hoydenish, I see," observed Judith. "And why are you sleeping up here, and not in the stables?"

For the first time, the little face showed a flash of regret. "There is a cat. He is a cursed nuisance. He managed to slice open my ankle a few days ago. I am safer here, but that is why my gown is so dirty; I have to drag it with me."

As a bat, Miss Cultor would be able to fly out the window but she'd have to carry her clothes between her teeth, or otherwise creep down in her human form. At least, Judith consoled herself, she wasn't so far devoid of propriety as to appear naked before poor Jimmy.

Judith considered. "Well, if you are set upon this arrangement, would you like me to escort you to the stables tonight?"

"Oooh, yes please." Miss Cutlor's face brightened. "That would be most helpful. I think Jimmy is gambling tonight with the visiting groomsmen. I don't want to miss it."

"Are you certain I can't sew up your hem first?" The ragged

edging was giving Judith a slight twitch. "Or brush your hair somehow?"

"I do miss my accoutrements," admitted Miss Cultor. "I don't suppose you have a vampiri comb?"

"No," said Judith. "You could try my fork?"

"I've tried that," said Miss Cultor cheerfully. "Doesn't work. Bird's nest it will have to be. Jimmy won't mind."

"I mind," said Judith, but she let it be. Mothering this little creature would probably annoy them both. Perhaps she missed her children more than she thought. "How do you keep hidden from Jimmy's friends? In order to respect the Edicts?"

"I watch from the rafters," replied Miss Cultor. "The other fellows don't look up, and if they do, they'll think I'm a faery."

Judith raised her brows. "I'm not so certain about *that*." She pictured a circle of inebriated stablehands and tutted. "At least you will be out of reach. I will pop you up there myself."

She rose and clicked her valise open, pulling out her blue and red paisley shawl. It had a handy pocket sewn into one side, used previously for a similar purpose. She showed it to Miss Cultor and carefully lifted the vampiri in, tucking her close and ignoring her questions about who else had previously ridden in such a way.

Judith set off down the passageway and stairs, hoping she would not be stopped.

She passed no one. The guests must all be eating or in the tap room. She sailed past the foyer with a regal air, knowing that her age and bearing of consequence would discourage any questions. Nobody was very curious about a middle-aged woman. Nonetheless, she stepped out into the night with a sigh of relief.

The carriage yard was quiet. One postboy kept watch for any late arrivals. Far above, a waxing moon rose in a clear sky. The air smelled of horses and hay, and Judith marched across to the arch leading into the stables.

Peering through the doorway, she saw five groomsmen sitting

round a table. Discreetly, she retreated back outside, taking shelter in the shadow of a wall.

"Are you *certain* you want to be left in there?" she hissed to Miss Cultor. "It seems rather unsuitable." She would not, for example, leave her own daughter in those circumstances, so why should she leave this little creature there?

"Pshaw." Miss Cultor's head emerged from the paisley pocket. "It is far less vulgar than the duke's residence I've just visited."

Judith looked down, surprised. "The duke's residence? Do you mean Sargenet?"

"Yes, my scholar visited there, hence I did too." Miss Cultor shuddered. "Ghastly experience. There were skulls floating about."

"Truly? I heard something like that, but I dismissed it as nonsense."

"Unfortunately true," said Miss Cultor regretfully. "Levitating through the ballroom. Quite tasteless."

Miss Cultor's voice was free of any deceit, but Judith's attention snagged on a detail. "The ballroom? I heard it was in the library."

"Oh, yes, there was blood on some books too."

Overhead, the lamps of the courtyard flickered, as if an unseen hand had passed across the wick. The cool night air slipped along Judith's collar bones, making her shiver. "Blood? Was anyone hurt?" She remembered, suddenly, the tobacco-man's tale of murder.

"Oh no," Miss Cultor grinned, showing tiny fangs. "Just a ghost, everyone says."

Judith let out a breath, relieved to hear that the tale of death was unsubstantiated. The postboy watched her curiously and she dropped her chin as if cold, turning her shoulder to hide Miss Cultor.

"A ghost?" she murmured. "Nonsense. It must be an Illusion, cast by a Musor."

Miss Cultor nodded, folding her arms over the sleeve of the pocket. "I suspected as much. I went to investigate the blood - a natural curiosity on my part, you understand - but I couldn't smell it. I usually have a good nose for such things, so I would say it was a weak Illusion only, despite the deep red trickles. In the library, of all places! Mr Nottley was most unimpressed."

"Mr Nottley?"

"My scholar, my last companion. He was incensed at the idea of blood near his precious books."

It was Judith's turn to shudder. "Dreadful. I wonder what purpose it served."

"A family prank," suggested Miss Cultor. "The duke's brother is there, with his wife and children. Though, come to think of it, they all seemed quite distressed by the occurrence. Now, can you please take me inside to Jimmy?"

"Oh dear," muttered Judith, ignoring Miss Cultor's request. How was she to conduct her business if the house was over-run by the duke's family? "Do you mean the duke's brother, the Earl of Triven, and his countess?"

"Yes. And a horde of young boys." Miss Cutlor raised a brow. "What does it matter to you?"

Judith paused, aware of the postboy. She must look like a madwoman talking to herself. It paid to be careful; she didn't want to fall afoul of the Edicts.

"I planned to visit Sargenet myself," she whispered to Miss Cultor. "Tomorrow. Now I wonder if I must delay."

"Well, no need to delay me too," said Miss Cultor acerbically. "Will you take me into the stables please? It is none of my business if you want to run headlong into a haunted house."

At that moment, a large white cat stalked out of the archway, its whiskers bristling. With a squeak, Miss Cultor vanished inside her pocket.

"Shoo it away!" came the muffled shriek.

Judith eyed the beautiful creature, prepared to chase it off if it showed any interest in having bat for dinner. The cat prowled over, its long tail lashing slightly.

Carefully, Judith bent to stroke it, hoping it now looked as if she were talking to the feline. "What else did you see at Sargenet? You say the family were distressed?" She paused. "Were the servants much discomposed?"

"The servants were blamed," said Miss Cultor. An eye appeared, then vanished. "Don't touch that bully!"

"Blamed?" Of course they were. Judith felt a stab of worry, even as she absentmindedly ran her fingers over soft white fur.

"Yes, the butler Broughton came under a lot of question."

"Broughton? I thought the butler was Fitzroy?"

"Not the one I saw," came the indistinct reply. Judith wondered why Fitzroy had been turned off. It was true that he must be elderly now. He had been rather old when Judith first visited Sargenet as a girl all those years ago. Or perhaps he had just seemed old to her youthful eyes.

Before she could question Miss Cultor further, however, the cat suddenly shot off in a blur of white. The sound of hoofbeats and wheels sounded beyond the yard. The postboy leapt to attention, running forward to greet the late arrival.

An equipage rolled through the gates: a high-strung curricle, drawn by two well-matched horses. Lanterns hung from the rear and front, glowing gold in the darkness.

The driver, a tall man in a riding cape, guided the horses to standing. He leapt down, handed the reins over and issued curt instructions to the postboy.

Judith stilled. The driver's face was apparent in the lamplight. It was a handsome face, classically cut, with dark deep-set eyes, black heavy brows, and full lips. His strong jawline was arrogantly tilted and age had cut lines down his cheeks. He was older than when she had seen him last, but Judith recognised him in an instant.

The Duke of Sargen.

He turned his back to her, to retrieve something from the curricle. Responding instinctively, Judith whipped round and bolted into the stables.

Through the arch, she darted behind some hay bales, keeping to the shadows. Her heart pounded. This was ridiculous. She was no longer some girl just out, to be afraid of the big bad duke. She was a matron; older, wiser, and nine years had passed since she had seen him last. There was no need for these dramatics. Why, then, was she hiding in the hay?

The smell was sweet and the sound of horses snuffling came from her right. From the gambling table, three pairs of eyes turned toward her. The others had passed her on the way out, having gone to help the postboy with the chestnuts.

"Are you orright, my lady?" said one of the stablehands; possibly Jimmy, for he looked young and confused.

Judith cleared her throat. Against her bodice, Miss Cultor was safe in her shawl pocket, if perhaps a little suffocated with the recent dash. Loosening the fabric a little, Judith stepped out from behind the hay bale, still very aware that the Duke of Sargen was outside in the courtyard. Had he seen her wild retreat? Would he come inside? Her pulse stuttered.

"I am fine, thank you," she replied. "I was simply, er, looking for some straw for a box - for my kitten."

"Plenty of hay here, my lady. Can I fetch some for you?"

"No, I will do it myself," she replied, and edged toward the rear wall where the hayloft ladder stood. Three pair of eyes followed her. Curse it, this was going to be more difficult than she'd thought.

However, the duke's horses provided a commotion. Two beautiful, exhausted, chestnut stallions were led in by the stablehands, immediately drawing the admiring gazes of all those present.

Quick as a flash, Judith opened her shawl and plucked Miss Cultor out. She placed her on the top rung of the ladder. "Shoo! Quick!" she hissed.

As a supernatural creature, Miss Cultor was fast. One second she was there on the ladder, the next she had shimmied into the loft. Judith let out a sigh of relief, tucking her shawl back round her and turning to face the music.

The duke was not there. Thank God. He must have gone inside for refreshment. Did he intend to keep travelling to Sargenet tonight? It seemed as if he were in a great hurry, pushing his horses and travelling after dusk.

He had probably heard of the trouble in his household and decided that skulls in the ballroom were not to be borne. As she watched, she saw the stablehands were preparing another two horses to drive the final leg. He must be willing to risk it in the moonlight.

Judith bit her lip, suddenly struck by a realisation. If the duke had returned, was her own visit still necessary? Surely now that his grace was home, he would rectify any wrongs that had been done in his name. He would see to it that Robert was treated better; he would do what she should have done a year ago.

Her hands twisted together. No: she owed it to Nicholas's memory and her own conscience to carry this through. And it galled her to think of the duke taking on this particular responsibility. She would continue on, and quietly approach the servant's quarter tomorrow. It would be difficult to manage, but then again, the duke would be storming around, shouting about skulls, so perhaps in the chaos of his return she could slip in and out unnoticed.

Of course, the duke would learn of her visit, but she doubted he would seek her out. Or would he be pleased to see her, after all? She could imagine his dark eyes lighting up as he strode forward to take her hand, and the ghost of his lips on her cheek.

She shook the thought off. It was a nonsensical thought, quite worthy of a girl in her first season. He had forgotten her. He had been gone for nine years, without word or letter. He did not care anymore.

Judith became aware that she remained standing by the hayloft, her fists clenched in her skirts. A few of the stable lads were giving her side-long looks. She glanced round and made a show of adjusting her matronly cap. Then she grit her teeth and gathered up a handful of hay. This is what came of indulging one's motherly instincts: one's sleeves were dirtied with grass.

"Cor," said one of the stablehands. "I think I just saw a faery!"

He was wide-eyed, gazing into the rafters. Judith glanced up, just in time to see Miss Cultor give her a smug wink and vanish into the shadows.

"Nonsense," said Judith crossly. "You've been drinking." Straw pricked through her gloves. She gave a nod to the assembled company, and marched out.

The courtyard was empty, the dust settled, the walls casting deep shadows. Her eyes searched the depths for a tall figure lurking to waylay her. But no one was there.

Relief, and maybe a touch of disappointment, made her shoulders droop.

She dropped the hay beside the drinking trough and scuttled back through the foyer, in stark contrast to her stately exit earlier. Heart beating fast, she darted along the passageway and up the stairs. Thank goodness, he must be still drinking his ale. She had escaped unseen and unknown.

Letting herself back into her little room, she tutted at her own reluctance to see him. Yes, they had fought terribly when they last spoke, but that was nine years ago. That heated conversation had long cooled. They were older, wiser, more temperate now. Water under the bridge, forsooth.

She was still hurt, she realised. The waters still roiled and seethed, for all that she was a matron now. She was still upset that he had left without a word, and stayed away for nine whole years. And long before that, he had shown himself to be unworthy of her affections.

The memories still rankled.

Interlude I

Twenty-three years earlier

The first time Judith saw the Duke of Sargen was at the Avely country party.

She had known that Nicholas counted the duke as a friend, yet she had not expected that his grace would deign to attend the small country ball. Wouldn't the duke be too busy seducing London ladies or fighting duels? She'd heard all the stories about him and although Nicholas dismissed most of them as exaggeration, she thought there must be some truth to them. She was only nineteen but her burgeoning Gift made her more cynical than her age should have allowed.

Nicholas had already danced with her once when the duke's name was announced from the door. It felt like half the occupants of the room turned to stare at his grace, all of them astonished that one of such esteemed rank should appear in their midst. He stood in the doorway, a vision of virility and power, ink-black hair curling round his ears, piercing eyes sweeping the room, booted feet in an arrogant stance. He did not see Judith, standing with her hand in Nick's, as they were near-hidden by the bulk of Mrs Peon.

"Oh, it's Dacian," said Nick. "Look at him posing for the masses. I'd best lend him some support."

Nicholas let go of Judith's arm to disappear across the floor and reappear next to the duke. They made a striking pair: Nick's handsome, relaxed countenance next to the duke's classical good looks.

She had turned away to talk with a friend and to dance with another. When it came to her favourite dance to a more stately tune, she looked again for Nicholas. It would not matter if they danced twice together, as soon all would know of their engagement.

Instead, the Duke of Sargen appeared before her. He had the Dowager Faudley in tow and wrangled an introduction on the spot. Lady Faudley introduced her as the Viscount Horis's oldest granddaughter, recently out in society. The duke bowed.

"May I have this dance?" he enquired, his eyes bright with admiration and possibly something else. Too much wine, Judith suspected. "I couldn't help but notice that you are uncommonly graceful on the floor, Miss Horis."

"Oh." Judith was flustered but immediately vowed not to appear as a blushing ingenue before his grace. After all, she had to make a good impression, as Nicholas's future wife. She inclined her head. "It would be my pleasure."

His grace led her onto the floor. As they waited for the music, he remarked teasingly that she seemed to smile less for him than her last partner.

"How could I not?" she replied, and mustered up a reluctant smile. "I do not know you at all, your grace. I suppose you commonly attract simpers merely for your title."

He grinned. "Oh, and here I thought they were for my good looks."

Somehow, this open arrogance was both infuriating and attractive. She frowned at him, squelching the wave of interest that swept through her body. The music began and she curtsied. "You are mistaken, your grace. Our society values your title more than your looks, and that is why everyone smiles at you."

He gave a mock sigh. "I believe you are right. I am unloved for myself; such is the burden I bear." He paused, passing by her ear. "Still, am I not handsome?"

She couldn't help but laugh. "A little handsome, yes." Clearly, also a little drunk.

Turning to look at him, she could admit to herself that he was more than a little handsome. His black hair was gleaming in the candlelight, his dark lashes unfairly long, his eyes sparkling. It was an alluring sight, even if the seductive glimmer was assisted by champagne.

He took her hands in his warm grasp. "Well, Miss Horis, you are lovely. And you are not a duchess, so you know my smiles are a true homage."

This time she gave him a cross look from below her lashes. Inebriation aside, surely the duke knew that he was flirting with Nicholas's intended? Had Nicholas not told him of his secret betrothal? She knew the two men to be good friends and Nicholas had seen the duke in the last week.

The cross look only made him grin again, lighting his face from a mystery to a radiance. "Don't you like being called lovely, Miss Horis?"

She let go of his hands. "I do not appreciate empty flirtations."

"It was not empty! You are indeed lovely."

She blushed even more rosily, for she could Discern that he was telling the truth. What on earth was she to make of *that*?

"Thank you, your grace," she said meekly.

He gave her a surprised look as the dance took him past her again. "Proper respect for my title, this time, Miss Horis?"

"Merely humouring you, your grace," she shot back. Perhaps he believed the lies he told; the most charming people had that facility, she had observed.

The music swirled round them and she felt a warmth and headiness. Perhaps she, also, had consumed too much wine this evening. As he escorted her off the dance floor, the duke began talking of the last ball he had attended in London, comparing it unfavourably to this one both in intimacy, dance partners, and quality of champagne. Judith entered into this badinage willingly enough, but when he claimed that all of London's beauties could not compete with herself, she frowned and told him that his lies did him no credit.

"It's not a lie." His dark eyes glinted at her and she smiled back patronisingly, and with some relief. This time she could hear the flat note in his voice. Unbeknownst to him, she could detect his empty flattery more than most, which would put her beyond his power. She was reassured to know it.

He stayed by her side but she avoided his gaze, looking over the dancers to see if she could spy Nicholas. She found him dancing with Miss Eaton, his head bent toward her.

"The smiles have gone again," remarked the duke. "What did I do this time? I hope it wasn't my dancing."

"You dance well enough," she allowed, for it was true. He was almost as good a dancer as Nick, who was light on his feet. The duke had danced with more languor, or perhaps it had been a slower tune. "I am merely wondering why you have attended such a humble ball."

"I've known Nicholas Avely since we were boys," the duke replied. "He asked me to attend, so here I am."

She was thankful when Nicholas's dance at last came to an end. She cast about for an excuse to leave the duke's side. However, at that moment, the supper bell rang.

Her insides tangled with opposing emotions: surprise, annoyance ... and, oddly, apprehension.

"Ah!" The duke's eyes lit up. "Are we being called into supper? I always have the luck. You must join me, Miss Horis."

She could hardly refuse. Curse it, where was Nicholas? He was supposed to have claimed the supper dance. Across the room, she caught sight of him again, corralled into escorting Miss Eaton. Nick gave Judith an expressive lift of his eyebrow and smiled. He glanced at the duke and then, strangely, winked.

Oblivious to this, the duke claimed Judith's arm again and they proceeded into the dining room.

She enjoyed that supper, against her best instincts. The Duke of Sargen was a good companion: witty, warm, and well-mannered, even as he knocked back several more glasses of wine. They found much to talk about, from the recent vote against further war in America, to the Spanish victory in Menorca, and the latest style of hats in London. He continued to flirt with her, and she continued to repress his attempts.

When the blackcurrant pie was served for dessert, he announced with mock arrogance that the Sargenet blackberries were far superior and offered to prove it by taking Judith to the blackberry bushes hidden at the edge of the woods on his property. Before she could decline, Judith's friend, Miss Turnow, sitting opposite, overheard and applauded the notion, inviting herself and her brother along for the expedition in two days' time. Judith laughed and admitted that she was fond of blackberries, but noted that they would have to wear old clothes, which might not suit his grace's consequence.

"Nonsense," said the duke. "I am handsome in any clothes."

He smiled at her. "And you will make a sackcloth look graceful, Miss Horis."

She gave him a derisive look at this lie and briefly considered telling him that she was betrothed to Nicholas. However, it was still a secret and she didn't want to presume too much in the duke's raillery. His grace undoubtedly would have flirted with any female supper companion, lovely or otherwise.

Yet, when she met his eyes, they were admiring, his smile expressive as he leaned toward her. She found herself smiling back, as if they shared a secret, as if they were somehow united against the rest of the party. As if they were boon companions on a private adventure.

Realising this, she gave her head a short sharp shake, as if trying to dislodge water from her ear. This would not do. Her adventure was with Nicholas. She had promised her life to him. He, at least, was a decent, responsible man, and not one to drink excessive amounts of wine, or kill someone in a duel.

"Did an insect land on you?" enquired the duke.

"Yes," she said. "A vexatious one, but I have vanquished it."

She was glad after supper when Mrs Miranda Bleau claimed the duke's attention. Judith had heard whispers of a liaison between the young man and the pretty, dark-haired widow, and she saw that the rumours were based in truth. Mrs Bleau placed a very proprietorial hand on the duke's forearm as she led him away, leaning her gleaming ebony head close to his. They looked very well together. Judith saw the duke dispense the same wicked smile to the widow and look down appreciatively at her low-cut bodice.

It was just as she had surmised and had been told: the duke was a rake. Nothing more and nothing less.

She was glad she had not been taken in by his charms. Nicholas might not have quite such a striking confidence, but at least within his regard she was safe from such fickleness.

As if the duke felt her censorious gaze, he glanced her way. When he saw her disapproving expression, his face stiffened. Later, he abandoned Mrs Bleau and returned to Judith's side, attempting to win another smile from her. Judith was cool, wondering yet again why Nicholas left her so exposed to the attentions of his disreputable friend.

NICHOLAS CALLED the day following the ball, to take her walking. Maid in tow, they strolled along the flowered path to the hills that unfolded behind her father's house. The air was warm with the flush of summer and even the grasses were full of tiny flowers and the movement of bees and insects.

"Why did you leave me with the duke?" she challenged him. "I had hoped to eat supper with you."

Nicholas gave a little grimace, holding her hand in his own as they stepped along the well-worn path. "You will think poorly of me."

"Tell me."

"I wanted Mother to see that you are comfortable in the highest circles. She only wants the best for me," he added apologetically.

Nicholas's mother wanted him to marry up. A rector's daughter, albeit a viscount's granddaughter, was not an ascension. Nicholas must have wanted some of the duke's nobility to rub off on her before he presented Judith as his bride.

"Was he an awful flirt?" Nicholas cast her a glance out of the corner of his eye.

Judith huffed. "Dreadful. Couldn't take his eyes off Mrs Bleau."

"They've been, er, intimate for a while now."

"So I gathered."

"Still, he's a good fellow."

Judith murmured something noncommittal.

Nicholas sighed. "I have bad news: I must go away to London tomorrow. I have a few things to attend to before we are married."

"What things?" objected Judith. "Surely they can wait?" A nearby sheep bleated in agreement.

"I must obtain permission from His Majesty, for a start," Nicholas smiled. "Though of course he cannot object to you, my darling."

It still seemed ridiculous to Judith that they needed a royal seal for their union, but as Nicholas served the Crown in a secret and important position, his marriage had to be vetted. In case she was a French spy, she supposed, setting out to seduce an English officer.

"I suppose I could cajole some secrets out of you," she teased. "Especially with my Gift. You'd better warn His Majesty."

"You don't need your Gift with your beautiful eyes." Nicholas bent closer and his lips brushed her cheek in a light kiss. Then he drew back, his eyes flicking to Betsy, who walked several paces behind them, her gaze discreetly lowered. "However, until I have royal permission, I cannot present myself to your father."

Judith sighed. She rather enjoyed having a secret engagement, but she also longed to tell the world of her happiness. "You can trust Betsy. How long will you be gone?"

"Two weeks at least. I leave tomorrow."

The warm sun suddenly felt tiresomely hot. "What shall I do without you?" she complained. "You were meant to come with us to the duke's blackberries." She paused. "Have you told his grace of our attachment?"

A brief look of discomfort crossed Nicholas's face. "I haven't told him," he confessed. "I trust Dacian, of course, but he knows the king personally. Better not risk it."

There was some odd note of discord in his voice which Judith dismissed. Most likely, Nicholas regretted not telling the duke of their engagement, after watching his grace flirt with her at supper last night. She tried not to blush, and nodded. "Very well, I won't mention it to him."

In which there is unsettling news

The barb and thrust of social interrogations can be an ideal place to practice Truth Discernment, though it may well leave you disillusioned with society.

   - from *Lady Avely's Guide to Truth and Magic*

JUDITH DIDN'T SLEEP until she heard the muted jangle and thudding hooves of the duke leaving the inn. He certainly was in a hurry. His grace was not one to be frightened by ghost tales, so there must be something else afoot, she thought, as she finally fell into a troubled sleep, old memories surfacing to plague her.

The next morning, she resisted the temptation to order break-fast chocolate, and made do with pound bread, ham, and coffee in her room. Halfway through the hot black coffee, Judith lifted her head to listen.

The faint snoring sound had resumed. Judith was relieved. Perhaps she could convince Miss Cultor to travel back to Devon with her, or even on to Cornwall. The castle would be an ideal place for the vampiri, especially as it was to be exempt from the

Edicts. Certainly, it was better than amongst these stablehands with that rascally cat. Furthermore, they could find something to brush her hair.

Finishing breakfast, she washed Miss Cultor's gown and hung it to dry (discreetly arrayed inside her cupboard). Then she literally and figuratively straightened her spine. There was no point putting it off any longer. She had delayed this duty for long enough, and the sin only compounded with time.

She dressed herself in deep grey. The gown was one of her more subdued pieces, suitable to a matronly chaperone, worn during her daughter's first season. Although Judith had not worn her weeds for several years, she still had a little widow's veil which would suit her purpose admirably today, concealing her features. She did not want anyone to recognise her, though she hadn't visited Sargen in the long years since her father's death.

The golden filigree of her lapis pendant gave an elegant touch but she tucked it into her bodice. Someone might see it and recognise its import.

Thus arrayed, Judith walked through the village, admiring the avenue of old buildings, and smelling the rich scents of the countryside. The houses were tightly packed together but softened by flowers, greenery, and the occasional old Tudor black and white fronting. Today was market day, so stalls were set up on the green and the local shops were bustling.

It was clear autumn weather, and by the time she reached the village green, she was quite hot in her high-cut gown and stifled by her veil. She meandered around, buying fruit and bread, and listening to the conspiratorial tones of speculation rising and falling between the vegetable stands. At one point, near the pumpkins, she clearly heard the duke's name mentioned. The village grapevine must be well aware that he had finally returned to Sargenet, with a skull to thank for this courtesy. She only hoped it wasn't anything more, though the voices held a sombre note.

Perhaps they were recalling the reason the duke had left: the sudden, fatal duel at Lord Garvey's estate, nine years ago.

The Duke of Sargen had left England under a cloud, and Judith knew the cloud had been brewing for years before he finally fled. Notoriously hot-tempered like his father, he had always been embroiled in fights as a boy, and as a man he had not abandoned the habit.

At the age of twenty - it was said - he had killed a man in a duel over some gambling scandal. That should have been enough to have him tried, but although duelling to death was a capital offence, it was rare that the law would pursue the matter - especially in the case of such lofty aristocracy. The officials politely looked the other way, allowing such gentlemen to settle their affairs of honour in their stupid, bloodthirsty ways.

Still, after that youthful mistake, the duke had made an effort to curtail his violent tendencies. More than two decades passed before he did it again. Except this time, instead of following the proper protocols of duelling, he had simply called out Lord Garvey on the spot and killed him.

Judith had heard the story told: how the duke had dragged his lordship outside and ordered him to take his paces, then shot him, his face a mask of cold fury. Lord Garvey had fallen on the gravel, dead through the heart.

She had her own reasons for doubting the story, but she knew at least some of it was true. She had been at the house party at Garvey House all those years ago. The sound of pistol shots had woken her, and she had stumbled to the window to see the moon bedraggled by clouds, but no sight of the culprits. Her window had looked onto the southern terraces, so she wouldn't have been granted a sight of Lord Garvey prone and lifeless.

She hadn't even seen the duke leave that night.

He had fled to Cornwall, it was whispered, and caught a smugglers' boat to the continent rather than risk the scandal of being hauled before the courts. For his grace's grievous disregard for duelling etiquette and the air of summary execution had gone too far. The authorities would act, especially as it came after another infraction.

No one was precisely sure what Lord Garvey's offence had been. Rumour said the duke had simply been offended by Lord Garvey's assessment of his horses. Or his wine. Or that they had some squabble about who had the best claim to a certain fair cyprian. Judith was inclined to believe the last. The duke was hot-headed about his romantic pursuits. There had been more than one attractive widow at the house party that night. Including herself, of course.

Judith sighed, wishing she could hear more of what was said on the village green. Her hearing was good, but not *that* good, in the hustle and bustle of the markets. People sensed, too, when a stranger was near and hushed their tones.

Overly warm in her stuffy gown, she paused to buy a cup of lemonade. Lifting her veil to sip the tangy liquid, she turned to watch the main street, wondering if any of the Sargen family would deign to visit the town on market day.

She guessed right. Two well-dressed ladies promenaded along the main avenue, with mincing steps on the cobblestones. Both of them were tall with their noses in the air. One, thin with dark colouring, was arrayed in a striking red gown with black trimmings, while the other, more plump and blonde, was dressed in a frumpish affair in purple.

Judith recognised the first as Lady Agatha, the duke's spinster sister, still as stylish and assured as ever, though age had dragged her striking features downwards. She had the same dark hair as her brother, with the Sargen height and regal bearing. The heavy brows did not suit her as well, nor did the angular shoulders, and she had never married. She had been left to pick up the management of Sargenet after the duke had left the country. And, it seemed, dismissed poor old Fitzroy and appointed Robert as footman. Judith felt a stirring of anger, examining Lady Agatha's aloof, aristocratic face.

Lady Agatha was accompanied now by Lady Mary, her sister-in-law, who was married to Lord John, the Earl of Triven, the duke and Agatha's brother. The countess was as tall as Lady Agatha, but more well-padded by nature, perhaps because she was usually lost in her books rather than horse-riding. Now she had her hand tucked into Lady Agatha's arm and they walked with their heads straight ahead, not deigning to notice the stir they were causing.

The two ladies turned into a shop door. Judith debated with herself. Her curiosity was piqued by the tales of the skull, and she might overhear something more. Yet she did not want to be recognised by Mary or Agatha.

Fortunately, she had her widow's veil. She gulped down the rest of her lemonade and put down the black netting. Carefully, she ensured that her lapis remained hidden. There was no need to wantonly display a symbol of her Gift upon her person, especially if she was trying to make subtle enquiries.

Judith crossed the road and quietly pushed open the door of the haberdashery.

The store was well lit by large windows at the front. It was a draper's shop as well, full of fabrics of all colours and quality, an array of patterns and textures. The two ladies were on the far side, examining some spools of thicker cloth, and they turned at her entrance. Judith's figure of mourning and bowed head must have appeared unthreatening, for they turned back to their cloth and sent the shopkeeper to fetch some ottoman fabric.

"This one, do you think?" declaimed Lady Agatha, pointing an imperious gloved finger at a red and grey pattern. "The drawing room needs cheering up. We must look at this as an opportunity."

There was a note of defiance in her tone. Judith wondered why they should need new fabrics. Any Illusions should dispel at the touch, leaving no trace behind.

"Not the red, please, dear," said Lady Mary, with a small shudder. "It recalls the blood in the library."

For a startled moment, Judith thought this must refer to some scene of violence, then she recalled Miss Cultor's tale of bloodied books.

"Oh yes," agreed Lady Agatha. "Perhaps this yellow one." She picked up a mustard yellow with green stripes. "The features will match the green curtains."

"You decide, Agatha dear, though we must give a passing consideration to what his grace would like, too."

Judith smiled behind her veil to hear the hierarchy so clearly stated, though the duke was not one to be bossed round by a mere sister, even if Agatha was the older. Perhaps that would all change now that he had returned. Judith edged closer, fingering a lovely blue silk that was soft as a sigh, thinking that it would look beautiful on her daughter Elinor.

Lady Agatha sniffed at Mary's comment. "Dacian cannot question my judgment when he has left me to run the house for the last nine years."

"So wonderful he has returned at last," murmured the countess.

Judith heard the lie in Mary's voice and allowed herself another small smile. It was little wonder that the countess looked with disquiet upon the duke's return. It would be like a lion arriving in a sheep paddock.

"He has been absent too long," agreed Lady Agatha with decision, yet not looking at Mary.

She had not spoken a lie, but Judith squinted through her veil. Lady Agatha was no sheep. She was a lioness, reluctant to give up her territory.

Mary frowned down at a pink striped fabric, her fingers worrying the edges. "I hope his grace has given up his habit of duelling."

This was a euphemism, Judith knew. Mary knew as well as she did that the duel when the duke was twenty was a complete fabrication. It was true that the quarrel had been over an accusation of cheating, but the violence had been instant and unpremeditated, erupting from his volatile Gift.

Nicholas had told Judith about it years ago: how the duke's family had covered it up with the story of a duel. Duelling was a far more honourable excuse, and in line with the Edicts that demanded his grace's powers remain a secret.

"I'm certain Dacian will restrain himself," said Agatha coldly. "He must make himself palatable in order to find a wife."

"A duke is always palatable," said Mary, wisely enough. "You think he will finally settle down?"

Judith was aware of a flash of resentment that these two should gossip about the duke's marriage prospects. Though she knew herself to be guilty of wondering the same thing over the years. When would his grace marry and provide the ducal line with heirs? If he did not, the title would pass to the Earl of Triven, Mary's husband - and then to their children. Felix was the oldest, if Judith recalled correctly, at school now. And his grace was not growing any younger.

"Dacian owes it to his lineage," said Lady Agatha pompously. "If he could be brought to stop philandering on the continent and marry a good English girl, we would all be better for it."

Even Lady Mary must have heard this to be a mere platitude, flat as a tin plate. Lady Agatha would detest having some young woman elevated above her as duchess.

Judith also found the thought depressing. His grace would be in his late forties now, being a few years older than Judith. She couldn't imagine he would be satisfied with a mere girl, even if such alliances were usually acceptable. He'd be bored. Especially after all his cavorting with exotic women farther afield.

She shook her head. Her mind was muddled from employing her Gift. She ought not let it drift about in such a fashion. Her focus must be on the matter at hand, not the duke's amorous exploits. Several though they had been, from all accounts. There was even a whisper that he had once seduced a young Italian count, and she could quite believe it ... and several beautiful widows, of course....

Judith frowned. He had always displayed a taste for widows.

Lady Mary lowered her voice. "I wonder that you don't return to London yourself, my dear, with all that has happened. I must say, I do not approve of a skull that throws books around."

Ah, so there *was* a book in the picture. It was a literary ghost, it seemed. A literary Illusion, Judith reminded herself.

"Don't be ridiculous," said Lady Agatha firmly. "How would a skull throw a book? It has no hands."

Judith nodded thoughtfully, now quite Bemused. The skull must be a distraction from the book. Yet what did a book have to do with anything? The ladies turned to look at her, and she pretended to be nodding at the fabrics. Anxious not to arouse their suspicions, she retreated to a corner where a coal-orange cloth flashed in a pile of silks.

At that moment, the shopkeeper returned with a dark-skinned assistant, both holding an armful of ottoman fabrics. Lady Agatha and Lady Mary lapsed into gentle bickering as the owner showed them the cloths. Lady Mary was holding her own, despite Lady Agatha's strident pronouncements. It might even be that the drawing room would end up clad in blue, as a compromise to suit both dark and blonde hair, even though the countess only visited Sargenet a few times a year.

A handsome young man with black hair entered the drapery, and the ladies called him over.

"Mr Lewis!" said Agatha. "You must help us decide! It is part of your duty as steward." She smiled at him warmly, and Judith examined Sargenet's steward more closely. He was a good-looking fellow, despite a rather terse mouth, with striking dark brows to match his black hair. He also looked strangely familiar - or perhaps that was the Bemusement confusing her senses.

The draper's assistant, tall and bespectacled, sidled up to Judith and asked if he could help her.

"Yes," murmured Judith. She rifled in her reticule for a coin, which she discreetly displayed. "I could not help but overhear a reference to, er, a ghost. Could you please tell me about it?"

"Ah." The assistant ducked his head and spoke in an equally low voice. "Sargenet has suffered a death and a spectre, my lady, but not in that order. It seems in this case, the spectre caused the death."

Her hand tightened on the coin, her heart suddenly thudding. "A death? Who? When?"

The man's lips pursed sorrowfully. "Three days ago, a footman. Hit on the head in the drawing room - by a book, if you can believe it."

Judith reeled backwards. She felt as if she were suddenly on the edge of a precipice, all her certainties plunging away from her.

"Which footman?" she demanded, fear clogging her vision and her voice growing louder. "Do you know his name?" For all her reluctance to make this errand, she would not be able to bear it if she had come too late. Her remorse would increase a hundredfold.

Suddenly, the black-haired steward stood next to the assistant. "What do you know of our footmen, my lady?"

The steward's voice was suspicious. Around her, the coloured cloth seemed suddenly too bright and garish. Lady Agatha and Lady Mary were still in heated debate with the shop-owner, oblivious to Judith's distress.

"I am friends with the household. Please put me out of my suspense," she begged the young man.

The handsome steward stared. "I am afraid I don't recognise you," he said, "and I am employed at Sargenet."

"Well, Mr Lewis," said the assistant mildly. "You've only been in your position for the last few years, remember. Mayhap this lady here knows the house from before your time."

"That is correct," said Judith, her eyes pleading. She felt as if she had cotton wool stuffed inside her ears as she awaited his answer.

Mr Lewis frowned. "Well, you wouldn't know Gilbert, the footman who died. Gilbert Drew."

The band round Judith's heart loosened. She dropped her chin to her chest, heaving in a deep breath. So Robert was safe, for now. "Thank you. Did I hear a book was involved? How can that be?"

"Yes, who found the body, Mr Lewis?" asked the assistant curiously. "Can you be sure the blow was dealt by a book?"

"Broughton found him; the butler," Mr Lewis replied shortly. Yet to Judith's ears, his words sounded flat and hollow.

A lie.

She licked her lips. "Did your butler see the skull too?"

"He says the attack was by a thief, not a skull," said Mr Lewis sharply. "Mr Keeves, I'll thank you not to repeat such nonsense."

"A thief?" Mr Keeves peered over his glasses, unabashed. "Ah yes, I heard that some vases were stolen, were they not?"

"That is the duke's concern, not yours." Mr Lewis glared at them both and turned his back, stalking over to the ladies once more.

Mr Keeves sighed. "Please excuse Mr Lewis. He has always been rather blunt." He shook his head. "It's a dark business, this death. Would you like some of that silk, my lady?"

In a daze, Judith bought a few yards of the orange-gold cloth, though she had no notion what she would do with it and could little afford the expense. Still, it was very pretty. She slipped Mr Keeves another coin for his troubles and put the cloth away in her black reticule. Casting one more glance at the ladies and the steward, she made her exit, trying not to bump into the door on the way out.

Interlude II

Twenty-three years earlier

Nick would have been more discomfited, she thought, if he had seen how attentive the duke was the next day at the blackberry picking expedition.

Judith arrived at Sargenet with her friend Miss Turnow and her brother, all carrying expectant baskets and dressed in old clothes. While they waited for Fitzroy to fetch his master, Miss Turnow whispered to Judith that last night the duke had flirted outrageously with the ravishing Miss Lowther, an heiress in the next county. Judith could quite believe it and only wondered what poor Mrs Bleau had done with herself.

Then the duke himself arrived, dressed only in old breeches, boots, and a brown shirt with his sleeves rolled up in a scandalously informal way. It certainly displayed his muscular forearms to advantage. He escorted them to the hidden clearing in the Sargenet woods where masses of wild blackberry bushes grew, their branches wide and bowed to the ground, generously laden with purple fruit.

It was like a secret faery glade, and Judith was enchanted. She forgot about the embarrassment of her old-fashioned, pale-yellow gown with its quaint frills and furbelows, until the duke teased her about it and said she was as pretty as a daisy.

She scowled at him. "Whereas you, your grace, look like a chimney sweep."

Judith did not want to admit, even to herself, how attractive his grace looked with his throat bare and his sleeves rolled up. He reached for more blackberries and popped one in his mouth. The Turnows had traipsed to the other side of the bushes.

The duke did not carry a basket and Judith chided him for it.

"Nonsense," he replied. "You're not supposed to take any home. Blackberries are best eaten on the spot, not saved for later. I should forbid your silly basket."

"I'm sure such heedlessness aligns with your general philosophy, your grace." She virtuously put several more berries in her receptacle. "I, on the other hand, know how to think of the future."

"You would benefit from my approach." The duke grinned at her and lazily ate another three. "You're missing out, Miss Horis. These are sinfully delicious."

The way he was eating them was sinful, but she capitulated and, avoiding the thorns, chose a fat blackberry to eat. The sweet fruit dissolved in her mouth and she closed her eyes with the rapture of it. It was true that they were the most delicious thing she had ever tasted.

"Good, aren't they?" said the duke.

She opened her eyes to see him watching her appreciatively.

"Divine," she admitted. "Proof of God's existence, I'd say."

"I don't know," he said. "I see the Devil at work too. You have delightfully stained lips right now, begging to be kissed."

She licked them hastily, blushing, and looked down, furious. Must he be so direct? She clenched her hands on her basket, feeling heat rush through her body. Nicholas, she must think of Nicholas, not the thought of what it would be like if the duke actually kissed her now under the blackberry branches. His dark eyes were laughing at her, a lock of hair falling onto his forehead. It looked rakish - because he was a rake. She ought to remember it.

"I beg you, your grace, not to overstep the bounds of propriety," she said, as coolly as she was able.

The duke turned back to the branches. "Sorry, my daisy. I couldn't resist. And you know my philosophy now."

She turned her back on him, making a show of industriously filling her basket. As she did so, she asked him about Nicholas, determined to turn the conversation to safer channels.

"You've known Mr Avely since you were boys, did you say?" she asked. "Does he know about this fruit?"

"Nick certainly does," said the duke. "He has gorged himself on blackberries often enough."

Judith huffed. "Mr Avely, I am certain, knows how to restrain himself."

The duke gave a bark of laughter. "Not always, I assure you."

"What can you mean?" she demanded, looking up from her basket.

The duke sobered, seeing her face. He cleared his throat. "Nothing, nought at all. Indeed, Nick is the embodiment of restraint."

She narrowed her eyes in confusion. The lie sounded like a gong in the duke's voice. Round them, the dappled sunlight moved sweetly on the ground, but she put down her basket unheeding.

"You are being sarcastic?" she queried. "Are you implying something against Mr Avely's character?"

"No, no." The duke looked discomfited. "I did not imply anything ungentlemanly, I swear."

Judith's eyes widened. He was lying again.

She dropped her gaze, confused. Her breath caught in her chest as she realised the implication. What did the duke know about Nicholas's conduct that she did not? It was true that they had been boys together. It must be something silly, like stealing a pie or eating too many sweetmeats, that he was thinking on. Still - why would he call that 'ungentlemanly'?

The duke turned back to his indulgences. "Do you know Mr Avely well?" he enquired. His fingers, she noticed, were stained red.

She debated whether or not to tell this miscreant that she was engaged to Nicholas, but decided against it. Nick had specifically said not to mention it.

"No, not that well," she lied. "He is in my circle of acquaintance, however, and I naturally object to unfounded accusations being implied against him."

"No unfounded accusations here." The duke raised his hands, grinning and placatory. This time his words rang true. Judith frowned.

"You speak of childhood misconduct then, I presume." She put a berry into her mouth and tried to muster a smile.

"Yes," said the duke. "Quite. Boyish pranks." He reached up to a higher branch, but not before she heard the hesitation and the flat note in his voice. It was no boyish pranks that he was thinking upon.

Judith swallowed. This conversation was making her head spin. It must be the Bemusement from employing her Gift when she was still learning. Perhaps that was it - she was mistaken, untutored. There had been no lie, after all. The duke had only spoken the truth when he said that Nicholas was the embodiment of restraint. Nicholas was a gentleman, the man that she loved, an honourable man who served the Crown and would marry her within the year. He was not capable of wrongdoing.

Then the duke spoke, his voice bitter. "I suppose you would rather picture someone like me as the villain of your story, Miss Horis?"

She looked over to him. "You said yourself that you do not prize restraint."

A dark look crossed his handsome face. Briefly Judith felt some kind of pressure gather in the air. "Oh yes." His jaw became rigid. "I cannot be a gentleman if I eat too many blackberries."

"It is not the blackberries that concern me," she snapped, "but your attitudes to women."

"Oh, is that so?" His laugh was harsh. "I constrain myself to widows, at least. I would never toy with a village girl's affections and make empty promises."

Judith faltered backwards, staring up at his angry face. "Mr Avely did this?"

"No, of course not," said the duke, his voice hard. "We are talking about me, Miss Horis."

It was a lie.

THE FOLLOWING DAY, both angry and fearful, Judith sought out her maid, Betsy. The duke must be confused or mistaken. It couldn't possibly be true that Nicholas Avely had toyed with a village girl, even if his grace thought it was. Of course, he would assume the worst, for it was the kind of thing the duke would probably do. Not Nicholas.

Betsy would know the gossip from the village, and she would have heard any rumours about Nicholas. Judith found her in the back garden, harvesting peas. She joined her, snapping off the bright green pods into the basket, and carefully framed her question.

"Betsy, do you know if Mr Avely ever courted anyone before me? Even in passing? I wish you would tell me, if so."

Betsy's face was obscured by the foliage. "Why do you want to know, miss?" She paused. "Only trouble will come of such questions."

"So there *was* someone." Judith's heart sank.

Betsy was silent a moment. "Well," she said reluctantly. "Mr Avely showed an interest in Anna Thane, from the village. But we all knew not to take it seriously. Just a gentleman's flirtation, nothing to worry your head about, miss. It's long finished."

Judith's stomach twisted as she heard the truth in Betsy's voice. Then anger surged through her. "What of Anna? Did *she* know not to take it seriously?"

Betsy pushed her cap back and peered around the climber. "I suppose you could say Anna's head was turned, but she ought to have known better. We warned her that Mr Avely was too high above her."

A pea snapped in Judith's hands, sharp and brittle. "How far did he press his attentions?" she asked coldly. She must know the worst. A terrible jealousy already spiked through her, but also an awful fear that Nicholas had taken advantage of this girl.

"Oh, not far, miss. It were innocent, I'm sure, just a few stolen kisses," said Betsy, and Judith felt both relieved and more angered. Betsy continued uneasily. "Mr Avely is a gentleman through and through, I believe."

Judith was starting to doubt it. "How long ago was this?"

"After Easter, miss. A while ago."

Easter was only four months ago. Mortification stung as Judith remembered the duke's complicit knowledge of this affair, innocent or not. Nicholas had been courting her for the last two months. She clenched her fists in her skirts.

"Anna is the seamstress's daughter, isn't she? How did they meet?"

Betsy's cheeks reddened as she bent over her basket. "I believe it was walking in the woods, miss."

The scent of turned earth was suddenly acrid to Judith's nose. Blindly, she continued to hunt for peas in silence, until Betsy told her there was enough.

"I'll shuck them now," said Betsy. "And don't worry about Anna, miss. Mr Avely walked away from her, which he would never do to you. You'll suit him much better."

Judith nodded and turned to leave the garden, but not before she caught the look of pity on Betsy's face.

THE NEXT MORNING, restless, Judith found an excuse to call upon the Thanes' stone cottage. She used the pretext of collecting charitable donations for the village school, a duty she regularly carried out for her father. She knocked on the door with trepidation, not even certain why she was there, except that she was desperate to know the full extent of Nicholas's entanglement.

Anna Thane herself opened it. Judith recognised her at once. She had not realised how very beautiful the girl was: green, luminous eyes, and a mass of brown hair tinted with auburn.

Jealousy churned in Judith's stomach. No wonder Nicholas had 'shown an interest' in this girl. Even in her plain green woollen gown, Anna's figure was shown to advantage, an apron cinched round a slender waist, her skin clear, her lashes dark.

A slender waist, at least. No curve of a belly. How long would it take for such things to reveal themselves? Judith did not know. Surely by three months?

Anna's green eyes narrowed in recognition. Judith spoke her collection speech by rote, wooden and uncertain.

"Please wait a moment, Miss Horis." Anna propped the door open and vanished, returning moments later with some coins. "A small token. We thank your father for the work he does."

Judith nodded numbly. They discussed the weather, as all good Englishwomen should, and the upcoming harvest. Judith barely knew what she said, looking into that beautiful face and knowing it would enchant any man.

"Good day, Miss Horis," said Anna, and suddenly she was closing the door.

"Wait. Please." Judith thrust the collection basket out.

The door paused. Anna arched her delicate brows.

Judith swallowed. "Can I ask you something ... rather intrusive?"

Anna looked down her nose. "I think I can guess what it is. You want to know about Nicholas."

The use of his Christian name was a painful confirmation. Judith drew a shaky breath. "He ... courted you?"

"He did indeed, a few months ago." The beautiful lips pursed.

"He didn't, er, take advantage of you?" Judith paused, knowing her question went beyond the bounds of courtesy. "Are you ... alright?"

Anna folded her slender arms. "He only took advantage of my naive heart."

Judith winced, for the same description could well apply to herself.

Anna continued, her voice hard. "I should have known better than to trust him." She sneered. "He was too scared to wed me. I've found a new beau now, Jack Steer, the blacksmith. We're to be married after the harvest, so don't you worry."

Judith was certain Anna had a queue of beaus. In the meanwhile, her own heart was crumbling. "Wed you? Did Mr Avely promise that?"

"All talk and no follow-through." Anna sniffed derisively, but

Judith could see hurt in the clench of her jaw. The girl stared at her for a long moment. "Too frightened of disappointing his mother. If it weren't for her, I'd be in your shoes right now, Miss Horis. I hope you're grateful for your position in life. Though, to be frank, I prefer my blacksmith."

Judith nodded, wishing she stood in some *other* shoes, even though she knew Anna was right to resent her privilege. Now it seemed a horrible place to be, where she was second best, a consolation prize, chosen to please Nicholas's mother. A place where her fiancé was a cad, a man who had promised marriage to another girl, then withdrew it. "I am sorry. If he hurt you."

"It's none of your business." Anna gave her one last measuring look. "Or maybe it is, if you'll have such a weak man."

In a swish of green, she shut the door.

Numbly, Judith turned away.

SHE WALKED ALONE through the fields, too distraught to stay still. The sun was out, impossibly, and the crops smelled sweet in the warmth. She did not see gentle vistas, her mind in turmoil.

Nicholas had loved Anna; Judith knew it with certainty. How could she doubt it, seeing that feminine perfection and that testing gaze? He would only have spoken of marriage if he had truly hoped for it; he was not a man to seduce a girl with empty promises. Achingly, she remembered how Nicholas had seemed withdrawn when she first met him. It had only added to his appeal, his sense of mystery and restraint. Now she knew it was because he was mourning Anna, his thoughts taken up with what he could not have.

Judith left the swaying barley fields and walked unseeing into the Sargenet woods, glad of the deeper shadows, lost in her own grief. How could she not have known this? How could she have believed that Nicholas truly loved her? He had always implied that there was no one else; that she was the only one for him. He must have been clever in his declarations, to avoid a direct lie that she would detect.

Footsteps sounded behind her. She was too lost in her own misery to turn around.

"Miss Horis!"

Judith turned blankly. As if from a distance, she saw the duke approaching, dressed in riding gear, a beaver hat set rakishly over his black locks.

She managed a curtsy. "Your grace."

"I saw you as I rode by and I couldn't believe my eyes! What are you doing here?" The duke halted, his voice faltering as he took in her pale face and empty eyes. "What is wrong? Judith, you poor girl, you look ill."

He put out a hand as if to take hers, then withdrew it, looking at her with concern.

She scarcely noticed his use of her name. She was suddenly agonisingly determined that the duke should not guess at her predicament. She mustered a smile and looked down, hunting for something to explain herself.

"What happened?" he asked again. "Why are you here in Sargenet woods? Were you on your way to visit me? Did you lose your basket, perchance? Though I cannot see how that would make you look so grief-stricken."

Judith cleared her throat. "I'm afraid I had some bad news this morning. My - er - my cat died." This had in fact occurred three weeks ago, which made the lie easy. The sadness of it was still present in her and she allowed her eyes to fill with tears, a simple feat in her overwrought state. "I was in danger of succumbing to too much melancholy, then I thought - who better to cheer me up than you, with your philosophy of the moment." She paused, swallowing the tears. "I apologise for setting off without my maid. I was distracted with sadness."

She was blinking at him as she lied, so she was taken aback by the delight that broke across his countenance, somewhat incongruous at her tale of woe.

"You were coming to me?" He smiled, his eyes warm. "I am honoured. What a precious duty I now bear, to help ease your misery. And do not concern yourself with maids, they are pesky creatures. We can walk now to the Dower House - no one shall even know we are there and I promise to look after your virtue. I am not as bad as I have been painted, you know."

He put out his arm and she acquiesced, placing her gloved fingers in the crook of his elbow. He fetched his horse and began the slow walk to Sargenet, talking lightly of this and that. Gradually she began to pay attention, forcibly putting thoughts of Nicholas and Anna aside.

They talked of the blackberry picking and how Mr Turnow had twisted his ankle on dismounting an oak tree, and how the Horis household had dined on blackberry pie, and how the song Four and Twenty Blackbirds could possibly refer to a real pie. His grace was adamant that it was possible to bake a pie large enough to hold a cage and that the birds could be placed inside once the frame was baked.

Judith even laughed. "Of course it would take a duke to dream of such extravagance," she mocked.

"I'll order my kitchen to bake you one," he vowed. "Though, on consideration, maybe not twenty-four blackbirds. Will two or three do?"

"No, indeed not, think of the poor birds!"

His black eyes glinted merrily, though there was still an undertone of concern in the way he kept his hand over hers. She smiled back. They arrived at the Dower House, its front windows shut between green ivy. He told her it was empty and locked, and led her past it, to the back of the house, where the gardens were ensconced by a low stone wall. Honeysuckle bloomed in a charming profusion, the golden colour lustrous in the summer sunshine.

The duke swept leaves off a wooden bench and invited her to sit. She realised, belatedly, that she was in fact alone with a man in a way that society would deplore. Yet she found she did not care. Her ordinary senses were dulled; she was simply relieved to be distracted from her pain.

She cast the duke a sidelong look. His striking coal-black hair, deep-set eyes, sensuous lips, and firm jaw combined to make an enthralling picture of masculine beauty. It was made even more heady by the warmth in his voice and the way he grinned at her. He was telling her some tale of how he had once stolen a jar of jam that ended up all over his person, but it was if he had never told anyone else the tale. Perhaps he had not.

He sat on the other end of the bench, not too close, but angled toward her, his long legs flung out. She sat primly, aware of the distance between them, and the closeness. Something strange was fluttering in her heart.

He was so handsome and quick-witted. And he had not lied to her.

He kept his promise. He did not move an inch closer, though his eyes lingered on her lips more than once. They talked and talked, until Judith became aware that the sun had reached midday and her stomach was rumbling. Reluctantly she stood. The scent of honeysuckle was sweetly intoxicating.

"I must walk home," she said, holding out her hand. "Thank you for cheering my spirits, your grace."

"Can I escort you?" Even as he took her hand, he shook his head. "No, you cannot be seen walking alone with me."

"I'll be fine by myself." She curtsied, bowing her head.

He did not let go of her hand. "Can I call on you tomorrow - to continue my chivalrous duty?"

Judith hesitated, awfully conscious that he might enquire of her household about her late, lamented cat. However, if he discovered her, she would be well served for her dishonesty. "I suppose you may."

"So loath with your favours!" said the duke. "I will be there in the morning."

He pressed her hand firmly, then released her.

In which a mansion looms

One soon learns to inure oneself against the trivial lies of strangers, even their larger transgressions. It is the deceptions of those close to you that cause more pain.

  - from *Lady Avely's Guide to Truth and Magic*

ON THE STREET outside the haberdashery, Judith set off slowly toward Sargenet, trying to clear her mind. Stumbling slightly, she found the gap in the hedgerow and turned on to the pathway that cut across the barley fields, now shorn.

The path was familiar: she remembered how she had wandered blindly through it after speaking with Anna Thane. Now those memories were tainted with an additional, awful sense of betrayal.

Two years after Nicholas died, she had found the letter from the duke, hidden in a book, the pages stained and creased. It was dated one year prior to her husband's death. She did not need the Gift of Memory to have the words seared on her mind.

. . .

DEAR NICHOLAS,

As you requested, I've put Robert Steer into Taunton's School for Boys, using the money you sent. It will be a step up in class for him, but I daresay that is appropriate. He looks like you. If you would like to see him, he will be housed in a cottage on my estate in term breaks. I trust that you are telling the truth when you say you have only just discovered his existence.

I feel sorry for his poor dead mother, but as you say, I have tried to respect her memory by not dragging her name through the mud. I have claimed my intervention is part of a new charity foundation for orphans, though I suspect there will be some speculation about his parentage regardless. The boy himself knows the truth. Let me know if there is anything else you want me to do for him; he should be safe enough at school until he reaches his majority.

Yours faithfully,
Dacian
Duke of Sargen

JUDITH HADN'T BEEN able to make sense of it at first, her mind blank with shock. Then she remembered the name of Steer: the blacksmith whom Anna had married.

Looking down at the stained paper, Judith had accepted the awful truth. Anna's son, born in wedlock, was in fact Nicholas's bastard child.

A terrible rage had filled her, overshadowing her grief. The husband she had loved was now the object of her revilement. All along, she had thought his courtship of Anna had been innocent. An unfulfilled love had been bad enough, yet now she had to contend with the knowledge that Nicholas and Anna had been intimate together. Worse, Nicholas had abandoned the girl after that, when honour demanded that he marry her.

Had he truly not known about Robert? And if he had indeed

only discovered it much later, how dared he keep the truth from Judith?

It was true that Nicholas had died unexpectedly, shot down in France a year after the letter. Perhaps he had intended to tell her, though he must have quailed at the thought. Then the chance had been taken from him.

She had been utterly furious with the duke. *He* had known the truth for years, and he had not seen fit to inform her, even when Nicholas passed away, taking him beyond the reach of her questions. She had confronted the duke at the Garvey House party, some months later, and they had fought bitterly.

Quickening her steps, Judith was glad to release some of the tension from her limbs as she strode through the shorn fields of barley. It was all so long ago now, but the memory of that fight still rankled. The duke must have known she was distraught, venting all her hurt and anger on him, the only target she could reach. There was no need for him to stay away for *nine whole years*.

Her eyes sought out the shape of the Sargenet woods in the distance, a dark mass of beech, yew, and oaks. After the duke's hasty retreat from England, she had tried to put it all out of her mind and concentrate on raising her own children. Robert Steer could take care of himself. She had enough to do with educating her own daughter, for she could not afford to send Elinor to school, although Peregrine would go to Westeller. The duke had told her that he had ensured that Robert would continue at Taunton, and she was too angry to question the arrangement. A discussion with her solicitor had revealed that the Avely estate regularly made payments to the duke, so she knew Nicholas had made some provision for it.

Yet eight years passed without the duke returning, and she started to wonder what would happen to Robert. An uneasy sense of guilt assailed her, that she had made no effort to check on the boy, so she wrote to Taunton. They replied that Robert Steer was no longer with them. He had been pulled out by Lady Agatha and given a position in her household as a footman.

Judith couldn't believe it when she read it. Nicholas's son, a footman, after all that? But of course, Lady Agatha wouldn't know of Robert's parentage. All she knew was that the duke had funded the orphan's schooling. No doubt she thought she was giving the boy a sought-after position, a stepping stone to greater things. Indeed, Lady Agatha probably thought a place as her footman was the highest of honours.

Judith's conscience was pricked. Work as a footman was menial, exhausting servitude. As much as she might deplore Robert's existence, she should intervene.

Yet, somehow, a whole twelvemonth had passed since she had discovered this state of affairs. She had been busy with Elinor's coming out, and navigating London society again. Moreover, Judith was at a loss of what to say to this Robert, and what to *do* with him. A whole twelvemonth passed while he worked as a footman, while his half-sister and half-brother supped with nobles.

Guilt churned in Judith's stomach as she drew closer to Sargenet. Guilt, and apprehension at the thought of actually meeting her husband's child for the first time.

The sun hid behind a blanket of soft grey clouds, and a chilly breeze chased the warmth away. When she reached the woods that marked the beginning of the Sargenet estate, she sat down on a rock by the tree line and unwrapped the food she had purchased at the market. She needed to gather herself before this approach.

Beside her, the forest was dark with shadows and rife with birdsong. The apple was sweet and crisp, the bread a welcome sustenance. The path beckoning through the woods was still familiar to her, even after all these years. Although the trees had grown, the rocks and shapes of the land had not changed, and the quiet peacefulness was the same.

She shook her head, putting the painful memories aside, and

turned her mind to more pressing problems. Gilbert Drew's death was unsettling news, and the rumoured skulls at Sargenet appeared in a more ominous light now. It must have been a mighty blow to the head to have killed the footman, and she had to admit she was curious as to which tome had been employed. It must have been a heavy one, wielded with decisiveness.

Judith shivered, relieved again that it had not been Robert who had suffered the blow.

Who had done such a deed? She took a thoughtful bite of her apple. Was it a thief surprised in the act of looting the drawing room, as the steward had implied? Vases were missing, she recalled. Surely it could not be anything else except robbery. Yet the ducal estate should be well protected against thieves, and not require the application of a heavy book. There were most certainly protections on the house, given the nature of the duke's Gift.

However, the duke had been gone for a long time. Perhaps the defences had worn down or been neglected. He would not be pleased about that. Nor would he be pleased about the skull that had presaged this death. Had the Illusion been seen on the same night?

There also remained the matter of why Mr Lewis had lied. Judith threw the apple core into a clump of harebell and stared unseeing into the dark forest.

The steward had claimed it was Broughton who had found the body. Broughton, she remembered, was the new butler mentioned by Miss Cultor. Had the butler gone to draw the curtains and found the body in the drawing room? It sounded plausible, but Mr Lewis's lie implied that someone else stumbled across the corpse first. Had it been Agatha, the mistress of the house, perhaps? Or Mr Lewis himself?

The steward, Judith decided, was a rather suspicious character, eager to avoid any questions, and all too calm in uttering his falsehood.

She brushed the bread crumbs from her gown and stood. A sixth sense told her that something was amiss; a horrible tangle in the threads that held Sargenet together. Furthermore, if there was some malignant force at work, her Gift might allow her to detect its source when no one else could. After all, she might be the only person who knew of Mr Lewis's lie.

She strode into the Sargenet woods, glad of her cloak and veil, as the shadows merged with the grey of the day. There was even more reason to hurry now to speak to Robert. It was possible he was in danger.

And perhaps the timeliness of her offer would make him look upon her more kindly than she deserved.

After a while, the path split, and she followed the lesser-used way past the Dower House, ignoring the walled garden with its honeysuckle vines and the memories it provoked. She passed the old disused well, boarded up but showing a gap of darkness between the planks. Finally, she reached the edge of the forest, overlooking the lawns of the house.

As she paused, a ray of sunshine struck out across the green. Beyond the lawn, the house loomed, still under cloud, the front archways arcing under a black roof.

She stared upon the visage of Sargenet.

The front door was ridiculous as ever: tall and wide enough to fit two oxen pulling a catapult. Lady Agatha had done her best to lighten the front aspect with roses and hedges, but they did little next to the sheer size of Sargenet. It was made of a central atrium, Judith knew, which vaulted in the back over a huge ballroom, the front taken up by the drawing rooms, library, and study. To the east lay the family wing; to the west the guest rooms and servants' quarters, and, further out, the stables.

To Judith's eyes it did not look any different to when she had last been there. No doubt the drawing room was spotless too and the library had lost its bloody decorations. All skulls and bodies would have been swept away.

As her eyes traced the shape of the house, she was distracted by the sight of three small boys running full tilt across the park, into the swathe of sunlight.

"I want to be the fox," came a shrill cry.

"No, I'll be the fox!" A stronger yell came from the boy ahead of the others, whose blond curls bounced round his face.

"You were the fox last time!"

A smaller child toddled behind them, too taken up with running to add his mite to the argument.

The blonde, curly-headed boy sprinted ahead. "I'll hide in the woods, you wait here."

The middle boy ignored this direction and followed his sibling as they all pelted toward where Judith was standing.

These must be Lady Mary's younger boys. They were followed by a woman who was not the bookish countess. A servant, by the looks of it, clad in serviceable brown with a high neckline, walking briskly, holding a basket, her head covered by a straw bonnet. She was not as old as Judith, yet no longer a maiden. The governess and a spinster, by appearances.

"Don't fall in the stream!" the woman shouted. "Otho! Cato! Quintus! You've already muddied your clothes once today."

Judith backed into the trees. Somehow, she did not want to be seen just yet, but if the boys were playing Hunt the Fox there was every chance they would find her. She ducked behind a large pollarded beech as the oldest thundered into the woods. Maybe she could edge along the tree line toward the servants' entry in the east wing.

Fortunately, the boys disappeared in the opposite direction.

Judith peered out from behind the trunk to see the governess set her basket down on the grass and roll out a blanket.

Then another figure crossed the green. A young man, with thick brown hair and a footman's green and gold livery.

Judith froze. A footman. How many footmen did Sargenet have? It could be Robert.

Her throat closed against the cool air.

The young man drew closer. His hair was a rich brown, coloured with a hint of auburn, a shade she remembered on Anna long ago. He had a straight nose, a slightly pugnacious chin, and an easygoing gait.

He looked so much like Nicholas that Judith's heart gave a wrench. Any doubt that had lingered in her mind now faded. Tears sprang to her eyes and she shrank a little more behind the tree, though unable to look away. She had known he would have reached maturity by now, but it was still a shock to see Robert was a man now, no longer the orphaned boy of her imagination.

The footman loped up to the governess. His deep voice carried clearly across the grass. "I'm sorry, Miss Atkinson. Lord John says the boys must come inside."

"What? Why?" demanded Miss Atkinson, pausing as she unpacked her picnic. A bird landed in the grass nearby and beadily examined the basket.

"He says they've been running wild the last two days and they must return to their studies."

"Nonsense," said Miss Atkinson crossly. "As if they could study Latin at a time like this. Only Lord John would say such a thing. The tension in the house is unbearable, it's not good for them. The boys are better off outside."

"I agree." Robert cast a wistful glance into the woods and Judith held her breath, afraid he would see her. She wanted to watch him unobserved for just a little while longer. He was taller than she had thought and he looked tired. Still, he did not seem to be full of resentment at his position, as she would have expected. Beside her, a creature rustled in the woods, a squirrel or something in the branches.

Robert continued. "I wish I could run wild like them sometimes, the lucky boys."

Miss Atkinson tipped her head in sympathy, the straw bonnet revealing brown hair in a more muted shade than Robert's. "You have double duty now, with Gilbert gone."

"Not that I mind it," said Robert quickly. "Poor fellow."

"It's a terrible thing," agreed Miss Atkinson, placing her wrapped parcels on the blanket and pulling out her knitting, with a flagrant disregard for Lord John's orders to return to the house. "The boys don't seem to care overmuch that there's been a death, to tell the truth, but *I* don't want to be in the house."

Robert gave a nervous glance back toward where Sargenet loomed its great bulk over the lawn. "Do you believe Broughton when he says it was a thief?"

Miss Atkinson gave him a surprised look. "Who else could it be? The crystal vases are missing, aren't they? And the terrace door was open."

Robert shifted, straightening his livery. "Yes, of course."

Judith frowned as she listened. So the terrace doors were open, were they? That explained how the thief had gained entrance. Had the doors been left accidentally unlocked? Did Robert suspect something else? He had shadows under his eyes, despite his youth, and his hands were restless. He was nervous, but that was understandable. He probably wanted to leave Sargenet far behind. Which was why she was here, if she could just gather her courage to step forward.

Still, her heart quailed. Even after the long years of growing accustomed to the brute fact of Robert's existence, seeing him now was a fresh pain. Especially when he looked so much like his father. Was this the son Nicholas wished for, if he could have stayed and married Anna? Or had he known about Robert all along, and callously abandoned them both so he could marry Judith? That was her deepest fear, that Nicholas had been someone else entirely, and her whole marriage was based on a lie. She, who was a Truth Discernor.

"Gilbert certainly didn't have many friends," Miss Atkinson was saying, giving Robert a shrewd glance as she gathered up her knitting again.

"He was a beast to you."

Miss Atkinson shrugged, dropping her eyes to her wool. "Such is the lot of a governess. It is not the first unwanted attention I have received and it won't be the last. I am lucky I had you and Mr Lewis to stand up for me."

Robert looked uncomfortable. "Anyone would have done the same, Miss Atkinson."

"Now don't you feel guilty for putting Gilbert in his place," said Miss Atkinson. "You weren't to know that he was going to die."

"No."

"We are all in a state of shock," she said calmly. "Which is why the boys need to be out in nature for a little longer. You can tell Lord John I promised them a picnic and we will return to Latin after lunch."

Robert nodded and turned to go.

Judith took in a breath. Had she not come all this way to see him? Straightening her widow's hat and veil, she stepped out from behind the trees and walked toward them. She adopted a decorous pace, though her shoulders felt tense and her heart was thudding in her ears.

Two heads whipped round in her direction. Robert started nervously while Miss Atkinson lowered her knitting to her lap and tilted her head curiously, like the bird on the lawn.

"Good day," said Judith, as calmly as she could manage. "Are you Robert Steer?"

He nodded warily.

"I would speak with you," said Judith, "on a private matter."

Robert cast a confused glance at Miss Atkinson, who gave an infinitesimal shrug.

"What can you have to say to me?" Robert asked. "My apologies, but I do not know you, my lady."

Judith hesitated, and took the roundabout route. "I knew your mother, Anna Thane. Before she was married."

"My mother?" Robert frowned. "She died a dozen years ago. How did you know her?"

"Not well," Judith confessed. "She was, er, better acquainted with my husband, Nicholas Avely."

Robert's eyes sharpened. "Nicholas Avely?" He paused. "You are his wife?"

"Yes."

They stared at each other, weighing one another up. Some communication passed between them: they each knew that they knew. Robert frowned, gnawing on his lip mulishly. Judith took another breath.

"Please," she said. "I can understand if you don't want to see me, but hear me out. I have some news that might interest you."

At that moment, however, activity from the house caused them both to turn. Another figure marched out from the huge front doors. This one was tall and masculine, his stride purposeful.

"Robert!" bellowed the figure. "Is that you? Come here at once!"

"Oh dear," said Miss Atkinson. "It's his disgrace."

"His grace," muttered Robert.

Judith's hands tightened.

The duke stood on the gravel and yelled. "Robert! Stop

dallying with the governess!" His coat was undone, his black hair bare to the sun. "I must speak with you! This is important!"

Robert sketched a bow at Judith. "I must go."

Was the duke going to dismiss Robert from his position, and grant him his freedom? Judith should only be glad of it, yet somehow, with Robert in front of her, she did not want to abandon her quest to help him. Especially not now that she had the means, and could rectify her neglect.

"Wait!" She put out a hand. "I must speak with you also! Tomorrow? I'll come again to these woods. Could you meet me there?"

Robert frowned, curiosity warring with wariness. "No, my lady, my apologies but I am too busy at the moment. The house is in an uproar and we are down a footman."

"I *must* speak with you. It is important. I might be able to help you."

The duke started out across the green. "Robert!"

"Such a patient fellow," said Miss Atkinson dryly. Her knitting had been completely abandoned at this point but she took it up now in a show of industriousness.

At Judith's offer of help, Robert's shoulders had stiffened. His face now closed, he turned toward the duke. "Sorry, Mrs Avely," he said over his shoulder. "His grace must take precedence."

Judith backed away, grinding her teeth. His grace always took precedence.

She tried not to run into the woods. A brisk, careless walk would be sufficient. The duke clearly had his heart set on talking to Robert, so maybe he would not notice her.

What a foolish notion. As if the duke would *not notice* an extra female disappearing into the trees. That was exactly the sort of thing that would pique his avid curiosity. Judith braced herself. He would follow her, she knew it.

If she ran now, she could hide in the forest somewhere.

No. That was ludicrous. She was not playing Hunt the Fox with the duke. She would merely make her way, decorously, back to the village, and if the duke wanted to accompany her, he could do so.

It was high time that they renewed their ... acquaintance.

In which old sins resurface

Truth Discernment is a subtle art, easily hidden, unlike some of the other more ostentatious Gifts.

   - from *Lady Avely's Guide to Truth and Magic*

Heart in her mouth, Judith quickened her pace, choosing a different path back through the wood, away from the Dower House.

About her, the trees grew densely, with only glimmers of light falling through the foliage. The ground was thick with roots and leaves. She felt like Red Riding Hood lost in the woods, about to be waylaid by the big bad wolf.

"Wait!"

The yell came from behind her. Judith rolled her eyes and continued walking.

"HALT! Judith! Is that you?"

She sighed and stopped.

"Madam! A few words, I beg you!"

She turned slowly, glad of her veil. It gave her a precious few moments to compose her features and examine his own.

The duke was storming toward her. He was frowning direfully, a line arrowed between his eyes, his admirable jaw clenched, his black hair now tousled. "Wait, please!"

She lifted her veil.

He ground to a halt. They stared at each other across the remaining gap. His gaze met hers, eager and somehow questioning. He took a step closer and she could see the lines that marked his cheeks and fanned from the corners of his eyes. There was a hint of grey in his dark hair, and a faint white scar marked his forehead, just as she remembered.

"Is it you?" His deep-set eyes searched her face. "Judith. I didn't believe it, as much as I wanted to. What are you doing here?"

"I came to see Robert."

He crossed the remaining distance with three quick strides. "So you are not here to visit me, then? You pierce my vanity."

"I thought you were in Spain, your grace. And I doubt your vanity is so easily pierced."

"I've just arrived from London." His eyes still searched her face and she was conscious of the new lines he would see. "You weren't there."

She tried not to interpret too much in this admission that he had looked for her. "I was in Devon for the last week. We must have just missed each other."

"Are you glad to see me?"

A wind brushed the tops of the trees, making a sound like the hushing of waves. "Of course," she replied, putting out her gloved hand.

"That is a namby-pamby answer, my dear." He raised her hand to his lips. "I, on the other hand, am very happy to see you."

She flushed a little, hearing the truth in his voice. So he wasn't still angry with her, then. Did he think that he could simply take up where he left off nine years ago?

As if reading her thoughts, he became suddenly serious, his hand tightening on hers. "I must apologise for my behaviour at Garvey House. For a long time, I have wanted to say how very sorry I am."

"I, too," said Judith stiffly, and withdrew her hand. Why had he not written, if he was so remorseful? "I was not myself. I hope you can forgive me as well."

The duke quirked an eyebrow. "You were perfectly within your rights." His tone was light and deliberate, but she sensed something hidden, a certain reserve in his manner.

Judith turned, beginning to walk again toward the village. "It was long ago. I am willing to put aside our arguments if you are."

She glanced back. He gave a short nod, and followed her.

Quickly, she changed the subject. "I came here because I heard that Robert was relegated to your upper staff."

"Ah, yes, I am sorry for that too." The duke kept pace beside her, his hands now clasped behind his back. "Agatha presumed too much while I was away. I thought Robert would still be at Taunton." He paused. "Agatha does not know his parentage, obviously."

"So I gathered."

"You may rest easy. I have told Robert he can leave, of course, but he insists on staying on as footman until we find some replacements. Then I will help him, on whatever path he chooses."

Boughs rustled overhead as they walked, and Judith felt the familiar flush of shame that the duke must take care of her husband's mistakes. "Did Robert say what sort of path he would choose?"

"Just that he will think on it. I suggested that perhaps I could buy him his colours, and he can join the fight against Napoleon. I will offer the same to my steward, who is another orphan Agatha decided to appropriate into service. The boys know each other well, and could join up together if they wish."

Judith frowned at the information that Robert and Mr Lewis were friends. Also, for some reason she did not like the eminently sensible suggestion that they join the army, especially after finally meeting Robert. He did not seem a military type. "Is that why you return to England now?"

His grace shrugged. Their footsteps sounded quietly on the leaves, and birdsong chimed. "I thought I might be of use if France grows bolder. Yet I come home to find that Sargenet is haunted. Have you heard?"

Judith cast him a side-long glance. "Yes. People are saying it is the old duke, who bashed a footman with a book." She didn't want to mention the talk of his own duelling victims risen from the dead.

The duke snorted. "Father is long gone, thank God. The apparition appeared as a skull - though I doubt it could wield a book." A flash of anger rippled off him, she saw, in the clenching of his jaw, and she felt his power gather briefly in the air.

"A book is an odd choice for a thief," she observed mildly. "They would more likely use a gun or a stick, having their own weapon handy."

He chuckled, his anger receding. "You are remarkably calm about it. Yes, it appears we have a thief, for some vases are miss-ing. Except...." he paused, "I'd have thought more would be taken."

"Who found the body, by the way?" She wondered if she should mention the steward's lie yet. It was suspicious enough to warrant warning the duke. Yet something held her back; a fear that Robert was somehow implicated, perhaps, if the two men were friends.

The duke shot her an acute look. "That's a rather particular question, Mrs Avely."

She cleared her throat. "Actually, my title has changed."

"Oh?" His head turned and the frown line deepened. His eyes suddenly went very dark. "You remarried? Judith, say it isn't so."

"No." Judith wet her lips. "King George granted a posthumous title of marquis to Nicholas, in gratitude for his services to the Crown."

The duke bowed his head, letting a silence pass. Then he said, "I'm glad you've accepted it. What lands come with the title?"

"In Cornwall," Judith replied. "Those connected with Lanyon Castle."

He let out a bark of laughter. "His Majesty has been trying to rid himself of that monstrosity for years."

They passed over a small wooden bridge, crossing the stream that ran through the woods. The water burbled merrily below, a soothing sound.

Judith lifted her head haughtily. "I am well aware that the castle is ... run down. I intend to visit it after I leave Sargenet. In fact, I was warned by the royal steward himself that I might find some things amiss. I want to inspect it before my children arrive."

The path ahead was partially blocked by a fallen branch, twice as long as Judith, and heavy with foliage. She directed her steps to go round it, but the duke held up a hand.

"Allow me, my lady." He approached the branch with a smirk, and Judith knew he was pleased at the opportunity to demonstrate his prowess.

With one smooth motion he lifted it, single-handedly, and tossed it out of the way. Judith felt the faint pressure in the air that marked the use of his Impact, the power that allowed him to manifest physical force at will. She sighed inwardly at the masculine display.

The duke looked back at her, a black lock over his forehead. "Impressed?"

"You've always been ostentatious."

"I can't help it if I naturally draw attention." He swept his arm to invite her progress. "As you have observed before."

She drew a breath, then saw that he was baiting her. Stepping forward, she smelled the sharp fragrance of broken wood. "Naturally."

He followed her. "Speaking of those who draw attention, where are your children now? I heard some interesting stories while I was in London."

"Elinor and Peregrine are staying with Lord Beresford, to whom Elinor is engaged." She didn't add any further details, such as the fact that Elinor was currently *pretending* to be Lord Beresford's wife, in a covert quest to the island of Sark. The less people who knew about *that*, the better.

"Ah, so you are free to gad about the countryside! What giddy liberation!" The duke walked by her side. "Do they know about Robert?"

Judith hesitated, ashamed. The path before them was hung round with ivy, so it felt as if they were enclosed in some private world. "No."

"Will you ever tell them?"

"I must, for I intend to offer Robert a place at Lanyon Castle."

The duke raised his brows, startled. "In what position?"

"As part of the Avely family, if he will have us." Judith drew her shoulders back and risked a glance at him.

He stopped walking and pulled at her elbow, forcing her to face him.

Reluctantly, she turned and met his eyes. Around them, the birds sang on, oblivious.

"Judith," he said gently. "You are not obliged to do anything like that."

"Robert is not your responsibility anymore," she argued. "Not now that I have inherited lands and title. It is only right that he benefit from them too."

The duke gave her elbow a little shake. "I can take care of him. As I promised Nicholas. No one would blame you for leaving it at that."

Judith felt the warmth of his fingers through her sleeve. "It should never have been your burden to bear. Especially once I knew the truth. I should have reached out to Robert long ago."

The duke dropped his hand, but his gaze still held her in place. "You did what seemed right at the time. And Robert was never a burden to me. I am a duke, remember, and I have connections you do not. I can ensure his future."

Judith shook her head, annoyed, for it was true. The duke would be in a better position to guide Robert than she. "Still, I must offer my help, as is my duty. I should have at least come a year ago, when I heard of his plight. I feel dreadful for having delayed so long."

The duke sighed. "You are so quick to condemn yourself. How you must revile *my* conduct!"

"*Your* conduct?"

"For all your guilt, your sins scarcely compare to killing a man and abandoning your duties for almost a decade."

Judith averted her eyes and shook her head slightly. "Your Gift is difficult. I cannot judge."

His voice deepened and roughened. "You do, nonetheless. As you should."

She could not deny it. He had killed a man in an act of barbaric savagery. He had fled the country rather than take responsibility for his actions. It was another reason why she should keep him at arm's length.

Looking up, she met his gaze. "I am certain that, after all this time, you have learned to control your power."

There was a flash of pressure in the air that just as quickly vanished into stillness. She saw his jaw tighten.

"What happened with Lord Garvey will never happen again," he said. "I can promise you that. I learnt a lot in Spain while I was away."

She wondered what exactly *had* happened with Lord Garvey. It must have been a repeat of his old crime, though the pistol shots that she had heard indicated otherwise. She let a silence pass, then said calmly, "I am sure you are right."

His face was grim, and he seemed about to say something more. Then he changed his mind and put out his arm in silence. She took it, and they began walking again. He pulled her closer to match her stride. She allowed it. They were almost out of the woods now and he must leave her soon. A little further and she would have managed this dangerous territory.

After a while, the duke spoke more quietly. "Where are you staying, Judith?"

She hesitated, guessing what was coming. "At the Gryffin."

He cocked an eyebrow. "You must stay at Sargenet, of course."

"I wouldn't want to impose," she replied mendaciously. "Especially now, with your household so troubled."

"Nonsense," he said. "Your presence would be a balm upon my soul."

"More accurately, you hope I will make your family behave themselves."

"They are being particularly tiresome," he agreed. "John is even more absent-minded than ever, spilling the coffee and spending all his time in his room. Mary seems worried about him. Agatha is tetchy and nervous, forgetting plain civility. And my manners are brusque at the best of times."

"Why are the earl and Lady Mary staying at Sargenet?"

"Apparently influenza is rife in their village," he replied. "Mary didn't want to expose her boys to illness, though frankly I think she is more concerned for her husband. John looks a bit peaked and he isn't much company. You will liven the place up." He paused. "And you must certainly come and stay if you are still practiced at your estimable Gift. I need it at this juncture. I have an excessively large household of servants and you can help me interview them. Your Gift will make it much easier to determine what happened with this skull and the footman's death, and whether they are at all related."

Judith hesitated. It was a tempting offer. She felt there was something dangerously amiss at Sargenet, and Robert had been there for more than a year. She would at least have more chances to speak with him, and help him if she could.

"Please," said the duke, tightening his grip. "We can unravel this matter together, Judith. And I can promise you something else."

"What is that?"

The corner of his mouth turned up. "Drinking chocolate, morning and night."

Judith laughed, despite herself.

He continued. "I know how you love it so, and I've brought home some particularly good quality cocoa tablets from Spain. I think you'll like the recipe they use."

"Oh?" She tilted her head, intrigued. "A different array of spices?"

"You'll have to taste it for yourself."

Judith frowned at him, but she capitulated at his cleverness. "Very well. However, you must give Robert permission for fifteen minutes away from his duties, so he can talk with me. He is overly committed to his post and will not give me the time of day."

"Done." A smile broke across his face like sunlight through the trees, edging his handsomeness with radiance.

They had reached the edge of the forest and the low stone wall that surrounded it. Judith turned to look at the view, to hide the fact that her breath had just been taken away by his smile. The fields and hedgerows lay before them, grasses bending in the wind. Clouds had gathered to sit heavily in the sky and a flock of ravens rose up in the air from a distant windmill.

Judith withdrew her arm. "You are needed at the house. I can continue alone."

He pulled away to face her. "You will return soon? I can send a carriage for you as soon as I reach home."

She hesitated, thinking of Miss Cultor. "Not tonight. Tomorrow morning, if you will. And what shall we tell Agatha as the reason for my visit?" Heaven forbid Agatha realise her connection with Robert.

"I will say I saw you in London last week and I invited you to stay as my guest - before I knew of our misfortunes. That will be plausible enough."

She nodded. "One more thing - if I am to help you question the servants, I do not think we should mention that I can Discern the truth."

"No," he agreed. "Yet does anyone know of your talent?"

"I don't know." She felt the weight of her lapis, hidden in her bodice. "Perhaps Lord John knows, from years ago?"

A frown creased the duke's brow. "I've never discussed you with John. Certainly, your husband's Gift was well known in the upper circles before he died. Perhaps yours was too, and John came to hear of it."

Judith had never advertised her Gift and she doubted a mere female's talent would be of much interest to Lord John. Perhaps his Lady Mary had been more attentive. However, since Nicholas's death twelve years ago, Judith had avoided the Musor circles, hoping to recede into obscurity while she raised her children. It was a long time since she had fraternised with Discernors. Yet both John and Mary were Gifted in Memory and might recall her involvement, if they had ever bothered to store the fact in their minds - which was unlikely.

She put a foot on the rock stile, preparing to step over the low wall. "Perhaps I should lay claim to a different Gift entirely? If I have a small talent in Diplomacy, it will explain why you wish to have me present while you are terrorising the servants."

"Not terrorise!" he objected. "I shall be very charming."

"You shall have to be, for I have no talent in Diplomacy at all."

"I don't know about that," he teased. "I think your Gift has taught you to hide your feelings well."

She raised her brows with an austere expression. He laughed and took her hand again. This time he did not raise it to his lips, just held it in his warm grasp, looking up at her. "Yet *I* will be open with you, Judith. I am glad to see you and I hope we can renew our old friendship, despite everything."

Her eyes dropped in confusion. Their 'friendship' had taken many different shapes over the years. Yet after nine years of silence, this sudden offer was disconcerting. She had not forgotten, either, how he had once broken her heart, at the beginning.

It was time to recall the role of a matronly widow, the one she had tried so hard to assert at Garvey House. Maybe that way she could repress his compulsive charisma.

She inclined her head graciously and withdrew to the next step. "Indeed, I am delighted to count you as a friend, your grace."

"Please, call me Dacian." He narrowed his eyes. "I see. You are determined to hold me at a distance. However, I am happy to wait, my dear marchioness. You will soften toward me eventually, despite my sins."

Judith smiled and lifted her veil so it dropped back over her face. "Your confidence is charming, your grace."

"I know." He laughed and strode off back through the woods.

Infuriatingly, he was right.

Interlude III

Twenty-three years earlier

The duke was assiduous in his attempts to distract Judith from the death of her cat, or, had he but known it, her grief over Nicholas. His grace called the very next morning and every second day of those fateful weeks while Nicholas was in London.

Judith did not repress his grace's attentions. Her heart and pride were so wounded by Nicholas's courtship of Anna that she welcomed the diversion and the balm to her self-regard.

The duke sat in her drawing room like a rare breed of lion, leaning toward her, his voice warm and admiring, and she felt like she was a rain-battered flower unfolding in the sun.

Furthermore, she could not fail to be aware of how his attention raised her consequence in the village. She was warned, of course, by everyone. Miss Turnow told her that his grace was a wicked flirt and had a dozen women in London. Mrs Pedlow pulled her aside and murmured that she shouldn't take the duke's compliments too seriously, and even Judith's father, the rector, found it necessary to seek his daughter out one evening.

"Are you certain you should encourage his grace?" asked Mr Horis, sitting by Judith and taking her hand. "He is a reprobate, by all accounts, and has even killed a man. He would not deserve you, Judith, my dear, even if he would ask for you."

"He won't ask for me," replied Judith, for she knew it was impossible that a duke should marry a rector's daughter, even if she was Viscount Horis's granddaughter and gently bred. Just like Anna should have known not to expect Nicholas's proposal. She repressed a stab of pain and anger. "It is just a passing flirtation. You must forgive me for enjoying it while it lasts, Father."

"Hmm," said the rector, frowning. "What of Mr Avely? I thought you were amenable to his suit."

Judith turned her head away. "I thought I was too."

"Where is he? What has happened?"

"Mr Avely is in London." She drew a breath. "Since he left, I have discovered that his affections were not what I believed them to be."

"Are you certain?" Mr Horis was perplexed. "I hope you will wait to see Mr Avely's intentions, and not rely on hearsay. Those who hear, speak of what they heard; those who see, know beyond mistake."

Judith reflected that the truth from Anna Thane's lips was scarcely hearsay. Nicholas had promised marriage. He would have married her if it had not been for his mother and his own cowardice. "Yes, Father."

"Don't let this duke turn your head," he warned. "Maintain a proper distance, my dear, even as you enjoy his attentions as your due."

The fact of the matter, Judith knew, was that the duke had already turned her head and a proper distance was *not* being maintained. They went for long walks and although she was now accompanied by her maid, Betsy would linger far behind, allowing for intimate conversation and glances - something she was well accustomed to doing from Nicholas's courtship. The duke did not dare a kiss, but even the warmth of his arm felt improper somehow, with the heat in his gaze.

They walked the very same paths she had strolled with Nicholas, but even further afield. She was thankful that those treacherous memories were being overlaid with a new pattern.

She still grieved Nicholas every night, composing the coldly furious set-down she would give him on his return. She had gone from love to hostility overnight, it seemed, and it festered in her when she had no other distraction for her thoughts. Better to feel anger than the aching grief of her heart.

Then gradually her last thoughts before sleep turned to the duke instead: how he had made her laugh, how he had clasped her hand, how he had made her think. Better to dwell on that than to remember Nicholas's guileful blue eyes.

His grace also invited her to Sargenet again, gave her a tour of the house and grounds, and took her riding. Always, when the duke entered a room, she was struck by his vibrancy and power, his effortless grace and charm, born of his position and upbringing, as well as his own personality. They talked of everything and nothing, and she enjoyed his bright, charismatic presence. Only slowly did she realise it was not just his own magnetism at work, but the sparkling energy between them.

Judith told herself not to take it too seriously. Like Anna, she must not be misled. The duke was an overt flirt, just as he had been the first night they met. This was all a delightful distraction, nothing more. She was vaguely aware that she was also being vindictive, seeking out a punishment for Nicholas that would suit his crime. Their engagement was over, as far as she was concerned, and she only hoped he would feel some prick of jealousy to hear that the duke had beguiled her days before leaving for London.

One afternoon, she and Dacian rode over the fields together, with Judith on a horse from his stables, and Betsy following at a distance on a placid mare. Reaching a glade by a river, the duke helped her dismount. As his hands tightened round her waist, he murmured into her ear that she was a fine horsewoman, a veritable Diana.

She turned, stepping out of his embrace and gave him a scornful glance. "Oh, do be quiet, your grace."

"Why?" His dark eyes gleamed, appearing to admire the picture she made in her old riding habit, standing on the bank of daisies, the river glistening behind her.

"I can tell you lie," she answered. "I don't like listening to empty flattery."

She turned away, more upset than she ought to be. After all, she knew she was only playing the role of country flirtation, a chance for him to practice his wiles. Why should she expect honesty from him?

"So mistrustful." He put his hand out to catch at her elbow. "Shall I try again, Judith? You are truly beautiful to me." He paused. "I have not met a more intriguing woman in all my twenty-four years."

His words rang with truth.

Inadvertently, she turned quickly to look up at him. He smiled, that same dazzling smile that she knew had felled many women. Yet this one seemed especially for her, containing them in some secret world. It was just them and the river and the warmth of the sun, and a strange heady magic enclosing them.

Despite herself, she smiled back. She felt his hand tighten on her arm, drawing her closer.

"Judith," he murmured. "Sweet Judith. Let me kiss you."

It wouldn't be long before Betsy would catch up to them. For these few moments, they were alone, with no one to see them except the willow trees and the insects skimming over the water.

Unable to resist, she raised her face to his. What harm would one kiss do? Nicholas had stolen as much from Anna.

The duke let out a sigh and pulled her into his body. His lips met hers and they kissed, tentatively at first, and then with more certainty. It ought to have been sweet, but the energy between them was like a magnet meeting iron, a strong grip that held them together even after their lips parted.

The intensity of it spun through her body, holding her in place. She felt both enraptured and exquisitely safe, like nothing she had ever felt before. Even Nicholas's kisses, as delightful as they had been, did not compare to the powerful lodestone of the duke.

They stood there for long moments, saying nothing, breathing each other in.

The sound of steady clip-clopping hooves broke them out of the enthralment. It was Betsy, arriving at last. Judith stepped out of his embrace and it was as if she had lost something precious.

He turned to busy himself with the stirrups. "So you learn to take a compliment, Miss Horis."

"So you learn to give one," she replied, and they smiled at each other like children.

"You must visit Sargenet tomorrow," he said. "The roses are blooming on the arbour; there is one corner in particular that I want to show you."

JUDITH WALKED up the drive at Sargenet, wondering if the roses were simply an excuse that the duke had invented to see her once more. Would he whisk her down a garden path to a hidden alcove in the rose arbour and kiss her again? She cast a glance at Betsy, knowing that her maid was equally invested in the courtship and would allow her some discretion.

Courtship? Was that the right word?

The memory of the duke's kiss had kept Judith awake until late the previous night. A kaleidoscope of emotions had twisted through her: guilt, desire, longing, and a burning curiosity. Did he experience their embrace with the same intensity that she had? Did he still regard her as a mere flirtation or had his feelings ripened into something more?

More, she felt a new guilt, toward Nicholas. She had never known any lips other than her intended's, and she had not officially broken off the engagement. Looked at dispassionately, her behaviour was that of a hussy. It had been easy to fool herself that it was a harmless flirtation when the duke was merely ravishing her with his eyes. Now it was a different matter and she felt both wretched and ecstatic. It was not a comfortable place to reside. She needed to tell the duke about her relations with Nicholas, and it was imperative that she inform Nicholas that their engagement was over.

She knocked on the imposing door of Sargenet. Fitzroy opened it. The butler's closed face was the first sign that something was amiss. She disregarded it; she was as light as a feather with the anticipation of seeing the duke again.

Fitzroy made her and Betsy wait in the cold entrance hall. After long minutes, he returned and led them to the blue drawing room. As she stepped in, Judith marvelled at the beauty of it, the light and space and elegance, the soft blues and creams set off by the wooden furniture.

"Miss Judith Horis," announced the butler.

The duke stood with his back to them, looking out the long windows.

As soon as she laid eyes on him, she knew something was

wrong. His shoulders held an unfamiliar tension and his body was taut.

The door snicked shut behind her. The duke remained staring outside. Judith exchanged a confused glance with Betsy.

The silence stretched out.

Judith stepped forwards. "Your grace?" she asked. "Is anything amiss?"

He turned. She almost stepped back again. His face was cut from stone, his eyes black coals, his jaw a rigid line. For the first time, she became aware of a faint pressure in the air.

He held a sheet of paper clenched in one hand.

"I received a letter from Nicholas this morning." His voice was like flint.

Her heart plummeted. She stared at the missive. "Oh?"

The duke cut his gaze to Betsy. "The contents are rather private. Perhaps while I share the news with you, your maid can pick some roses to take home. Fitzroy will show her the arbour."

Betsy bobbed a curtsy and hastily fled from the room, giving Judith one last wide-eyed look at this autocratic and improper dismissal.

Judith took a few tentative steps forward. "What does Nicholas say?" She paused. "Whatever it is, I can explain, Dacian."

He flung the letter up before him. "Shall I read it to you? *'I have been detained in London longer than I expected. Please, my friend, in my absence, I ask you to keep a watchful eye on Miss Judith Horis. She is most dear to me. I have not wanted to tell you the news until now, but we are secretly engaged to be married.'*"

Dacian's eyes flicked up to her and the accusation in them was like the sting of a horsewhip.

"Is this true?"

Judith swallowed. "Yes, we were engaged. But no longer! It is finished!"

"Not in Nicholas's mind, I observe." His voice was icy.

"Nicholas left for London two weeks ago," she said, struggling to retain her composure. "And soon after he left, I discovered his relationship with Anna Thane. As far as I am concerned, from that moment on we were no longer betrothed. I have not been in honour bound to him, though I have not had a chance to tell him yet."

"His relationship with Anna Thane?" The duke's brow furrowed. The letter fell to his side. "How did you discover it?"

"Through you." She was relieved at his calm question. "I haven't told you, but I am Gifted in Discernment. I could hear your lie about Nicholas that day by the blackberries, so I asked my maid about it."

"You share the same Gift as Nicholas." His tone was bleak. "You are well matched."

She ignored that. "Regardless, you must see why I regarded myself as freed from the engagement, if he has been in love with Anna all along."

Dacian's face hardened again, into grim lines. "You are too hasty, Judith. Nicholas doesn't love Anna anymore; he renounced Anna months ago. Even in this letter he writes how his feelings for her have faded."

"Ah," said Judith. "So his feelings *were* very strong."

"It was before he ever met you," snapped the duke. He shook the letter like a threat. "Admit it: you were simply jealous and you used *me* to feel better about yourself, and to punish him - and me." He laughed, a bitter sound. "I suppose you thought I deserved it. You've always thought I was the insincere one."

"That's not true!" She took a breath, knowing that honesty was necessary now. "Perhaps initially I welcomed your attentions to soothe my hurt. Yet my feelings for you have grown to be much more than that. Please don't look so harshly upon me."

"You should have considered my good opinion before you

betrayed your fiancé," he said cuttingly. "And I cannot seduce his betrothed behind his back. I've been friends with him since boyhood! You must see it is impossible."

His voice broke on the last sentence and he turned away from her again, walking blindly to a chair and grasping the back of it, like a blind man on a stormy deck.

Judith felt as if the heavy door of Sargenet had fallen on her. Impossible? She couldn't quite understand the meaning of his words.

"Do you mean - you think I must marry Nicholas?" She hated the quaver in her voice.

"Yes."

As he spoke, there was a silent crack like felt thunder, a sharp, reverberating shudder through the air. The wooden chair in his hands shattered. Shards of wood flew outward, splintering the space. Instinctively, she threw her arms up. When she looked through them, she saw the duke's hands and forehead were bleeding.

"Judith, are you alright?" He was white, stricken. "My cursed power still escapes me. I would never forgive myself if I hurt you."

"Dacian." She ran over, almost glad that she had something real to tend to, pulling her handkerchief out of her reticule and pressing it on his forehead. The white cambric soaked red.

She looked for the bell, but Fitzroy was already in the room, having felt the silent thunder. After one glance, the butler retreated to fetch cloths and bandages. Judith stripped off her gloves, and when he returned, held the padding to the duke's hands, forcing him to sit down on the couch.

Despite his hurts, it was a relief to be close to him again. She only wished she could stroke his black hair, brush her lips over his, and tell him it was going to be alright.

He stared grimly down at their clasped hands. "I almost hurt you."

"You hurt yourself," she corrected. The cut on his forehead still weeped a trickle of blood.

They sat close together, thighs touching. She dared to hope, and slipped an arm round his waist.

He dropped his head on her shoulder, sighing deeply. "Judith."

"Yes?"

"We cannot do this."

In which a storm wails

One lie can give rise to a cascade of untruths.
  - from *Lady Avely's Guide to Truth and Magic*

JUDITH STEPPED over the wall and made her way slowly through the fields. She could not deny that she was a little flustered from her encounter with the duke. The truth was that she *was* very glad to see him again. Their rapport had not faded, even after all these years.

When Nicholas had died, and she had discovered the truth about Robert Steer, she had thought ... well, she didn't even want to admit to herself what she had thought. That the duke might renew his attentions. That once she was a widow, he might pursue her in earnest again. Which was ridiculous. Instead, he had initially avoided her, until their encounter at Garvey House. Their fight then might have been her fault, but afterwards he had left England without another word, and stayed away.

Clearly, he did not care for her. She must not be misled by his charm now. It was simply that she was conveniently close by: low-hanging fruit to entertain his grace while he repaired at his country estate. Judith nibbled on her lip. She was determined not to be low-hanging fruit.

Sighing, she remembered that his hair had seemed blue-black in the sun. And his shoulders somehow broader, his skin faintly tanned. Whatever he had been doing in Spain suited him, as did the lines at the corners of his eyes. His air of authority had only increased. And his eyes still laughed at her, as they always had.

She became aware that she was meandering in her thoughts again, so she set on a brisk pace toward the village. Passing under the bows of the beech trees, she remembered Robert's straight-forward gaze instead, and felt something soften within her.

For so long, she had wrestled with Nicholas's secret, feeling besmirched, furious, and ashamed. Yet there was nothing to be ashamed of in Robert. He appeared to be a fine young man, one who had sought to protect Miss Atkinson, and uphold his debt to the duke. Judith knew, of course, that an illegitimate child did not bear the taint of their birth. It was more her *own* grief that loosened a little, seeing those blue, unflinching eyes. Perhaps good had come from Nicholas's misdeeds, after all.

If only she could be sure that Robert and Anna had not suffered too much, and somehow rectify the wrong.

Soon, she reached the stile that joined with the main road. A cart rumbled by, wheels clacking over the dirt. The clouds were growing ominously dark, and she feared that rain might be imminent.

Turning to look back, she saw that a man was walking along the road, head bent, lost in thought. He was clothed as a gentleman, his black hat low over his face. She walked faster, but found that he kept pace with her, thirty feet behind. Not liking the feeling of a figure lurking behind her, she slowed down so he could pass her. The man also slowed.

Frowning, she stopped, and bent as if to fix something on her gown. The man's footsteps approached and she looked up, once more glad of her veil.

It was the earl, Lord John. She had thought so, but now she could be sure, seeing the thin shoulders and black hair of the duke's brother. John's face had thinned with age, though he was younger than the duke, and it looked as if he hadn't been eating enough. Too much time with his books, perhaps. She knew that Lord John was Gifted in Memory, content to spend hours in the vast regions of his mind. Ironically, perhaps he'd been forgetting to eat. Or maybe he *was* ill, as Mary had suggested.

Frown lines marked his eyes and he seemed unhappy or worried. He stopped as she fiddled with her gown. "Good afternoon, ma'am. Can I help you with anything?"

She bobbed a curtsy. "Good afternoon, my lord. It is but a trifle, I thank you."

His eyes sharpened a little at her voice, but she bent her head again, unwilling to expose her identity. She hoped he did not remember her. It had been a long day and she did not fancy explaining her situation once more. She made a show of rifling through her reticule, effectively dismissing him.

He paused a moment, then continued on his way.

She followed behind him as they walked to the village. Oddly, Lord John's destination was the same as hers: the Gryffin, the only inn at Sargen village. Rain was beginning to fall gently. She hurried after him, hoping to see what business concerned him.

His lordship went through the yard and continued inside. When she quietly followed, she saw him talking, low-voiced, to the innkeeper. Judith stood as if awaiting her turn, straining her ears. Despite her acute senses, she could not make out their conversation, especially against the sound of rain now splattering on the roof. It sounded as if Lord John had a question. The innkeeper looked impassive in response, and Lord John looked round nervously at Judith, sharpening his eyes on her once more, rather as if he wished he could rip off her veil.

With dignity, she stepped forward and asked the innkeeper some trivial request. Lord John turned and stalked off.

She was glad to go upstairs to her bare, but now familiar, little room. After shedding her damp clothes and bathing, she requested a large supper, telling herself she could afford to be a little indulgent this evening, for she could rely on the hospitality of the duke going forward. Still, she did not order any chocolate, feeling a little guilty to be so easily bought.

Tired after the long day, she lit the fire and leaned back in the armchair. Outside the rain had turned into a storm, the heavy clouds obscuring the sunset. Wind whipped around the inn, creaking in the eaves. Judith ate her dinner, washed, and waited for Miss Cultor to arise. Perhaps she could give the vampiri the orange-gold cloth purchased today. It might make Miss Cultor more amenable to the rather forward request that Judith intended to propose.

"No," said Miss Cultor, her hands on her hips as she stood on the bed. "I won't go back there, thank you for asking, my lady. I don't hold with skulls. Or skeletons wearing nothing but a helmet."

Outside, the storm wailed, the rain loud on the roof.

Judith was momentarily distracted. "Oh, did the apparition appear with a helmet?"

Miss Cultor nodded. "Marching down the upper gallery in the ballroom with a black feather waving from it. The rest of its bones were as bare as a branch in winter. I regretfully decline your invitation."

Judith folded her hands in her lap patiently. "Perhaps I should explain a little more."

"You could do that," allowed Miss Cultor. She sat down cross-legged. "Why do you want to go to that heathen house? I thought you were more proper than that."

Judith decided not to mention Robert, and to appeal to Miss Cultor's sense of adventure instead. The vampiri's yellow gown was once more dirtied at the hem, her hair a wild tangle of brown curls. Once more Judith resisted the urge to comb out the knots.

"The duke has asked me to help him solve a mystery. There was a murder at Sargenet two days ago."

Miss Cultor sat straighter. "Murder? Two days ago? That was just after I left with Mr Nottley!"

"Yes, I thought you might be interested to know - a footman was killed in the drawing room, by the concerted application of a book."

Miss Cultor's eyes widened. "Oh dear. That lends even more vulgarity to the residence. Not a proper use of a book, and so Mr Nottley would say." A window pane rattled.

"Indeed. Yet I am a Truth Discernor, so the duke wants me there as he questions everyone."

"Hmm," Miss Cultor frowned thoughtfully. "The duke has returned, has he? I suppose when a duke is on the scene, all accusations of vulgarity fade away. What has this all to do with *me*, may I ask?"

Judith leaned forward. "If I am to use my Gift continually over the next few days to question everyone, I will need the help of a vampiri bond to ameliorate my Bemusement. I would be honoured if you would become my blood companion while I stay at Sargenet, merely temporarily. Afterwards, I could return you to your stablehand, or give you passage to Devon or Cornwall, which is where I travel next - whichever you prefer."

Miss Cultor raised her brows. "You mean you want me to return to the scene of a murder and poke round until we find the murderer?"

Judith bit her lip. "Not exactly. I'll be the one poking round, not you."

"Are you mad?"

Judith winced. "No?"

Miss Cultor folded her arms again. "Of course I'm going to poke round. I am a creature of the night, ideally suited to the task. I'll be a shadow in the darkness while you are sleeping. I can hunt for a suspicious character creeping about with a book." A smile of anticipation spread across her piquant face. "And if anyone sees me, they'll think I'm merely a faery."

Judith shuddered, beginning to regret her invitation. "I hope you will do no such thing. I do not intend for you to be in any danger."

As if provoked by her words, lightning flashed through the gap in the curtains. Moments later thunder boomed in the distance and Judith stood restlessly, aware of a desire to keep her hands busy. She went over to rifle through her valise, pulling out some knitting that she had begun in Devon, in soft creamy wool. Her daughter would require marital stockings and there was no time to waste, with the wedding in less than a month.

Miss Cultor watched from her seat on the bed. "What of yourself? You are not taking into account the danger *you* might encounter."

Judith settled into the armchair and began to knit. "I will be fine." As she said it, she realised it was because she knew she would have the duke by her side. She was indulging in some foolish notion that he would protect her, and she shook off the thought irritably. Regardless, no one would dare approach a middle-aged widow with violence.

Miss Cultor seemed to read her mind. "You are mighty thick with the duke, my lady."

"I have known him for many years," replied Judith primly.

"Oh? And what is the duke's particular talent?"

Judith hesitated, but the information was well known in the upper Musor circles in London, though kept a secret from the general populace. "He is an Impactor."

"A dangerous fellow himself then."

"I suppose. He has a certain ... reputation for violence. Though he tells me he has grown out of it by now." She started another row, frowning down at the wool. Age did seem to have mellowed him a little, softening the rawness of his power to a warmer edge. Unfortunately, it was even more attractive than the volatility of his youth. When she was young, she had been silly enough to think that his unbridled power was a sign of his love for her. Now she knew that his ability to contain himself was a better gauge.

She pushed those memories away, frowning at herself. She had been so foolish back then. Those few weeks, so long ago, felt as if they had happened to another person. At the very least, they had no bearing on her present relationship with his grace. She was doing herself a disservice to imagine that he could remember it all as clearly as she could.

Miss Cultor pursed her lips. "What of you? Do many people know of your particular talent?"

"Not my ability to Discern lies," admitted Judith, looking up. "I drew away from the Musor circles twelve years ago, when my husband died. However, even when I partook of the salons I did not bandy about the particulars of my Gift. People don't like to be caught out in their little falsehoods." She had even kept it secret from her own children, until they had discovered it.

"Good," said Miss Cultor. "Better that no one knows that you can sniff out lies, if there is a deadly ghost loose."

Judith frowned at her knitting. Was the person behind the 'ghost' also responsible for the murder? They could be separate matters entirely, but she was curious to solve them both. "Yes, if anyone asks, I am posing as a Diplomacor when I help the duke interview the servants."

"Lord John and Lady Mary are Memors, are they not? Mr Nottley told me they have long shared his interests."

Judith nodded. "Yes, and I believe that Lady Agatha has a measure of Impacting like the duke, though not as strong."

It was another reason Lady Agatha had not taken on the marriage mart. Those in the know considered her Gift unladylike, especially as it rendered her stronger than most suitors.

"Useful for wielding a book effectively," suggested Miss Cultor.

Judith smiled, unwinding her wool. "I cannot imagine Lady Agatha committing such an act and bringing scandal to Sargenet." She bethought herself of something else that might be useful. "*You* might be able to sniff out the Illusor, with your ability to sense when someone is Musing."

Miss Cultor propped her elbows on her knees, resting her chin on her hands. "I was there for the skull's first appearance, you know. It happened after I arrived with Mr Nottley a few weeks ago."

"Tell me about it." Judith tilted her head to listen, while continuing the intricacies of sock-work. Rain continued to pour down outside.

"I didn't see it myself," Miss Cultor warned. "I heard about it the next day. The housemaid said she saw a skull hanging from the ballroom chandelier. It was tied with a red ribbon and swinging slowly, though there was no movement of air."

Judith imagined the vast, empty ballroom at night, a skull swaying as if to invisible music. She wrinkled her nose. "I see what you mean. Did the skeleton appear there too?"

Miss Cultor nodded. "Yes, waltzing about the ballroom floor - that's the one I saw. Our ghost likes to dance, it appears. I was too taken aback to think of sensing for magic."

"A shame. I wonder what the significance of the ballroom may be." Judith rather suspected it was a matter of accessibility. The upper gallery of the ballroom joined with both wings of the house on either side.

Miss Cultor had a more dramatic turn of mind. "Has anyone died there, do you suppose?"

"Not that I am aware. Any Sargens probably died in their beds or on a battlefield."

"A ballroom can be a battlefield," said Miss Cultor sagely. "What about the old duke, how did he die?"

"A hunting accident, a long time ago. Certainly not in the ballroom." Thunder still cracked at intervals. Judith put her knitting aside, and placed more wood on the fire. "So, will you join me tomorrow, Miss Cultor?"

The vampiri smiled broadly, showing a glimpse of tiny fangs. "I would be delighted."

Judith brushed dirt from her hands. "Perhaps," she suggested, "we can begin our blood bond now. I suspect my mettle will soon be tested."

Miss Cultor agreed and deigned to feed from Judith's wrist. The prick of little teeth tickled and Judith settled back, glad that the vampiri would not be making another treacherous trip to the stable-yard tonight. They both needed rest. Tomorrow, Judith suspected, they would be hunting a spectre and a murderer.

Interlude IV

Twenty-three years earlier

When the blood stopped flowing, Judith bandaged the duke's hands, her fingers gentle. The light from the drawing room windows showed the wound on his forehead all too clearly as he sat beside her.

"I still can't control my power." His voice was rough. "Do you forgive me?"

She smiled at him, afraid, but not for the reason he thought. "Only if you forgive me."

He dropped his eyes. Carefully, he lifted her hands and returned them to her lap. "There is nothing to forgive. It was a mere flirtation that we can now forget."

"Don't say that."

"Why not? It's true."

"I can hear when you lie, remember."

He stood abruptly. "Well, then, it has to become true. You have to leave now, before we create any scandal. We do not want anything to come to Nicholas's ears that would give him room to doubt you."

"Never mind that *I* doubt *him*!"

"You should not. He loves you." The duke would not look at her. "You should marry him."

Judith swallowed. Was she meant to keep all of this from Nicholas and proceed as if nothing had happened? It felt as if the shard of wood was lodged in her heart, along with a terrible, doubting guilt. Had she made an awful mistake?

"You must go now," he repeated. Judith opened her mouth to object, but at that moment Fitzroy appeared at the door, informing them that Betsy had returned with the roses.

Judith stood mechanically. "Thank you, Fitzroy." The sight of Betsy's armful of red and pink flowers was a fresh pain.

"I hope you enjoy the blooms." The duke stood with his bandaged hands behind his back. "Good day, Miss Horis."

Like a mourner, Judith left Sargenet, blinded by tears.

As well as her heartbreak, Judith had to bear with the indignity of the local gossip, in an ironic echo of what must have been Anna's experience after Nicholas abandoned her.

Those who had been displeased to see a mere rector's daughter catch the attention of a duke were maliciously glad to see that his interest was as quickly lost as gained. His grace was no longer seen calling at the Rectory, or riding or walking with Miss Horis. The duke, in fact, was heard to have closed the doors of Sargenet, refusing all callers, drinking to excess, and riding recklessly. Rumours said he planned to return to London soon.

Furthermore, it was remarked that Miss Horis looked quite miserable, when she ought to have known better than to have set her cap at a duke, especially such a rake as Sargen. Even the return of her other suitor, Mr Nicholas Avely, did not seem to cheer her spirits.

Nicholas returned three days after the dreadful scene in the

Sargenet drawing room. Judith barely slept for those nights, her innards twisting as she considered the import of the duke's words. Was he right? Did Nicholas in fact love her, not Anna? Had she utterly betrayed him?

Her heart rebelled at the thought, for her heart now longed for Dacian. Reluctantly, however, her mind began to accept the truth of what he had said. What affairs Nicholas had conducted before he met her were Nicholas's own business. She could not hold him to an impossible standard of purity before their courtship; never mind that she was supposed to be so chaste. If what Dacian said was true, Nicholas had put Anna behind him. He been loyal to Judith and proposed marriage in good faith, even if he had first loved another.

Gradually, her old anger faded away to a terrible apathy. Very well, Nicholas had done no wrong to her directly. Very well, she had no real excuse to break off the engagement, other than jealousy and pride.

Yet she found she could not bear the thought of marrying him, not when Dacian had kissed her. Guilt surged through her, at her recklessness and faithlessness, yet all she wanted was Dacian's embrace and for the smile to return to his eyes when he looked at her.

When Nicholas called on the third day, she received him in the Rectory parlour. She could see from the hallway mirror that her eyes were sunken, her face pale, but she could not bring herself to care. The icy set-down she had laboured over had deserted her. She didn't even know what she would say; she had no idea where to begin, or if she should even say anything at all.

Yet when Nicholas walked into the room, her heart gave a strange lurch. He was smiling, his handsome countenance open, his blue eyes so glad to see her. He wore a new coat he must have purchased in London and he took off his hat and eagerly grasped her hand.

"Judith! Are you well? I am so happy to see you again."

"Well enough," she murmured, gladdened somehow by his cheerfulness even as it cut at her heart. Seeing his smile reminded her of all the time they had spent together, in those innocent days from before. "Was London to your liking?"

"Not as much as returning home to you, my beautiful muse." He paused, eyes fixing on her face. "My dear, you don't appear to be at your usual vitality."

She sank back into her chair, retrieving her hand. Nicholas was forced to step back but he remained hovering anxiously over her.

"Judith, are you ill? Tell me what is wrong."

She looked up at his worried face, his familiar eyes creased in concern. The chair felt hard and unforgiving, and her lungs didn't seem to be working properly.

"Nicholas, I know about Anna Thane."

His face transmuted into shock. Finally, he fell back a step. "What do you mean?"

"I know that you love her."

She kept her tone even but her lack of anger seemed to frighten Nicholas more. He went pale.

"What?"

"I can Discern the truth, remember," she said dully. "I spoke to her. I know that you loved her and would have married her, if not for your mother."

Nicholas swallowed. "I spoke of marriage - I never promised it. She knew as well as I did that it was unlikely."

"Because you were too much of a coward."

"No! It was because I need a wife who will be able to move in the highest circles in London! My position requires it."

Judith raised her eyebrows in scorn.

Nicholas waded on. "And Anna is not Gifted." He paused, uncomfortable under Judith's glare. "Don't forget that the Avely motto is *Vincit Prudentia*. I have the family line to consider. It was not a matter of cowardice; far from it."

Judith had thought it was a happy accident that her Gift aligned with his. Now she knew that she had been chosen simply to uphold the Avely maxim, 'Wisdom Conquers', which pointed to a long heritage of Discernment. Nicholas - and his mother - were clearly determined to ensure his children also carried on that noble tradition.

"So pleased my Gift is useful to your bloodline," Judith snapped, "and that I am necessary for your position! I thank you for the kind sentiment."

He flushed, and knelt at her feet. "That's not what I meant! I love you quite aside from all that. Please," he begged, "you can hear it in my voice, I know it."

She could, but it was cold comfort, now that she would rather hear the words from Dacian. Twisting her hands in her lap, she avoided Nicholas's gaze.

"Judith, I could not bear if this were to drive us apart," he said earnestly, placing his hands over hers. "Please forgive me."

She looked round the tidy drawing room, searching for words.

"It has already driven us apart. It has been a shock to me, to find that you already love another - that I was your second choice, for such stupid reasons."

Nicholas shook his head silently, a pained expression on his face as he realised he could not voice a denial without her hearing the lie.

"I do not think we should proceed with our engagement," she said shakily. She did not want to reveal her own unfaithfulness, even as guilt dug into her. At least she knew how to keep her voice even, and phrase her words to be oblique. "As it stands, I cannot marry you. You must give me time to think."

Nicholas swallowed hard and stood. "Yes, of course. As much time as you need."

He left the Rectory with his head bowed, and Judith felt remorse twist her heart anew.

AFTER HE LEFT, she spent many days in turmoil. It was a disagreeable task to reflect more closely on her own motivations. If anything, Nicholas, with his one indiscretion - a foolish courtship - was a beacon of morality compared to Dacian's multitude of affairs. Although Dacian had implied he would never mislead a village girl, he had committed other indiscretions with women of his own class. Why, then, did she judge Nicholas so harshly for his stolen kisses?

Was she, a rector's daughter, so easily swayed by jealousy and pride?

Yet below those ugly whirlpools, and transcending them, was love. She was certain of it. How else could she describe this yearning to see Dacian again, this ache in her heart, this sense of despair at his continued absence? She longed to see him and explain, to beg him to see things differently.

Or was this simply passion, not love?

She had only known the duke for a few weeks, she realised. How could this have happened? Had she allowed heightened feelings, stoked by pain, to carry her away? Rationally, she owed Nicholas loyalty and a second chance.

Irrationally, all she could think of was Dacian.

Late in the restless hours of the night, Judith decided that she had to speak to the duke. It was imperative, utterly essential, that she talk with him before she made any irrevocable decision.

She would have to be quick, before he left for London, as the rumours promised he would. She sat up in bed, suddenly gripped by a certainty that he would leave the following morning. What if she were too late? What if she missed him? Agonised by the thought, she got out of bed, pacing restlessly.

Half an hour later, she led her father's horse at a quiet walk through the Rectory gate. The countryside was dark, lit only by a waning moon. It was safe enough, she reasoned, for no one would be abroad this late. No one would notice a young woman riding to Sargenet, dressed as if for a morning ride even though it was past midnight.

Her progress was nerve-racking, nonetheless, and when she reached the woods, it was too black to ride further. She tethered Milly to a tree and proceeded on foot by lantern-light, mutinously ignoring the shifting darkness, driven by her insistent need to talk to Dacian.

Finally, she emerged onto the front lawns of Sargenet, her hem damp from dew. Everything was grey and black, the trees casting long shadows over the grass. The mansion was a looming darkness except for one window burning with light. It must be the duke, she reasoned, and she took some hope from the fact that he too was awake, perhaps burdened with her own agitation.

She marched across the drive, determined that her nerve should not fail her now. The front door had never seemed so large as she clanged the knocker down as loudly as she could, and set down her lantern.

After a long wait, Fitzroy opened the door part way, his eyes widening in astonishment when he saw Judith on the step.

"Miss Horis! What are you doing here?"

"I have come to see the duke." She aimed for a brazen noncha-lance in her voice, though allowing her eyes to plead. "Please, Fitzroy, let me speak with him privately. It is an urgent matter."

Fitzroy's bushy eyebrows lowered. "I'm afraid it is impossible, Miss Horis. His grace is asleep."

"Nonsense. I saw his window lit."

"Indisposed, then." Fitzroy changed tack. "Unfit to see a lady,

I can assure you. And we have the hour to consider too. Most irregular. You ought to be safe at home."

Fitzroy had never been so loquacious before. Dacian must be drunk, and in a state of disarray. All to the good; if Dacian were three sheets to the wind, he might be more open about his feelings with her.

"I must see his grace," repeated Judith. She tried to push the door open and pass Fitzroy, but the butler was redoubtable and remained undefeated by this tactic. His elbows suddenly seemed to gain pointier ends.

"My apologies, Miss Horis, but I cannot allow you in." Fitzroy's voice held a note of finality.

Judith stared at him, wondering if she should fall to her knees and beg. A moment later she was glad she did not, for the duke's voice came from the great hall.

"Fitz, who is at the door at this ungodly hour?"

Fitzroy turned to acknowledge his master, blocking Judith from view. "An unsuitable caller, your grace. You may return to your bed."

"Dacian," called Judith. "He won't let me in."

"Is that Judith, or did I imagine it?" drawled the duke. "Are you obstructing a lady, Fitz?"

Judith drew a ragged breath of relief. Dacian did sound drunk, but not displeased to see her.

"Yes, let me in." This time she pushed past Fitzroy without encountering resistance, though the butler's face was tense with worry.

The hall was lit only by one sconce of candles. The duke held another aloft in his hand. The light cast a flattering glow over his face, warming his handsome features and flinging a glitter into his eyes. Or perhaps that was the drink.

He raked his gaze over her. "Judith." He stepped forward until he was towering above her. "Come into the library."

She followed him meekly and when he closed the door she was suddenly lost for words, for all that she had to say. The smell of leather and old books was strong in the gloomy light. And she was alone with him at last.

He put the candles down and turned, his pupils dilated. "Judith. You've come to give me one more kiss before you marry Nicholas, haven't you?"

Her breath caught. "I don't want to marry Nicholas; I've told him so. You can kiss me if you like." Hope burned in her chest. He had forgiven her. He still wanted her.

She had been right to come. She dared him with her eyes, feeling the strength of their attraction as a palpable force between them.

A step brought him close. With a sigh, he swept an arm round her and pulled her in.

The warmth and hardness of him made her head swim. His masculine scent was heady: the smell of whisky, skin, and smoke. She lifted her face, inviting, and he kissed her.

It was rough and hungry this time, a devouring insistence. She revelled in it, opening her mouth to his, pressing against him, starved herself. Her hands lifted to curl over his shoulders and tangle in his hair. The same powerful magnetism bonded their bodies together again, as if they would never part.

Until, suddenly, Judith found herself pushed away.

His mouth reddened, the duke glared, black hair falling tousled over his brow. His pupils were enlarged with lust and drink.

"There," he said. "Now go."

"Don't be cruel." The cold of the library sucked at her but she held her ground.

He turned away, enunciating clearly. "I am drunk, my dear, but even I know that you should not be here. Are you trying to compromise me?"

She stared, nonplussed by his abrupt shift in mood. "I wanted to speak to you. Not just kiss you."

"There is nothing more to say," he said harshly. "Nicholas is awaiting his bride. It is time for you to leave."

He went to stand behind his desk, as if to keep it between them. His expression was grim and the candlelight now cast unflattering shadows across his face. Yet she could hear the lie in his voice, see the hurt in his eyes, and sense his regret for what he had just done.

"Dacian," she said, "I love you. You must know this. How can you expect me to marry Nicholas as if nothing has changed in the time he was away? You might be right that jealousy clouded my thinking. It might be true that I allowed myself to be beguiled into impropriety." She took a deep breath. "But the fact remains that I love you."

"Beguiled? That's an interesting choice of word," said Dacian coldly, ignoring her declaration. He leaned forward, gripping the desk, his fingers biting into the wood. Power hovered in the air, but his eyes were now unflinching. "If I recall correctly, you claimed that your cat died to disguise your real grief. That was when you discovered Nicholas's affair with Anna, was it not?"

Judith bit her lip. "I was upset and ashamed. I didn't want to tell you."

"So you lied to me."

"Only once!"

He released the desk and gave a sharp laugh. "You've been lying to me for our entire acquaintance. You didn't think I'd like to know that you are engaged to my friend?"

A wave of frustration swept over her. "I was going to tell you."

"When?"

"That very day you received Nicholas's letter. I knew things had progressed too far."

"You finally had me on your hook, you mean?"

"Don't demean us, Dacian." She clenched her hands into impotent fists. "Don't make me abase myself again."

"Abase? Is that how you feel about it?" Dacian stepped back, folding his arms across his chest. His face darkened. "Would you still love me if you knew I have a woman in my bedchamber at this very minute?"

Judith stared at him. His words were like a knife in her stomach. "Is that true?"

As if she had to ask.

"Yes." He paused, letting the word sink in. "As you know, without even having to see her, for you have such a useful talent. Quite convenient, really."

Judith swallowed. "Who is it?"

"The Widow Bleau." Dacian sat down deliberately and leaned back in the chair. "Victoria heard that I was in some distress and came to offer her sympathies. I do enjoy the ministrations of a beautiful woman. And I confess that my vanity was in need of soothing."

Judith felt the blood drain out of her face. "How could you?"

His face was a mask of stone.

"How could I not?" he countered. "You are promised to Nicholas. I am promised to protect his interests. What else is left for me to do? I am saving us both, by making the picture eminently clear."

Silence stretched thick between them. The looming bookshelves now felt cluttered and imposing, the darkness frightening.

"You are ruining us both," she said at last, with certainty.

He gave a harsh laugh. "I am sure your supposed *love* for me will fade in time. It was never built on strong foundations. It lacks common respect at its core."

"That is not true!"

"You are not the only arbiter of truth, Miss Horis. You have always thought me a wastrel and a rake, so I doubt your momentary infatuation would have lasted. Your sense of self-preservation and moral discernment would have prevailed."

She gripped her hands together, aware that she had entertained that very thought a day ago.

He raised his brows. "Don't look at me with those lost eyes. I will accept your thanks later, when you realise that your agonising decision is now made easy."

At this, she straightened. "Don't you dare use me as an excuse for your peccadillos, your grace!"

"We are back to 'your grace'," Dacian observed. His lips twisted wryly. "Very good. Now if you would kindly leave, Miss Horis, as you are keeping me from the comforts of my bed."

She gasped in outrage. Turning abruptly, she gathered up her skirts even as tears gathered in her eyes. She refused to look at him as she stalked toward the door.

"Good bye, Miss Horis," called the duke. "I do wish you well, you know."

It was true, she could hear it in his voice, with some other note she couldn't place. Mockery, most likely.

She wrenched the door open and marched out into the cold night, her heart breaking.

IT WAS A TERRIBLE REVERSAL. Now it was Dacian who had broken her heart and ground down her pride. Now it was Dacian who had behaved like a rake and scoundrel - just as she had surmised he would from the start.

This time, it was Nicholas who had proved faithful and steadfast. He took her empty eyes and miserable demeanour to be a judgement on his own character, which he bore in humble patience. After a while, she relented a little, suggesting that they return to their walks to see if they could recover their former affection.

So they returned to their habitual strolls across the fields and along the streams, enjoying the sunlight and movement, the flowers and birdsong, and, gradually, their sense of a renewed companionship. Nicholas remained intelligent, kind, thoughtful, and loyal, just as he had always been. He would be a good friend, a good father, a good husband. They shared so much in common, even their Gift, and he swore to her that he loved her regardless, with truth ringing in his voice.

She could not deny that they were well-matched, as Dacian had said.

Meanwhile, rumours soon filtered through of the duke's outrageous flirtations and improper liaisons in London. He had left Judith behind for good, cast her aside, and her heart burned with a bitter fury. To think she had been deceived by his charm and charisma, and laid out her heart before him, only to have it ruthlessly defiled.

The duke was despicable, wicked ... and her heart ached with the loss of him, even as her cheeks flamed with anger.

Now it was Nicholas's tender solicitude that became a balm on her soul. The irony was not lost on her and she squirmed with self-recrimination, ashamed that she should turn from one man to the next and back again. For a while she considered staying a spinster, abjuring all men, and staying with her father in the Rectory, resigned to being an old maid. Yet the pull of motherhood was strong. She longed to have a family of her own and the comfort of her own household. It was self-defeating to spend her whole life as a spinster, grieving her broken heart, when she could marry a man who loved and respected her, even if a corner of his heart still belonged to another.

As they walked and talked together, something deeper also rekindled: her love for Nicholas. It had not vanished entirely, she realised, but had simply gone underground. The familiar patterns of their courtship allowed the current to re-emerge. His steadfast regard gradually cleansed the taint from it, and she began to believe again that he had given her his heart, and would guard her own carefully.

So she married him.

If it was not with the giddy joy she had felt months earlier, it was with a sustaining happiness, love, and a sense of relief. Within a year, she fell pregnant. Her adoration for the baby filled her days, and Nicholas's companionship was a steady rock, their friendship a boon.

If, late at night, her thoughts returned to Dacian's smiling eyes, the phantom was soon vanquished. It wasn't hard to remember his cruelty. When she saw him, inevitably, in London, the pain was sharp. Dacian avoided her, though he kept up his friendship with Nicholas, meeting him in the clubs and on horseback. Judith did not find it difficult to show her disapproval, as the stories about the duke increased.

In which the outlook is gloomy

In some respects, "Truth Discernment" is a misnomer, as the Gift is honed on discerning lies, not truth. Sometimes it is possible to piece together the truth from knowing the lies, yet this is not always the case.
  - from Lady Avely's Guide to Truth and Magic

THE NEXT MORNING the ducal carriage arrived at the Gryffin rather early. It was accompanied by a break in the dark clouds, and Robert.

Judith had not expected to speak to Robert again so soon. In the dim light of the inn, he looked even more like Nicholas: his rich brown hair tied back, his dimpled chin thrust out.

"Good morning, Lady Avely," he said, in the careful neutral tones of a good servant. There was no hint of curiosity as to how she had transformed from Mrs to Lady overnight, but she detected some new reserve in him nonetheless. "His grace sends his carriage and says I am to accompany you back to Sargenet."

Judith was impressed by the duke's dexterity. This way she would have a private space with Robert and an opportunity to speak to him at length. She nodded rather distantly, feeling apprehensive. Perhaps the duke was right, that Robert was better off without her patronage.

At least she must say her piece and do her duty. It would be a blessing to put the burden down. She was guiltily aware that one of her motivations to act now was to lessen her own guilt. Even in her righteousness she was selfish.

She was dressed in a grey silk morning gown, the best she could find for the occasion, and she had tied a matching mobcap over her hair. She rather thought she resembled a matronly mushroom and repressed any regret she had about this mortifying fact. Her valise was neatly packed with Miss Cultor tucked into the top right corner, in her bat form, her yellow gown and the paisley shawl folded round her to provide some cushioning.

Still, Judith handed the case over carefully. "Please pack this inside the carriage. It contains some precious, fragile belongings." She wondered if Miss Cultor was listening, jolted awake by the movement, and if she appreciated the description. Of course, now that they shared even a temporary bond, Judith was obligated to care for Miss Cultor, providing sustenance and shelter. Miss Cultor would return the favour by protecting Judith from Bemusement, and, one hoped, provide an extra pair of eyes and ears at Sargenet.

Robert took the valise. Judith added, cautiously, "And if you would be so good as to travel in the carriage with me, rather than on the back, I would welcome a chance to talk with you."

He nodded reluctantly and led the way outside, where rain was beginning to patter down again.

Once he had stowed the valise and handed Judith up, he leapt into the carriage himself and sat in the opposite corner. He stared out as they whisked through the village, clearly a little uncomfortable. The valise was wedged on the floor between them. Outside, the road was thick with mud from the storm.

As the village gave way to fields, Judith gripped her hands in her lap and wasted no more time.

"Mr Steer," she began. "Please listen to me for a moment."

"Of course, my lady." Robert turned his blue eyes upon her warily.

"As we both know, you are my husband's illegitimate child. I have come to apologise to you and to make you an offer."

Robert's brow creased slightly. "What do *you* have to apologise for, my lady?"

Outside, the sky was heavy, the stripped barley fields flattened by rain. Drops pattered on the carriage roof.

Judith cleared her throat. "Your position as a footman, for a start. I should never have allowed it to happen. It must have been an awful shock for you, after Taunton."

Robert's smile was rueful. "Taunton was a shock for me, my lady, when I started there. I never quite believed it would last. Footman duties bother me less than most, I suspect. Easier than blacksmithing."

Judith felt a flash of shame that he had always doubted his place at the school for privileged boys of the gentry. "I am sorry. I first learned of your existence after my husband died and I ought to have come to see you while the duke was abroad, especially when I heard of your position at Sargenet a year ago. I apologise for my laxness."

Robert's expression became opaque. "Well. Don't bother yourself about it too much, my lady. The duke has said he will look after me, now that he is home."

She sat up straighter and ploughed on, determined to say her piece. "There is no need for that, if you do not wish to be beholden to his grace. I have not told you the real reason I am here. Your father was granted a posthumous title for his service to the Crown. He died bravely in service of his country, and the king decreed that I am to take possession of a large property in Cornwall. I wondered if you would like to live there too. There is an income to support you. That is what Nicholas would have wanted, I am certain." She paused and added stiffly. "It is what I want also."

Robert turned to look at her, his expression surprised and wary. "You would have me live in Cornwall?"

"Yes. As is your due, as my husband's child." Judith clenched her hands in her lap, her fingernails digging even through her gloves. She cursed Nicholas, for the hundredth time, for putting her in this position, even as her gaze softened on Robert's face. He had suffered far more than she.

Silence fell in the swaying carriage, apart from the relentless rain overhead.

Robert turned to stare outside at the sodden landscape. After a long moment, he spoke. "I cannot leave. Not now. Sargenet needs me. I have told his grace I do not mind the position of footman for the moment, while the house is in such disorder."

Judith carefully undid the tight grip of her hands, feeling a mixture of relief and, oddly, disappointment. "Of course, we could wait until his grace employs some new footmen."

"It will be hard to find willing bodies when the last one died," said Robert wryly. "And even so, I don't like to leave Sargenet, not with things as they are. The duke requires my presence, and I owe him a debt of honour."

Judith could hear this was the truth, but she could sense something else beneath his words. She remembered the conversation she had overheard on the lawn. "Mr Steer, may I ask a question, perhaps related - do you entertain some doubts about how Gilbert died?"

Robert darted a nervous look toward her. She raised her brows. After a fraught pause, he gave a slightly theatrical sigh and dropped his stiff shoulders. "No - it is simply - I suppose death always seems like a terrible mistake."

Judith was suddenly reminded of her daughter Elinor and felt a strange pang. Robert was Elinor's half-brother, after all. Perhaps he shared Elinor's penchant for misdirection when it suited her. Misdirection was difficult for a Truth Discernor to catch. A person could be telling the complete truth and still be concealing something else.

"A terrible shock indeed," she said. "Who found Gilbert, do you know?"

Robert's eyes bulged slightly and he glanced sideways again. "Broughton, I believe."

It was a lie. Just as she had heard from Mr Lewis, the steward. Yet Robert appeared to be more nervous in uttering it, compared to Mr Lewis's casual confidence. Was the whole household lying about this little matter? Or were Mr Lewis and Robert hiding something? It was as she had suspected: the arrogant Mr Lewis had roped poor Robert into his deceit.

"Who is Broughton?" asked Judith carefully.

"The butler." Robert seemed to be relieved to be able to tell the simple truth this time.

Judith raised her brows. "Not Fitzroy anymore?"

"No, Lady Agatha dismissed Fitzroy a few years ago, I believe. He looks after the Dower House now, where Mr Lewis resides."

Judith thought of Fitzroy's silver head and kindly smile. The duke would not be happy with Agatha's impertinence in replacing him.

"And how did Broughton discover Gilbert?" she pressed.

Robert swallowed. "Er. He went into the drawing room late at night and found Gilbert dead on the settee by the fire."

Judith winced. Miss Cultor would not approve.

And Robert's recitation remained a lie. Furthermore, he seemed edgy, almost guilty. She supposed it was a good sign, that he disliked lying so much. Or perhaps it was an indication that he was hiding something worse.

Judith decided to go for the direct attack. "Did *you* find Gilbert's body, perchance?"

Robert's eyes widened in shock. "No!"

She leaned back, confused. His voice did not ring with the hollowness of an outright lie, but something coloured it nonetheless. If not deceit, perhaps it was just uncertainty? But how could one be *uncertain* if one had found a dead body?

Judith massaged her temples, hoping that her Gift was not playing her false at this juncture. She had not, after all, given it much usage since Nicholas had died. It had seemed unwise to Muse too much, especially given the Edicts and her lack of a blood companion to help counter the effects of Bemusement. Besides, she had plenty to occupy her in raising her children. Discerning their little untruths was the most she had practiced, apart from the whirlwind of Elinor's introduction to society and the chaos *that* had wrought.

Perhaps she was too used to her own children's deceptions, so it was difficult for her to read Robert's voice. Still, there was something out of key in his denial. She chewed on her lip. The carriage was now driving alongside the dark, impenetrable woods and soon they would reach Sargenet. She was running out of time.

She cleared her throat, speaking louder against the thick rain on the roof. "I believe you, Mr Steer, but if there is any way I can help, please allow me to do so. And please consider my offer to travel to Cornwall. My son and daughter will be there: your half-brother and half-sister. You could meet them."

Robert's face became as closed as stone. "Thank you, Lady Avely, for your very kind offer, but I am bound to Sargenet."

The undertone of refusal was clear. He had shut her out.

Judith sighed. She had made a mull of it. She had hoped to feel better after this conversation, but instead she felt worse, saddened and uneasy.

The carriage rolled past the last of the woods and up the long driveway. Ahead, Sargenet scowled under the grey sky, its black roofs glistening with rain.

The butler came out to greet Judith, who examined him with interest, glad to give her thoughts another direction. Broughton was a sturdy, dark-haired man with porous skin and grey streaks in his hair despite the energy in his stride. His manner was impeccable and he seemed quite unruffled, befitting a duke's butler, as he led Judith inside. Broughton was not unduly affected by recent events, it seemed.

Judith repressed the urge to ask him if he had found the body. It would be good to know if Broughton believed this to be true, or if he was also complicit in the lie. She pursed her lips in frustration. Perhaps under the duke's aegis she could make more direct enquiries.

Robert followed them into the house, carrying the valise. The high front windows were dim with rain and the atrium was cold. In the darkness of the vast entrance hall, it took Judith a moment to realise the duke was not there to greet her and to feel a moment's disappointment. She shook it off. No doubt the duke had plenty of business to see to upon his return to his ancestral home. He was probably in deep discussions with his steward.

Broughton led them up the right-hand staircase to the west wing. Judith expected to be shown to a small guest room, but the butler opened the door onto huge quarters of warm opulence, coloured in creams, yellows, and maroons. An elegant vase of autumn roses stood on an oak dresser by the bed.

"My lady," intoned Broughton, "the Gold Room."

The huge bed was covered with a cream-gold quilt. A long chaise sat by the tall windows, and next to it stood a steaming cup of chocolate.

Judith frowned. She hoped the duke didn't think she was so easily seduced. Did he imagine that she would invite him into this room later, to say thank you for this indulgence? Had he put other widows in here, before her? Mrs Bleau, perhaps, and all the others since then?

Not recently, at least, she told herself. It was merely ducal hospitality. She need not put her hackles up. Even if this room was far too extravagant for her, despite her new title of marchioness.

Broughton spoke. "Lady Agatha will be pleased to see you in the Green Drawing Room in half an hour."

Judith nodded a cool thank you and waited for Broughton's and Robert's footsteps to recede. Then she set about transferring Miss Cultor from the valise. She had to achieve this without exposing Miss Cultor to daylight, but it was a preferable risk to a zealous maid unpacking the vampiri later.

Miss Cultor blinked blearily from the valise, peering round the opulent room, the curtains now closed against the rainy day. "What's that? I smell spices." She froze. "Is that ... cocoa?"

Judith carried her across to the dresser, borne aloft on a pillow of paisley shawl. "Yes, the duke has provided me with a cup of chocolate. A special recipe from Spain, I hope."

Miss Cultor's eyes widened. "Don't drink it!"

Judith cast a look at the steaming cup. "What is wrong with Spanish chocolate?"

"*Any* chocolate!" The vampiri sat up straight in her nest of fabric. "It makes you deaf! It is something to do with the properties of the cocoa nut."

"Nonsense. Who told you that?"

"My mother saw it happen! She had a companion who drank chocolate like water." Miss Cultor paused ominously. "The lady went as deaf as a plank."

"Mere coincidence," Judith assured her, stepping back. "I've drunk plenty of chocolate in my time, and my ears are rather good. You said so yourself."

"Hmm." Miss Cultor looked unconvinced.

"Now, will this do for a sleeping place?" Judith indicated the dark space behind the large oak dresser.

Miss Cultor sniffed. "No skulls?"

"None that I can see."

"Very well." She yawned, showing tiny pointed fangs. "I will sleep. Drink that foul brew at your own risk. And you who needs your ears in particular!"

On that parting shot, Miss Cultor vanished behind the cupboard and appeared to fall asleep instantly, from the soft snores that soon drifted out. Judith opened the curtains again and looked over the rain-washed grounds. Come to think of it, the chocolate *was* much appreciated. It would help her to forget the wariness in Robert's eyes and the lie in his voice. And maybe it would give her some insight as to how else she could help him, if he would not come to Cornwall.

She took the warm cup in her hands and sat on the couch by the window. Ah, chocolate at last. Taking a sip, she revelled in the fragrant spices: cardamom, cinnamon, and a hint of pepper and nutmeg. As well as the usual flavours, there was some other taste she could not place. Not the traditional rose-watered sugar or the touch of anise, or even the rich nuttiness of pistachio. She peered into the cup, noting that the cocoa had a slightly golden colour to it. What could it be? It added a lovely note to the palate.

Judith sighed with pleasure. The duke was right. The Spaniards knew how to do chocolate exceedingly well. The kitchen had added cream too.

She took another long, luscious sip, and smiled at Miss Cultor's superstitions. The chocolate was a timely fortification against coming events. For soon Judith would have to face Lady Agatha.

In which our heroine is warned

One advantage of being a Truth Discernor is that one learns how to disguise one's own mendacities more effectively.

- from *Lady Avely's Guide to Truth and Magic*

SETTING DOWN HER EMPTY CUP, Judith straightened her mobcap. It was time to make some discreet enquires about a villainous skull and a dead footman. Lady Agatha must know something about one or the other.

They had seen each other in London recently, but only from a distance in the whirlwind of the season. Judith had been busy chaperoning her daughter and Lady Agatha had seemed to avoid them both, perhaps from awareness of their difference in social station. On the few occasions that their paths crossed, Agatha had been coolly civil but indisposed to talk. Perhaps she even guessed a little of Judith's history with the duke.

Now, Judith made her way downstairs to the Green Drawing Room, the smaller of the two drawing rooms at Sargenet. She paused at the threshold, wondering if it was the scene of Gilbert's death. Ah yes, Agatha had mentioned the need to match the green curtains to the new fabric.

Lady Agatha was seated in front of the fire. The steward, Mr Lewis, was standing in front of her, his hands clasped behind his back, listening to some instruction.

Looking round curiously, Judith spied a gap where a settee must have once stood next to the fireplace. The carpet still held the impression of long-standing furniture and a faint smell of soap lingered in the air. Other than that, there was no sign of the violence recently wrought here.

The terrace windows were closed against the rain. These were the doors that had been left unlocked, presumably allowing the thief entrance. Or did the intruder enter the Green Drawing Room the same way Judith did now, only to escape through the window?

Agatha finished her conversation with Mr Lewis, and beckoned with an imperious hand. Her sharp eyes measured Judith's demure grey gown and matronly cap.

"Judith Avely!" exclaimed her ladyship in a falsely cheerful tone as Judith came forward. "What is this I hear about you becoming a marchioness?" She gestured to the armchair opposite her. "Sit and tell me all about it. Mr Lewis, you may go now. Tell Robert to fetch some tea things for us, would you?"

The young, dark-haired man gave Judith an unsmiling nod and left the room. She went forward to take her place by the fire, struck anew by his appearance. Why did Mr Lewis seem so familiar? Was it just because she had seen him in the village that she felt she recognised him?

She explained her change in circumstances to Lady Agatha. Her ladyship listened, back straight, her striking features impassive.

"Well," Agatha said, "I wish you luck of Castle Lanyon.

Terrible rambling place, if you ask me. You'll have your work cut out for you. Worse than Sargenet, I daresay."

"Indeed," replied Judith, trying not to take offence at this rudeness. Agatha spoke the truth, after all. Judith decided to return the insult. "I hope it is not haunted, at least."

Lady Agatha sniffed and cast her a sharp look. "I suppose you've heard about our ghostly skull. A lot of nonsense, you will agree, seeing as you've decided to stay at Sargenet. How long will you be here, do you think?"

It was a change of subject and also a hint that Judith was not particularly wanted. "A se'enight at most, Lady Agatha."

"Hmm." A week seemed too long, for Agatha's mouth twitched disapprovingly. She leaned forward and lowered her voice. "*Lady* Avely, I think it is best you leave within a day or two. We are at sixes and sevens with the duke's arrival, and, to speak frankly, you will be in the way of his grace resuming his duties."

Judith was surprised by this direct approach. However, before she could formulate a response, Robert entered the room, bearing a tea tray. He set it down carefully on the small table between them. Lady Agatha ignored him, and he retreated, expressionless, as Mr Lewis came through the door again.

The steward bowed. "Lady Agatha, I'll be at the Dower House. If you want to discuss matters further, Robert can fetch me."

"Of course." Agatha's eyes softened on Mr Lewis. "I'm sure his grace has plenty for you to do."

Mr Lewis nodded and left the room.

Judith covertly watched the young man withdraw. With that strong cut of the jaw, the thick, black hair, and the masculine deep-set eyes, she suddenly realised who he resembled. The Duke of Sargen.

The surprise of it left her speechless for a moment, distracted from Lady Agatha's machinations. Dazedly, she accepted a cup of tea and half-listened to her ladyship's strident pronouncements about the events of the London season.

Lewis was of Sargen blood. Judith could not doubt it, looking at the distinctive hair and striking eyes. The only question was - whose child was he? The duke's? Or Lord John's? Or even, possibly, Agatha's? Lady Agatha also shared the duke's deep-set eyes, black hair, and prominent cheekbones. The thought that Agatha had borne a love-child was absurd, but Judith had seen for herself how Agatha's eyes softened upon Lewis.

It appeared there was a bastard entrenched at Sargenet. Judith wondered how Lord John felt about that, but of course an illegitimate child usually offered no threat to the line of succession - as much as Lewis really did look like the duke had twenty years ago. He had the same sense of barely contained virility and arrogant pride. No wonder he had seemed familiar.

He looked like the duke's son. Judith felt a stab somewhere in the region of her heart. The thought that the duke had committed the same indiscretion as Nicholas was painful, though not surprising. She should have expected it, really, with all his grace's dalliances.

Agatha was still talking, asking Judith about her daughter's betrothal. Judith gathered her composure and discussed the wedding, avoiding Agatha's probing questions about the scandal that had accompanied Elinor earlier in the year.

When the conversation upon nuptials lulled, Judith cleared her throat. "Can I ask where the ghostly apparitions have been seen, Lady Agatha, so that I may avoid them?"

Agatha waved a thin hand dismissively. "Here and there. You need not worry. They do not travel near the Gold Room." The last was said with a bit of a snap. Her ladyship clearly thought that the duke was pandering to Judith's new title, and did not like it.

Judith was more interested to note that the phantoms seemed

to stay in the main part of the house, or the ballroom. They avoided the guest wing, it seemed. She was secretly glad to hear it. She was not as eager as Miss Cultor to face down a skull.

"You don't seem very troubled by them," observed Judith. "You are not concerned that the hauntings could be connected with your footman's death?"

Agatha stiffened. "A preposterous suggestion!" Her voice was coated in tin.

Judith tried to remain expressionless, though it was intriguing that Agatha believed the two events were connected. Or perhaps she *knew* it, if she had something to do with them.

Agatha continued in a more even tone. "My dear, I must ask you, was there a particular reason you decided to visit us now?"

It was an abrupt change of subject. It occurred to Judith, too late, that her presence at Sargenet might seem as if she - an available widow - was pursuing the duke. If only Agatha knew that Judith wanted nothing to do with a man who had seduced half of England and had the by-blows to prove it. She put down her cup with a clink.

"I merely wished to break my journey to Cornwall, Lady Agatha," she replied. "His grace was very kind to offer me his hospitality. I did not realise that my visit would coincide with your time of trouble."

Agatha's hands clenched on the arm chair. "The trouble is all passed, Lady Avely, but I would appreciate it if you would make your visit a short one." Agatha looked nervously over her shoulder, her eyes going to the door.

She was lying again. Moreover, her voice rung with fear as well as falsehood.

AFTER ANOTHER STRAINED cup of tea, Judith was relieved when the duke strode into the room. Then she saw that he was angry.

He loomed in front of Agatha, his brow black.

"That cursed butler!" he growled. "Agatha! What possessed you to replace Fitzroy? This Broughton fellow doesn't know twaddle. The defences I left on the stables have been completely neglected."

"Dacian." Agatha winced slightly but she waved a deflecting hand. "You see that Lady Avely is here."

He gave Judith a short nod of acknowledgment and turned back to his sister. "Don't try to distract me, Aggie. We must discuss your high-handed dismissal of Fitzroy. I never gave you permission to do so."

Power rose in the air ominously. His fists were clenched. Judith's own hands tightened in her lap. He had promised he was able to control his temper now, but his mood seemed to indicate otherwise.

Lady Agatha drew herself up tall in her chair. "You were not present to give me permission, brother!"

The duke towered over her, eyes hard. "You knew I wouldn't like it. He's been with the family since I was a boy!"

"Exactly! Fitzroy is old!" snapped Agatha. "Too old. He can barely make it up all the stairs anymore. It is unfair to ask it of him. I had no choice! I've given him Dower House to care for instead, where he can look after Mr Lewis."

The duke suddenly seemed to return to his normal size. "Oh." Remorse crossed his face briefly, then he rallied. "So instead you employ this jackanapes, Broughton. Does he even have any of the ... *accomplishments* traditional for a butler?"

Judith knew that he was referring to the Gifts. Usually servants were not Gifted. The Musing only showed itself in a small portion of the population and the power it gave inevitably led to yet other types of privilege. Over time, the Gifts had coalesced most strongly in the noble families - the laws of succession had contributed to this - but the Musing continued to disregard rank, hence Miss Cultor's stablehand with a strain of Diplomacy.

Ordinarily, a Gifted member of the lower classes would quickly rise to the position of a higher servant, such as a butler, housekeeper, or head groomsman. Even then, they could not afford to employ their Gift regularly, as it would affect their ability to perform their other duties. A butler, nonetheless, would ideally have some modicum of magic to call upon in times of need. Impacting, perhaps, to deal with unwanted visitors or threats. Or Diplomacy, to cast a warm, amenable glow over gatherings. Or Illusion, to paint over any mishaps.

Agatha looked down, her cheeks flushed. "Of course. I am not a fool, Dacian. Broughton is perfectly suited to his position, in both *accomplishments* and age."

Judith wondered if she implied that Broughton was an Impactor or an Illusor. Either one made the butler a suspect for the ghostly skulls, or, indeed, the blow to Gilbert's head.

Agatha continued. "If you dislike Broughton so much, we can train Robert up to take his place. Surely that will be sufficient advancement to satisfy him?"

"No, it will not. We will discuss that matter later." The duke took a deep breath and let it out, visibly calming his temper, his shoulders lowering. The faint pressure in the air faded. Turning to Judith, he smiled down at her. "Lady Avely. I apologise for my rudeness. I'm glad you are warming yourself by the fire. Let me show you our library as I promised."

Judith kept her expression benign at this patent ploy, only hoping that Agatha did not think they were making a romantic rendezvous. Lady Agatha watched, a line between her brows like her brother's, as the duke positively dragged Judith out of the drawing room.

He pulled her into the library. It was a large room placed next to the Green Drawing Room, also overlooking the front terraces. Its high walls were crammed with books and the corners were fitted with reading alcoves, complete with cushioned insets and candle sconces.

Judith shook him off and looked round, repressing another memory as her eye fell on the wooden desk. There was no sense in dwelling on the past of more than twenty years ago. His grace, certainly, would have forgotten it.

"Now," said the duke, turning. "We need to talk."

"Yes, we do," she said sharply. She wanted to know if Lewis was truly his son, and possibly give leash to some of the anger stirring in her. No wonder he advised she should forgive her own sins, if he had so many of them.

Before either of them could say anything more, movement from one of the alcoves caught her eye. A startled Lord John rose to his feet. He was wearing a brown coat and worn trousers, obviously in his comfortable clothes for a day reading about the house. He blinked at his brother and bowed to Judith, holding a book in his hand and a question on his face.

"John," said the duke impatiently. "Are you moldering in here again? This is Lady Judith Avely; I'm sure you will recall her from our more sociable years, before duels or books dragged us away from London. She has recently been elevated to the rank of a marchioness."

Judith came forward to greet Lord John with a small curtsy, slightly shallower than she would have made as Mrs Avely.

"Ah," said Lord John in his dry voice. "How do you do, Lady Avely?" He looked at her carefully and she wondered if he connected her figure with the one he had seen walking. In the light from the windows, his face looked even more drawn and tired.

"I am well," she replied. "I am sorry to hear of your troubles."

John's jaw tightened, then he dropped his gaze. "You mean the footman. Poor boy. What was his name again?"

"Gilbert Drew," the duke interposed, coming to stand next to them. "I believe you are more upset about this damnable phantom business. Tell Judith about it, John."

John shot his brother an irritated look then turned to Judith with a resigned air. "We have a prankster, Lady Avely, who finds it amusing to drip blood from these walls." He flung a thin hand out toward the wooden panelling above a fireplace. "I left books on that mantlepiece and found them desecrated."

"Not really," said the duke. "Just *appearing* to be desecrated."

"That is just as bad!" snapped John.

"Yes, but as soon as you touched them, the Illusion disappeared."

John looked uncomfortable and glanced at Judith then back to his brother, his brows faintly lifted.

"Don't worry," the duke assured him. "Lady Avely knows we are dealing with the Musor arts. She was married to a Musor, and she is familiar with the magicks, having a small talent in Diplomacy herself. She is going to help me question the servants and keep everyone calm."

Judith carefully remained neutral in expression. It was dangerous to pretend a talent she did not have, especially to one Gifted in Memory. She had hoped her deception would only concern the servants, but John might remember her from the salons when Nicholas was still alive.

The weight of her lapis hung on her neck, hidden in her bodice. But the lie seemed to pass muster. John nodded.

"Ah yes, a bit of Diplomacy wouldn't go astray, brother, if you are going to bang some heads together."

The duke cleared his throat. "No need for that."

Judith also coughed. "It shouldn't be too hard to unravel it all," she remarked. "We all know how Illusion works: it must be cast within sight of the Illusor and it will not usually withstand direct physical touch - unless the Illusor is herself holding it in place with her own hand. Or if the Illusion emanated from an enchanted object - and Illusion charm - it will likewise vanish upon contact. Did you touch the bloodied books, John?"

John wrinkled his nose. "No, I did not. I called a footman. His cloth destroyed the trick."

"Which footman?" asked Judith.

There was an infinitesimal pause. "Actually, I believe it was the steward who managed to destroy the Illusion. Lewis. Though I'm afraid my shout of outrage was heard by others."

Judith took a seat on an armchair, thoughtful. "And which books were so desecrated, if I may ask?"

John was happy to answer, putting his hands behind his back as if he were about to give a lecture. "Shakespeare's play *Julius Caesar*, a biography of Constantine the Great by Triste, and a commentary by Polonetheus." He paused. "Oh, and a few of Agatha's trivial novels were also lying about and caught some of the splatter." His black brows came together in a frown like his sister's.

Judith risked another inflammatory question. "While we are on the subject of books, may I enquire which one dealt the fatal blow to Gilbert?"

The duke's lips quirked. "I had the same burning curiosity, Lady Avely."

John sniffed. "It was Polonetheus's commentary on the Odyssey." At Judith's blank look, he explained. "Polonetheus was a Byzantine scholar - a Memor, we suspect - who wrote a lengthy accompaniment to Homer. The thief chose well."

"It makes for heavy reading," interpolated the duke. "Weighty stuff."

Judith frowned him down. "So it was the same Polonetheus's

commentary that was subjected to desecration in the library, Lord John?"

"Yes, actually," admitted Lord John.

"So how did the book make its way into the drawing room?"

Lord John shrugged. "Someone must have carried it over. My wife Mary, perhaps, or even Miss Atkinson, or Mr Nottley, who left the day previously. Though no one can seem to recall doing so, which means it was probably Mr Nottley. Polonetheus is his area, after all."

"It wasn't you?" asked Judith, detecting a false note in his voice.

"The Odyssey is not my interest," said Lord John stiffly.

Judith privately wondered at this, even as she noted his avoidance of the question. Surely all ancient writers were in the same hay field? True, Homer was Greek and Ovid was Roman, so perhaps Judith shouldn't corral them all in the same pen. It sounded as if Mr Nottley preferred the Greeks and Polonetheus. John seemed eager to implicate this Mr Nottley.

The duke leaned on the mantelpiece. "Scholars are always leaving their books about, unfortunately."

Judith speculated whether an academic was more or less likely to use a book to bash someone on the head. Given Lord John's affront about the sullying of Shakespeare, he, at least, she suspected, would refrain from hitting a footman with a book. Unless John harboured particularly violent thoughts about Polonetheus and Odysseus?

"And what are the servants saying about it all?" she asked. "Do they know the blood on the mantelpiece was an Illusion?"

The duke shook his head. "They think it a ghost and I'd rather keep it that way, given the Edicts."

Lord John dropped his chin. "The blood appeared again the following night, higher up on the wall. It was harder to reach and most of the household witnessed it."

Judith stared at the wooden panelling, wondering at the significance of it. In the daylight, it showed only the whorls and grain of wood, framed by an ornate mantlepiece that was now clear of any detritus. Below the mantlepiece, a small fire blazed, warming the library.

She could imagine it, however: the stack of books with blood dripping down the side, obscuring the titles and pooling on the topmost book. Could there be some reason behind the ghost's tricks - some message that they could not yet decipher? Yet if that was the case, someone in the house could be the intended recipient, and knew all too well what meaning was implied.

"Lord John," said Judith. "Which book was on the top of the pile?"

"*Julius Caesar*," said John reluctantly.

"And can you speculate as to the message of the Illusion?"

His lordship drew in a sharp breath and lowered his eyes. He shook his head slightly, shrugging self-deprecatingly.

Silence filled the library. The duke thrust his chin forward. "Well, go on, man. A fool could see you have a theory. Tell us what you think."

Judith leaned forward. "Perhaps you see a connection between the Illusory tricks and Gilbert's death? After all, the same book was involved in both."

John swallowed and looked up. "On the contrary, *Julius Caesar* could indeed be significant."

"Why is that?" demanded the duke.

John's voice was low. "It could warn us of betrayal."

In which a butler is inscrutable

As a Truth Discernor, one may discover secrets which others prefer kept hidden, hence one must employ discretion.
  - from Lady Avely's Guide to Truth and Magic

AFTER HIS DRAMATIC ANNOUNCEMENT, Lord John sealed his lips. He would not say anymore as to what sort of betrayal he suspected. His announcement had been no lie, thought Judith. Could he mean betrayal by Lewis, the steward who was so intimately connected with the family?

More and more, Judith was inclined to suspect the young man's involvement. He also appeared to be very cosy with Lady Agatha. Were they hiding something together?

She was somewhat woozy from listening with her inner sense, and she sat on the edge of an armchair, frowning while the duke escorted John to the library door, telling him to go eat some food and stop talking nonsense.

Returning to Judith, the duke stood before her. "Do you think John is right?"

Judith bit her lip. "About betrayal? He believed it to be true, but that doesn't tell us much."

The duke tossed a piece of wood onto the fire and poked at it so it burned a little brighter. He sat down next to her and stretched out his long legs. His foot rested perilously close to Judith's. She resisted the urge to draw her feet in like a virtuous maiden. She was a matron now, after all.

"By the way," said the duke. "That is a lovely cap you are wearing."

She shot him a suspicious look. "Sarcasm doesn't suit you, your grace." Carefully, she did not reach up to touch her mushroomly mobcap.

"Not at all," he replied. "I like that cap - because it provokes me into imagining what it would be like to remove it."

Judith gasped. Now she *did* draw her feet in like an outraged matron. "Your grace!"

The duke smile lazily. "Yes, how it would be to untie it - pulling the ribbons loose and slipping it off your head...."

Judith shook her head sharply. "You are impertinent - because I am a widow now, I suppose."

His eyes rested on her for a long moment. "It's been twelve years, Judith. Have you mourned him enough?"

Judith gave a tiny nod. "Nevertheless, I am not your flirt."

The duke's face shuttered and he drew his own feet in too. "Very well, marchioness." There was a fraught pause, then he spoke in an even voice. "Let us instead consider a more pleasant topic of conversation - perhaps the books that were drizzled in blood. Do you think a clue lies in their subjects?"

"Polonetheus's commentary on the Odyssey, you mean?" Judith gratefully followed the change of subject. "It will be difficult to parse a clue from such a long text."

"A warning not to anger the god of the sea?" he suggested flippantly.

"Or to be faithful to one's husband?" she returned, thinking of Penelope, who had turned away over a hundred suitors while she awaited Odysseus's return. Then she realised what she had said, and stiffened with embarrassment.

The duke didn't seem to notice. "Or maybe it is the biography on Constantine the Great that is crucial."

"The first Roman emperor to convert to Christianity," she said. "He waited until his deathbed to be baptised so that it would wash away as many sins as possible."

He laughed. "A strategist to the end."

"I'm sure his sins were too varied to give us a clue."

"John also mentioned Agatha's novels," he pointed out. "Maybe we should find out more about them. I've seen a few Gothic romances lying around. I'll ask Agatha. You had a chat with her this morning, did you not? And Robert? How did it go?"

Judith took a moment to collect her thoughts. The library felt quite warm, the fire flickering next to her, its flames a cheerful dance. She sighed. "You were right. He did not want to come with me to Cornwall."

The duke said nothing, just looked at her sympathetically.

"He says he feels he is bound to Sargenet," she added. "Can you make him understand that he is free to leave? He feels he owes you a debt, but surely it is repaid by now."

He hesitated. "Yes."

She heard a strange note in his voice, one she could not decipher. Did he somehow believe that Robert should stay at Sargenet? She raised her brows.

The duke ignored her questioning look and changed the subject. "What of Agatha?"

"She believes the Illusions have something to do with the footman's death. She seemed ... afraid."

"Hmm. Perhaps she suspects one of the staff. Shall we interview the servants now? We can start with Broughton."

Judith nodded, though she rather thought it would be more efficient to start with Lewis. However, she was also curious to see if the butler knew of Lewis's lie. And it would give her time to determine how to question Lewis without implicating Robert.

The duke added, "I have already discreetly mentioned your *minor* talent in Diplomacy."

"You are rather free with your lies, for someone who is allying with a Truth Discernor."

He grinned. "A few of the housemaids are threatening to leave, so Broughton quite saw the need for a soothing presence."

"Is Broughton himself Gifted?"

"Yes, Illusion, a little."

"I suppose that makes him a prime suspect for the skull." She paused, wondering if Lewis was Gifted too, but she was reluctant to ask. If he was an Impactor, it made it all the more certain that the duke was his father. "I hope you will remain polite, for if things become heated I shall look like a terrible Diplomacor."

The duke snorted. "I shall be a veritable paragon of courtesy."

"You may be confusing courtesy with authority," she suggested tartly.

However, she was surprised to see that the duke managed to be quite affable to his new butler, despite his grace's anger about the supplanting of his old retainer.

Broughton, called to the library, was the epitome of a good upper servant: well spoken, reserved, respectful. He stood in front of them, his grey hairs glinting in the light from the window, his hands held neatly by his sides.

After a few more general enquires, the duke's questions became more pointed. "My good sir, you are modestly Gifted in Illusion, are you not?"

"Yes, your grace." Broughton inclined his head slightly, his voice even and true. Judith watched from her armchair beside the duke, listening carefully.

"And forgive me an impertinence, but have you by any chance been Illusing skulls around the place?"

Judith fought the impulse to roll her eyes at the duke's attempt at 'courtesy'.

Broughton's expression did not change. "No, your grace."

It was the truth. Judith sighed. It would have been nice if the butler had done it. Fitzroy would have been pleased. She spared him a thought for where he had been relegated to the Dower House.

"And what do you know about Gilbert's death?" enquired the duke. "Don't suppose you killed him, did you?"

This time Judith did roll her eyes. But Broughton did not deign to reply directly, which was vexatious. Instead, he shook his head and said, "If you are implying that I left the drawing room windows open, your grace, I can assure you that I did not. It was not by my agency that a thief entered the house."

His voice was untarnished. It was the truth, as far as he knew. Or, perhaps, a misdirection.

"Then how did the thief enter?" Judith asked quickly. "Are you suggesting that he came into the house through the front door?"

"I could not say." Broughton turned to her and offered a thin smile. "Perhaps the thief was indeed a ghost, who came through the walls."

Judith narrowed her eyes. Deceit now coated the butler's words. He certainly did not believe in the ghost. Was that because he himself had been the 'thief'? But what on earth would moti-vate Broughton to kill Gilbert?

She tried another tack, finally reaching the subject that inter-ested her. "Did I hear that you found the body?"

"Yes, my lady. It was quite the shock."

His eyes were unreadable but his voice sounded clear.

So Broughton had not known of Lewis's lie - or Robert's. As far as he knew, he was the first one to stumble across Gilbert's corpse. Still, Judith couldn't shake the feeling that the butler was hiding something. She bit her lip, examining him closely. A bead of sweat had appeared on his porous brow. He avoided her gaze, turning his face back to the duke.

Judith folded her hands in her lap, defeated. Whatever the butler was hiding, he was too butlerish for her to discover it.

The duke spoke up. "Ghosts aside, how would a person enter the house? If the windows, as you say, were all locked."

Broughton cleared his throat. "I have only one speculation, your grace, if you will permit it." His grace nodded and Broughton continued. "If someone possessed a copy of the key to the window locks, they would be able to enter the premises as they liked."

"You cannot be accusing Mrs Bunn." The duke's voice took on a stony quality. He was referring to the housekeeper, who carried a chatelaine of keys. Mrs Bunn had been with the household for a very long time.

"Not at all," said Broughton hastily. "A foolish speculation only, your grace."

Judith blinked. "What of the steward?" she asked. "Does Mr Lewis have keys?"

"Yes, my lady," said Broughton. "He does."

The duke cast a quick look between them. "Lewis is trustworthy," he said firmly. "I will warn him to keep his keys under tight watch. As must you, Broughton. You may go now. Send in Mrs Bunn."

Broughton left. Judith leaned her head against the armchair, her mind feeling murky, even as she felt triumphant about gathering more evidence against Lewis. She was dreadfully out of practice in Musing. Thank goodness she had found Miss Cultor to assist with the blood bond, as well as wearing her talisman stone. Still, it was an unaccustomed strain.

Fortunately, interviewing Mrs Bunn was a straightforward

affair. The older woman was professional, truthful, and knew nothing about ghosts or murderers, thank you very much. She certainly hadn't unlocked the drawing room windows. His grace even managed to ask this question without provoking offence.

When the housekeeper left, the duke turned to Judith. "We must rest for lunch. I don't want to overtax you."

Judith rubbed her forehead and agreed. The duke ordered some trays of food, promptly delivered by Broughton. Once they had made a substantial reduction to the pile of meat and cheeses, she decided it was finally time to broach the subject of Lewis's perfidy.

She set about pouring tea, and handed the duke a cup. "Yesterday in the village, your grace," she said carefully, "I overheard Lewis tell a lie."

"Hmm. Dacian, please, I beg you." The duke accepted the tea and examined her narrowly. "And what lie was this?"

"That Broughton found the body."

"Ah."

She raised her eyebrows, took a sip, and waited. Silence was often the best interrogation technique; something she had learnt as a mother. Besides, she was still a little hazy herself, despite the luncheon. She kept her eyes fixed on Dacian.

He took a moment to drink his own tea. "Lewis is a good man," he said at last. "Even if he is a trifle arrogant and hot-tempered."

Like father, like son, she thought dispassionately. The duke's *hot temper* had led to a man's death more than once. His illegitimate son could take after him in that respect too.

"He must have a reason for lying," she said.

"I cannot think why, but I doubt it implies that he killed a footman."

"You are eager to defend him," she said bluntly, her usual reticence somewhat marred by Bemusement. "Is he your son?"

The duke raised his brows, his eyes growing hard. "Of course, you *would* assume that, marchioness." His voice was harsh.

Judith bristled but tried to disguise it with another sip. "It is a natural assumption, your grace. Lewis could be the fruit of any number of your past unions. If I were to guess, I would say he is the progeny of your affair with that opera singer - what was her name? Lily Siltreed? He has the same sulky mouth."

Just after Judith had married Nicholas, the duke has embarked on a scandalously public affair with Miss Lily Siltreed, a flashy blonde actress with full lips and a full figure. It had irked Judith at the time, and it irked her now, with a strange pain in the region of her solar plexus. She was still angry, still affected by emotions she had thought long dead. She gritted her teeth together and put her cup down abruptly.

The duke's mouth turned up at the corner. "Jealous of Lily, were you, Judith? Sorry to disappoint you, but no, Lewis is not her child, nor mine." He took a sedate sip.

"I was not jealous!" Belatedly, she heard the truth in his words. Her breath expelled in a whoosh. "Not yours? Whose child, then?"

"John's." The duke grimaced. "Yes, the little devil. A year before his marriage with Mary he was indiscreet with an actress. So you weren't too far off with your guess about Lily. Just a bit off on your paternity."

"I am sorry," she said stiffly.

He shrugged and took another gulp of tea. "I did my best for Lewis; I put him in school with Robert, if you must know, at Taunton, and housed them together when they were on break. They grew up like brothers. Then Agatha roped Lewis into his position of steward while I was away. It is a gentleman's position, at least. I will recommend him to another great house if he wishes to distance himself from the Sargens."

"Agatha must know the truth, I presume."

"Yes, otherwise she would have made him a footman too, no doubt, along with Robert. Yet everyone else thinks Lewis is *my* child, most likely."

Judith winced, even as she wondered at the repercussions of that. Did anyone fear that Lewis would be adopted by the duke and fritter away the income of the estate? Usually, the laws of primogeniture would forbid a bastard from inheriting any title or entail, but there were other ways to dilute the assets.

"Does Lord John ever acknowledge him when they stay here?"

"No, John ignores him. For Mary's sake, I imagine."

Judith felt a rush of sympathy for Mary, who must find Lewis's presence at Sargenet grating. She knew all too well the pain of discovering a husband's misdeeds. "Does Lewis know his own parentage?"

The duke nodded. "Fortunately, John and Mary only visit twice a year, and he doesn't have much to do with them."

An uncomfortable silence fell, then Dacian cleared his throat. "Did you hear any other lies - from Broughton or Mrs Bunn, for example?"

Judith shook her head, and explained that the only lie from Broughton was his reference to the ghost.

Dacian frowned and put down his cup. "We need a signalling system."

"What do you mean?"

"I need to know when you detect a lie. You are very good at hiding your thoughts."

She was pleased to hear that. "I suppose so."

"It cannot be too obvious." The duke leaned back on his chair. "Maybe you could press your finger against your bottom lip."

Judith tried it. Dacian's eyes fixed on her mouth.

She quickly withdrew her finger. "No."

"You could lick your lips instead," he suggested.

Resolutely, she did no such thing. She glared at him.

"Or bite them?" he said, a gleam in his eye. "Or, perhaps, start undoing your mobcap ribbons, seeing as you won't let me do it?"

Despite herself, she imagined his long fingers pulling the lace away and undoing her hair, as he murmured outrageous things. She mustered a stony gaze. "No, your grace. I think, perhaps, I will just clench my fist on my lap. As a warning."

Dacian nodded, chastised. "Very well. Shall I send for Lewis now? We can see if he is hiding anything else."

In which a dream is ominous

Usually, Musing takes conscious will. However, sometimes Discernment can speak through dreams, though the messages may be unreliable.
  - from *Lady Avely's Guide to Truth and Magic*

THE DUKE RANG the bell and gave Broughton instructions to fetch Lewis to the library.

Judith occupied herself with pouring herself another cup of tea. She was already a bit befuddled and now she had to employ her Gift once more. The duke stood by the mantelpiece, his back to the fire while she settled in her armchair, holding the warm cup.

Lewis came into the library, appearing the same as before: expressionless, good-looking, with a sense of coiled energy. Judith was reminded again of the duke at the same age and consoled herself that she could not be blamed for jumping to conclusions.

"Yes, your grace?"

"I am making enquiries into Gilbert's death," said the duke. "Can you tell me who found the body?"

"Certainly. Broughton did." The lie came as before, smooth and ready. "At around midnight on Thursday night."

Judith realised she had to make a fist. She set the teacup in one hand and curled her fingers into a ball on the armrest.

The duke saw and hesitated. "How do you know this?"

Lewis's eyes darted to Judith, as if he suspected some communication had passed between them. "Everyone knows it, your grace. You could ask Broughton yourself."

The duke ignored this evading tactic. "So Gilbert was found at midnight. When was the last time you saw him?"

Lewis hesitated. "He was at the servant's supper that night. I eat with Broughton and Mrs Bunn, but I saw Robert and Gilbert at the lower table." His voice rang true. Judith uncurled her hand reluctantly, though she narrowed her eyes at his wording. Had he skilfully evaded the question?

The duke nodded, pleased. "Come to think of it, when did Gilbert start his employment here?"

"Just before Robert," replied Lewis. Emboldened by the duke's frown, he added, "I never liked Gilbert; not many of us did. I know I shouldn't speak ill of the dead, but Gilbert was rather ... inopportune."

Judith raised her brows, interested to note that Lewis felt comfortable enough to make his opinions known to the duke; almost like a nephew instead of a steward, even though the duke had been absent for the last nine years.

"What do you mean, inopportune?" asked Dacian.

A faint sneer crossed Lewis's face. "Gilbert pestered Miss Atkinson with his attentions and he wandered about the woods when he should have been working. And I know for a fact that sometimes he would sleep in the library or the drawing room, preferring to be close to a fire than in the attics where he belonged."

That might explain why Gilbert had been in the drawing

room, thought Judith. She shivered slightly, realising that the footman might have been sleeping even as the book came down on his head. That made it possible that the assailant was a woman, unafraid to attack while Gilbert was already unconscious. Or perhaps a man who was a natural coward. Lewis, she had to admit, did not seem like a coward.

The duke was focused on another matter. "The library? Are you suggesting Gilbert might have had something to do with the hauntings?"

"Yes," said Lewis. "You can't deny that since he died, we have not had any more ghosts appear."

Judith gave the duke an enquiring look and he nodded shortly.

Yet there was something in Lewis's tone that she mistrusted. His voice sounded different somehow. Not a lie, but a misdirection perhaps, or an evasion. For some reason, he wanted them to believe that the ghosts were possibly Gilbert's doing.

She could not go so far as to curl her hand into a fist, but she decided to probe. "Excuse me, but how would Gilbert have managed such a thing? From what I hear, you've even had a skeleton wearing armour in the ballroom."

Lewis did not lower himself so much as to shrug, but he turned his head to give Judith a cool stare. "I do not know, my lady. I would never attempt such a stupid trick, especially not in this household."

This, Judith believed. At least that ruled out Lewis as the cause of the apparitions - though not necessarily Gilbert's death. She clung to this certainty, her mind reeling from too much effort in expending her Gift. Her newly wrought bond with Miss Cultor was not enough to prevent her becoming entirely Bemused. She needed to excuse herself before she embarrassed herself.

She bowed her head. "I'm afraid I feel a headache coming on, your grace. I must retire to my room." Her head was spinning, but at least her Bemusement gave her an excuse to delay the interview with Robert until the morrow. "What time is dinner?"

"In a few hours." Dacian looked concerned. "You must rest, of course."

Determined not to totter, she left the two of them standing by the fire with identical frowns on their faces.

BACK IN THE GOLD ROOM, Judith closed the curtains and collapsed gratefully on the large bed. In the dark and warmth of the room she fell asleep immediately. She had been more tired than she realised, with the long journey, the gruelling interviews, and the previous late evening with Miss Cultor.

As she slept, she dreamed. A skeleton wearing nothing but a helmet lurched toward her. Black feathers protruded from the silver dome and the face was a blank sheet. The skeleton's bare bones rattled below, in a ghastly approximation of nakedness.

Judith was frozen at the end of the passageway, watching in horror as the skeleton drew inexorably closer, its feet tapping hollowly on the ground. The white bones gleamed, but Judith found her eyes somehow fixed on the soft black feathers. They protruded from the helmet, swaying above her.

A bony hand reached out to touch her. *Second-best*, a voice whispered in judgment. *Second-best.*

Judith woke with a start, her heart thudding in her ears. Her body was stiff with fear. She lay breathing deeply, keeping her eyes resolutely closed. Compared to the lumpy mattress at the inn, this bed was firm, and she tried to take comfort from it and recover her equilibrium.

A shiver ran through her as she remembered the blank face of the helmet. Why had her dream given it a crest of black feathers?

Then she recalled that Miss Cultor had mentioned that detail. Strange that her dream should linger on it.

She listened carefully for any sign of Miss Cultor. No betraying snore emanated from the oak dresser. One thing to be grateful for, at least, that the vampiri would keep well hidden.

"Hsst," came a small voice right next to her ear.

Judith's head jerked and she turned to see Miss Cultor standing on the bed, with only a scrap of orange-gold cloth wrapped round her. She looked like a tiny doll.

"Good afternoon," whispered Miss Cultor. "I could tell by your breathing that you had awakened."

"Shouldn't you be asleep?"

The curtains were closed, shrouding the room in darkness, allowing only a dim light to seep along the edges.

"We need to confer!" Miss Cultor blinked with excitement. "Dusk is settling earlier, after all, and I can be up and about after another nap. We must determine a plan before you go down for dinner."

"We must?"

Miss Cultor seemed to sense Judith's lack of enthusiasm and she deflated a little, the orange cloth flouncing. "You can't bring me back here, then bid me to twiddle my thumbs while you eat dinner and converse. That is what I had to do with Mr Nottley."

Thumb twiddling sounded rather soothing to Judith at the present moment, but she sat up and rubbed her eyes. "Very well. What sort of plan? Shall you start with the ballroom?"

Miss Cultor's eyes brightened again. "Yes, I shall flit from eave to eave. I shall be a shadow in darkness." She tilted her head, considering what this might, in fact, achieve. "I shall lie in wait for the ghost."

"The ghost seems to have died since the murder," pointed out Judith. Then she paused at the import of her own words. "Goodness. I wonder if Lewis was right. Maybe Gilbert *was* the ghost. I was so Bemused this afternoon that I didn't give his ideas enough credence."

"Who is Lewis?"

Judith explained what she had discovered so far: that Mr Lewis (the illegitimate son of Lord John) had disliked Gilbert and claimed he was always where he shouldn't be, implying that Gilbert had caused the phantasms. "Yet Lady Agatha believes the opposite: she is afraid the ghost will reappear."

"Oh, I do hope it does," said Miss Cultor, twitching her cloth with excitement and showing a glimpse of bare leg.

"I thought you disapproved of the ghost."

"Well, this time I mean to *catch* it. I'll tell it exactly what I think of it. An unclothed skeleton displays bad taste, and so I shall say."

Judith shook away an image of Miss Cultor scolding a penitent skeleton. "I suppose it would be useful if you can inspect the ballroom chandelier, to see if there was some way the Illusion of the skull was fixed to it. Your wings will be able to take you where I cannot reach. And if you cannot find anything attached to the chandelier, search the upper gallery for hiding places. The Illusor would have to be within sight of the chandelier to cast the image."

"Excellent notion," agreed Miss Cultor. "Aren't you glad we made this arrangement? I can do all the dangerous wingwork while you are having dinner."

"Indeed. I am most grateful." Judith nodded and rubbed her temple. She still felt tired and the evening was yet to be endured.

Miss Cultor folded her arms. "Why are you rubbing your head? Did you drink that chocolate?"

Judith hastily put her hands down. "I am merely fatigued."

"You drank it! After I warned you!"

"Don't be ridiculous," said Judith. "It was just chocolate.

Perfectly harmless and delicious. I was simply Discerning too much today."

"Hmm," said the vampiri skeptically. "We'll see. Don't blame me when you can't hear a thing." Suddenly she held up a hand, almost dropping her silk in the process. "Hush," she whispered. "Someone approaches, not that *you'd* know!"

Judith listened but could not hear anything. She suspected Miss Cultor of pulling her leg, but the thick carpet in the hallway would dull any footsteps. Miss Cultor stood stiffly, her hand held up in warning.

A quiet knock fell on the door.

Judith swung her legs off the bed. She was aware of a treacherously hopeful thought: could it be the duke? Yet he would not knock so gently. It must be a servant.

Miss Cultor hissed a direction. "Put me in the drawer! I shall listen to this rendezvous!"

Judith frowned. "It is not a rendezvous," she muttered under her breath, but did as she was asked, carefully placing Miss Cultor in the bedside drawer and sliding it shut.

She padded to the door and opened it.

Robert stood there, hands clasped together in front of him. "My lady, may I speak with you a moment?"

Judith stared, taken aback. "Of course."

He looked apprehensively down the hallway. "In private?"

"Certainly." She opened the door further and invited him in with a gesture.

Robert took only a few steps in and stood uneasily, shifting from foot to foot in a way that was unbefitting of a footman, or indeed, of a gentleman. He was still in his green and gold livery, but his thick brown hair fell across his forehead and a frown marred his blue eyes. Judith felt pain twist inside her as she looked at the young man. If Nicholas had known about Robert, would he have taken a different path, setting Judith aside? Or worse, had he set Robert aside?

She went over to the window and pulled the red curtains open. Outside the rain had ceased, but grey clouds still filled the sky with heaviness. She clasped the fabric in a gold tassel and turned to face Robert with a questioning look.

His eyes became more blue in the clear light - just like Nicholas's - but he looked away.

"I have been thinking on what you said this morning, Lady Avely." He seemed now to balk, and rubbed a hand on his coat nervously.

"Yes?" Could it be that Robert was now willing to go to Cornwall with her? Judith held a breath.

He swallowed. "I wonder if you could tell me more about my father." He hurried on before she could respond. "The duke has told me that Nicholas Avely was a Discernor. I want to know: did my father ever show signs of Illusion as well?"

In which a ring is cursed

A person may tell you the complete truth and nonetheless be concealing something else.

  - from *Lady Avely's Guide to Truth and Magic*

JUDITH STARED AT ROBERT, her mind reeling, and sat down with a bump on the couch by the window.

Of course, she had often contemplated whether or not Robert would be Gifted. She had asked the duke when they had fought at Garvey House, and he had replied in the negative. Yet she ought to have known that the boy may have developed his talent as he matured in the duke's absence.

Robert's question now implied this was the case. For Musors were not supposed to discuss the Musing with anyone, unless they possessed a Gift also.

She let out a breath. "No," she said slowly. "Your father was not Gifted in Illusion, only in Discernment. It is very rare for someone to possess two Gifts."

Robert's shoulders fell. "His grace didn't tell me that."

It sounded like she needed to have another chat with his grace.

"Why do you ask?" she enquired gently. "I take it that you must also be Gifted, if the duke made you privy to such information about your father."

He nodded. "I am an Illusor. But you can see why I don't want anyone to know that, with the ghost."

It was clear, now, why he had been so nervous. Judith frowned. "You are not responsible for the apparitions?"

Robert's eyes dropped. "I don't think so."

Again, the unclear note sounded in his voice, one she could not decipher.

"You don't *think* so?"

He worried at his lip again. "Well, it is just - could I be doing them in my sleep, my lady? His grace says it is not possible, but I confess to doubting myself. I was hoping you might have some wisdom on the matter."

Judith shook her head. "I'm afraid I don't know much about Illusion, to that extent." She considered thoughtfully. "However, sometimes Discernors have dreams that act as Discernments. I suppose it is possible that an Illusor's dreams could work similarly."

"My Gift is not well practiced," said Robert. "It doesn't seem likely that I could do it in my sleep, but the thought has worried me nonetheless. I cannot remember my dreams, and when I do, they have been troubled."

Judith pursed her lips, remembering her own disturbed dream. "Does the duke know of your Gift?"

Robert smiled, with the first hint of mischief she had seen from him. "I told him yesterday, and I can tell he is suspicious. But I asked him to keep it a secret."

Judith cast a look round the Gold Room with its indulgent accents of deep red. No wonder the duke had wanted her

Truth Discernment on hand. What other secrets was he guarding?

"I appreciate you telling me," she said. "Have you thought any more on my offer to go to Cornwall? We will be able to help you learn more of your Gift there."

Robert's expression became closed again. "No, my lady. The duke requires my presence, and I am honour bound to help him."

Judith narrowed her eyes. What did that mean? Was Dacian trying to interfere?

She tried a tentative question. "I am under the impression that the Avely estate still supports you, with money sent regularly."

Robert flushed. "Yes, that is true. Since mother died."

Judith couldn't help herself. "But not before?" *Had* Nicholas not known? Her hands gripped tightly together in her lap, hoping she could determine the answer.

Robert's lips twisted. "My mother only wrote to Mr Avely when she knew she was dying. He did not know about me before that."

Judith blinked, tears starting to her eyes with an overwhelming sense of relief. Nicholas had not known; he had not deliberately walked away from his own child.

"Why didn't she write earlier?"

"Mother had her pride, and she didn't want to bring trouble to her marriage." Robert shrugged. He seemed to sense the gravity of the matter, and added, "She told me that she only realised the truth herself when I was two years old. That's when I started to look like him, she said."

Judith's shoulders sank, almost with a sense of bewilderment. Even Anna had not known. Therefore, Nick had not callously abandoned her, and he had done the best he could when the truth came to light.

A great burden was lifted off Judith's soul.

She sighed, meeting Robert's thoughtful gaze with a new sense of clarity. Nicholas would have wanted him to see Castle Lanyon, she was suddenly sure of it.

Before she could say anything, a faint noise came from the bedside drawer. Robert's head moved sharply. "What was that?"

"A mouse, perhaps?" Judith folded her hands in her lap, accepting the change in subject, though she was determined to return to the matter later. "I know these old ducal houses are full of such creatures."

The drawer went quiet.

"I can set a trap, if you like," offered Robert.

Another gesture, perhaps, of reconciliation. Judith would take it, even as tiny as it was.

"Yes, please, if you would be so kind." She smiled tentatively at him. "Where do you sleep? Would you be able to cast an Illusion from there into the ballroom or library?"

"My bed is in the attic in the servants' quarters, in the east wing," he replied readily. "We are on the top floor - quite near the ballroom, actually."

Judith scratched her head, which was now bare of her cap. "I'm sorry you have been shunted there. Do you ever use your Gift in your daily duties?"

"No, my lady," said Robert. "As I said, it is not well practiced, and I cannot afford the Bemusement it causes me. Sometimes I experiment with it on my days off, making paintings on the attic wall, or simple pictures in the air. I have never made a skull," he hastened to add, but blushed rosily as he said so. "Only portraits and landscapes. I can paint a good likeness of Lewis's face, for example."

Judith was impressed. "Does anyone else know of your Gift?" she asked. "Other than his grace?"

Robert dropped his eyes to the ground and didn't answer.

"Oh dear," said Judith. "Who else knows? Who else is Gifted?"

Robert bit his lip. "It is not my secret to tell, my lady."

She sighed. "Mr Lewis."

Robert's eyes leapt to hers, startled. "How did you...?" Then he reddened again, realising that he had given her certainty. "Yes, Mr Lewis."

"Being of Sargen blood, he is likely to have inherited a power," she agreed. "Is he an Impactor like the duke, or a Memor like his father?"

"An Impactor," admitted Robert reluctantly.

Judith sat on the couch by the window, feeling a headache coming on again. These new revelations cast all sorts of possibilities into the air. "Could Lewis accidentally have killed Gilbert? Did they get into a fight in the drawing room, perhaps? An Impactor could crush a person's skull in a matter of seconds."

"No!" Robert shook his head vehemently. "Lewis would never do that."

"I do not say he would intend it. Accidents happen," said Judith. The Duke of Sargen knew this all too well. "Was Lewis perhaps defending Miss Atkinson's honour?"

"No!"

Again, the uncertain note in Robert's voice. Judith tried to put him at ease. "Or perhaps Lewis was expressing a dislike of Polonetheus?"

Robert shook his head with a faint air of belligerence. "I know Lewis didn't do it. He told me so and I believe him."

"Oh?" Judith raised her brows. "Why did you even ask him such a question?"

Robert clamped his lips shut, looking uneasy.

Judith continued. "You are much better off confiding in me, Robert, despite having no reason to trust me. I am here to help the duke come to the bottom of the matter, and concealing things will only make you or Lewis look guilty." She paused, taking a risk.

"I know Broughton was not the first person to stumble across Gilbert."

Robert stared, wide eyed.

"And," continued Judith inexorably, "I want to know why, having found Gilbert when he still lived, you kept that fact to yourself."

Robert's head drew back in shock. "He wasn't alive! He was dead, I swear it!"

"Ah, so you did find him!" Judith sighed, cross and also relieved that she could hear the truth in his voice this time. "Why did you keep it a secret? What else did you see? Tell me at once."

Robert looked unnerved. "Fine, I'll tell you - but only because it will come out anyway. Miss Atkinson will notice, you see."

"Notice what?"

Robert abandoned his pose as an orderly footman and began pacing. "Gilbert's ring."

"His ring?"

"Yes, Lewis won a ring from Gilbert a couple of nights ago in a game of cards." He threw an angry look over his shoulder. "Gilbert had it from his father and he was always calling attention to it. He thought of himself as superior to Lewis, even though he was only a footman."

Judith winced. "Because he was born in wedlock?"

"Of course," said Robert, still pacing. "You can imagine how we both hated it, and the sight of that gold ring on Gilbert's fat finger at supper. So Lewis let Gilbert join us in a game of cards, and won it off him. Then *Lewis* was flaunting it about, driving Gilbert purple with anger."

Judith could imagine the tensions running high. "What does this have to do with you finding the body?"

Robert's lips pressed together and he came to a standstill. "That night, I knew Gilbert hadn't come back to his room yet, so I went to look for him. I was worried he was ... getting up to mischief." He hurried on, and Judith wondered if he had been anxious for Miss Atkinson. "Then I found him lying there on the settee. It gave me a terrible shock, as you can imagine. I tried to wake him. I shook him and spoke his name. His gloves were off, but his flesh was cold. That's when I saw that his ring was back on his finger."

"Ah."

"You see how it looks," said Robert defensively. "So I asked Lewis about it afterwards - there are no secrets between us. He is like a brother to me - we lived together for a while and went to school together, you see. He told me he also came in to look for Gilbert, and when he saw him dead, he felt sorry about the ring. So he put the ring back on Gilbert's finger. That's all. He didn't hurt him."

Judith, listening, could only hear the truth this time. However, it was a second-hand truth and therefore unreliable. She had learned that to her detriment before.

"Has Lewis told anyone else about this?"

Robert shook his head. "Only me, because I asked him. But it will come out. Miss Atkinson knew about the ring; all the servants did. If they show the body at the funeral, everyone will see it and wonder how it got there. But Lewis just wanted to make sure the cursed ring was buried with Gilbert. He didn't want to have it hanging on his conscience."

Judith thought Lewis might have something worse hanging on his conscience. It was entirely possible that Gilbert had challenged Lewis to return his ring and came out dead for the encounter.

Robert seemed to hear her thoughts. "I can tell you one thing," he said angrily. "Lewis would never have killed Gilbert in the Sargenet drawing room. He would never be so careless of his position. If he was going to kill him, he would do it outside."

Judith gave a reluctant smile. Robert believed this to be true, she could hear, but it did not mean that Lewis had not forgotten himself in a moment of rage or jealousy, even in the ducal drawing room. He was an Impactor, like his uncle. They were prone to losing their tempers with disastrous results.

Another chat with Lewis was clearly in order. *After* she had a chat with the duke.

Robert looked restlessly round the room. "Anyway, that is why I left Gilbert lying there. I considered removing the ring, but thought I should speak to Lewis. Then Broughton found the body before I could do anything more."

Judith rubbed her forehead. "Well, the more I know of what really happened, the more likely it is we will find the truth." She paused as her stomach rumbled a more pressing concern. "Now, however, I must ready myself for dinner."

Robert straightened abruptly, remembering his footmanly duties. "Dinner! I must go." He paused. "Please don't say anything to Lewis. He would be angry if he knew I told you."

Judith nodded grudgingly. It was the least she could do for him, especially when he had trusted her with his confidences. Robert took a ragged breath and bolted from the room, though careful to close the door quietly behind him.

She waited a moment and then shut the curtains once more, closing out the dreary landscape. It took her a moment to remember that the whole conversation had been heard by her silent listener. She crossed to the bedside drawer and slid it open and blinked, for Miss Cultor was lying quite at her ease, completely naked, on her stomach on the orange-gold cloth. Her chin rested on her hands and she looked quizzically up at Judith.

"That was quite a tale," observed Miss Cultor. "Was it all true?"

Judith sat on the bed, averting her gaze while Miss Cultor

arranged her cloth more modestly. "Yes, what Robert said was true." She sighed. "At least I have the advantage of knowing that, and not being tricked by lies."

"Lewis sounds like a suspicious character." Miss Cultor hopped out of the drawer and onto the table. "Is he the dark, brooding steward?"

"Yes." Judith smiled at this description. "And possibly prone to violence. He can't be our ghost, however, if he is Gifted with Impacting. He wouldn't be able to cast an Illusion."

Miss Cultor held up a finger. "Ah, but you can obtain objects with Illusion attached to them, can you not? Could he have purchased the Illusions and put them in place?"

Judith considered. "Yes, I suppose that is true. But he denied it to me, truthfully."

"A shame." Then Miss Cultor brightened. "He didn't deny the murder though?"

"No." Judith laughed. "I had the same thought. He seems the most likely member of the household to have killed anyone."

"Ah, but it is the innocent-seeming ones that we must suspect." Miss Cultor yawned. "I am excessively tired after all that eavesdropping. It's my turn for a nap. I want to be ready for adventures tonight."

Judith returned the vampiri to the nook behind the dresser and prepared herself for dinner.

With foresight, she had packed one fine evening gown, a navy-blue silk with lilac edging and embroidery on the lower skirts. She had been very pleased with it when she had purchased it in London last year. Now, looking at it, she was aware of a sense of dissatisfaction. It was a drab colour, after all, and the sleeves were rather puffy.

She dressed and regarded her reflection suspiciously. At least she had a bit more colour in her cheeks after her afternoon nap, and her hazel eyes were clear. And she could not wear a cap with her evening gown. She only hoped the duke would realise it was a matter of dinner etiquette and not her being unduly influenced by his opinions.

In which there is a frightful visitation

An Illusion is a visual lie. Hence, it will be undetectable to the Truth Discernor, who relies upon her ears.
  - from *Lady Avely's Guide to Truth and Magic*

JUDITH MADE her way down for dinner. Downstairs, the entrance hall was lit with several candelabras but it remained cold and uninviting. Broughton stood by the doors to the dining room, staring straight ahead as Judith passed him. Judith wondered if he ever employed his Gift of Illusion for respectable duties.

The dining room was as she remembered it: excessively large, with a massive oak table. It was flanked by ornate wooden dressers and large oil paintings of hunting scenes. A log fire burned along one wall, struggling to warm the high-ceilinged room. On the table were platters of peaches, cheeses, and bread.

The duke stood by a dresser with his back to the room, but he turned his head and gave Judith a smile as she came in. Judith looked round at the other occupants of the room.

Lady Agatha was already seated, with Lady Mary diagonally

opposite her, both fitted out in fine gowns in bright colours, and nibbling desultorily at peaches. Beside Mary, Lord John rose to his feet, still looking pale and gaunt. Opposite, an unfamiliar gentleman followed suit in standing.

"Lady Avely," said Lord John. "Good evening. May I introduce you to Mr Nottley? He is our guest tonight, and an old family friend."

Judith curtsied a greeting and examined Mr Nottley with interest. He was a spare little man with a bald head, bright eyes, and a neatly trimmed beard. His well-tailored clothes were a little old-fashioned, yet fit his figure well.

"Good evening," said Mr Nottley. "Yes, I quite treat Sargenet as my own home, after all these years." He turned and gave a gracious little bow toward Lady Agatha, and then seemed to recall that it was in fact the duke's house and twisted so his bow included his grace.

Lady Agatha allowed herself a small smile at this acknowledgement of her seniority. "Yes, Mr Nottley, it seems you cannot stay away!"

Judith found her own place at the table, guided by Broughton to sit opposite Lady Agatha and above Lady Mary. She felt a momentary embarrassment that she was now placed in precedence at the right hand of the duke, instead of further down, where she would usually sit in the midst of the hoi polloi.

To distract herself, she wondered why Mr Nottley had returned to Sargenet. For he was the boring scholar whom Miss Cultor had previously accompanied, the one who had supposedly left four days ago for London, the morning before the footman died.

As if hearing her thoughts, Mr Nottley smiled as he sat. "I was at Sargenet last week. After I departed, I realised I had left a precious book behind, one I could not do without. Hence, I returned - though also to spend a few more days in such a fine household. And one with such a fine library." Here he nodded to Lord John, as if to include him in the compliments.

Lord John looked glum. "A fine library, if it will stop raining blood."

"John!" snapped Lady Agatha. "Do not refer to such vulgar subjects at the dining table."

Lady Mary came to her husband's defence. "When else shall we refer to them, Agatha? Mr Nottley may have some insights to help us."

Lord John did not look as if he appreciated his wife's interjection.

"Oh?" Mr Nottley preened a little, stroking his beard. "Still having ghostly visitations, are we? I am not an expert on such matters, I confess."

The duke spoke up, from where he had been pouring himself a glass of wine at a side table. "Not just ghosts, Nottley. A death."

Mr Nottley looked as if he had swallowed a whole peach. "Pardon me?"

"One of our footmen," said Lord John. "Brained to death. The night after you left, actually."

Mr Nottley looked from face to face, eyes narrowing. "And you think the ghost did it?"

The duke walked to take his place at the head of the table. "Ghosts can't bash a man with a book."

"Please, Dacian," said Agatha, a harsh note in her voice. "Let us maintain some decency. Otherwise, whoever committed these atrocities is winning another point against us."

With that pronouncement, Agatha changed the subject, asking the duke how his visits to the tenants had been received that morning. Robert entered the room to help serve the first course. Steaming cauliflower soup was ladled into bowls and fresh bread served on a platter with hunks of butter.

Just as they were about to start eating, a clatter at the door announced the presence of the governess, Miss Atkinson. Her straw bonnet had been replaced by a cap rather similar to Judith's earlier, and the governess herded her three charges before her: Otho, Cato, and Quintus. The oldest boy - Otho? - looked as if his unruly blonde curls had been vigorously brushed, perhaps after another stint as a fox. They were all neatly clad as they lined up, eying the company and the food with interest.

Miss Atkinson curtsied, unfazed as all eyes turned toward her. "Good evening, my lords and ladies. The children wished to say goodnight."

"Goodnight," chimed the three boys, in differing levels of enthusiasm and volume.

Lord John nodded in acknowledgment but Mary held out her pillowy arm. Each boy came forward for a cuddle and a kiss on the cheek. This duty endured, they returned to the side of Miss Atkinson.

The duke spoke up. "Miss Atkinson, would you like to join us for dinner after you put the boys to bed?"

Miss Atkinson blinked, momentarily flustered. "Oh, no, I thank you, your grace. That is very kind of you but I will have my dinner in the schoolroom, as usual."

She curtsied again and briskly led the boys out before anyone could argue. Judith, seeing Agatha's disapproving look, imagined that it was her ladyship's decree that the governess eat separately to the family.

The table turned to their dinner. Judith ate hungrily and conversed with Lady Mary, asking after her elder sons. Felix and Maximus were at school, with Maximus apparently showing some of the same academic brilliance that characterised his father. Judith wondered if this meant that Maximus was also a Memor.

Judith smiled at Mary. "Surely Maximus could have inherited his scholarly aptitude from you too, Lady Mary. I know you share Lord John's interests and capacity." Lady Mary was a Memor too, though perhaps not as Gifted as her husband. Or perhaps she had been given less opportunity to develop her skills.

Mary's eyes seemed to focus on a point far away beyond Judith's shoulder. "Lord John is far more clever than I, of course. We are very happy that Maximus is showing the same bent." She took a sedate sip of soup.

Mr Nottley interposed from the opposite side of the table, smiling at Mary. "One out of five isn't too bad odds. I am certain Maximus has inherited his mother's acuity."

A blush stained Mary's cheeks.

Lord John spoke with coldness in his voice. "I hope the others will also develop their intellects, particularly Otho."

Mr Nottley ignored him. "Remind me, Lady Mary, did you name Quintus after the Roman poet or after his place in the family?"

Mary's lips parted but Lord John answered for her. "Horace, of course. He was the ancient's most superior poet, even above Ovid."

Mr Nottley took playful exception to this and Judith let them wander down a more scholarly dialogue, though it quickly became heated. She gathered it wasn't the first academic disagreement between Mr Nottley and Lord John, as vicious mentions were made of inadequate citations and poor research. Lord John's fist even clenched on the tabletop.

The duke provided a welcome distraction.

"Lady Avely," he paused over his soup. "Did you enjoy the chocolate I sent up, to warm you after your journey?"

"Indeed," she replied, "Most delicious. What is the recipe, do you know?"

Dacian waggled his eyebrows. "Ah, the secret of the Spaniards. I do not know if I should divulge it."

Judith raised her brows, her spoon paused over her bowl. "Why would you not?"

He lowered his voice, though no one was listening. "It gives me something to tempt you back to Sargenet. I know I am insufficient."

She did not want to deny it. Instead, she took a measured sip of her soup.

Dacian's lips twisted wryly. "I also have some chocolate infused with cayenne pepper," he continued. "It is quite spicy. I can send up a cup after dinner, if you like."

"An unnecessary indulgence, your grace."

"You must be indulged," he returned. "After all those years raising your children as a widow, you deserve some cosseting."

When Nicholas had died, she remembered suddenly, the duke had come to the funeral and offered his support. It was a year before the Garvey House party, when she was still wretched with grief, and unsuspecting of the second blow that would fall. She remembered how his grace had stood next to her in the front pew, dressed in unrelieved black, his face pale, his eyes sunken. He could not have looked worse than she had, but her ravaged face had been hidden by her veil. Afterwards, he had offered to plump out her widow's pension, as a duty owed to the wife of a dear friend. She had refused, thank God.

She had treated Dacian with blank coldness, reeling from Nicholas's death, and the duke had gone away in silence.

Judith had somehow forgotten it until now, wiped out in the shock and pain of that difficult time. She stared at him, remembering his stiff words and quick retreat then.

"Yes," she said slowly. "There were some hard years."

He smiled. "Are you revelling in your new freedom from your children?"

Judith spread butter on her bread. "It is strange to have my children out of my reach and beyond my advice."

"I'm sure it is excellent advice."

"It is easy to give good advice," she replied. "Harder to follow it."

Dacian looked away. Robert leaned between them, serving the next course, while Broughton on the other side of the table served Lady Agatha.

The rest of the dinner passed in uncomplicated chatter, the duke claiming most of Judith's attention. After the dessert (custard ices and pear tarts), Lady Agatha rose in a rustle of silk and led the ladies out, this time to the large drawing room near the dining room, decked out in pale blue and yellow.

Judith remembered this drawing room from a scene long ago. Her eyes involuntarily went to the duke, looking for the crescent-shaped scar that marked his forehead, but she pushed the memories down and kept her face politely neutral. This was not the time to dwell on youthful follies.

She had hoped for a private word with Agatha, but the gentlemen were hot on their heels. Judith found Dacian sitting next to her again, and wondered if anyone else noticed his attentions, or if they simply expected it. Lady Agatha was now entertaining Mr Nottley with her London tales, and Lord John was conferring with his wife on some private matter. There appeared to be some marital tension.

The duke leaned closer to Judith. "I'm delighted to see you without a cap, marchioness."

Judith raised her eyes and slayed him with a glance.

He smiled. "Truly. It is a pleasure to see your lustrous hair."

"Your grace!" She turned her head away. "Stop with your tarra-diddles."

He laughed under his breath. "My dear marchioness, if you will not call me Dacian, at least call me duke, not this insipid 'your grace' nonsense. And you know very well there are no tarra-diddles here! When I know you can Discern lies, what can I do but tell the truth?"

"Ha!" she retorted. "No need tell lies when you have been *omitting* the truth, *your grace*." She lowered her voice. "When were you going to tell me about Robert and Lewis's Gifts?"

Dacian's expression became shame-faced. "Ah, I, er, I was going to tell you, after our interlude with Lewis. I had hoped we were going to have a nice *tête-à-tête* after that, but you retreated to your bed. I hope you had a pleasant rest." He picked up her hand and kissed it, in a blatant attempt to distract her.

Even though she knew it for a ploy, she felt a tingle run through her hand, hearing his warm voice refer to her bed. She blinked crossly. This would never do. She withdrew her fingers sharply. "Well, Robert sought me out and told me an interesting tale." He had asked her not to tell Lewis, but she must inform Dacian, if only to clear Robert's name from any suspicion.

"Oh." Dacian raised a brow. "Do tell."

Hurriedly, Judith recounted the story that Robert had told of Lewis and the contested ring. Hearing it again, it sounded even more unlikely. "Robert told me the truth as he believed it, but I think there may be more to it."

Anger clenched in Dacian's jaw. "Robert didn't tell *me* this."

"I tricked it out of him," Judith explained hastily. "He was protecting Lewis, that is all."

The duke frowned. "Stupid young men. Did Robert say anything about ... his Gift?"

"He said he did not cast the skull, unless he did it in his dreams."

"Hmm. Well, I trust him, *and* Lewis. It is the rest of them that I am not certain about." Dacian gestured to the assembled company in the drawing room.

"You think one of them could have killed Gilbert?"

"I don't know." His voice hardened. "The very fact that he was killed in the drawing room indicates that the culprit is intimately involved in the household. We still haven't determined how any thief would gain access to the drawing room, with the Defences on the window."

Dacian's hand gripped the armchair and she felt a frisson of power. She placed her own gloved hand over his to calm him. "You're home now. You can rectify it."

The duke stared at her, his hand relaxing under hers. "Thank you, Judith."

She met his eyes and found herself suddenly without words.

At that moment, Lady Mary turned away from her husband and cleared her throat. "Why don't we play a few rounds of whist? We have even numbers with Lady Avely and Mr Nottley here tonight."

"Excellent notion," agreed Lady Agatha, and she clicked her fingers for Robert to fetch a pack of cards before anyone could say otherwise.

The duke led Judith over to the table, managing to arrange it so they were facing each other. Judith felt a little uncomfortable at this continued attention, especially when Dacian hadn't seen his family for nine years. True, Mr Nottley was not kin, and he was monopolising Lady Mary with scholarly discussions.

Perhaps it was simply that Judith was the only available female. Dacian was accustomed to having feminine attention fixed upon him. She frowned to herself. She did not like the role of pandering to his masculine ego.

The game began with the duke shuffling and dealing the deck. A silence fell as they all gathered up their cards.

Dacian looked to Lady Agatha at his left. "What's it to be, Aggie?"

Agatha examined her cards thoughtfully, pursing her lips. Then she looked up and her eyes widened. She went pale, her mouth slightly ajar, her answer dying on her lips.

Judith twisted quickly.

Behind her, a skull hovered in the middle of the drawing room.

The dome of its head was luminous white, with two black holes for eyes. The teeth were in a painful grimace, the jaw clenched. As Judith watched, the jaw hinged open as if to speak.

Lady Agatha let out a gasp. Lady Mary screamed.

Judith hastily looked round the circle. Everyone was staring, horrified, except for the duke, who also examined everyone's expressions. Lady Agatha looked as pale as death. Mary was red and quivering. Lord John was grim, while Mr Nottley's eyes bulged.

Looking back at the skull, Judith could not see a likely anchor for it, or any Illusion charm that could have triggered its appearance.

By the door, Robert stared wide-eyed. Broughton was nowhere to be seen, but Judith speculated that he could be standing just outside the door, within view of the Illusion.

The skull grew brighter and drifted toward them.

Then with a jerk, it snapped its teeth shut and dropped to the floor. It rolled in an arc and came to rest right in the centre of the room. Rather smugly, it lay there as if waiting for someone to touch it.

Agatha spoke, her voice rough. "Don't go near it!"

"I don't intend to," replied the duke, leaning back in his chair. He still watched everyone closely. "Touching it will simply make it disappear. It is an Illusion."

As if he had commanded the words, the skull vanished, with a theatrical puff of smoke.

Everyone turned to stare at Dacian. He held up his hands. "It wasn't me. I wasn't here for the earlier appearances, you recall."

"No," said Lord John, his voice quivering with rage. "It was Mr Nottley."

In which our heroine waits in the dark

Sometimes, one's own mind supplies the lies.
   - from *Lady Avely's Guide to Truth and Magic*

EVERYONE TURNED to look at Lord John, who had just accused his guest of a terrible vulgarity.

Lord John pointed a shaking finger at Mr Nottley. "You were here for the other ghosts. You are here tonight. And in your absence, we have had not a single visitation. I think that logic speaks for itself. Do you have some unacknowledged Gift for Illusion? Your Memory is poor enough to warrant it."

Mr Nottley drew in his bearded chin with affront. "How dare you, my lord! I am a guest in your household!"

"Yes, and until you came here, we had no other problems!" shouted Lord John.

The duke spoke up from where he lounged in his chair. "We must not jump to conclusions, brother. It may simply be a convenient coincidence, setting up Mr Nottley as a scape-goat."

Mr Nottley grew even more red at this suggestion. "A scape-goat!"

"Yes, for murder."

"Murder!" His eyes almost popped out of his head and he gobbled incoherently, sounding much like an insulted turkey. "You go too far, Johnny boy, if you think you can pin that footman's death on me!"

He stood as if willing to enter a brawl on the moment. Lord John also stood, knocking into the table as he did. A glass of wine spilled, running red over the wood. Robert leapt forward to tend to it.

Lady Agatha drew a shaky breath. "Calm yourselves, gentlemen. We will not blame you for murder, Mr Nottley."

"Speak for yourself," said Lord John, curling his thin fingers into a fist.

Beside him, Lady Mary reached out to cling to his coat. "No, John!"

Judith looked round at the shocked faces. Despite the mixed expressions of disgust and anger, any one of those present could have cast the Illusion. She was listening for a tell-tale lie, but so far no-one had directly denied responsibility. Even Mr Nottley's spluttering had not explicitly denied Lord John's accusations.

Lord John, at least, must be innocent, for Judith could hear no lie in his voice.

But there was something slightly off in the whole tableau, something that Judith could not quite put her finger on. Lord John and Mr Nottley were glaring at each other as if they would gladly like to kill each other.

The duke raised a hand. "Please do not be hasty, my friends. I know all too well the dangers of rushing into a fight. We are gentlemen, remember."

Lady Agatha cleared her throat. "You have been badly frightened. I am certain we will all calm down in a moment."

Mr Nottley twitched his shoulders, as if tossing something off them. He sat down again with a thump. "I am calm," he growled. Judith swallowed a smile at the lie.

Lord John stared at him angrily. Then he stalked away, going to the drinks table. "I need a drink."

Well, that was true.

"I think we all do," said the duke. "Broughton, a whiskey please, and fetch that sherry I brought back from Spain, so the ladies may try it."

The reminder of the presence of servants was enough to make everyone look away and soothe their ruffled feathers. Robert, Judith saw, was pale but composed as he cleared the spilt wine. His eyes met hers for a moment, and he shook his head slightly, denying responsibility for the skull.

Soon Broughton returned with the sherry. Judith was glad of the sweet liquid burning down her throat. She felt shaken by the apparition, even though she knew it was not some visitation from beyond the grave. The all-too-human intention behind it was more frightening, and the sudden spark to violence unsettling.

Lady Agatha insisted they continue with the game of whist, but nobody's heart was in it. Agatha's hand, Judith noticed, quivered slightly as she placed down her tricks. The duke, as if sensing Judith's unease, gave her a reassuring smile.

But Judith could not shake off her sense of foreboding, even as she concentrated on her cards.

Was the reappearance of the skull another warning? And could it portend another death?

THEY ALL RETIRED EARLY. Lady Agatha stood abruptly and excused herself, claiming a headache. Lady Mary followed soon behind, and Judith was glad to depart as well, leaving the gentlemen behind. She needed time to think over what had happened. Lewis, her favourite suspect, had been the only one *not* present tonight, and besides, he had scornfully - and truthfully - denied casting any Illusions. Or could he be in cahoots with someone else, who was using the skull to distract everyone?

Perhaps the whole performance was a distraction from the real reason for Gilbert's death. Lewis, at least, had some motivation to attack Gilbert, with his well-known enmity, and Lewis's ignominious defeat. But it appeared there were other hostilities at play at Sargenet.

Judith walked slowly up the stairs, lost in thought, until she heard the duke at her heels.

"Wait, marchioness!"

She paused, her hand on the bannister.

When he gained her side, he spoke under his breath. "Who was it? Could you tell?"

"I couldn't detect a lie. But something strange is going on."

"Really?" He smiled down at her and took her arm. "I am astonished to hear it."

She allowed him to escort her up the next flight. "I mean between Lord John and Mr Nottley. Is there some other animosity between them?"

Dacian shrugged. "Perhaps some scholarly disagreement? I don't see what bearing it would have on the Illusions or Gilbert's death."

"No," she agreed thoughtfully. "Unless the two are disconnected. Could Mr Nottley wish to unsettle or distract Lord John with the Illusions? For John does have a point, in that Mr Nottley's presence has coincided with the ghost."

"Mr Nottley is a Memor," said the duke thoughtfully. "Illusion and Memory are adjacent Gifts. I have heard that there are rare occasions where an adjacent Gift can show itself in a small measure alongside the dominant one."

"Yes," agreed Judith. "And even without that possibility, he could empower a token of Illusion."

"Then Lord John and Lady Mary could equally well have done it," he said. "They are both Memors as well, if we are to talk of adjacent Gifts."

"And all of them were there tonight, including Broughton." She did not mention that Robert, too, had been present and able to cast Illusions. "But Mr Nottley had left Sargenet when Gilbert was attacked, so that rules him out."

"Unless he returned that night, unbeknownst to anyone."

They were now at her door and she turned to face him, withdrawing her arm. "But why? Why would anyone kill Gilbert?"

"The servants might know something. We can question them tomorrow."

"We must talk to Lewis again, too."

Dacian nodded reluctantly, and she bobbed her head. "Goodnight, your grace."

"Dacian, please."

"Goodnight, Dacian," she managed. Their eyes met and a wave of energy passed between them.

"Shall I send up some of the cayenne chocolate?" he asked.

"Oh no," she demurred. "That won't be necessary. I am replete."

However, as he took his leave, she was aware of a tingle of dissatisfaction, and an urge, even, to invite the duke into her bedchamber - to continue their discussion over a cup of spiced chocolate. Perhaps he was not so bad; she had misjudged him about Lewis, after all. But no - nothing would change the brute fact of his silence over the last nine years.

Regardless, she was no Mrs Bleau.

As she let herself into her room, she belatedly remembered that Miss Cultor was out and about, investigating the ballroom.

Judith would have to wait til the morrow for news, or hope that Miss Cultor woke her if she discovered anything of interest.

Yet sleep was evasive, with her afternoon nap not being conducive to slumber now. She was also restless from the events of the evening, her mind going over the reactions and interactions she had witnessed. She tossed fitfully in the darkness for an hour, then resolutely sat up.

Why wait for Miss Cultor? Judith could visit the ballroom herself and see if there was anything of note, and then escort Miss Cultor back. Everyone would be abed by now, surely.

She stayed in her nightgown, merely throwing a cloak over the top and putting on her evening slippers. Creeping from her bedroom, lantern in hand, she took the righthand turn. The large ballroom was flanked on either side by each wing, and a corridor from the guest floor connected with the upper gallery around the ballroom.

Judith stepped through the door, exiting the west wing. Immediately, she sensed the dark void of the ballroom before her. To either side stretched the gallery, forming an upper level for guests to circulate far above the dancers. She could make out large rectangles of the paintings, the subjects obscured in the dim light. Before her was the low wall and railing that jutted out over the ballroom, gilt edges glimmering. The lantern light showed the waterfall of steps of the grand staircase descending from the southern end of the gallery.

Cautiously, she stepped forward, holding the lantern aloft. Further above, in the open space, hung the chandelier. It was rich with glass crystals, now glimmering in the light. Its candles were doused, the ballroom silent. She could see the expanse of the wooden floor, thirty feet below.

There was no skull, thank goodness.

A black shadow moved out of the corner of her eye. Judith looked round sharply. She felt a sense of unseen eyes watching her and shook herself. It would be Miss Cultor, of course. None-theless, the air in the deserted ballroom seemed suddenly cold. She shivered.

A soft thud came from behind. Judith whirled round.

Miss Cultor sprawled on the carpet. She was stark naked, no doubt after a difficult landing and transformation. She scrambled to her feet, brown curls standing out round her little face.

"What are you doing here?" the vampiri hissed. "You're scaring off the ghost!"

Judith beckoned, moving down the gallery. She knew from past experience that there were several alcoves set into the wall. She pulled the drape back from one and slipped inside, waiting for Miss Cultor to follow.

Miss Cultor stalked in, apparently oblivious to the fact that she was as bare as nature made her. Judith sighed. Clearly, she would have to start carrying a small spare gown if any sort of decency was to be maintained. At least that gave her an excuse to find the creature some better clothes.

She let the curtain drop, ensconcing them in a cosy circle. The lantern lit the alcove, showing a bench inset, covered in rugs and cushions, and a little wooden table. She knew it to be the scene of private trysts; in fact, Nicholas had once waylaid her into one of these alcoves at a Sargenet ball after they were married. She shook the memory off like a sigh, the sensation of Nicholas's arm over her shoulder fading away into the darkness.

"We can talk here," Judith said. "Did you find anything?"

Miss Cultor huffed, staying on the floor. "I thought you were the skeleton! No such luck. How am I to find anything if you stomp round like a herd of goats?"

Judith decided not to take offence at this description and laughed. "My apologies. I presumed you were waiting long enough. Did you see any Illusions?"

"No," said Miss Cultor, bare shoulders drooping. "No skulls or blood of any kind. Though the ballroom provides a dark, atmospheric setting."

Judith sat down on the bench, putting the lantern on the table. "We stole a march on you. A skull appeared in the drawing room."

Miss Cultor looked up sharply. "Really? That's not fair! Was there blood?"

"No blood. There was, however, a large audience for the appearance. It was just after dinner and the servants were there too."

"You mean to say it could have been any of them who cast the Illusion?"

"Exactly, because I could see no anchor for the image. It was cast from thin air."

Miss Cultor's lips pursed thoughtfully. "I couldn't find anything attached to the chandelier. That indicates it, too, was a live Illusion, not a stored one."

"Unless the perpetrator has since removed the anchor," suggested Judith.

Miss Cultor paced round the alcove. "I suppose this means the ghost has gone to bed now," she said morosely. "My vigil has been in vain. What am I to do now?"

"You could investigate the library and the drawing room," suggested Judith. "There might be something I missed. I was surrounded by people, so I couldn't poke around."

"Hmm," said Miss Cultor disconsolately. Then she stiffened like a plucked string. "Wait! I hear something!" She shot Judith a look. "Unlike you!"

Once again, Judith listened intently but could hear nothing. Remembering last time, however, how Robert had crept up to the door unheard, she could not doubt Miss Cultor. The vampiri's face was intent, her hand raised, a finger pointing as if she were a governess about to instruct a child.

"Wait here!" whispered Miss Cultor.

Before Judith could do anything, the vampiri collapsed in on herself, becoming a bat and flicking out her wings. Miss Cultor crawled up the drape which separated Judith from the gallery, hunched her way through the thick cloth and disappeared.

Alone, Judith sat as still as a rock, listening. She could hear nothing and cursed her all-too-human ears.

The silence did not lessen the feeling that someone was out there, either in the ballroom or the gallery itself.

Very slowly, she stood and edged toward the curtain. She desperately wanted to look out, but if she opened the drape even an inch, the light of the lantern would betray her presence. She could not bear to think of putting out the light, so she would have to trust Miss Cultor to be her eyes.

Carefully, Judith grasped the curtain edge between her thumb and forefinger, feeling the soft velvet fabric. She was ready to dart out there if she heard any squeak of distress. No noise came, however, just deathly silence.

The quiet, she decided, was somehow more unnerving.

Long minutes passed. Where in seven hells was Miss Cultor? Was she playing some trick on her? Growing cold and stiff, Judith gripped the curtain tightly, but still hesitated. She didn't want to chase the ghost off again with her goat-hoofed feet.

Damn the goat-like consequences. She couldn't stay here all night. Miss Cultor shouldn't have abandoned her.

Slowly parting the curtain, she stepped out, thrusting the lantern before her.

In which there is a gloomy presence

As a Musor, one soon grows accustomed to nakedness. However, I advise you to always carry a large handkerchief.
  - from *Lady Avely's Guide to Truth and Magic*

THE GALLERY WAS EMPTY. The dim lantern-light showed only the shapes of paintings and the carpeted floor. The flower pattern looked uncanny in the flickering light, like crawling lizards. Beside her, the chandelier was motionless over the dark pool of the ballroom.

Miss Cultor must have chased off any apparitions. Judith sighed. It was time she went back to bed.

Tiptoeing in her kid slippers, she made her way along the corridor, holding her breath. Then, just as she was about to step back into the safety of the west wing, the door swung open in her face.

She fell back with a startled gasp, her heart thudding. A tall, dark figure emerged.

It was the duke, his face stark in the shadows cast by her lantern, the lines on them seeming deeper. He loomed over her, frowning.

"Judith! What are you doing here?"

She lifted the lantern, equally taken aback. "I came to look for ghosts," she replied. "And you?"

"The same, but Judith, are you mad? You can't wander about unattended in the pitch of night!"

She bit back the observation that she had Miss Cultor attending her and pulled her cloak closer over her nightgown. She was aware that her white petticoats were showing. One hoped the duke would not look down.

He looked down. "You're not even dressed!"

Her anxiety from the last half hour morphed into anger. "I have a cloak! Furthermore, I am no longer a young maiden and I may move about unattended!"

"No, you may not!" he said. "There is a killer in the house, threatening us with skulls, and you thought you'd waltz round after midnight?"

"If you must know," she retorted, "I was in here for a discussion with my vampiri companion."

His brows shot up and he looked round in a pointed fashion at the empty gallery. Shadows danced wildly as the lantern flickered. "And where is this vampiri companion?"

Judith lifted her chin. "She heard something and went to investigate."

"Ah, I see." His voice dripped with sarcasm. "And the ballroom is a perfect place for a discussion. Have you forgotten the Edicts?"

A new voice spoke, equally sardonic. "A black kettle, your grace."

It arose seemingly from behind the duke. Judith's eyes widened. She craned her neck to see but she could see only shadows.

"Who was that?" she demanded. "A vampiri?"

"Very good," came the voice. "A pleasure to make your acquaintance, if I may say so, Lady Avely."

The voice did not sound particularly pleased about it; if anything, the greeting was uttered in mournful tones, with a faintly foreign accent. Still, she could not see the owner, even though she lifted the lantern higher and looked all about her. No vampiri head protruded from the duke's pockets or from behind his shoulder.

The duke sighed. "On my boot. May I introduce you to his gracel, Wooten Willoughby."

Judith looked down. There, on the duke's tan leather boot, sat a small figure with black wavy hair and swarthy skin. His face was long with sensitive features. He sat in a negligent pose on the duke's boot, his black eyes opaque as he stared at Judith. He was dressed all in black, except for the miniature white cravat tied with great finesse round his neck and contrasting with his olive complexion.

"How do you do?" she said.

"Well enough, I suppose," said Wooten gloomily. "Though this method of transportation recalls the plunging of a boat at sea."

Judith looked more closely and saw that Wooten held onto a string that hung from the turned-down top of the duke's boots. He must hold onto it to keep his balance as the duke strode about. Judith wondered how the string was attached to the boot and hoped it wasn't tied to the ducal toe.

Dacian retorted, "You were the one who suggested it, to save your cravat."

Wooten lifted a graceful hand to his neckcloth. "My cravat is worth saving. But I would be obliged to you, Lady Avely, if you would occupy his grace in conversation a moment longer, so I can recover my equilibrium."

The duke rolled his eyes. "None of us should be conversing out here. Lady Avely, let me escort you back to your room."

"No, I beg you," said Wooten in faint accents.

Dacian put his arm out in a peremptory fashion. "Come, Lady Avely. Hold tight, Wooten."

"No," said Judith. "I cannot leave without my own vampiri. She may be in some sort of trouble."

Just then, a brown shape dropped from the ceiling. It swept over their heads and then circled back to zoom round Judith's cloak, only to disappear under the hem. Judith blinked and stayed still. She did not even have a handkerchief on her person to assist Miss Cultor's embarrassment. A moment later, the vampiri popped her head through Judith's white petticoats, holding them to cover her modesty.

"I am here!" Miss Cultor announced cheerfully. Her brown curls bobbed like a halo round her head. Judith cursed inwardly, to have more attention drawn to her night clothes.

Wooten stared in horror, while the duke peered down at the tiny figure with interest.

Miss Cultor examined them with equal curiosity. "*You* must be the duke and his companion. Good evening, your grace and gracel. I am Miss Cultor."

"At your service, Miss Cultor." Wooten stood on the boot and gave a very creditable bow.

The duke restrained himself to a respectful nod. "A pleasure to meet Lady Avely's companion."

"We have bonded temporarily only," said Miss Cultor. "And I see you have a full head of hair on you."

The duke stared. "I confess, I cannot see the relevance of that particular observation right now."

Wooten coughed. "It is always apt to observe a gentleman's hair." Wooten's locks were carefully arranged in a windswept style,

Judith noted, which would also be difficult to maintain when squashed in Dacian's pocket - or indeed, riding the boat of his grace's boot.

She shook her head. "Why are we discussing gentlemen's hair?"

Miss Cultor smiled smugly. "It is only that I just saw a gentlemen with a bald head, vanishing into the east wing."

Judith stood up straighter. "Mr Nottley!"

Dacian raised his brows. "You think he is the one behind the phantoms?"

"Unless he is visiting the family wing for some other reason," said Judith thoughtfully.

Miss Cultor huffed from the petticoats. "I don't believe Mr Nottley is a killer, though I saw that bald pate with my own eyes," she declared. "He has no imagination for such things, being only obsessed with his books. The whole time we were here together he cloistered himself in the library."

"Oh really?" said the duke. "How are you acquainted with Mr Nottley?"

Miss Cultor explained that she had temporarily been Mr Nottley's companion, joining him on his last visit to Sargenet, but that she had found his obsession with ancient history a trifle boring. "I was always left in Mr Nottley's room while he engaged in scholarly debates. He seemed to have some long-standing quarrels with Lord John."

"Hmm," said Dacian. "It seems that Mr Nottley might be up to more than scholarly debates."

"We must follow him!" said Miss Cultor. "He shut a door in my face, so I could not pursue further. You could assist, your grace, by opening a door for me."

Judith repressed a smile, wondering if the duke would agree to be put to such menial service.

"No," said Dacian. "My apologies, Miss Cultor, but I've had enough of this foolishness. Let us return to our beds, for God's sake."

He put out his arm for Judith and she took it this time, holding the lantern again in her other hand. Dacian rotated slowly, so as to not dislodge Wooten, and Judith stifled another smile. Then she cleared her throat as Miss Cultor ducked beneath her petticoats, but the vampiri re-emerged as a bat and attached herself to Judith's cloak. Thus arrayed, they made their way back to the Gold Room.

At her door, the duke halted abruptly. "Promise me you'll stay abed for the rest of the night, Judith."

"I promise," she said meekly.

He glowered. "And all the nights following."

It was time to voice an objection. "How am I to discover anything if I am to keep to my bed?"

"Hear, hear," said Wooten from his boot perch, though he looked a bit queasy. "Clearly we are required to stalk this Mr Nottley tomorrow night."

Miss Cultor nodded eagerly as she hung upside-down as a bat on the cloak.

Dacian folded his arms. "Wooten, *you* can stalk Mr Nottley, if it makes you happy. Lady Avely will not be so improper, nor so incautious."

Wooten coughed. "What of the doors? We may need your assistance with doorknobs, your grace, as much as I regret the necessity."

Judith smiled. "Indeed. What is the harm in opening a few doors, your grace?"

"Plenty, when a murderer could wait behind one."

"Very well," she allowed. "If I sneak around at night-time, you may accompany me."

Dacian's eyes rested on her for a moment. There was a silence.

"Deal."

Judith went to bed feeling like she had somehow bartered away her virtue. Yet she was a matron now. There was nothing untoward in investigating the house at night in the presence of the duke. He could scarcely ravish her in the gallery.

Well, she wouldn't put it past him. But she wasn't going to allow it. And Wooten Willoughby would certainly frown upon such disgraceful conduct.

THE FOLLOWING MORNING, Judith awoke late after troubled dreams. A knock at the door heralded a maid, who entered with a steaming cup of chocolate.

"Thank you." Judith sat up to take the cup, gratefully feeling its warmth. Its presence somewhat mitigated the annoyance she was feeling toward Dacian.

She looked round to see if Miss Cultor was watching this indulgence with judgment. However, the vampiri must be asleep behind the cupboard, returned after her night-time adventures. At least, Judith hoped so, for the maid swept the curtains back to let in the morning light. Outside, the sky showed an unaccustomed blue.

Judith sat in bed and drank slowly, savouring the rich creaminess and sweetened spices. The faint taste of some unrecognisable ingredient still lingered in her mouth; the mysterious Spanish ingredient which once again coloured the chocolate a beautiful golden colour.

She mulled over recent events. Mr Nottley had seemed genuinely angry at Lord John's accusation, but his bluster could point to his guilt. Or was he hiding something else? Miss Cultor had seen Mr Nottley disappear into the family wing. Could he have gone there for a romantic tryst rather than a ghostly one?

Judith took a contemplative sip, her eyes dwelling on the vase of autumn roses by her bed, the red blooms expansive and fragrant. Yes, a romantic tryst would explain Lord John's antipathy. The dapper scholar had been quite attentive to Mary at dinner, and Lord John had been unfriendly even before the skull had made an appearance.

Her eyes glazed over, resting on the flowers. Could such an affair have any bearing on the murder of Gilbert? Could Gilbert have witnessed the torrid coupling and tried to blackmail Mr Nottley or Lady Mary, threatening to tell Lord John of his wife's indiscretion? Perhaps Lady Mary was finally wreaking revenge on her husband for his own indiscretions.

Judith sighed, taking another fortifying sip. As much as she was loath to abandon Lewis as her prime suspect, it looked as if Mr Nottley must now claim that position. She found it hard to imagine Lady Mary having the strength to brain someone, much less a young man. Unless Gilbert had been weakened beforehand with drink or some kind of drug ... or simply asleep, as Lewis had suggested, enjoying a warm slumber on the drawing room settee by the fire. Still, it would have taken either strong resolution or temper, and Judith doubted Mary contained such steel. Unless she was very desperate to keep her husband from discovering her affair. If indeed, there *was* such an affair.

Soon there were only dregs of cocoa left in the cup. Judith readied herself for the day, dressing in another drab gown. It was made of worsted wool of a fine quality, but a dull ash colour; a purchase made last season with her role as a matron in mind. It was high cut and rather stuffy looking with its lace collar. She sighed. A season ago she had not minded. It was only all the memories from her youth that were muddling her judgment now.

The grey woollen gown had a grey mobcap to match it. Judith swung it from her fingers with indecision. Would the duke make inappropriate comments about this one too? Surely, he would not dare. She had reprimanded him once already, and that should be enough.

Hmm. However, what choice did she have? As a matron, she ought to wear modest headgear. This mobcap was large, floppy, and decidedly unbecoming: eminently suitable for a matron interviewing the servants. Firmly, she tied the lace ribbons round her chin, trying to ignore the vision that filled her imagination: of the duke standing close behind her, his warm breath on her neck, his fingers undoing these very same ribbons, another arm snaking round her waist and pulling her close.

She frowned at herself in the mirror and carefully did the clasp for her lapis pendant, tucking the deep blue stone under the lace collar.

Thus armoured and recapped, Judith marched downstairs and partook of the breakfast spread. Lady Agatha was sitting, pale but composed, at the head of the small table in the parlour; purely from habit, Judith imagined, as that seat should now by rights be reserved for the duke.

Lady Mary sat at her left, looking tired and showing her age in the morning light. Lord John sat next to his wife, sipping coffee, his plate empty, his cheeks hollow. Mr Nottley was happily eating some bread and conserves, dabbing jam off his beard. The duke was nowhere to be seen.

Broughton served the coffee while Robert stood to attention by the door, his young, handsome face looking rather worried. Judith smiled at him, but he did not return the compliment. Perhaps, like her, he was feeling anxious about the appearance of the skull last night in the drawing room. Somebody in the house clearly had an unhealthy disregard for what was appropriate to the dignity of ducal rooms.

Despite her own anxiety, Judith felt hungry and made substantial inroads into a plate of eggs, toast, and butter. Twenty minutes later the duke came in from an early morning ride and helped himself to a massive plate of food. He glanced sideways at Agatha, then ignored her and sat down by Judith. His appetite and healthy colour made Lord John look even more gaunt and listless.

After breakfast, the duke interrupted Judith's perusal of the morning papers and the news of Napoleon's latest impertinences.

"Come, marchioness," he said. "We have work to do."

In which ladies commit falsehoods

The power of Discernment can be imbued within an object, but it takes great skill and capacity, and usually the effect is rather clumsy.
  - from *Lady Avely's Guide to Truth and Magic*

INSTEAD OF THE LIBRARY, this time the duke led Judith into his study.

She had only seen the study once before, long ago when Dacian had first shown her round his house with youthful pride. The room was half the size of the library, commanded by a large oak writing desk. A heavy armchair sat next to it, on a thick Turkish rug patterned in red and brown.

The duke threw himself on the chair behind the writing desk. "Nice mobcap."

She gave him a disapproving look. Her fears had been realised.

"That one begs even more to be ripped off your head," he added as she took her place in the armchair at right angles to the desk. "Are you trying to pass yourself off as an old woman? You're younger than me, for God's sake."

"Behave your age then," she retorted. "This is no time for badinage."

"No, that will be tonight, when we are skulking around in the dark, trailing Mr Nottley." He grinned.

Again, she regretted her concession. It would be much easier to follow Mr Nottley without the duke underfoot making inappropriate comments.

"Perhaps we should leave that task to the vampiri," she suggested reluctantly. "My talents are better used in conversation."

"I wouldn't say that," said the duke, then he looked away and straightened some papers on the desk. "Still, let us continue with the interviews. Don't forget your hand signals."

Judith nodded and rested her hand on the armrest, visible to the duke but behind the line of sight of anybody facing the desk.

They proceeded to question the lower servants first, including the scullery maid and house maids. These interviews went smoothly, without any sign of deception. None of the maids knew anything relevant about Gilbert's death or the spectres, so Judith was happy to keep her hand uncurled.

Then, after a cup of tea, it was time to speak to Lewis again, with Judith's new knowledge. She wanted to hear the story of Gilbert's ring according to the steward himself. She only hoped she could keep track of it, for her mind was starting to blur at the edges, as it were. Fortunately, she would only have to listen in silence while Dacian did all the talking.

When Lewis was standing before them, the duke became suddenly forbidding. "I have a few more questions, Lewis," he said. "It is in your interest to answer truthfully."

Lewis nodded shortly, his black locks gleaming much like his uncle's but without the strains of silver. Judith's eyes tracked between the two. Really, although they were so similar, Dacian was so much more attractive than that callow youth. She sighed.

Dacian shot her a glance but continued. "I have gathered from the household gossip that you won a ring from Gilbert last week. Is that right?"

Judith hoped she would not be suspected as the source of household gossip, nor Robert, and she tried to make herself as inconspicuous as possible.

Lewis answered readily enough, though his eyes narrowed. "Yes, your grace. Fair and square. I invited him to join a game with Robert and me, and that was the outcome."

"Yet the ring has since been returned to Gilbert's finger. Could you explain how?"

Lewis did not blink. "I put it back myself. I found him dead and I felt sorry for him."

This time, the lie sounded like dinner plates clashing together. Judith winced slightly and clenched her fist on the armrest.

Dacian's eyes flickered. "I'm afraid I don't believe you."

"Why not?" Lewis stiffened.

Dacian considered. "I don't think you would have had the presence of mind, let alone the inclination, to put a ring back on a dead man's finger."

"I certainly would."

Judith flexed her hand and curled it back into a fist.

The duke's voice was like iron. "Come now, Lewis. The truth please."

"It is the truth."

"No, it is not." He paused, his voice softening. "Listen, if your Gift escaped you, I will understand. I have made the same error myself in the past, so I can scarcely punish you harshly if you did the same."

Lewis's eyes widened.

Dacian continued. "However, I need to know the truth. So speak."

The steward's chin lowered to his chest. "Very well. Gilbert won the ring back, the little rotter." He paused. "He was a cheat."

"Go on," said Dacian grimly.

"The night Gilbert died, he came up behind me as I was returning to the Dower House after dinner. He jostled me on the shoulder, trying to start a fight, called me a few names and threatened me. He said he'd fight me for his ring. I know I should have walked away but I thought it might do us both good to clear the air." Lewis cleared his throat under Dacian's disapproving gaze. "He was desperate to win that cursed ring back. I should have suspected something, as usually there was no chance he would win. But he must have slipped something in my drink at dinner, because I felt all strange and unbalanced. I kept missing my punches. He got me down and took the ring. He left me lying on the grass, feeling like the world was crashing."

This time, Lewis was telling the truth, his words clean and uncoated. Judith watched his profile carefully and laid her hand flat on the armrest. She was reluctant to believe him, despite the evidence of her ears. Perhaps it was not the whole truth. Perhaps this ignominious defeat had enraged Lewis and he had exacted his revenge later, furious at being cheated in his own game.

Dacian was shaking his head. "You know you're not allowed to fight. Especially you, Lewis."

"I know," said Lewis, without much remorse. "That's why I didn't tell anyone. Also, I was worried I had somehow killed him."

"How?" asked Dacian.

Lewis shrugged. "Maybe a blow had worked more damage than I knew. He seemed fine as he walked away from me," he added nonchalantly. "Last I saw of Bert, he was disappearing into the house."

This was the truth. Judith kept her palm flat. This meant Lewis was innocent, unless, like he said, his fists had caused fatal damage that was not immediately apparent.

None of this explained how Gilbert had ended up on the settee in the drawing room with a book lying next to his head. Judith frowned, wondering who else might have a grudge against Gilbert.

"When was this?" asked Dacian.

"Close to eleven at night," replied Lewis. "After the servants' supper."

"Hmm," said Dacian. "So Gilbert was alive before midnight."

"You believe me now?" asked Lewis, with a hint of insolence.

Dacian glanced at Judith's relaxed hand. "Yes."

Lewis's shoulders relaxed infinitesimally.

Judith spoke up from her armchair. "May I ask a question?"

Lewis turned, his jaw tightening.

She held his gaze. "Tell me what you know of Miss Atkinson."

Lewis's surly demeanour showed a crack of surprise. "Nothing much. She's been governess for those boys for the last few years. On your mother's recommendation, no?" he asked Dacian.

Dacian nodded. "She is the cousin of my mother's friend, Mrs Atkinson. Perfectly respectable, as far I know."

Judith said, "What of her relations to Gilbert?"

Mr Lewis was discomfited. "Oh, she didn't like him. None of us did. He took a fancy to her, though."

"She rebuffed him?"

"Firmly," said Lewis, with a reluctant grin. It made him look even more like his uncle.

"Oh," interjected Dacian. "With a book, perhaps? If Gilbert came inside, giddy with victory from your fight, and tried to force his attentions upon her?"

Lewis shrugged. "Maybe, and if so, who can blame her?"

Judith tended to agree. If Gilbert had been trying to rape Miss Atkinson, he deserved a well-placed book to the head. Surely the law would allow it as self-defence. Yet society was not so forgiving of scandal. Perhaps the governess did not trust she would emerge unscathed from such a sordid affair. Perhaps she feared losing her position if she was known to execute lecherous men with books.

She fell silent, her mind even more woolly now from exerting her Gift in such a prolonged manner.

"Thank you, Lewis," said Dacian, casting her a concerned glance. "You may go now. Don't talk of this to anyone."

Lewis clicked his heels together and left, with another sidelong look at Judith.

Once he had gone, Judith sighed and laid her head on the armchair backing. "We must talk to Miss Atkinson, and congratulate her on bashing that lecherous footman."

"You are rather jumping to conclusions," said Dacian with amusement. "Perhaps you should gather your wits again."

She sat up with dignity. "I am perfectly fine."

"You have a becoming flush in your cheeks."

Her hands went to her face. "I do?"

"It makes your cap look even more ridiculous."

"Stop criticising my caps," she said crossly.

"Stop wearing them."

"I am a matron!"

"You're not in your dotage. Stop hiding under those silly confections."

She stared, unable to think of a response. Cursed Bemusement, muddling her senses. His smiling black eyes, crinkled at the corners, did not help her state of mind.

"Do we need to talk to Robert?" She tried to return the conversation to safer channels. "I have already heard his story."

"There is something else I need to tell you about Robert," replied the duke. "Perhaps while you gather your wits?"

"My wits are perfectly gathered, thank you very much."

"Indulge me." He looked away, and she saw an expression of discomfit flicker across his face. "Do you know about the *Lapis Veritas?*"

"No." She frowned. "What is that?"

He stood. "I've been meaning to show you. I only hope you will not be angry with me again."

He strode across the room to where a portrait of the old duke hung over a low bookshelf. Judith watched Dacian's shoulders flex as he moved the painting aside, wondering what he had done to rouse her wrath now. Then her attention was captured by the steel safe set in the wall. Placing his hands on the metal, Dacian unlocked the Defences on it. The metal quivered briefly and a faint echo of power tingled round the room, rattling the window panes.

Judith sat up straighter. Whatever was in that safe must be very valuable to warrant such a spell. Dacian swung the steel door open and pulled out a smaller wooden box from within.

The box was carved ornately, with an elegant wind rose depicted on the lid. Opening it, he presented the contents to Judith.

She looked down at a long, thin stone of blue lapis. It was in the shape of a divining rod, hanging on a silver chain, the midnight blue set against cream silk. Reaching out a finger to touch it, she guessed that it held some kind of magic. Discernment, most likely, given the nature of the stone.

Gold veins sparkled in the deep blue. "What is it?"

"It is a tool of Discernment," Dacian replied. "Nicholas made it."

She looked up sharply. "Nicholas?"

"He gave it to me as a gift, as a repayment for the arrangements I made for Robert, little though I did. Please," he held up a hand, "do not be angry that I kept the knowledge of it from you. I thought it would only cause you more pain."

Judith stared at the stone, anger indeed stirring in her, aimed diffusely at both Nicholas and Dacian, and the secrets they had kept together.

Dacian continued. "I tried to return the stone, but Nicholas insisted I keep it. So I have been more than compensated for the duties I undertook on his behalf. The *Lapis Veritas* is a priceless treasure."

"How does it work?" Judith asked coldly.

"It can give you the answer to any question you ask."

She drew her head back in disbelief. "I doubt that. Discernment is not usually so generous or wide-ranging."

Dacian put the box in her hands and retreated to the desk once more. "Well, perhaps not *anything*," he agreed. He began playing with a letter-opener that lay on the desk, its sharp thin blade gleaming as he tossed it from hand to hand. "The Eye of Truth has its limitations. One has to ask the question three days in a row and hope it gives you a consistent answer. And it requires one of Avely blood to wield it."

"*What?*" Her fingers tightened on the heavy box.

Dacian nodded, spinning the blade through the air again. "Yes, Nicholas was clever. He took seven nights to imbue this stone with his power and link it to his bloodline. He wanted to ensure that I would always be bound to look after Robert, for I would need him to wield the Eye."

Judith stared down at the stone. "Yet it also binds Robert to you."

"Indeed. It must be what Robert meant when he said he cannot leave Sargenet." Dacian put the knife down with a clatter. "But I will tell him he is free to go. After all, if he is in Cornwall, I will know where to find him."

"Thank you." She appreciated the sentiment but she doubted Robert would heed it. He was stubborn, like his father. She ran her finger over the beautiful pendant again, thinking of Nicholas. He had tried, in his own way, to do his best by Robert. If only he could have told her about it.

Dacian moved away from the desk and flung himself in one of

the deep-set armchairs. "Robert wants me to use the Eye of Truth to find out who killed Gilbert, but it is not so easy."

"No," she agreed. "Yes or no answers, I suppose? And three nights to wait for each answer? You could be here for months."

"Your Gift is much quicker and more precise," he acknowledged. "Has your mind sharpened once more? I don't want to drive you too hard, but we could question the head groomsman before lunch."

"I suppose so," she allowed, and handed him the box. He stowed it away in the safe again, straightening the painting so the old duke once more gazed sternly over the study.

The head groomsman was even less helpful than the maids, as he kept to the stables and knew nothing of ghosts or thieves except for exaggerated gossip heard from the main house. He told them that a skull had tried to devour Lady Agatha as she slept in her boudoir, and that another one was seen trying to draw water from the old well in the woods. Judith wondered at this latter story, the first she'd heard where the ghost appeared outside the house. Both tales were probably pure fabrication.

Her mind wandered, trying to make sense of the puzzle. Lewis, her favourite suspect, had proven himself innocent of both the spectre and the murder. Who else, then, would have wanted Gilbert dead? She thought of Lord John, who had been anxiously pursuing some business at the inn, and, moreover, was so quick to accuse Nottley of the phantoms. Yet why would Lord John kill an innocent footman? And did the frightful skulls have any bearing on the death?

Unfortunately, her mind was too befuddled to think of how they could possibly be connected. She was glad when the duke called a halt to the interviews and escorted her to lunch. The family and guests gathered again in the breakfast room, helping themselves to the repast set out on the board.

Mr Nottley was once more eagerly consuming a healthy plate

of food and chatting to Lady Mary about the intricacies of translating Latin. Even Lord John was eating this time, sitting close to his wife and glowering at Mr Nottley. The duke was ravenous again, though Judith could not imagine why, for he had simply been sitting in the study for hours with her. Broughton hovered anxiously while Lady Agatha ate bread and meat that she did not appear to enjoy.

Judith ignored them all, keeping her head down while her mind was foggy. When Dacian had finished wolfing down his food, he told her that he was duty-bound to visit some more tenants that afternoon with Lewis, so she was free to do as she liked. She gave him a narrow look, suspecting he was worried for her state of mind. Nonetheless, perhaps another nap was in order. Perhaps she should form a habit of afternoon naps, as befit her advanced age of past forty.

As Dacian strode away to fetch Lewis, she reflected that it was notable that Lewis was so involved in the running of the estate. The duties of a steward combined with his obvious connection to the family made it look, to a suspicious mind, that he stood a chance of being formally adopted into the Sargen clan. Judith stole a glance at Lord John, to see him staring woodenly at his plate. Did he fear Lewis would supplant his own sons in the line to inherit?

She shook her head, for the notion was ridiculous, with the ducal estate entailed and Lewis a bastard. Then she remembered his Gift. The ordinary laws of primogeniture were sometimes overridden to keep the musor powers within the great families. As an Impactor, Lewis held the same power that the ducal line had nurtured for centuries. He was both of Sargen blood and Sargen power. Inheritance of the title was not as impossible as she'd first thought. It would certainly solve the problem of speedily providing Dacian with an heir.

But no. It was far more likely that Dacian would marry some

young woman and beget tens of children with their own Impacting power. Neither Lewis nor John's children stood a chance of inheriting the estate.

Lady Agatha cleared her throat from her end of the table. "I will be busy this afternoon - writing letters in my room, Lady Avely. I hope you will forgive me for not being about to entertain you."

Judith looked up in surprise. Not only was Lady Agatha being a rude hostess, but she was also lying. She had no plans to write letters today, of that Judith was certain. Her voice had sounded with the hollowness of deliberate untruth.

"Of course," Judith murmured. "I am happy to entertain myself."

Agatha gave a short nod. "You may borrow books from our extensive library. Perhaps Mary can find you something instructive."

The countess put her napkin aside. "I'm afraid I am feeling rather poorly, Lady Agatha. I, too, will be retiring to my room to rest."

Judith looked with curiosity at Mary. She too was lying.

Lord John spoke up. "I will be at my studies," he said, "but I would be happy to assist you in selecting a volume, Lady Avely."

He, at least, spoke the truth. Judith smiled at him and replied that it would not be necessary, that she knew how to choose a book for herself.

The ladies excused themselves, leaving Judith alone with Lord John and the servants, and half a slice of bread on her plate. She bit into it thoughtfully. Perhaps a nap would be ill-timed. Both Mary and Agatha had lied, and both had rooms in the east wing. If only she could somehow keep watch to see if either of them tried to leave on clandestine business. Perhaps what her Gift could not Discern, plain old snooping could discover.

She knew that the east wing had a rear stairwell, with a door opening onto the back gardens. Pushing her chair out, bread still in hand, she informed Lord John that she would be out in the grounds and left quickly via the entrance hall.

In which there is a graveyard tryst

The problem with Truth Discernment is that there are many layers to truth.

 - from *Lady Avely's Guide to Truth and Magic*

JUDITH SLIPPED OUT into the cool autumn sunshine. Quickly, she followed the gravel path round to the back of the house, feeling the crunch of stones under her slippers.

The rear door to the east wing was in shadow. It was still closed. Judith looked round for a likely hiding place. If she hurried, she could place herself in secrecy before Mary or Agatha likewise came out the door.

She scuttled over to a large hawthorn hedge, its leaves thick and glossy enough to hide her. She nestled close behind the branches and let a breath out, peering through the chinks in the hedge. A rather perfect vantage point, if she did say so herself. She had a direct line of sight to the rear door and yet she was concealed from view from the house. She ate the remainder of her bread and licked the butter from her fingers, wondering how long she would have to wait.

Mary, of course, could have arranged a tryst with Mr Nottley somewhere else in the house. Yet surely, with the day so fine, they would snatch a chance to meet outside, away from any prying servants. As for Agatha, her lie was probably just to cover the fact that she would spend all morning reading gothic novels in bed.

Judith started to wish she was doing the same thing instead of enacting her own intrigues. Half an hour passed. Her legs began to weary and her mind began to doubt. She was staring absent-mindedly up at the white clouds piling over the house, thinking on old memories, when movement from the east wing caught her eye.

The rear door opened with a snap. Not Mary, but Agatha stepped out. She was dressed for walking and she looked round imperiously.

Judith shrank into her hedge, though she was certain Agatha could not see her. Yet, horrifyingly, Agatha stalked toward the hawthorn shrub. Judith held her breath, wondering how she could explain her presence. The hawthorn wasn't even flowering! Then Agatha passed by, close enough for Judith to see the frown lines on her brow.

Agatha continued following the path marked by the hedge, quickly disappearing into the rose arbour. Laden with late blossoms, the elegant archways soon concealed her figure.

Cautiously, Judith followed. What lay in this direction? She cast her mind back to the extensive tours of Sargenet that the duke had once given her, years ago. Beyond the rose arbour was a small, pretty pond and a few apple trees. Oh, and beyond that was a cemetery, the final resting place of many a Sargen and even their servants. Perhaps Lady Agatha was going to pay respects to her long dead father, the old duke.

But why should she lie about such a dutiful act? Was she, after all, the one behind the phantoms? She was the one known to read gothic novels - maybe that was her fear, that she would be discovered in her tricks. Or was she up to something more ominous?

Judith crept through the curve of the arbour, smelling the delicate fragrance of overblown autumn roses. Unbidden, she remembered how once, long ago, the duke had promised to show her the arbour, and how he had failed to keep that promise.

She shook her head sharply. What was done was done. And when it was done by a duke it was even more unassailable. He couldn't change his mind, click his fingers, and expect her to come running back into his arms now that he was returned to England. She had some pride, after all. She ignored the beckoning pathways to either side of the main avenue and hurried on after Agatha.

Emerging from the laden arches, Judith slipped behind one of the apple trees, thick with large green apples. Agatha's tall figure remained in sight, turning briskly at the pond. Just as Judith had guessed, she was following the narrow path that led over the hill to the cemetery. A flock of crows rose up as she strode through them.

Judith dithered. She did not want to crest the rise and be seen by Agatha. Instead, she cut round the hill and approached the cemetery from the back, through a copse of beech trees.

She kept to the shadows and trunks. A wind plucked at her hair, sending cold tendrils along her neck. She came in view of the cemetery and ducked behind a beech. A crow called nearby, startling her with its harsh sound. After a few moments, she peered round the trunk, in search of Agatha.

White gravestones shone bright in the sunshine, evenly placed, with the grass clipped neatly. A row of crypts lined the back of the graveyard, the stone houses bare and unadorned, and backed by a row of tall pines that whispered in the wind.

It was against the crypts that she made out the silhouette of Agatha.

Not just Agatha. The lady of the house was entwined in the embrace of another. Leaning in the shelter of a large stone that loomed over them both, Lady Agatha rested in the arms of Mr Nottley.

Judith squinted, not trusting her own eyes. Yet it was certainly the dapper figure of the scholar, his bearded face against Agatha's pale cheek. Even as Judith watched, he bent to kiss Agatha's neck and her ladyship tilted her head back in pleasure, her hands grasping at his coat.

Grimacing, Judith stepped behind a trunk to gather her thoughts. Mr Nottley was having an affair with Lady Agatha? Recalling the dynamics of dinner the night previously, Judith remembered how Agatha had smiled so smugly when Mr Nottley said he could not keep away. His attentions to Lady Mary must be a feint to cast suspicion away from his true object.

How long had this been going on? Mr Nottley was an old family friend: it could be years of dalliance, or a more recent diversion.

Judith was aware of some sympathy for Lady Agatha. It must not be easy, being a duke's daughter and unmarried after all these years. She must long for company and intimacy. Judith scarcely blamed her for welcoming Mr Nottley's enthusiastic caresses.

Yet, it made Agatha equally vulnerable to blackmail.

A duke's daughter was meant to be beyond reproach, even - especially - at Agatha's advanced age. Had the new footman Gilbert discovered her affair and threatened exposure? Had she killed him to keep his silence? Or asked Mr Nottley to do it?

Judith narrowed her eyes, casting another glance round the tree at the unlikely couple. Agatha *could* have asked Mr Nottley to do the deed. His coincidental departure from Sargenet could have been orchestrated by her to give him an alibi, even as Agatha instructed him to return that evening and meet with Gilbert. Perhaps she had asked Gilbert to attend to some trivial evening duty in the drawing room, appointing him to his death. Perhaps her fear and her lies were covering her own culpability.

The lovers ceased their passionate embrace and began talking. Judith, burning with curiosity, crept through the beeches to where the trees thinned. She was hidden from their line of sight by the slab of the crypts. Agonisingly slowly, she quietly tiptoed up to their particular crypt, until its mass squatted over her.

The stone was cold, as yet untouched by sun. She leaned against it, listening intently, smelling the sharp fragrance of the nearby pines. Her heart was beating fast at her own temerity.

At first there was silence. Judith kept very still, fearing that she had been heard. But it seemed that the lovers were simply absorbed in each another's company again. Judith grimaced to herself, not liking the position she found herself in. Yet Gilbert's death remained unresolved and her abhorrent behaviour might gain a vital clue.

Finally, Agatha spoke, her voice roughened. "You must be careful, my sweet. You should leave Sargenet."

Judith caught her breath. If only Agatha would confide in Mr Nottley the reason for her fear.

"Such a loving nature," said Mr Nottley fondly, if somewhat erroneously in Judith's opinion, and indeed in the faint accents of a well-intentioned white lie. "Why would I leave when I could stay close to my beloved Venus?"

"John is getting suspicious, after all this time. He almost called you out last night. For all his Romans, he is a prude. I do not know what he will do when he realises the truth about us."

That was one reason for her fear, thought Judith. Agatha was concerned that all the questions would reveal her amorous activities.

Mr Nottley chuckled. "I'm less worried about John than the

duke," he said, and Judith could hear that this was the truth. "His grace is the one who fights duels willy nilly, isn't he? Will he drive a sword through me if he realises I have captured your affections?"

Agatha tittered, a strange sound to Judith's ears. "You have captured more than my affections, my Eros."

There was a small silence (filled with passionate kisses, Judith reluctantly imagined) then Agatha spoke again.

"The duke seems to have invited Lady Avely into my house at the worst possible time."

"Who is this Lady Avely, by the way?" asked Mr Nottley. "His grace seems very interested in her. Could ducal nuptials be on the cards?"

Judith grimaced to herself. It was somehow worse to be eaves-dropping when the subject of conversation was herself. Especially joined with such a nonsensical notion.

Agatha's voice responded with a bite in it. "Don't be foolish. Judith Avely might be recently elevated to marchioness, but her father was the rector in the village. The duke has flirted with her for years but nothing has ever come of it, thank goodness." Agatha paused. "Her presence at Sargenet is very unfortunate. I've already tried to give her a strongly worded hint to leave but she is pretending to be deaf."

Miss Cultor would have a theory about *that*, thought Judith.

"Why is her presence so unfortunate?" asked Mr Nottley. "She might soften the duke and make him see the world in a rosier glow."

Behind the slab, Judith tilted her head. She, too, would like to know why Agatha was so opposed to her presence.

Agatha hesitated. "She tends to have a volatile effect on Dacian. He starts ... brooding."

Judith hunched her shoulders against the stone. *Ha.* Dacian was probably just mulling over his latest horse purchase.

"I can't see why she would captivate his attention," said Mr Nottley soothingly. "Lady Avely is just a drab widow."

Judith raised her brows and crossed her arms. Mr Nottley was not being entirely honest, by the echo in his voice.

"Hmm," said Agatha. "Drab or not, I want her gone from Sargenet. Maybe you should say something to her - warn her off, tell her something uncanny is going on. She might listen to you."

"I'm surprised she wants to stay with all that has happened," observed Mr Nottley. "What's all this about a ghost swinging books about?"

"Poor dear Gilbert," said Agatha. "I feel terrible. He was my own man in the house, you know. I can't quite believe he is gone."

Judith frowned. Agatha's voice was genuinely regretful as she mourned Gilbert's absence. So it was unlikely that he had been blackmailing her.

"Well, I don't like the sound of all these spectres," tutted Mr Nottley. "Are you able to protect yourself?"

His words, too, were sincere. Judith's frown deepened. It appeared that Mr Nottley was innocent too - of the Illusions, at least.

Agatha replied with a hint of tartness. "I possess the Impacting Gift, remember. Besides, no one would dare raise a hand to a duke's daughter."

Ah, so Agatha *was* an Impactor. It meant she was capable of killing Gilbert, but reluctantly Judith put that possibility aside. Why would Agatha take a book to his head, when she relied upon him for all her private errands - and no doubt to arrange her secret liaisons?

"Quite right," said Mr Nottley. "Still, a skull might not realise you are a duke's daughter. I wouldn't want any ghosts propositioning you."

"They are just Illusions," said Agatha scornfully. "I can't

imagine who might be responsible, but if I simply ignore them they will go away."

The lie seemed to echo in the empty graveyard, lifting up on the faint breeze with an undercurrent of fear below Agatha's defiance. Judith frowned. What did Agatha suspect about the skulls that she was unwilling to mention even to Mr Nottley?

The couple in the graveyard fell silent. Only when Judith heard the rustle of fabric and some panting breaths did she move. Gingerly, she rose to her feet, inch by inch. One of her joints gave an audible crack and she froze. But it seemed the faint sound had not been heard by the lovers. Gritting her teeth, she backed away quietly and fled down the hill, keeping to the trees.

She was half-way back when she realised that Agatha had not been entirely honest. Gilbert was not her only 'man in the house'. She had also appointed Broughton a few years ago.

Perhaps it was Broughton whom Agatha feared.

In which there is a cry for help

We all have a duty to truth. It is the foundation of all other virtues, alongside love.

  - from *Lady Avely's Guide to Truth and Magic*

RETURNING TO SARGENET, Judith rubbed her forehead as she walked, trying to make sense of this new revelation. From the tenor of their discussion, neither Agatha nor Nottley had killed Gilbert, and both knew nothing of the phantoms. Why kill Gilbert, if he was assisting in their affair? Why kill Gilbert at all?

It would make more sense if Lewis had been the victim. He, after all, was the upstart bastard who might inherit the estate. Judith frowned with a sudden thought.

As she drew closer to the house, she espied Robert raking in the rose arbour, making neat while the sun lasted. His rich brown hair gleamed in the dappled light, the now familiar profile bent to his work. He looked up as Judith approached.

"Good afternoon, my lady," he said respectfully.

She attempted a conversation. "It is a lovely day. Not one for skeletons, I hope."

He lowered his voice. "It wasn't me, Lady Avely. I'd know if I had made that skull."

She had almost forgotten about the skull, for Lady Agatha's conduct this afternoon had overshadowed it.

"I didn't think it was you," she replied, but it was good to know it for certain. The bell of truth had sounded in Robert's words. "I have a question for you, however: did Gilbert look at all like Mr Lewis? Could someone have confused the two?"

Robert rested his rake. The roses framed him with large, nodding blooms of colour. He tilted his head, considering. "Yes, they were similar. Both of the same height, with dark hair. Bert wasn't as handsome as Lewis, I can tell you that." He paused. "I could show you, if you like."

"What do you mean?" Even as she spoke, she had an inkling.

"Here." Robert propped the rake against a wooden post and made a show of drawing out his pocket watch, as if finding the time for her. He held the small clock-face in his palm. As she bent toward it, the timepiece transformed into an image of a stranger's face, with shoulders showing the green and gold of the Sargen footman's livery.

It was a clever Illusion, detailed and life-like even in miniature. Judith cast a quick glance at Robert, to see a hint of pride in his expression, even as he frowned in concentration. She was glad he had softened enough to share his Gift with her.

"You are talented," she observed. "This is Gilbert?"

He nodded. The portrait showed a young man with dark hair and eyes, as Robert had said, but with thin lips, a slightly bulbous nose, and a supercilious expression. Gilbert lacked the strong bone structure that gave Lewis (and Dacian) such a striking appearance.

Judith glanced round at the grounds, apprehensive that

someone would see Robert's display. The tips of pine trees protruded from the graveyard hill but there was no sign of Agatha or Mr Nottley yet.

She looked back at the cameo and used a finger to trace the outline of it. The Illusion did not vanish, held in place by Robert's own hand.

"I see what you mean," she said. "A surface resemblance only. Still, I wonder if a stranger with instructions to hurt Lewis might have mixed them up by accident."

Robert shook his head, waving the pocket watch for emphasis. Gilbert sneered up at them. "Why would anyone want to hurt Lewis?"

She raised a brow. Perhaps Robert didn't know of the exceptions made to keep certain Gifts within the noble families. Lewis was endowed even with the same rare Gift that the Sargens had carried for centuries, which made him a possible heir to the Sargen title. He was also older, even, than John's heir, Felix, and ensconced in the Dower House, groomed to rule the estate. If Dacian decided to formally adopt him, Lewis could be in line to inherit the ducal title and lands. And undoubtedly, many believed that Lewis was the duke's son.

She said nothing, not wanting to burden Robert with her thoughts.

"Lewis is just the steward," he said mulishly. He looked down at the portrait and it vanished. He tucked the pocket watch away. "He doesn't want to be a noble."

"Doesn't he?" Judith found this hard to believe. Lewis had the same barely veiled arrogance of his uncle. She could imagine that he, likewise, managed to aggravate jealousy or fear.

"Lewis might seem a bit swaggering." Robert coughed, taking his rake and leaning it into his side. "But he had a hard time of it. Harder than me. Being Lord John's by-blow and all, and his mother abandoning him. At least I had my Mum for longer."

Here Robert shifted uncomfortably. "And Lewis looked after me."

Judith ignored the reference to Anna. "How old was Lewis when he came here, do you know?"

"Just a mite, I believe. He's been living on the estate much longer than I. Yet he has always been treated like an outsider, strangely enough, even if he has more right than any of the servants to be here."

She could imagine that to be true: Lewis caught in a no-man's land between the servant classes and true acceptance into the gentry, especially before his Gift began to show. "Does everyone know his parentage?"

Robert nodded. "Every time Lord John's boys visit Sargenet they are eager to show their superiority."

"You mean Felix and Maximus?"

"Yes, they are Memors like their father, which irks them, as they'd rather have the Impacting Gift. Lewis is not so easy to cower, of course. I remember one winter Felix and Lewis got into a terrible fight, and Felix ended up out cold in this very clearing under the rose thorns."

He gestured around at the circular rose arbour, with its abundance of flowers, the petals strewn under his rake.

"Oh dear." Judith pictured the arbour in winter, with the roses pruned and bare, framing a scene of fisticuffs between two boys. She could imagine Lewis, the scorned outsider, deploying the power of his Gift to deal a punishing blow. "Was Lewis reprimanded harshly?"

Robert began raking again, vicious strokes against the gravel to relieve his feelings. "Not in the ordinary fashion. The duke had said that no one was to whip Lewis or me, so Lewis just went without supper for a few days. Then Felix pushed him into the well in the woods, the little worm. Which to my mind just shows how inferior he is," added Robert bitterly, thrashing the gravel a little more.

Judith could see that Robert was deeply loyal to Lewis. It was understandable if they had grown up together, with Lewis like an older brother to him.

She cleared her throat. "Have you thought any more on my invitation to Cornwall?"

Robert glanced away and continued to rake. "Er, a little reflection, my lady. The fact remains that my duty lies with Sargenet."

Judith remembered, suddenly, how the duke had shown her the *Lapis Veritas*, and what he had said. Here, at least, was one concern she could alleviate. "His grace told me about the Eye of Truth."

Robert looked up, startled. The rake stilled. "He did?"

"Yes, and he absolves you of that binding. He told me that he can always visit Cornwall if he needs your help. You must think on what you would like to do with your life, Robert. Do you have any ambitions?"

His eyes dropped. "His grace asked me that too."

"And?"

There was a long pause. "I'd like to paint, if I could. On real canvas, not just Illusions that vanish."

Judith considered, remembering the talent Robert had displayed in the small portrait of Gilbert. "Then Cornwall would be perfect. You'd have plenty of landscapes to study, and a place of your own. Perhaps you could eventually apply to the Royal Academy, once you have built up a collection of work."

A light appeared in Robert's eyes, then just as suddenly, it faded. "I can't abandon Lewis. Especially if someone means him harm. I have to watch out for him, just as he has done for me." A stray white rose petal drifted down to the ground behind him.

"I don't want you in danger too." She realised that it was true:

she could not bear it if Robert were hurt. She had come a long way from reviling his existence.

"That's kind of you, my lady." He tilted his rake, ready to resume work again, his voice firm. "But I cannot leave Sargenet and I cannot leave Lewis."

Judith pressed her lips together. Here was another reason to determine who lay behind the troubles at the ducal estate, if it would put Robert's mind at rest. Her duty, and her growing affection for him, demanded that she pursue the truth. She harboured, too, a fear that Lewis was in danger. The man was annoying, like his uncle, but she didn't want to see him dead any more than Robert.

"When will the duke and Lewis return from seeing his tenants?" she asked. She felt restless that she could not continue with the interviews, as if time was of the essence somehow.

"They went on horseback," said Robert. "His grace might be another hour at least. You could walk for a while and return to meet him at the stables."

Judith nodded and left as Robert resumed his methodical raking.

She skirted the house and walked briskly into the forest as he suggested, trying to walk off her sense of urgency and unease. The ancient trees cast a thick canopy overhead, blocking out the blue sky and casting cold shadows. The last time she had walked this path had been with the duke, and the woods had felt welcoming. Now she felt lonely and anxious.

Robert had reminded her of the apparition of the skull and the menace it had conveyed. It was possible these portents of death were more than trifling trickery, and had foretold Gilbert's death. What if the reappearance of the skull was another warning? She had been distracted by Lady Agatha's indiscretions from the real matter at hand. And why must the duke be so conscientious about visiting his tenants, when they had a murder to solve?

She saw a narrower path cutting across and took it, turning right. A cool wind managed to stir gusts through the woods, piercing through her woollen gown. Clouds gathered overhead, making the forest grow dim. The thick scent of damp earth rose up.

Did her presence at Sargenet simply complicate matters, rather than clarify them? She had hoped to be useful, but her Discernment was hampered if several people were lying. Her Gift could pick out the falsehoods, but it couldn't tell her which one was crucial. Furthermore, with all the obfuscation, her mind was in danger of becoming befuddled. She had not spent so much time in Discernment for a while, and she was in danger of over-taxing herself.

Perhaps now was the time to employ some deductive reasoning, rather than rely upon her Gift. Slowly, she went over the lies she had heard so far.

Both Lady Agatha and Lady Mary had lied about how pleased they were at the duke's return, but that was scarcely enough to indict them for murder. Lady Agatha, on the other hand, had fraudulently dismissed any connection between the phantoms and Gilbert's death. Did she simply fear the two were related, or did she have a more direct hand in it? She had never lied directly about her affair with Mr Nottley, but she had certainly concealed it. Try as she might, however, Judith could not see what motive would have moved Agatha to kill Gilbert or concoct the Illusions.

Gilbert, as Agatha's trusted footman, had most likely known of the affair. But Agatha had truthfully said that Gilbert had been her loyal retainer, and she had sounded genuinely sorry about his death. Broughton too, might know of his mistress's affair, but Judith could not imagine how that would bear on the Illusions or the murder.

Lewis, then Robert, had lied about who found the body. But those lies had simply been covering up Lewis's violent fight with

Gilbert before he died. Judith was inclined to believe Lewis when he said that the last time he saw Gilbert, the footman had still been alive. And Lewis had categorically - and truthfully - denied any responsibility for the Illusions.

Broughton, too, had denied a hand in the Illusions, despite his Gift. The butler's only white lie had been to suggest that a ghost had done the deed. But perhaps his little joke and his careful truth-telling concealed a more guilty secret. He had avoided a direct answer about Gilbert, instead turning the conversation to the locks on the windows, suggesting that someone might have obtained a copy of the key.

Judith nibbled on her lip, only vaguely aware of the dark forest around her as she followed the circle of her thoughts. Who was Broughton trying to implicate? Members of the family would simply have entered the drawing room from within the house, not requiring a key to unlock the windows. Then again, Lord John and Lady Mary, although members of the clan, were just visiting. Perhaps one of them had obtained a copy of the key, and Broughton knew it.

Either Lord John or Lady Mary had a motive to attack Lewis.

Could she be right that someone had mistaken Gilbert for Lewis? Robert's Illusion had shown a surface resemblance only, yet with the same thick dark hair. If Gilbert had been sleeping in the drawing room, his face turned away, someone might have thought they had caught the steward unawares - for what footman would dare to take such a liberty?

She pursed her lips. Lord John had avoided a direct answer when she had questioned him about how Polonetheus's commentary had ended up in the drawing room. He had been behaving suspiciously at the Gryffin. He was nervous, and quick to accuse Mr Nottley of the spectres. Could he be the one who had raised a book to Gilbert's head, mistaking him for Lewis? Would he have a motive to kill his own illegitimate son?

With Dacian gone so long on the continent, John might have begun to hope that the title would pass back to himself and his oldest son, Felix. If he feared Lewis would supplant him, would he have taken drastic action?

Judith's thoughts were cut short as she suddenly became aware of a sound drifting through the trees. It was a mewling cry, faint on the wind.

Help ...

She stood still and listened with every sense pricked. All she could see was the thick trunks and the suffocating canopy of the woods. The birds stopped chirping. The faint cry weaved its way again on the wind, obscured by trees.

Help ... Help ...

It sounded like the high-pitched wail of a child. Or a ghost. But that was nonsense. Could one of Mary's boys be in trouble? It must be Otho, Cato, or Quintus.

It could be a trap, she realised. The calls for help could be intended to lure her to a greater danger. Or it could be intended to lure another.

She followed the cry, regardless. She could not sit by while someone called with such desperation, especially a child. She remembered, too, the old well, and Robert's story of Felix pushing Lewis into it. It was closed up now but the gap in the planks might fit a small child through, tumbling into the dark depths.

Her steps quickened, her ears straining. The sound did indeed come from the direction of the Dower House.

Twigs cracked in the forest behind her. She glanced round warily. A rustle from a bush died away.

Help ...

The wail was louder in the silence. It echoed slightly, sounding uncanny. A sudden thought occurred to her: could Illusion cast sound?

She had never considered that matter before, always assuming that Illusion was limited to visual foolery. Perhaps if it did, the sound would echo in that fashion, slightly at odds with the scenery around it. Yet to her ear of Discernment, the distress in the call sounded true.

As she hurried on, her eye caught on a small splash of white and red on the path. Heart in her mouth, she saw it was the pale body of a mouse, sprawled in the centre of the track.

It was decapitated, the neck weeping a sickly treacle of blood.

Judith swallowed, horrified. She leaned in, despite her first impulse to jump a mile. She was aware of the urge to hurry, to find the child in distress, but a sixth sense caused her to examine the mouse more closely. What, or who, could have done this? The placement right in the middle of her path was suspicious.

Steeling herself, she moved her foot, nudging the tail with her slipper. The grisly vision crumbled away.

It had been an Illusion, just as she suspected. A warning.

She looked up sharply, searching for the culprit. The dark mass of trees surrounded her, providing plenty of concealment. The cry came again, raising the hair on the back of her arms, and she hurried forward again.

Then, as if in a last-ditch effort to stop her, the skull appeared.

It floated out of the trees before her, a disembodied head larger than life. The white bone was stark against the gloomy backdrop of the forest, the bare teeth in a rictus grin. Blood streamed from its eyes.

Miss Cultor would be unimpressed, thought Judith, gathering her courage. This spectre would *not* be enough to sway her from her path. It was only another ghastly Illusion.

Help ...

The skull drifted toward her, its awful eye-sockets fixed upon Judith.

She gritted her teeth, much like her adversary. Then she kicked off her slipper, reached down, and threw it.

It missed the skull, sailing past and landing in the undergrowth. Curse it. Then, to her relief, the apparition floated upwards, as if affronted. Blood trailed from its eyes, evaporating in the air. Judith winced, expecting it to bash its head on a branch, but it did nothing so ignominious. It simply transposed itself over the canopy, until it drifted out of sight.

Good riddance. Quickly, she fetched her slipper and rushed along the path, now unhindered. She was close to the well, it turned out, and soon she stumbled across the clearing with its squat sentinel.

The exposed rocks were rich with green moss. A black gap slashed across the circle, where a plank of wood had been removed.

She stopped, cautiously examining the clearing. The call came again, louder, resonating from the well. Abandoning prudence, she strode forward to peer into the twenty-foot drop.

A pale shape lay in the darkness. Her eyes made out a small figure with a curly mop of blonde hair. It was Otho, Mary's elder boy.

"Hello?" she called. "Otho, is that you?"

"Help!" His voice echoed hollowly. "Yes, it's me! I'm stuck!"

She felt faint with relief that the call now sounded reassuringly human, even as she glanced behind her into the shadows of the forest. "I can see that. Are you hurt?"

"My arm is sore," he confessed. "I think I might have broken it."

Judith winced and leaned against the cold stones. "How did you land down there?"

There was a short silence. "I fell."

"Oh dear," said Judith. At least he had not said he'd been pushed, though she detected some prevarication in his voice. "Why were you looking down the well in the first place?"

"Just exploring," came the answer, too quickly and with an

undertone of untruth. Judith frowned but did not press the matter. The most urgent thing was somehow lifting him out.

There was no longer any rope or bucket attached to the well, though there were iron pegs just below the wooden planks for such a purpose. Even if there had been a rope, Judith doubted her strength would be enough to haul the boy up. She would have to go for help, little though she liked leaving Otho there alone in the dark and damp. Yet any lurking killer would not be able to reach him, either, she reasoned. And the Dower House was close by, with Fitzroy on hand.

"Otho," she called. "I will fetch some rope and assistance. I'll go to the Dower House, and I'll be as quick as I can."

She thought she could see him nod, then his voice floated up. "Yes, my lady." He paused again, drawing a breath that was audible as it echoed up the well. "I don't suppose you could not tell my mother?"

The age-old request of boys in trouble, thought Judith wryly. Or perhaps there was more to it in this instance. What would Mary say when she heard that the well had claimed one of her own this time?

Judith leaned into the aperture again. "I can't promise that, Otho. Your mother is bound to hear about it."

There was silence from the well and Judith called a goodbye, promising again to return as soon as she was able.

She walked briskly along the path, on the lookout for any more skulls or grisly mice. Soon, to her relief, the rear of the Dower House appeared, its brick walls covered in ivy, a quaint two-storey cottage with white-framed windows and gabled roofs. It was intended as a residence for the duke's mother, but as far as Judith knew, the dowager duchess had chosen to live with her sister in North England when her husband died, leaving the Dower House empty for years. Agatha must have installed Lewis there after his schooling finished, with his appointment as steward.

Examining it now, Judith thought that the rear gardens looked well -tended, with large square beds of herbs and vegetables backing onto the woods. Fitzroy's devoted work, no doubt. She paused on the edge of the tree-line. The honeysuckle vines were now burdened with round, red berries, the only sign of their summertime extravagance.

A figure was kneeling by one of the vegetable beds, with white hair and stooping shoulders. He appeared to be digging, his knees dirty in the soil.

Judith knew that profile, from long ago. The hair was shaggier, the posture more bent, but she could not mistake that long nose and bushy eyebrows. She cleared her throat and stepped out of the trees.

The old man looked up quickly, two blue eyes fastening on Judith. He stood abruptly, almost nervously.

"Who goes there?"

Judith walked forward. "It is I, Judith Avely." She was willing to gamble that Fitzroy would remember her face regardless; he had always been an excellent butler. She glanced down to see that he had been digging potatoes: they were scattered at his feet in a medley of brown, grey, and maroon.

The old butler brushed the dirt off his hands, his eyes widening. "Mrs Avely! A pleasure to see you again at Sargenet."

A faint blush infused her cheeks. Fitzroy knew rather too much of her history at Sargenet. She did not pause to explain her change in title. "I am glad to see you again, Fitzroy, but I have come on an urgent errand. Otho, Mary's boy, has fallen down the old well. Do you have any rope we could use? And perhaps you could fetch some men from the house to pull him out."

Fitzroy blinked again, his brow furrowing in confusion. Then his old shoulders went back. "Certainly, my lady. I'll find rope at once."

He went round the side of the house. Judith's eyes fell on the turned earth, reflecting that it was a long way to fall from the glory of a duke's butler. At least lady Agatha had not turned him out entirely.

Fitzroy emerged again, holding a long, thick rope looped round his arm.

"I'll take that," she said. "You hurry to the main house."

He nodded, his face solemn, and handed her the heavy rope. They parted ways along the woodland path and Judith strode briskly back to the well. Putting the rope down, she leaned over the pitiless black hole, reassuring Otho with her presence and the news that help was on its way.

In the meanwhile, she found the nearest tree and set about knotting the rope, hoping it would be long enough. Just as she had finished doing so, she was surprised by a voice behind her.

"Judith?"

In which a secret is revealed

Do not be so concerned with judging the timbre of a voice that you fail to take into account the objective facts at hand.
  - from Lady Avely's Guide to Truth and Magic

SHE TURNED to see Dacian at the edge of the clearing. Relief sagged her shoulders. "Oh, I'm so glad you're here."

The duke was in his riding clothes, a cape round his shoulders. He strode forward, a frown creasing his brow. "What happened?"

"Otho is in the well."

His head turned sharply to the stone monument. "Is he hurt?"

Otho's voice floated up, eerie in the quiet glade. "Uncle Dacian? Don't be angry. I only broke my arm."

"It serves you right, you little rascal." Dacian went over and peered into the dark hole. "Why wasn't this boarded up properly?"

"There was a plank loose," said Judith.

He frowned, wrenching another plank away with ease. "Careless. I've been gone too long."

"How do you come to be here, for that matter? And where is Lewis?"

Dacian cast the plank aside and looked round at the gloomy woods. "Lewis set off before me; he must be home by now. I saw a skull rising up from the trees as I was riding over the fields. Did you see it?"

"Yes, it was crying blood." She shuddered.

"That's the one." He gave her a closer look. "Did it see your mobcap, do you think?"

She smiled at his attempt to cheer her spirits. "Don't be rude."

"I am merely pointing out that the skull agreed with me that it is too dowdy. It's even worse than the one you wore yesterday."

Judith resisted the urge to pat her hair. "It's hardly any different."

The duke cocked his head. "It's quite different. It doesn't frame your face so nicely."

"Uncle Dacian," called Otho. "Are you trying to seduce a lady right now?"

Judith raised a brow to echo the query.

Dacian chuckled. "Of course. You be quiet, Otho."

Judith gave him a reproving look. Of course. She was a female, therefore he would flirt. She'd best not forget it. Nor the nine years he had spent flirting - or worse - with other women, without a word to her.

The duke's face sobered too, as he tightened the knot round the tree. "In all seriousness, what does this damn skull mean, floating about like that?"

Judith shrugged wordlessly. She didn't want to mention the gruesome mouse. That had felt like a threat particular to her. A shiver ran down her spine but she kept her silence. The duke had enough to worry him at the moment.

They turned their focus to the difficult task of lifting an injured boy several metres up into the air. Under the duke's instruction, Otho tied the rope round his waist then looped it under his legs and his uninjured shoulder. Dacian, with his Impacting power, had strength to spare, but it was a delicate matter to avoid hitting Otho against the stone walls. A few yelps of pain echoed up at them, with Judith wincing each time, while Dacian remained frowning with concentration.

At last, the boy's curly head appeared over the lip of wall. He gave a brave smile, but collapsed weakly into Dacian's arms as he hauled him out.

Dacian stood there, effortlessly holding the boy against his chest. "What happened, Otho? Did someone push you in? Tell me."

"No!" said Otho. "No one pushed me, I swear!"

It was the truth. Despite not hearing any note of discord, Judith's motherly intuition suggested that Otho was concealing something. She raised her eyebrows, and Dacian, seeing this, butted Otho gently with his head.

"So how came you to fall into the well? The whole story now, boy."

Otho hesitated, then spoke in a rush. "It was my own fault. I saw the parcel tied to the iron pegs, and I tried to fetch it out and I fell."

"What parcel?" demanded Dacian.

"At the end of the rope." Otho jerked his head.

The rope still dangled into the shaft. Judith hurried to pull it up, finding it surprisingly heavy. At the end, as promised, was a large brown parcel which Otho, in his ingenuity, had tied up so it could join him in his escape.

The parcel was wrapped in canvas and appeared to have been unwrapped and rewrapped. String and rope made a tangle round the awkward shape.

At a nod from Dacian, Judith bent down and began untying. After a small struggle, the parcel gave up its contents. Three crystal vases lay glimmering in the dim light of the woods, one of them cracked and broken.

"See," said Otho proudly. "The thief hid the vases in the well and I found them."

Dacian's frown deepened. "So it appears."

All was still and quiet, with no birds singing. Judith wondered if anyone was watching from the trees. She exchanged a glance with Dacian over Otho's curly head. The vases were proof that whoever killed Gilbert was no passing thief. Whoever had left them here was someone closer to home, just as Broughton had implied.

As they stared at one another, they heard voices in the distance.

"Quickly, wrap them up again," ordered Dacian. "Otho, I don't want you to tell anyone else about this, do you hear? Not even your brothers or your governess. Or your mother."

Otho nodded eagerly and Judith set about tying up the vases again. It was tricky with their cumbersome shapes but she had just managed it when Lord John marched into the clearing, flanked by Miss Atkinson and followed by Fitzroy.

Quickly, Judith stood over the package so her long skirts hid it from view.

"What's this?" Lord John demanded. "Otho, were you down that hole? We've been looking for you!"

Otho hung his head. Lord John made no move to take him from Dacian's arms but stared angrily, his eyes darting from his son to the black gash in the well. "You've been warned not to play here before! No dinner for you tonight - do you hear that, Miss Atkinson?"

Miss Atkinson rushed forward. "He is hurt! Look how pale he is. Otho, my dear boy, are you alright?"

"I hurt my arm," sniffed Otho, suddenly appearing much

younger. Tears welled in his eyes in the face of this familiar feminine concern. "I think I broke it."

"Lucky it was just your arm," said Dacian callously, still holding the boy tightly. "It might have been your neck."

Lord John turned round, looking for someone to blame. Judith wondered if he was really angry because his secret had been discovered - had he been the one to steal the vases, after misapplying Polonetheus? John's gaze passed crossly over Fitzroy, who stood quietly observing.

"Miss Atkinson." Lord John landed on a scapegoat. "Why was Otho out here when he should be studying his Latin? I specifically asked you to keep the children indoors."

Miss Atkinson dropped her eyes, looking remorseful. Her hand still rested on Otho's arm. "Yes, my lord. I was most remiss."

Judith, however, could detect a hollow note under the apparent sincerity. Perhaps Miss Atkinson did not truly believe she was misguided in allowing the children to play. Come to think of it, she seemed an odd choice for a governess employed by two such devoted scholars as Lord John and Lady Mary.

"Boys will escape their governesses," said Dacian. "I'm sure Miss Atkinson cannot be blamed for this, John. And Otho has been punished enough by his injury."

"Don't tell me how to manage my own son," snapped Lord John.

Otho was still aloft in Dacian's unyielding arms. Dacian gave his brother a flinty look and then pushed past him, carrying the boy back to the house. He was followed by Lord John, muttering, and Miss Atkinson, maintaining a dignified silence.

Judith stayed behind, hoping that she would not draw attention as she stood, seemingly transfixed, by the well.

Fitzroy, however, also stayed. "May I help you with anything, Mrs Avely?" he enquired, looking at her curiously.

Judith bit her lip, biding for time. "Actually, Fitzroy, I am a marchioness now. My husband was awarded a title for his services."

The old butler gave a little bow. "I am glad to hear it, Lady Avely." He paused. "Would you like me to gather up the rope?"

She was standing on the rope. After a moment's hesitation, she decided to trust him. She lifted her skirts slightly and stepped away from the parcel, gesturing downwards. "Otho discovered the missing vases, as you can see. We must keep it secret for now, but I would appreciate it if you could take them to the Dower House for safe-keeping."

Fitzroy's eyes bulged slightly. His next words showed that his wits, at least, had not frayed with age. "Otho found them in the well? But that means the killer is still about."

"I'm afraid so. Which is why you must not speak of this to anyone - apart from his grace, of course."

Fitzroy nodded sombrely. "Of course, my lady. I will keep them discreetly."

"Thank you."

The butler gathered up the parcel, then cleared his throat. "One more thing, my lady, if you will permit me."

"Of course."

He coughed gently. "I am glad that you are helping his grace in this matter. He has always held you in high regard."

Judith flushed at this little speech. What did Fitzroy mean, exactly? And how would the old butler know the duke's opinions - he, too, hadn't seen his master for years. Most likely, the old butler was stuck in the past, remembering a time long ago when they were all much younger.

"Thank you, Fitzroy," she said stiffly.

He nodded and bore the parcel away.

Turning, Judith followed the path that curved along the edge of the wood, rather than plunge into the depths again. A bird flitted in front of her, its plumage sleek and brown. She watched it with envy, feeling rather ruffled herself. To her relief, the sensation that someone was watching her had now dissipated. Only the memory of the ghastly apparitions remained to unsettle her. Could it really be Lord John, with a secret minor talent in Illusion? Possibly he had been trying to scare the boy away from the loot, or, failing that, scare herself away before she found them both. He had appeared at the scene not long afterwards.

She shivered. Surely, he had not intended for his own son to fall in the well. Or was his mind addled by illness and guilt, so that his actions had become erratic? Yet the dead mouse on the path had seemed coldly calculated.

Making her way into the house, she nodded at Broughton by the door. Mary and Miss Atkinson were in the entrance hall, talking in low voices, and they both looked up as Judith passed.

"Thank you, Lady Avely," said Mary, her face drawn and pale. "For finding Otho."

"It was nothing," replied Judith. "Is his arm indeed broken?"

"I suspect it is just a sprain," said Mary. "I've sent for the doctor." She sighed deeply. "Maybe John can be convinced to see the doctor too. I am worried for his health."

Miss Atkinson folded her hands together. "What about you, Lady Avely? Were you hurt at all? You look rather mud-stained."

Judith denied any harm and glanced down at her gown, seeing that it was indeed marked from her adventure. Then she saw, with a stab of horror, that her lapis lazuli stone had fallen out from its hiding place. It must have done so in the activity of the rescue.

The large oval pendant rested on her bosom, clear for anyone to see, framed in gold filigree.

She did not want to draw further attention to it, so she quickly made her excuses and retreated upstairs. Once she was safe in her room, she tucked the stone back into the lace collar, cursing to herself. Who else had seen the pendant? Would anyone recognise its import?

Any Musor would know that the lapis talisman stone assisted Discernment. Agatha, Mary, Lord John, perhaps even Miss Atkinson, would suspect her Gift now, and know that her claim to Diplomacy was an arrant lie. Yet they would not know her particular talent was in detecting falsehoods. Perhaps they would think she could Discern something innocuous like jewels, like her daughter Elinor.

She stared anxiously at the mirror, her face smudged with dirt, her blonde hair escaping from her cap. Ironically, she could only hope that no one would guess the truth.

THERE WAS BARELY time to change her clothes before a sharp rap sounded on the door. It was the duke, carrying a tray of food in his capable hands. He too, looked a bit disheveled, with dirt emphasising the slant of his cheekbone.

"Marchioness." He loomed in the doorway, concern etched on his face. "Are you alright?"

"I'm fine. Is Otho in bed?" She let him in and shut the door with a careful click.

He put the tray of fruits and cakes down on the rosewood table by the window. "Yes. The doctor just arrived." He turned, still frowning. "Where are the vases?"

"In the safekeeping of Fitzroy."

Dacian strode over and grasped both her hands. "I should send you home. You know what this means: the murderer is among us. And you were alone in the woods today near the phantom."

"Not for long."

He squeezed her fingers, a smile emerging. "You were happy to see me. Don't think I didn't notice."

"Perhaps," she admitted.

"It is a shame that it takes Otho spraining his arm for you to gladden at the sight of me."

"Nonsense."

He grinned. "Maybe I should push Quintus into the well next time."

Judith shuddered, pulling her hands free. "Don't say such things."

Dacian walked over to the window and threw himself down on the elegant chaise. "Come, you need some sustenance to rebuild your strength."

She felt a little self-conscious to be entertaining him alone in her bedchamber, but it was fairly innocuous, really. It was fanciful to imagine any impropriety attached to having a man in her bedroom when she was past forty.

He patted the chaise next to him invitingly, but she drew up a spindly chair to the rosewood table, rather than risk sitting too close. She eyed the ripe pears but did not want to end up with juice all over her chin, like a child, so she reached for a cake instead.

The duke, perhaps guessing her dilemma, set about carving up the pears into neat slices, giving her time to eat. A comfortable silence rose between them. As she chewed her plum cake, she surreptitiously examined his powerful hands, so dextrous and strong. Perhaps it was more dangerous to sit opposite him, where she was exposed to the full extent of his masculine beauty. The lines at the corners of his eyes had softened his face from its old arrogance. It was undeniable: he had only grown more attractive with age, his power settling into a deeper groove. He probably knew it, too.

Eventually he spoke, laying the knife down. "Lewis was shoved down that well once, when he was a boy. By Felix, years ago. That was why we boarded it up."

"I know. Robert told me."

"Was Otho telling the truth when he said he wasn't pushed?"

"Yes." Judith finished a mouthful of cake and reached for a slice of pear. "He fell all by himself. Unless you count the temptation of the parcel."

Dacian leaned back, threading his fingers behind his head. His black hair glinted with threads of grey. "Any ideas who put it there? Have you talked with anyone else this morning?"

Judith hesitated. "I spoke with Robert, as I said. He showed me his skill at Illusion. He is quite talented." She nibbled on her pear, the fruit sweet and soft. "He told me he wants to practice art."

Dacian raised his brows. "I am glad that he is confiding in you. Are you still determined to win him over to your castle?"

"Yes. You must not interfere, Dacian."

He shrugged. "If you say so. I just don't want you to be unnecessarily burdened by Nicholas's mistakes."

"We have all made mistakes," said Judith quietly.

Dacian met her eyes. "Indeed." There was a fraught silence. "Have you forgiven Nicholas for his, then?"

She sighed and took another slice of pear. "Almost. Strangely, my mind has eased a little after meeting his son."

"Robert is a good sort. He takes after his father."

Judith's lips twisted. "Yes, I see now that Nicholas did the best he could."

Dacian gave her a sympathetic look. "Passion can lead even the best of us astray." He untwined his fingers and leaned forward, seemingly about to say something more.

She stiffened, and reached for a diversion, in case he should try to excuse his own behaviour. "Even Agatha has been swayed by passion, it seems. I found her trysting with Mr Nottley in the graveyard." It was unhandsome to expose Agatha, but the affair could have some bearing on the whole matter.

"Agatha and Nottley?" Dacian's eyes widened in horror, as if he had sighted another skull.

"Your sister deserves some happiness, you know, for all that she is a spinster." Defiantly, Judith took a bite of her pear.

A cloud passed across Dacian's face. His lips clamped shut and he angled his head away. She wondered what thought had caused this plunge in his mood. She took another bite, unconcerned if he was going to be prudish about Agatha's affair. It was not like he had any leg to stand on, with all his amours.

After a long pause, he said, "I suppose women are entitled to their own dalliances, especially at her age. But will Agatha marry him?"

Judith finished her mouthful. "I gather the affair has been going on for some time, and it would be a come-down in her station to marry him. Mr Nottley is not titled and Agatha has always had a high opinion of her bloodline."

Dacian sighed. "You're right, she is probably just taking advantage of him." After a thoughtful pause, he suddenly glinted at her, in a mercurial change in mood. "I wish you would take advantage of *me*, marchioness."

Judith almost choked on her pear. "Your grace!"

"You might give me a chance, Judith, now that we are both unencumbered."

His handsome face was serious for once, his dark eyes intent. Yet indignation rose in her. She had given him a chance, a long time ago. She had laid her heart out before him. He was the one who had pushed her away.

She gathered her composure, swallowing the pear that now felt dry and flavourless. Then she spoke.

"Your grace, you are never *unencumbered* for long."

He did not deny it. His eyes dropped. A bitter sense of triumph soured in her chest. Dacian was not made for love: he was made for passion.

She changed the subject. "I think we should talk to Agatha immediately. I should be present."

The duke's lips pressed together. "You think Agatha might lie about Nottley? Let us go now, then, before anyone else is hurt."

He stood and led the way out, his shoulders stiff, his expression closed.

Judith followed, bitterness mixing with remorse for having spoken so pointedly. Yet she had only spoken the truth.

In which a lady has suspicions

Unfortunately, when one is on a search for truth, one may become rather befuddled.

   - from *Lady Avely's Guide to Truth and Magic*

As Dacian knocked on Agatha's door, Judith cringed, hoping that they would not discover a scene *en deshabille* with Mr Nottley.

The door remained closed and silent.

"It's Dacian," he called, knocking again loudly. "Let me in, Agatha. We need to talk."

After a minute, the door opened slightly to reveal her lady-ship. She was no longer wearing her walking cloak or boots, and her irritated expression became even more suspicious when her eyes fell upon Judith.

"What do you want?" Agatha's fingers tightened on the edge of the door. "What is *she* doing here?"

Dacian pushed past her. "Is your lover Mr Nottley in this room?"

Agatha fell back, her face going red. "Pardon me? How dare you insinuate...!"

Judith awkwardly followed Dacian into the room, braving Agatha's gimlet glare as she did so and closing the door quietly behind her. The room was larger even than the Gold Room, and hung with paintings of nature scenes. Judith looked round in vain for the gothic books that Lord John had mentioned as Agatha's reading material, but they were well hidden.

Doorways led off to other spaces. Clearly Agatha had laid claim to a whole suite. It was ideal for entertaining gentlemen callers, set so far into the east wing as it was. Only Agatha's personal servants and the housemaid would dare venture here.

Dacian marched round, twitching drapes aside and peering behind furniture as if to espy the errant Mr Nottley. Agatha watched in fury as he opened the other doors and even went so far as to look in the cupboards.

Agatha spoke icily. "You may desist, brother. I am not hiding a man in my curtains."

This was true.

The duke straightened from peering under the bed. "Don't bother with your pretensions, Aggie. I know that you have been intimate with Nottley. We will discuss it soon enough, but right now you should know that Otho was found hurt in the old well - just after that damn skull made another appearance."

Judith cursed inwardly. It would have been more opportune to ask Agatha what she knew of Otho's whereabouts, or the skull, to see if she would lie. The duke, bless his innocent soul, did not seem to entertain any thought that Agatha could be the guilty party. Judith was not so sure. Agatha might not have killed Gilbert, but she knew something about the apparitions.

Agatha gasped, her mouth falling open. "Oh dear, is Otho alright?"

It was an estimable act, if it was one.

"He sprained his arm," snapped Dacian. "Where is Nottley? And where has he been for the last few hours?"

Agatha drew herself up angrily. "Nottley is an old family friend! Are you suggesting that he had anything to do with it?"

"I don't know," retorted the duke. "However, I *am* guessing you can vouch for his presence when this skull appeared. Which is what you will do, if you want him to have an alibi. The time for cutting a wheedle is long past."

Agatha was frowning deeply. She jerked her head toward Judith. "You still have not explained her presence here. This is a private matter."

Judith bowed her head. "I understand how you feel, Lady Agatha. Believe me, I do not wish to intrude upon your privacy. However, I promised I would help the duke discover who is behind these accidents."

Agatha narrowed her gaze. "What help could *you* possibly give my brother?"

Dacian interceded. "Lady Avely has some ability in Diplomacy, Aggie, so she has been assisting my enquiries, to make sure I don't lose my temper, as you well know I am wont to do. Now tell me what's really going on."

Agatha's suspicions were not abated. "I do not feel the effects of any Diplomacy."

"Lady Avely is very subtle," said Dacian firmly. "Now stop prevaricating, or I'll have to ask her to increase her effect. Tell me Nottley's whereabouts, or I'll traverse the house while shouting for him."

The wind seemed to go out of Agatha's sails. Her shoulders dropped a little and her eyes lowered. She gave a heavy sigh. "Nottley left me an hour ago," she confessed, and her words were true. "But he could not have cast the Illusion. He is only Gifted with a modicum of Memory."

The duke leaned on a tiny table that looked as if it might

break beneath his weight. A pair of knitting needles rolled off, landing silently on the thick carpet, their thin points gleaming wickedly. "Memory is adjacent to Illusion. Nottley might have both."

"Such an occurrence is very rare." Agatha folded her arms and ignored the fallen needles.

"Furthermore," added Dacian, "even if Nottley is only a Memor, Illusions can be bought. Particularly a simple one like the skull. He could have picked it up in some disreputable London shop."

Agatha's lips thinned. "Nottley has no reason to cast such things. He is a scholar, remember, part of that ancient history society with John. Nottley only dabbles, because he has other interests." She put her chin in the air.

"Is Nottley fond of Polonetheus?" suggested the duke. He bent, picking up the steel needles and placing them back on the table. He refrained from snapping the metal with his power, though Judith could tell he was still irritated. She gave him a warning glance: it did her pretence of Diplomacy no good if he were to lose his temper.

"I believe he reads Polonetheus," admitted Agatha. "But so does Mary. "

The duke folded his arms to match his sister. "And when did you grow intimate with Nottley, Aggie dear?"

Agatha licked her lips and cast a glance at Judith. "A few years ago, if you must know."'

"That long?" Dacian seemed more outraged by this than the fact of the affair. "Is it serious then? Will you marry him?"

Agatha glared. "No. Though I will have you know that he *has* asked me."

This was the truth, as far as Judith could hear. Her own head was beginning to fill with clouds again. She had already used her Gift several times today and the Bemusement was quicker to return. She was past due for an afternoon nap. "Why not marry him?" she asked, before she could stop herself.

"It is none of your business," snapped Agatha. "Dacian, I must protest again. Lady Avely has no right to be here asking me these intrusive questions. Neither do you. I have conducted my affairs with the utmost discretion, which is more than I can say of *you*."

Affairs, plural? Judith blinked, and sat down on a convenient armchair.

Dacian held up a hand. "We are just trying to see if Nottley has anything to do with it," he said. "That's all. I admit you can do what you like, Aggie. Just as long as he isn't blackmailing you or using you against your will."

Agatha drew herself up. "Certainly not! What an odious suggestion. You insult me, Dacian. Nottley would not dare. He wants to marry me, not besmirch me!"

Again, Agatha's words rung with righteous truth. Judith blinked blearily, trying to listen carefully to every sentence.

Dacian bowed his head penitently. "Sorry, Aggie. I'm just trying, in my bumble-fisted way, to look after you."

Agatha was not mollified. "Well, I don't need your belated patronage. Leave me in peace, as you've done over the last nine years. And don't go asking Nottley questions - I won't have it. He has already been hounded enough by John."

"I can't promise that," said Dacian. "I still don't know where he is, Aggie."

Further questions to Agatha revealed that she had stayed with Nottley at the cemetery for another twenty minutes after Judith had left her there. Judith did not want to ask too closely about what had occupied Agatha, and the duke skirted the issue too, looking deeply uncomfortable.

Suffice to say, there was plenty of time for Mr Nottley to have left his inamorata in the graveyard and cast skulls and mice in the woods.

Of course, that also left Agatha enough time to do the same deed.

Agatha wanted to know the details of Otho's adventure down the well. Dacian, not seeing any harm in telling her, obliged with a very brief account of the rescue and the fact that Otho was now in bed with a sprained arm.

Agatha, her lip between her teeth, tottered to a chair and sat down.

She put a hand to her brow, shielding her face. "The poor boy. It is a coincidence, surely, that these misfortunes have come together?"

"Unlikely," said Dacian shortly. "Do you know anything about the ghostly apparitions, Aggie?"

There was a silence, then: "No." Agatha kept her head bowed, away from them.

A lie. Judith widened her eyes at Dacian, forgetting that she could curl a fist to mark the falsehood.

Dacian didn't need the signal. "You're lying, I can tell. Who is behind the skulls? I promise I won't murder him, if it is indeed Nottley."

Agatha looked up, her face stricken. "Not Nottley. Broughton."

"Broughton?" repeated the duke. He cast a wild-eyed look at Judith, who shrugged minutely. As far as she could tell, Agatha believed this. It was as Judith had suspected: Agatha feared her own butler. She did not know that the duke had already pursued this question and Judith had heard Broughton's truthful denial.

"Yes," said Agatha. "He is accomplished in Illusion. I have charged him with it and he denies it vehemently, but who else can it be? I fear he is plotting against me. He never liked Gilbert."

Dacian turned away abruptly, avoiding Agatha's eyes. "Surely he would not have killed him for a mere dislike. Why would he do something like that?"

"I don't know." Agatha put her head in her hands. "I am at my wits' end. I have missed Fitzroy too, you know. You're not the only one who valued his service."

This was true. At the same time, Judith wondered why Fitzroy was relegated to kneeling in the dirt, especially if Agatha claimed his knees couldn't cope with the stairs.

Dacian strode restlessly to the window. "I think you can rescind your suspicions of Broughton, Aggie, as much as I am loath to say it. I believe he is innocent as he claims."

"Why?" she demanded.

"I have my reasons," he replied. "And until we find the real culprit, I think you should stay in your own rooms for the rest of the day."

Agatha narrowed her eyes.

Judith nibbled on her own lip, aware of a desire to retire to her own room for the rest of the afternoon. Her mind was foggy and she felt as if she had consumed a bottle of bad wine: queasy and unbalanced.

She stood shakily. "I, too, must retire."

Dacian turned sharply. "Are you alright, Judith? You look pale."

She waved a hand. "Perfectly fine, just a little Bemused. Some time in your bed will sort me out." Her eyes widened. "My bed. The gold bed. Sleeping."

He grinned, coming over to her side. "Whatever you want, Judith."

Judith blinked at him. Suddenly, the idea of doing as he suggested and *taking advantage of him* had a mesmerising appeal.

Agatha tutted.

Judith drew a breath. "I should rest." His masculine presence was rather overwhelming in her current state. Her eyes went to his broad chest.

Dacian's lips quirked and he took her elbow, pulling her toward the door. "Stay here," he threw over his shoulder at

Agatha. "I will find this skull and sort it out, after I put Judith to bed."

Agatha followed them to the door. "She shouldn't be here," she warned. "Send her home, Dacian, not just to bed."

DACIAN LED Judith back to the Gold Room, his warm hand over hers. At the door, he grasped both her arms.

"Rest now," he said. "Don't move from this room until dinner."

Judith smiled up at him woozily. "You could come inside. Not to take advantage of you. Just to discuss matters."

He stared down, his expression unreadable. "You are muse-drunk, Judith. Best sleep it off." He let go of her arms. "Then see me with a clear mind - as much as it may work against me."

"Sleep does sound attractive," she admitted.

His mouth twitched. "Always the blows to my vanity."

She poked him in the chest, noticing that it wasn't squidgy at all. "Your vanity can take it."

"Don't be so certain." He pulled himself up, puffing out his pectorals. "You have certainly reduced my ego to tatters over the years."

She squinted at him, hearing truth in his voice, but too Bemused to believe it. "Yes, tatters for a duke serve very well for most men." She yawned.

"Poor Judith," he said. "We've quite worn you out. Shall I send for more chocolate before you nap?"

The duke was turning out to be a sensible man, after all.

"Will you tell me the secret ingredient?"

"No."

"Hmph." She yawned. "I think I'm too tired even for chocolate."

"Sacrilege." His dark eyes gleamed. "Sleep, Judith. You'll need it, for I am planning to enliven things a little tonight."

She peered at him. "How do you mean? No duels or *ostende de vi*, I beg of you."

He smiled at her Latin reference to his Gift. "No, I will simply reveal the contents of the parcel to everyone after dinner. You will need to listen with all your acuity to the responses."

Judith nodded, a little apprehensively. Was it wise to throw the vases on the table, as it were?

He took one of her hands and squeezed it. "Please lock your door until then. I don't want that skull bothering you."

"Very well," she said with dignity. "Though I think it *does* like my cap."

"Make sure you take it off while you sleep," he murmured. "You wouldn't want to crease it."

She ignored this sally and stumbled into her room, falling onto her bed and into a deep sleep.

The skull did come back to haunt her. In that strange afternoon slumber, she dreamed of the helmet, the black feather swaying as before. This time, however, the head was not attached to its skeleton, but floating through the Sargenet library, as if looking for books.

As she watched, transfixed, the blank face of steel became Lord John's gaunt features, which then transformed into those of Lewis, who distorted into Mary. Mary scowled at Judith, her teeth bared. "Go away," said Mary the skull. "You are not wanted here, Mrs Avely. Leave Robert alone."

Bloody tears leaked from Mary's eyes and then the voice changed again. *Help.*

It was Otho's young voice, high-pitched with fear.

In which there are fearful undercurrents

JUDITH AWOKE WITH A SHIVER. The room was now cold with the onset of evening. The light from the window had faded to a dusky pink. She must have slept for a long time, hours even. She sat up guiltily. What had happened while she wasted the afternoon away?

She blinked the sleep from her eyes, relieved to feel that her mind was once more clear. Unfortunately, that meant she could recall with disastrous clarity inviting the duke into her bedchamber, and his careful rejection of her. So much for her vain presumption that she was an attractive, available widow, ripe for the plucking. He could have done some plucking today. But no. Instead, he had retreated down the cold corridor as fast as he could, while she was left to fling herself onto an empty bed. Why had he asked her to give him another chance and then tossed it back in her face again?

Perhaps he was just being honourable, she told herself. She *had* been rather befuddled. She tutted to herself. More likely Dacian was being vain: he wanted to seduce her while she was in her right mind. She would be a better conquest that way. He had always liked a challenge.

Cringing, she told herself that she must re-establish a proper distance the next time she saw him. He must think her an utter fool, to be poking him in the chest and coyly referring to her mobcap.

"Psst," came Miss Cultor's voice from behind the cupboard. "You awake, marchioness? Close the curtains, if you would be so kind."

Judith stood and crossed to the curtains, pulling them closed with a swish of heavy fabric. Turning, she saw Miss Cultor pop her head out, followed by her body, once more gowned in yellow.

"You were out like a lamp," observed the vampiri. "An eventful day?"

"Yes, quite tiresome." Not to say mortifying.

Miss Cultor trotted out. "Is it time to stalk Mr Nottley?"

Judith had quite forgotten about this plan. She sat down with a plop on the chaise, rubbing a hand over her forehead. "No need. I - er - stalked him this morning. It turns out he is having an affair with Agatha."

"What?" Miss Cultor's eyes bulged from her head. "An affair? That dry old stick?"

"Perhaps when he claimed to be having scholarly arguments he was having a different sort of intercourse."

Miss Cultor looked revolted. "Eww."

"I think it is nice for them," said Judith, a tad wistfully. She'd had her fair share of being married. Maybe an affair might not be so bad, after all. Especially if it involved Dacian sprawled on her bed and teasing her about nonsensical things. Or sprawling her on the bed and demonstrating his *ostende de vi*.... The thought was suddenly riveting. Perhaps she had not entirely recovered from her Bemusement.

Miss Cultor marched over to the dresser and demanded to be lifted up. "So is Nottley blackmailing Lady Agatha?" she demanded. "Tell me what you heard."

Judith renounced her distracting daydream and lifted Miss Cultor, then put her own feet up on the spindly chair. "Mr Nottley appears to be genuine in his pursuit. He has even asked Agatha to marry him." She recounted the conversation she had overheard at the graveyard, and also told Miss Cultor about Otho's mishap, the hidden parcel, and the floating skull.

"Ridiculous," seethed Miss Cultor. "Bloody tears, really? Has this ghost no taste at all? It is positively juvenile. I hope you weren't frightened."

"Not for a second," lied Judith, recalling the bloodied mouse corpse.

"Well, it's been a difficult day," observed Miss Cultor. "I suppose you'd better feed me now so that you can strengthen your mind. Besides, I'm hungry."

Judith slipped off her glove and held out her wrist. The prick of Miss Cultor's little teeth was like the nip of a kitten, and oddly reassuring.

When Miss Cultor finished, she dabbed at Judith's skin with the hem of her yellow dress. "Thank you. I suppose you should call me Marigold, now that we have progressed beyond mere acquaintance."

"I would be honoured," said Judith, setting her back on the dresser, and vowing internally to find a new gown for the vampiri as soon as might be practicable. "Call me Judith. And if we are friends now, I can tell you that I made a fool of myself today because I was so Bemused. You have arrived just in time."

"How did you make a fool of yourself?" Miss Cultor - Marigold - sat cross-legged and cocked her head with interest.

Judith sighed heavily. "I invited the duke into my bedchamber this afternoon."

"Sounds like a sensible suggestion to me."

"It was a stupid notion, for so many reasons. He doesn't even like my caps."

"Nor do I," said Marigold. "So he is a man of taste. That is a good thing."

"Well, he fled down the corridor as fast as he could."

"Strange," tutted Marigold. "Perhaps he is scared of widows."

"Quite the opposite, I assure you," said Judith morosely.

"He strikes me as a starving man who was offered a feast but didn't believe his luck," said Marigold bracingly.

Judith sighed. She was the one who was starved. Still, dinner was soon, so at least she could satisfy one type of hunger. She rang the bell to ask for some hot water. As she refreshed herself and slowly dressed for dinner, various thoughts plagued her, which she shared with Marigold. Why had she seen no novels in Agatha's room? Who had moved the Polonetheus? And could someone have mistaken Gilbert for Lewis?

She dressed in a grey evening gown, though this one was brightened by cream trimmings. At least she didn't have to decide about a mobcap tonight. She brushed her blonde hair until it shone, tying it back in an elegant knot, and slipping on her matching cream gloves.

When Marigold heard of the duke's plan to reveal the vases to the assembled company, she insisted on hiding herself in the drawing room, to witness the event.

"I can sense any Musing!" she pointed out. "If there is another phantom, I might be able to tell who is casting it this time."

Judith agreed and carried her downstairs, hidden in her reticule, and detoured to the drawing room. Marigold promised she would abide by the Edicts and stay hidden in the curtains so

Judith left her there, hoping that the evening would not unfold any more unpleasantness.

THE COLD, vast dining room filled up slowly with the family, with Mr Nottley arriving last in a dapper waistcoat with silver stripes. Judith thought the duke's plain waistcoat and dark blue coat tails were far superior, but perhaps that was Dacian's tall figure and broad shoulders setting off his clothes to advantage. Mr Nottley's slighter form and pointed beard made her think of some kind of silver-striped bee.

From her place by the duke's side, Judith watched the outsider with interest. Now that she knew the truth, she could see the warmth in Mr Nottley's gaze when it rested on Agatha, and notice his little gestures of attention. Agatha was wearing an extravagant evening gown of yellow satin, a creamy mink stole over her shoulders, and two spots of colour on her cheeks as she enjoyed Mr Nottley's compliments.

Mr Nottley also, however, turned his smiles upon Lady Mary and talked at length with her about his interpretation of Triste. Opposite, Lord John glowered at his wife, though Agatha did not seem to mind Mr Nottley's diversions. Mary was dressed in a much plainer gown of blue sarcenet that nonetheless clung to her rounded figure in various places.

Could Mr Nottley be amusing himself with both ladies? Judith wondered. She soon dismissed the thought, for she could detect a level of coolness in Mary's demeanour toward the scholar. Perhaps Mary was putting on a cold face to placate her husband's suspicions, but Judith could hear no subterfuge in the aloof tone she reserved for Mr Nottley. Her disdain was real. Perhaps Mary knew of Agatha's affair and disapproved. Or perhaps she disliked his silver-striped waistcoat.

Miss Atkinson came in with Cato and Quintus to say their goodnights. Otho was already in bed with his sprained arm and Judith hoped he had been fed dinner despite Lord John's ruling. Cato and Quintus seemed subdued, with Miss Atkinson holding onto their elbows tightly, perhaps to prevent them wandering off and falling down any other available holes. The governess wore a pretty mauve gown that suited her. Judith could see why Gilbert had been attracted, with Miss Atkinson's brown hair now curled into glossy ringlets and her lips a warm pink.

Lady Mary gave her boys their kisses with a touching display of affection and asked after Otho. Miss Atkinson replied that he had been administered some laudanum and was fast asleep. Once again Dacian invited the governess to eat at the table and was refused.

"Then you could join us in the drawing room," he suggested. "After dinner?"

Agatha looked on disapprovingly. Miss Atkinson, however, declined the invitation. Judith thought she looked a little anxious under the pretty dress and glossy hair; she was probably hoping for an early bed after the excitement of the day.

Dinner was brought out. Judith felt rather awkward to be served by Robert. He seemed unperturbed, quietly carrying out his duties - which was something she could respect. She was very hungry again, and ate the salmon and potatoes with relish, hoping that Robert would be served the same later.

Dacian was a little distant at dinner, apart from the occasional pleasantry, absorbed in his own thoughts. When the ladies rose to depart for the drawing room, Agatha once more led the way out.

As she followed, Judith was aware of a faint feeling of unease, prickling ominously at the back of her neck. The discovery of the vases meant that she had been right: the 'thief' and murderer still lurked nearby. Now Dacian intended to provoke them.

The blue drawing room was already warmly lit with candles

and a fire. Judith took an outer armchair, ready to observe. She glanced at the pale blue curtains, hoping that Miss Cultor was well-hidden with a good vantage point.

Conversation was desultory and soon the gentlemen joined them, the duke going to stand by the mantelpiece. A stir at the door soon caught everyone's attention.

Fitzroy had arrived, bearing the parcel, his silver head held with dignity. However, Broughton was clearly taken aback at the appearance of the old butler and barred the way. After a muttered exchange, Fitzroy pushed his way in and presented his burden to the duke.

"Ah, thank you, Fitzroy," said Dacian genially.

Lady Agatha sat up straight in her chair. "Dacian! What are you doing? You ought not to be dragging poor Fitzroy into the house when we have another butler now."

"Fitzroy is assisting me in a small matter."

"Really, is that wise?" asked Agatha, her eyes darting to where Broughton stood stiffly by the door.

Dacian ignored her and laid the parcel on a square table by the fire-place. "Everyone, do you know what I have here?"

"I cannot imagine!" said Agatha, and her voice rang true.

So Agatha did not know that the vases were contained in the canvas - which implied her innocence.

Everyone else remained silent and did not venture an opinion, which was vexatious. Lord John's widened eyes and Broughton's implacable ones could not be tested for pretence. Lady Mary merely raised her brows and waited, while Robert watched with a slight frown from the corner of the room. Mr Nottley alone remained incurious, pouring himself a glass of whisky. He yawned. "I'm sure you are going to show us, old boy," he said. "I didn't know you enjoyed parlour games."

"Not a game," said the duke. "Something most intriguing, however. Fitzroy, if you may do the honours?"

Fitzroy bent to untie the rope and pull the wrapping away. In a swish of fabric, the vases lay revealed, firelight throwing orange flecks through the crystal. The broken edge gleamed.

Judith did not spare the glittering vases a glance. She was too busy looking at the faces around her. All showed surprise and confusion, but that was easy enough to enact. Judith surreptitiously placed her hand on her bosom, to touch the lapis pendant that lay hidden under her bodice.

Agatha spoke first, incredulously. "Those are our vases! Have you apprehended the thief, Dacian?"

Listening carefully, Judith did not think she was shamming it.

"I'm afraid not," said Dacian.

Lord John licked his lips. "If you have not ... how did you come by them?"

Mr Nottley was frowning at the vases. He looked round at the company and then questioningly at the duke. Broughton was staring at the crystal as if Fitzroy had brought in a parcel of donkey excrement. Fitzroy stood by impassively, not allowing himself the satisfaction of a smirk at his successor's affront.

Robert had unconsciously taken a step forward, his jaw tense.

Dacian said, "Otho found them in the well."

Mary said, "The well in the woods?" She had gone very pale. Her eyes darted round the table.

"Indeed." Dacian leaned on the mantelpiece casually. "You see what this means."

"What?" spluttered John. "What does it mean?"

Mr Nottley raised his brows. "It means your thief is closer to home than we thought. Isn't that right, your grace? We must all be careful."

Agatha spoke, clenching her fists on her lap. "Do you mean to say the thief will return? Why else would he hide the vases in the well?"

Mary swallowed, her eyes fixed on the glinting crystal. Dacian did not reply, as he waited to see what the others would say. Judith listened carefully, while also trying not to over-exert herself. She did not want to lose her wits and start misinterpreting things. Or worse, poke Dacian in the chest again.

John answered. "Because the theft was merely a pretence." His voice was grim but true. "The vases were stolen to explain away Gilbert's death."

A breath was drawn in, perhaps by Mary. Judith could not tell.

Everyone else stared at Lord John. He turned to Dacian angrily. "Are you trying to say that Gilbert was murdered by someone in the village?"

This time, Judith could hear a note of mendacity in John's voice. He didn't believe the village theory, but he was offering it up in the hopes that it would turn attention away from Sargenet. His cheeks were flushed and his eyes bright.

"Perhaps," said the duke.

Everyone went silent, hearing what he had not said.

Agatha said, "I don't like it. Not at all. It doesn't make sense."

"I don't like it either," said Mr Nottley. He looked at Agatha with concern. "Lady Agatha, should you perhaps repair to London?"

"Nonsense," said Agatha sharply. "I am not going to drift about London in the off-season. I will not be frightened out of my own home." Her belligerence, however, was mixed with agitation.

Mary spoke up at last. "I think, however, that *we* should leave. John, let us return home tomorrow. The influenza will surely be gone from Tithrow now."

The countess dropped her eyes. Judith could hear no direct lie, but Mary looked very pale and nervous, her hands clasped tightly in her lap. Judith considered whether or not those slender hands would be able to wield a heavy tome. It was possible.

Yet John was also lying.

Either one of them, Judith realised, could be trying to cover for the other. She bit her lip. She didn't like the way this was turning out. Apprehension grew in her, filling her stomach as if she had swallowed one of the vases.

She was only glad that no apparition had made itself known tonight. Glancing over at the curtain, she saw Miss Cultor's curly head peering over the top of the railing, inquisitive glee on her face. Judith looked away quickly.

Mr Nottley took a swig of his drink. "What did you suppose to gain by showing us these, your grace?"

Agatha stood in a rustle of satin, the yellow glowing in the candlelight. "Dacian simply likes to destroy an evening. We should have expected it of him, I suppose." She paused. "I am going to bed, and furthermore, I am going to lock my door."

"Good," said Dacian, still leaning on the mantlepiece. "As should the rest of you."

Mary followed Agatha, her shoulders in a tense line. John cast Dacian an angry look and trailed after his wife. Mr Nottley sketched a bow and tutted to himself as he left. Broughton stood like an effigy as everyone trooped past him. Fitzroy outdid him in wooden inscrutability.

Robert stared straight ahead in his corner.

Dacian raised his eyebrows at Judith and said, "Well?"

She stood and shook her head slightly. She did not want to speak of it before the butlers. Furthermore, one of the others could be listening, lingering outside the door. "I am tired," she lied. "I will repair to my bedroom as well."

Dacian nodded.

As she walked through the cold entrance hall to the stairs, Judith saw that someone *had* been listening. A glimpse of a skirt disappeared behind the library door.

It was not the yellow of satin, or the blue of sarcenet. It was mauve, the colour of Miss Atkinson's gown.

Judith hesitated only for a moment before following her.

In which there is an eerie scream

When listening for the lies of others, it is easy to miss the lies we tell ourselves.

    - from *Lady Avely's Guide to Truth and Magic*

THE LIBRARY WAS dark except for one lamp and the coals in the fireplace. Judith soon made out the figure of Miss Atkinson standing near the windows, her hands clenched together in front of her.

"Miss Atkinson?" Judith said gently. "Is that you?"

The governess turned and dropped a curtsy. "Yes, my lady. I came to fetch some evening reading material." She waved vaguely at the shelves, looking embarrassed at the lie that sounded in her voice.

Judith stepped closer, examining Miss Atkinson's face in the uneven light. "Did you happen to overhear the scene in the drawing room? I would not blame you for being curious."

Miss Atkinson hesitated. "I confess, I considered for a moment joining you all, seeing as the duke so kindly invited me.

Yet when I heard the raised voices ... it seemed inadvisable." She paused. "Did I hear that his grace discovered the missing vases?"

"Otho did - in the well. It is what lured him in there."

Miss Atkinson blinked. "Oh dear. I can see how that might have happened."

"A skull also appeared nearby. It wept blood at me. I don't suppose you know anything about either of these things, do you?"

The governess's eyes widened. "Uh, no. Not at all."

A tinny sound coated her words. Judith's eyes narrowed at the lie, but Miss Atkinson turned her back, ostensibly to examine the books.

"Goodness, what a dreadful day it's been," Miss Atkinson babbled on. "My nerves are a little strained - I shall need something to put me to sleep."

She reached randomly for a book on a low shelf. It was a large, leather-bound specimen, and Judith could not help but notice that the governess had no difficulty tucking it under one arm. Miss Atkinson backed away toward the door.

"Wait," said Judith. "Please, I want you to know: if you were cornered by Gilbert in a lecherous mood, you will not be blamed if you lashed out in self-defence and killed him."

Miss Atkinson's eyes widened and she froze on the doorstep. "Oh, my goodness. Thank you, Lady Avely. You are very kind."

Judith watched her impassively, wondering if she would confess.

Seeming to understand that more was required, Miss Atkinson lowered her gaze respectfully. "Your concern is much appreciated, my lady, but Gilbert did not press his advances on me that night. Robert had previously warned him off, so I was quite safe."

"Indeed." Judith frowned.

"And now," continued Miss Atkinson. "I must see the children. Good night, Lady Avely." She dropped a curtsy and vanished.

Left alone in the darkened library, Judith chewed on her lip. It seemed that the governess was innocent. Yet Miss Atkinson knew *something* of the apparitions. Did she guess who was behind them? Or was *she* behind them?

It was quite possible that Miss Atkinson was Gifted. Perhaps that was why she had been employed by Lord John, despite her apparent misalignment with his lordship's ideas of how small boys should be governed. If she were Gifted in Memory, Lord John would hope she would know how to tutor his sons in the art.

If so, the governess might also know how to work tokens of Illusion. Or have that rare confluence of two minor Gifts.

Judith realised suddenly that if Miss Atkinson had been lurking outside the drawing room tonight, she might very well have been lurking outside the previous evening too. She could have cast the spectre of the skull herself. And she could have been in the woods, supposedly looking for Otho while in fact casting those ghastly visions.

The question was: *why?* And did it have any bearing on Gilbert's death?

Judith looked round at the gloomy library, an old memory surfacing to taunt her. The dim shelves, the smell of leather and wood, the faint light, all was the same as it had been that night twenty-three years ago. The desk, where the duke had barricaded himself, was still in the same place. It was here that Dacian had kissed her and then broken her heart.

The wisp of a warm embrace teased at the corners of her mind and she shook it off. She had played that scene in her mind so many times over the years, trying to make sense of it. Now, as then, she failed. She could not understand how he could have betrayed her like that. She could not match the Dacian that she knew with the rake that the world had promised her, even when he delivered it to her with a resounding slap.

Even now, she was in danger of falling under his spell again and forgetting his true nature.

Straightening her spine, Judith turned to leave the cold library.

Yet just as she was about to cross the threshold, her eyes were drawn down by smear of red at her feet. Involuntarily, she let out a small shriek and leapt backwards. A dead mouse lay in her path, its tail bent unnaturally, its head a bloody mess.

Her bosom heaved and a sick feeling rose in her throat. It was not real. She knew that. It was too similar to the mouse she had seen in the woods. Yet it made her heart thud, even as an Illusion. It was clearly intended for her.

She ought to run out into the hallway and find the culprit. Somehow, she couldn't quite manage it, and consoled herself that at least she was not a foolish gothic heroine to run out into a dark hallway where a menacing presence lurked. The truth was that the mouse alone cowed her. She'd never been fond of mice and a dead one was even more repulsive. It lay inert and deformed, ominous in its crushed fragility.

After a few deep breaths, she crept forward to examine it.

Reluctantly, she admitted that the artistry was superb: life-like in its portrayal of death. The soft furry body, the limp paws, and the bloodied neck were all painted with realism and detail. Judith shuddered. Though perhaps the head was missing because the artist did not feel capable of rendering a rodent's face. Still, whoever had cast it was talented and particular. Involuntarily, her thoughts turned to Robert.

Whoever had cast it must still be within sight of the door. Judith retreated to grab the poker from beside the library fireplace. Thus armed, she tiptoed up to the mouse and prodded it.

The Illusion wavered then dissolved.

She waited a few more breaths, then proceeded through the door, holding the poker aloft. After all, she had to return to her bed at some point. The mouse was out of the way, so now she could deal with the impertinent member of the household who had cast it. If they received a poker to the head for their trouble, she could scarcely be blamed.

The hallway was dark and empty. Her heart thudded in her ears, making it difficult to hear any retreating footsteps. Tentatively, she walked forward, the poker looming next to her ear. Slowly, however, her pulse slowed. The sense of a watching presence receded. Whoever it was, they must be daunted by the sight of her weapon. A matron on the warpath was not to be trifled with.

Still holding the poker, she cautiously made her way to the drawing room where she had left Marigold.

The vampiri peeped from beneath the curtain. Her eyes widened when she saw the poker. Miming for silence, Judith put it down and lifted the vampiri into her reticule.

"What's going on?" hissed Marigold.

"I saw a mouse."

Marigold frowned in confusion, but Judith did not elucidate. She was feeling more at ease now. She had allowed her nerves to get the better of her. Cursed mouse. It couldn't hurt her. Even the skulls had shown no inclination to reveal their master. The Illusor was a coward, hiding behind puppets.

She propped the poker by the drawing room fire, leaving it as a puzzle for the maid in the morning. Ensuring Marigold was out of sight, she made her way upstairs with all due decorum, but there was no further sign of any skulls or decapitated creatures. Turning into the second floor of the west wing, she trod quietly along the corridor.

The soft carpet swallowed her footsteps. As she passed one of the other guest rooms, she heard voices talking in low urgent tones. Despite herself, she paused outside the door, listening. It was dishonourable to eavesdrop, but this case surely warranted an exception. Whoever was skulking in there might be the culprit.

Leaning closer, she heard the sharp voice of Lewis.

"He will blame me for it. You watch, he will say it is *my* fault."

"Why you?" came Robert's voice. "I'm the footman at the moment. If the duke should have asked for anyone's assistance, it ought to have been me."

"Broughton will make snide comments about *me*," said Lewis. "He hates it when Fitzroy comes into the house, and he will think I'm in cahoots with him now."

There was a sound of a piece of furniture being kicked, and, because Lewis was an Impactor, moving across the floor with a grating thud.

"Don't retaliate," said Robert warningly. "Otherwise he will make life difficult for you. Push the bed back, for God's sake. You must be careful of your power."

"I won't be here, I'll be leaving soon, if I can manage it. Now that the duke is back, he can recommend me to one of his friends."

Still, there came the sound of the bed being dragged back into position.

"Where will you go?" asked Robert.

"London," snapped Lewis. "Far from here."

Judith leaned a little closer. So Lewis wanted to run, did he? Marigold also emerged partially from the reticule and listened, agog.

After a moment, Robert spoke again. "Maybe I'll come with you."

"Really? I thought you never wanted to leave your home county."

Robert's voice drew closer to the door. "I don't, but...."

Hearing Robert approach, Judith leapt away like a bat in sunlight. She scuttled down the corridor, almost dislodging Miss Cultor, who was half hanging out the reticule. Fortunately, the door simply clicked shut behind them. Robert must have closed it to ensure privacy as he talked with Lewis.

Judith drew a deep breath. Robert was thinking of going to London. She ought to feel relieved, but somehow she felt disappointment.

She reached her room and let herself in with a sigh - only to be taken aback by a vision of the duke lounging on her chaise, still in his dark blue coat tails, open to show a loosened cravat. A brass candlestick on the table cast his handsome features in a soft glow. The room was lit with another candelabra, the red and gold furnishings bathed in warm light. He looked up with an expression of concern.

A rush of affection and desire coursed through her. Perhaps he was here so she could take advantage of him, after all? Then she saw that Wooten sat on the armrest, once again impeccably dressed in black, and sporting a beautifully arranged cravat in miniature, his legs elegantly crossed.

"Where were you?" Dacian stood to greet her. "I hope you weren't hunting ghosts without me. You promised."

She went over to the large bed, repressing her disappointment and debating whether or not to mention the grisly mouse. She helped Marigold out of the reticule and the vampiri stepped out, straightening her stained yellow gown. Wooten looked on with a faint look of disapproval as Marigold bobbed a curtsy.

"I followed Miss Atkinson," replied Judith. "She was going to enter the drawing room when she heard all the fuss. She retreated into the library and I took the opportunity to ask her about the apparitions and the murder."

"Oh?"

"She claimed to know nothing, but it was a lie." Judith sank onto the bed and pulled off her cream gloves pensively. Miss Atkinson had also been present just prior to the appearance of the dead mouse. "Is she a Musor, do you know?"

Dacian squinted and sat down again on the chaise. "Probably. The cousin of an old friend of the family's. I can ask John. But she would most likely be a Memor, not an Illusor. Surely, *she* hasn't been the one conjuring skulls."

"Unless she has some reason we can't see yet."

Marigold piped up. "My money is on Lady Mary. I saw everything in the drawing room and she behaved oddly."

Judith was thoughtful. "She was hiding something, that much I could tell. And now she wants to leave Sargenet in a hurry." Mary was not the only one; Lewis, too, was eager to leave.

Wooten nodded sagely, recrossing a handsomely booted foot. "A sign of guilt. Mary fears discovery."

"Or she is frightened," suggested Judith. Maybe Lewis was too. Maybe he had remembered that Gilbert bore a passing resemblance to himself. Or perhaps his mind had returned to an earlier memory: that of being pushed into a well. Her own thoughts had turned to that more than once.

"Are *you* frightened, Judith?" asked the duke. "Do you want to leave? I confess I think you should go tomorrow, even though I want you to stay."

His dark eyes were fixed on her in worry.

She ignored his confession even though the truth in his voice gave her a flush of pleasure. "I have an uneasy feeling," she admitted. "The discovery of the vases will precipitate something, I think."

Wooten wrinkled his nose. "Maybe it will be an iron fist this time."

Judith turned curiously. "Why do you say that?"

Wooten tugged at his lapels. "Oh. Well. It just appears that the apparitions are in the vein of *The Castle of Otranto*, that ridiculous novel by Horace Walpole. Not that I read such rubbish, of course, but everyone knows that a helmet falls from the sky with a black feather in it, and a skeleton appears in a cowl. It's all rather familiar, you know."

Judith stared. She felt foolish for not noticing the connection earlier. Elinor and Peregrine had read *The Castle of Otranto* a few years ago and she had heard some of it read aloud. It was a ghastly story, full of death, ghosts, and turgid masculine pride. Arguably the masculine pride was the most loathsome aspect.

She rubbed her forehead. "The black feather in the helmet - no wonder I dreamed of it. You think our ghost has a literary influence?"

"I suppose it is *literary*," said Wooten disparagingly. "It is grim enough."

Marigold sighed. "I suspect it rules Nottley out, simply because of its modern provenance. He would never read anything that wasn't boringly ancient, much less cast it into an Illusion."

"Nor John," said Dacian. "Agatha, however...."

"That's right," exclaimed Judith. "Her gothic novels. Someone else must be reading them. Mary, perhaps, or Miss Atkinson. Yet why would they amuse themselves with such trickery?"

Dacian shrugged. "Let's not jump to conclusions. The similarities could be merely a coincidence."

Wooten disagreed. "From what I hear, *Otranto* is definitely an influence on our ghost. All we need now is the armoured hand of God appearing as a warning of the dissolution and corruption of the nobility."

"Steady on," objected the duke. "I hope you're not referring to me."

"Of course not," soothed Wooten. "Prince Manfred in the story is ultimately dispossessed by a peasant holding the bloodline. That won't happen to you, will it?"

Judith and Dacian stared at him.

"Lewis," said Judith.

"Oh yes," put in Marigold excitedly. "The illegitimate steward. Is he the noble peasant in this scenario?"

Dacian's lips thinned. "I don't think he sees himself like that."

Judith nibbled on her lip. Prince Manfred was a revolting character and bore no resemblance to the Duke of Sargen. Not in her mind, at least. Especially not now that he was older and wiser. Yet could someone hold a grudge toward the duke, and have expressed it through the apparitions?

At that moment, a tap came at the door. Judith gestured for Marigold to hide, which she did so by jumping down and slipping under the bed. Wooten, likewise, hid behind the chaise.

Assured that the vampiri were out of sight - and abiding by the Edicts - Judith opened the door a crack. Robert stood there, bearing a tray with a molinet of chocolate and two elegant cups. She stood aside and let him in with a tentative smile.

"Ah, good," said Dacian. "We need to bolster our constitutions. This chocolate has cayenne in it, marchioness."

Judith took the tray from Robert, eyeing the molinet with interest. However, some things, as loathe she was to admit it, were more important. "Robert, is Mr Lewis about? I have an important question to ask him."

Robert's eyes dropped. "Ah, yes, I can fetch him if you like." He turned and left.

Judith put the tray down on the rosewood table and sat in the spindly chair. "Cayenne, you say?"

Dacian gave her a dazzling smile and set about pouring. The delicious waft of spices drifted through the room. Marigold poked her head from under the bed with a disapproving look.

"Disgusting stuff."

"Cayenne?" asked Dacian. "Have you tried it?"

"She means the cocoa," explained Judith. "Miss Cultor *erroneously* believes it causes deafness."

"My mother told me." Marigold folded her arms defensively. "She knew a woman who lost her hearing that way."

"Don't be ridiculous," said Wooten, popping up from behind the chaise.

Dacian raised his brows as he poured the second cup. "Hmm.

Come to think of it, my uncle drank hot chocolate by the gallon, and he went deaf. You might be right, Miss Cultor."

"Oh, for goodness' sake," said Judith. "Don't encourage her. My ears are perfectly good. Excellent, in fact."

"Are you certain?" asked Dacian. He leaned across the table toward her, holding out the mug. "I can murmur in your ear if necessary."

"That will *not* be necessary."

"As you wish." His fingers skimmed hers, sending a tingle through her. She took a long gulp of the warm milk, glad of something to soothe her nerves. The taste enveloped her mouth: cinnamon, cardamom, nutmeg, almond, pistachio, and some additional peppery taste.

"It is superb," she acknowledged. The heat in the sweetness was delightful.

Marigold wrinkled her nose. "An evil drink."

"I, at least," said Judith with dignity, "do not consume blood."

Marigold folded her arms and glared.

A knock came at the door. Marigold and Wooten ducked out of sight again and, at Judith's command, Robert entered with Lewis. Both of them looked rather apprehensive.

"My lady, you wished to speak with me?" Lewis stood sullenly in the centre of the room, his hands behind his back. Robert hovered just behind him.

"Ah, yes," said Judith, putting down the chocolate. "I have a question."

However, before she could phrase it, a faint, unearthly sound floated through the room: a woman screaming somewhere in the night.

In which a plan is foolhardy

THE UNCANNY WAIL drifted through the open door.

Judith's skin pricked with the eeriness of it. They all looked at each other, startled. Abruptly, the sound stopped, cut short by a muffled thud.

Dacian strode to the door, head cocked. In the aftermath of the ghastly shriek, the house was more deathly silent than before.

"Wait here." He cast a grim glance at them all and disappeared down the dark corridor at a run.

"Boys, *you* wait here," muttered Judith.

She picked up the brass candlestick from the table and hustled after him. Despite her command, Lewis and Robert followed behind her.

She saw Dacian running to the door that joined the ballroom, aiming to cut across the gallery to the other side of the house. He must think that the sound had come from the east wing.

Seeing his trajectory, Judith took a different route, hoping to cut off anyone who might retreat to the entrance hall. She bolted to the stairs of the west wing, holding the candle aloft. At the top of the stairs she paused, overlooking the hall, hoping she would not see another tearful skull floating before her.

Her heart rose to her throat.

A figure lay sprawled at the bottom of the eastern staircase. In the dimness of the entrance hall, Judith could see that it was a woman, face up, eyes closed, her complexion ashen. Her arm was flung out at a strange angle and her blue gown lay in disarray.

Lady Mary.

A book lay a few yards from her head, pages open and bent in equal disarray.

Judith clattered down the stairs, careless of noise. "Lady Mary? Are you alright?"

No answer came. Judith rushed over and knelt by the prone figure, putting the candle down. Mary lay utterly still, her lips bloodless, her hair messed. Sickeningly, Judith was reminded of the dead mouse. Her skin shivered with horror. Carefully, she picked up a limp wrist and then put it down again, fearing Mary had broken something, or worse.

The duke appeared at the top of the eastern stairs.

"Good God. What happened?"

"She must have fallen." Judith did not voice the alternative.

Dacian's face was furious as he bounded down. Agatha appeared on the stairs behind him, her brow creased in worry.

"What was that sound?" Agatha saw the tableau and froze. "Mary!"

A gasp hissed. Judith looked round and saw Lewis standing at the top of the western stairs that Judith had descended. His fists were clenched. Robert was just behind him.

Behind Robert, Mr Nottley emerged, blinking, from the west wing. Miss Atkinson appeared next to Agatha, presumably also drawn out of her room. Broughton stepped into the entrance hall from the servants' quarters.

It was hard to see everyone's expressions in the poor light. Judith stared round, wondering who had pushed Mary. Or if it were Lord John, who was nowhere to be seen.

Dacian knelt beside her. "Is she alive?"

Judith bent over Mary, making a show of putting her face near the pale lips and listening for a breath. Holding a thick wrist up, she placed her other hand at Mary's bosom. After a long, tense moment, she raised her head.

"She is dead." Her voice carried low and clear. "Lady Mary is dead. She must have fallen and knocked her head."

Agatha gave a small, gasping cry. She tottered down to the eastern landing. Miss Atkinson followed close behind, her face contorted with shock.

Dacian met Judith's eyes. Impassively, he too bent his head to Mary's face, putting three fingers to her exposed neck.

"Yes," he said evenly. "She is gone."

"No," shrieked Agatha, clutching the bannister. "She can't be dead. Call for a doctor, Dacian, I insist. There must be some mistake."

Dacian shook his head. "Mary is no longer breathing, Aggie. It is too late. Her heart has stilled."

"Surely not," said Miss Atkinson faintly, from the landing.

"I'm afraid so." Dacian spoke with all the authority of his position, his words falling like stones. He slid his arms under Mary's frame. "I will return her to her room. May she rest in peace."

Judith stood. "I will sit in vigil for the first half of the night."

Everyone stood staring with horror. Dacian lifted Mary, his Gifted strength making her pillowy form seem light and fragile. Bowing his head, he carried her up the eastern stairs, cradling her against his broad chest. A tangle of blue sarcenet and feet drooped over his arm. It was the second body he had carried in his arms today: Otho's discovery of the vases had indeed provoked a violent response.

While all eyes were on Dacian and his tragic burden, Judith bent to pick up her candle and the fallen book. Quickly, she tucked the tome under her arm. It was large and leather-bound, with a long title which she could not make out. Something about Constantine the Great. Perhaps it was even the same book that had been subjected to the bloody Illusion in the library. Or perhaps it was the book that Miss Atkinson had borrowed earlier.

Slowly, like sleep-walkers, Agatha and Miss Atkinson parted before Dacian on the landing. Judith, following close behind, saw tears sparkling in Agatha's eyes. Miss Atkinson was dry-eyed, her jaw rigid as she gazed upon Mary.

Judith looked carefully at the limp figure. Mary's blonde hair covered her face and lay stark against Dacian's dark blue coat. Her hands hung lifelessly, pale and ungloved. She must have begun to undress for the evening before she was drawn out of her room again.

Glancing round, Judith saw that Lewis and Robert were retreating up the western staircase. Robert looked stunned, Lewis angry. Judith jerked a thumb at them, indicating that they should return to her room.

Mr Nottley stood staring after Dacian, frowning deeply. He caught Judith's eye and gave her a hard look, folding his arms, disbelief writ upon his face. Clearly, he did not believe it was an accident that had befallen Mary. His gaze moved to rest anxiously on Agatha.

Dacian turned to face them all again at the top of the stairs and spoke over Mary's head. "It is late. There is nothing you can do for her now. You may pay your respects in the morning, but for now everyone must go to bed."

"Will you tell John?" asked Agatha, in a querulous voice.

Dacian nodded shortly.

Stiffly, everyone obeyed his orders, disappearing one by one. Judith stood quietly by Dacian, not saying a word but turning to accompany him as he carried Mary through the third floor of the east wing. He shot her a sideways look but also remained silent.

They reached a door and at Dacian's gesture, Judith opened it for him.

A sumptuous room met her eyes, feminine in its excesses. Cushions piled on the bed and books leaned on the bedside table, next to a bowl of sweets and a vase of white roses, overblown and drooping. It was lit with many candles, indicating it had been recently occupied. The thick carpet glowed in oriental patterns and the curtains were deep blue. It was more cosy than Judith had expected of Mary's character.

She put down the candlestick on the dresser and next to it she placed the book she had found by Mary's head.

In the candlelight she could read the title: *An Extensive and Complete Biography of Constantine the Great.* The Roman Emperor. Lord John's interest.

Perhaps just a coincidence. Constantine the Great could very well be within Mary's purview too, if she shared her husband's scholarly pursuits, rather than the Greeks of Mr Nottley. Perhaps Mary had simply been carrying the book when she fell, tripping on the staircase. Judith didn't believe it, however.

She could see no trace of Lord John in the bedroom, in person or effects. This must be Lady Mary's private room, with Lord John sleeping in other quarters. The bed was large and Judith set about clearing it of cushions, so that Dacian could set Mary down.

He did so gently, while Judith shut the door and returned to his side.

"She still lives?" she asked quietly.

Mary's pale face looked somehow younger as she lay there,

unconscious, her careworn lines relaxed. Judith arranged her limbs more neatly and tucked two blankets over her, tutting.

"Thank you for going along with my lie," she said. "I suspect she was pushed."

"By whom?"

"I don't know. But I feared another attack on her life."

"Did they all believe us, do you think?"

Judith's lips twisted. "I think we should be prepared for a visitor here. Whoever tried to kill Mary might want to see if he succeeded."

"You've set a trap, in fact. Well done, Judith."

She looked up, pausing as she straightened Mary's covers. "I just hope we don't expose her to more danger. We must send for a doctor, but perhaps you should move her to the west wing - far from here. We effectively announced to everyone that she would be left vulnerable in her room, except for my vigil."

"Forget that. I'm not carting Mary off and leaving you alone in here, waiting for a murderer to knock on the door. Especially with the murder weapon still at hand." He nodded at *The Extensive and Complete Biography of Constantine the Great.*

"Yes, I wonder if it was chosen deliberately to wield the blow. Lord John studies the Romans, and I'm afraid I've recalled something about Constantine."

"What is that?"

"He killed his own son," said Judith. "Crispus always stuck in my mind. It takes a certain coldness to execute your eldest son, even if he was illegitimate."

Dacian grimaced. "I hope you are not suggesting a particular relevance here. John would never hurt Lewis."

"Can you be sure?"

Dacian's eyes dropped. "I would have said that no one in this house could harm another."

"Maybe Mary knows something crucial and we risk her being killed in truth."

"Not if I'm here." Dacian puffed out his chest.

Judith ignored this masculine self-importance. She bit her lip worriedly. "Maybe we should use Robert's Gift to help us."

"Illusion?" Dacian frowned suspiciously. "What are you thinking?"

"Lewis could carry Mary to the west wing, if you are determined to stay here. Then I could lie in the bed and pretend to be Mary, with the help of a little Illusion from Robert." She held up a hand, forestalling objections. "He can be hiding in the curtains. You can hide there too, both of you ready to leap out if the murderer comes by. This way, we catch him in the act of trying to silence Mary, which will give us the proof we need to accuse him. Or her."

"Absolutely not," said Dacian. "Categorically, definitively not."

"Why not?" she demanded. "It's a perfectly good idea." One worthy of her daughter Elinor, who would be proud. "As you said, we set a trap, but without endangering Mary."

"While endangering you!"

"I am not unconscious and injured!"

"You are a woman, however, and unable to defend yourself against violence."

This patronising remark annoyed her but she tried to stay patient. "You will be there, ready to defend me."

"No," said Dacian. "*I* will be Mary."

"*What?*"

"Robert can Illuse me just as well as you. Then I am right beneath the murderer's hands, ready to leap up and grab him."

Judith stared. "That's a ridiculous idea."

"No more ridiculous than yours."

He had a point. Yet her instincts told her that the killer would come that night to see Mary. *Someone* had to be waiting.

"Right then," said Dacian, folding his arms. "That's decided. I'll be Mary - she is almost as tall as me, after all - you are too short."

Judith pursed her lips. It was unfortunately true.

Dacian continued. "Can you find Lewis and send him here? We will need him to move Mary. Do you trust him now?"

"Well, he can't have been the one who pushed her," she pointed out. "He and Robert were with us when we heard the scream. I'll be quick; we might not have much time."

The duke came round the bed to her side, and took her hand. "Be careful, Judith. I don't want anything to happen to you."

She rested a moment, enjoying the warmth of his grasp despite herself. "You too. Watch out for weighty books."

"Oh, I usually avoid the heavy stuff."

She squeezed his hand admonishingly and let go.

Slipping out of the room, Judith looked around. The corridor was empty. Mary's room was on the third floor, which joined with the upper gallery in the ballroom. Quickly, Judith hurried past the black pit of the dance floor, making her way to the west wing.

Her bedroom door stood ajar. She pushed it open cautiously, relieved to see Lewis and Robert waiting inside in a tense silence, the tray of abandoned chocolate between them on the table. Marigold and Wooten were nowhere to be seen.

"Mr Lewis." She saw him jump slightly. "The duke needs you in Mary's room."

"Of course." He made as if to leave.

She held up a hand. "But answer me this first: who pushed you into the well, all those years ago?"

Lewis frowned. "Felix, I think. Lord John's eldest."

"Are you certain?"

"I didn't see whoever it was," he admitted. "I was perched on the stone wall, daydreaming, looking into the black depths. I felt two hands on the small of my back, pushing me, and then I was falling. I didn't have time to look round."

Robert spoke up. "Of course it was Felix. Who else could it be? You pummelled him the day before, remember, in the rose arbour? He was humiliated. He hated being bested by you."

Judith tilted her head, considering. "I wonder. Everyone must have known of that fight." She paused. "And you swear you did not kill Gilbert, Mr Lewis?"

"Not to my knowledge," he replied uneasily.

Judith nodded. He spoke truly. "Very well, you must hurry. The duke wants you to carry Mary here, to hide her safely. She still lives and we are setting a trap for the person who pushed her."

They both stared in astonishment. Behind them, Wooten's head emerged from behind the settee.

"A trap?" said Wooten mournfully. "I shall be required, if there is to be violence, much to my abhorrence."

Lewis and Robert whipped their heads round to stare at Wooten.

"Who are you?" demanded Lewis.

"I am Wooten Willoughby," said Wooten. "You may address me as your gracel. And you may carry me to the duke."

"This is the duke's blood companion," explained Judith. "His presence will assist Dacian, should Dacian be required to use any force."

"Dacian, is it?" said Lewis.

Judith was saved from answering when Marigold popped her head out next to Wooten. "And I am Miss Marigold Cultor."

Judith sighed. "My companion." The bat was out of the bag now. One hoped Lewis and Robert would be discreet about this night's adventures. "Mr Lewis, once you bring Mary here, you must fetch a doctor from the village."

Lewis eyed the dapper vampiri.

"I will go with you," said Wooten austerely, "if you are careful of my cravat."

Reluctantly, Lewis went over and put out his hand. He kept stoically still as Wooten sashayed up his arm and sat on his shoulder.

Wooten tugged Lewis's left ear. "You may proceed."

The steward set off impassively. Judith was glad to see he had *some* training in good manners.

"What about me?" piped up Marigold. "I want to be part of the fun. You will need me to listen for villains, Judith, with your hearing so diminished."

Judith ignored this sally and turned to Robert. "I have a task for you, Robert. Could you paint a likeness of Lady Mary's face over the duke's?"

"What?" Then Robert frowned. "Faces are the hardest."

"It need not look exactly like her. Mary is meant to be dead, after all. You could afford a little waxiness."

"In that case...." Robert rubbed his hands together. "This will be interesting. Shall I bring the chocolate?"

Judith cast a longing glance at the two cups. "Better not. This is meant to be a death vigil, not a tea party."

"Of course, my lady."

She gave him a wry look and led the way out.

In which a trap is set

Unfortunately, sometimes when one Discerns the truth, one is forced into deceit.

   - from *Lady Avely's Guide to Truth and Magic*

MARY WAS BORNE AWAY by Lewis, her figure heavy with sleep. Fortunately, Lewis had the strength of an Impactor, and found no trouble manoeuvring her through the door and across to the west wing. He was under urgent instructions to fetch the village doctor and bring him up to see Mary in the Gold Room, discreetly via the back door.

Meanwhile, the rest of them took their places in Mary's boudoir.

Robert was in the cupboard. He had tried hiding behind the curtains, but he stood out like a footman-shaped blob. In the large wooden wardrobe, he had a direct line of sight to the duke if he kneeled next to the keyhole, which made it easier to project his Illusion.

They arranged it so that Robert would trigger the Illusion

when Marigold gave the signal from the door that someone approached. Marigold had a sewing basket strategically leaned against the wall, providing a pocket of darkness in which to hide.

When Robert practiced, a simulacrum of Mary's face transposed over Dacian's. The life-like mask hid the duke's striking features. It was creepy, despite - or because - of its effectiveness. Robert managed the likeness quite well, if with a little stiffness in the cheeks.

Fortunately, Mary was a tall woman, so the duke's long figure didn't seem too out of place in her bed.

"How do I look?" The duke's voice came disembodied from Mary's pale lips.

"Dreadful," replied Judith. "Your head is too big."

"My head is perfectly shaped, thank you very much."

"Perfectly for your ducal self-importance, but not for Mary's more reserved character," Judith whispered back. "I'm going to put a mobcap on you to disguise the effect. Hold off for a minute, Robert."

"Ha," hissed Dacian, his handsome face revealed. "You're just trying to punish me for my remarks."

"Why would that be, I wonder?" asked Judith innocently, foraging through Mary's dressing table.

She found a purple silk cap that would suit nicely, and set about tying it round the duke's inarguably large head. She lingered at the bow, then patted his cheek patronisingly.

He winked. "See? You want to take it off, don't you?"

Judith stepped back and admired the result. "Not at all. Robert, if you please."

The visage of Mary melted onto Dacian's face, appearing marginally more to scale this time.

"Well done, Robert," said Judith. "Especially when you are working with such dull clay."

"Ha," said the duke.

Wooten was perched on the corner poster of the bed. "I am afraid that while the face is passable, his grace's bosoms are insufficient."

A snort of laughter came from the cupboard. The Illusion vanished and Dacian glared.

Judith bit her lip. "You are right, Wooten. Lady Mary is more ... bolstered at the top."

"As much as it pains me to say," said Wooten, wincing, "perhaps you should use his cravat."

Judith stepped forward and drew Dacian's white cravat from his neck. She set about stuffing it into the top of the blanket, trying not to notice how hard the duke's chest was underneath.

"Is that better?" she asked Wooten, avoiding Dacian's gaze.

The vampiri shook his head. "More."

"Must we?" snapped the duke.

Repressing an hysterical urge to laugh, Judith found another shawl and inserted it, then patted it.

"That's better," pronounced Wooten.

"I don't know about that," muttered the duke.

Wooten leapt gracefully off the bed post to vanish under the bed. Marigold leant against the door, her arms folded over her untidy gown, grinning.

Judith retired to her chair by the bedside. "Now we wait," she said. "I will stay watching in vigil."

"No, you won't!" Dacian shouted in a stage-whisper. "Go, Judith, I beg you! The whole point of me wearing these blasted bosoms is so that you'll be out of danger."

"I told everyone that I would wait in vigil!" she hissed back. "If I'm not here, whoever comes will suspect a trap."

"No, they won't! They will grab the opportunity to murder me."

"Well, forgive me if that sounds inadvisable!"

Wooten's voice came hollowly from under the bed. "Hush, you two."

Marigold had her ear against the door. "Yes, be quiet! How am I supposed to hear anything if you two are squabbling like old ladies?"

Judith held up a hand. "I'll pretend I've fallen asleep, so they are free to murder you, does that suit?"

"No, it does not suit!" hissed Dacian.

"Quiet!" hushed Marigold. "Someone approaches!"

"Too late now," whispered Judith with satisfaction. "Robert, ahoy! Dacian, remember our signalling system!"

The pale mask descended upon Dacian, hiding his glare with the appearance of black lashes closed upon a white cheek. Dacian audibly ground his teeth. It was an uncanny sound coming from Mary's dead face.

Judith put her head on her shoulder and tried to feign sleep. Her heartbeat quickened even as she listened intently. She could hear no footsteps but Marigold had been proven right before.

Finally, in the tense silence of the room, a faint tap sounded at the door. Then came the sound of the door opening, swishing over the oriental rug.

The door edged over the carpet slowly. Beneath her lashes, Judith watched the gap widen. A boot emerged.

Mr Nottley stepped into the room.

He was still dressed in his evening attire, his silver-striped waistcoat glinting in the candlelight. He had his chin down, looking cautiously around. He took in Judith's lolling head and the prone figure of the duke.

Quietly, he drew closer.

Judith tried to breathe evenly. Was Mr Nottley the murderer? Would he try to strangle or bludgeon Mary right before Judith?

He paused by the bed, then looked around the room. He

stepped toward the dresser, where the book on Constantine lay. Was he going to use it again? Judith's eyelids fluttered anxiously.

In the silence, Mr Nottley suddenly cleared his throat loudly. It sounded like a dog growling.

Judith jumped slightly, her eyes shooting open.

"Ah, Lady Avely," said Mr Nottley pleasantly. "I hope I do not disturb you."

That was a lie. He had meant to wake her up with that aggressive noise.

"Not at all," she said, hoping that Dacian had not jerked in reaction as well. "I was just, er, resting my eyelids, in this sad time."

"You are very good to sit in vigil for poor Mary," said Nottley. "You must excuse my intrusion. I have come to fetch Agatha's shawl. She said she left it here - a white one."

Judith, surprised, heard that he was telling the truth. Carefully, she laid her hands flat, hoping Dacian would see her signal through the Illusion.

"Oh," she said. "Certainly." She only hoped that the missing shawl wasn't currently stuffed down the duke's shirt.

Fortunately, Mr Nottley turned and picked up a white stole that lay over a seat. "Ah, here it is - I recognise it." He paused, sighing as he looked down at the figure prone on the bed. "Mary looks serene in death, does she not?"

Judith, casting a glance at Robert's Illusion, thought that Mary did indeed look more poetical than she had in life. Her cheeks were smoother and her lashes darker.

"May she rest in peace," said Judith piously. She kept her hands flat.

"Mary was always beautiful in her own way." Mr Nottley still stared at Mary. "Intelligence is attractive, don't you think?"

Judith could detect no subterfuge and tentatively agreed. Mr

Nottley obviously possessed *some* taste. She took the opportunity to ask a question. "Had you known her long?"

"For years now." He shook his head sadly. His eyes drifted to Mary's 'bosom'. "But do not misinterpret my admiration, Lady Avely. It is pure in its nature. Despite Lord John's suspicions, I have never made any lustful advances toward his wife."

Again, Judith could hear only the truth. It was as she suspected, Mr Nottley was devoted to Agatha.

Then his gaze sharpened on her. "Tell me, do you really think it was an accident? Mary's death?"

Judith widened her own eyes. "Mr Nottley! What else could it be?"

He frowned and did not answer, looking instead around the room again. His eyes lighted on *The Extensive and Detailed Biography of Constantine the Great*. He huffed.

"That was the book in the entrance hall, wasn't it? Lying next to Mary?" He shook his head and muttered sadly. "John's book. Ah, perhaps it was divine retribution after all."

Judith stared. "What do you mean?"

"Oh, well, the young man, Mr Lewis, also fell from a great height, did he not?" Mr Nottley raised his brows. "Lord John's illegitimate son? Perhaps this is a divine settling of that old account - though far more tragic, of course."

Judith frowned. Did Nottley know something? It certainly sounded as if he knew quite a lot about the secret history of the household. "Mr Lewis fell, did he?" she asked, trying to lead him to further revelations.

He nodded. "Down that old well. Haven't you heard? I would have thought it was all raked up with Otho meeting the same fate. Though Lewis was pushed, of course."

Judith kept her hands flat, for Nottley was simply recounting the truth. "Who pushed him, do you know?" This was the very question that plagued her.

Nottley gave a small, regretful shrug. He ran a hand down his silver stripes, hesitating. "Everyone says it was Felix, Lady Mary's eldest son. He was jealous of Lewis, and they came to fisticuffs the day before."

Judith noted the evasive phrasing of his speech, even as she realised why this story of Felix had never sounded right to her. "If Felix was unafraid to come to fisticuffs with Lewis, why would he sneak up on him and push him into the well?"

Nottley's eyes glinted. "I'm sure I cannot guess. I've known the family for a long time, but it is not for me to say how such an exalted bloodline should choose to act."

He stood, having clearly planted the seeds he wished to sow. "Well, Lady Avely, I must bid you goodnight." He gave a last sorrowful look at Mary. "Dear Mary, to be punished so harshly."

With that last suggestion, he tenderly bore the white stole away like a funeral shroud.

The door shut behind him with a snap. Marigold had given it an extra shove on the way out.

The vampiri waited a few moments before she gave vent to her scorn. "That sneaky old waggle-head," she hissed. "What was he trying to say?"

"I'm not sure," said Judith slowly. "Perhaps that Lord John pushed Lewis into the well. And then hit Mary on the head to prevent her from exposing him."

The Illusion evaporated like a cloud around Dacian's dark, handsome face. He was frowning. "I don't believe it. John would never do anything like that."

"I agree," put in Robert, muffled from the cupboard. "Lord John doesn't even notice Lewis. He wouldn't bother trying to kill him."

Wooten stuck his head out. "Maybe that is a pretence. Maybe he wanted to rid himself of an awkward illegitimate child."

"Never," scowled Dacian, darting his eyes meaningfully to the cupboard, where another awkward illegitimate child was listening.

Judith spoke. "Mr Nottley has only voiced my own doubt. I asked Lewis this evening about it, and he told me he never saw who pushed him."

Perhaps it was as she had thought: Lord John was as cold as Constantine, and had sought to eliminate his own illegitimate son, for fear that the boy would oust his other children. On several occasions now John had evaded her questions, or even lied. She hadn't thought he was capable of such violence, but perhaps with a book in his hands he had become vicious. Perhaps his illness had made him slightly mad, and with Dacian returning home he had thought to put an end to Lewis.

Mary must have threatened to expose him, and he had grown angry. Judith shivered, wondering if John would come to the room now to make sure his work was done. She shook her head faintly. Somehow, she could not quite see it.

Robert cracked the cupboard open slightly. "I'm a bit cramped in here. My knees hurt."

"Come out," allowed Judith. "Stretch quickly."

Gingerly, Robert emerged, his long limbs unfolding. "I feel a bit woozy, to be honest. I think I'm getting Bemused."

"Well, don't do anything stupid," said Dacian, from the bed. "I look silly enough for both of us."

Robert swallowed a grin. "Certainly, your grace."

"Are you agreeing that I look silly?"

"Certainly not, your grace."

Wooten popped up from under the bed. "You certainly do. Or like something from a nightmare."

"Says the vampire bat," said Dacian. "Any more rude commentary from you, Wooten, and I will make you ride in my pocket from now on."

Wooten clamped his lips together.

"Now," said Dacian with dignity. "Judith, I think you've done enough here. You should return to the Gold Room and watch over the real Mary."

"Nonsense. Lewis and the doctor can look after her. If I hadn't been here, Mr Nottley might have looked too closely at you. And I think we will have another visitor soon."

"All the more reason for you to go."

"I'm not leaving. In fact, I think I need a weapon." She looked round, wondering if she could wield *Constantine* effectively. That would take two hands, however, and she might have only time for one. She was starting to feel a little Bemused herself.

"You do *not* need a weapon," snapped Dacian. "*I* am your weapon."

"Currently covered in blankets," she pointed out, her eyes drifting down. "And rather ... encumbered. You might be too slow."

"I will not!"

She stood up to examine the glass vase on the bedside table, where the white roses were starting to discolour. In a pinch, it might work to create a distraction. "Do you think I could smash this vase on someone? Or perhaps the brass candlestick?"

Dacian's brow became thunderous under his ribbons. "No! If anyone is going to smash something, it will be me!"

Judith rolled her eyes.

Robert said hopefully, "I could smash something, if required."

"You - back in the cupboard now," said Dacian sternly.

Robert hopped with alacrity into his hiding place. The door swung shut with a bang.

Dacian turned his attention back to Judith. "Watch me."

He flung the bedclothes back and released his hands. Within a second, Judith found herself suddenly jolted backwards and pressed against the cupboard by an invisible power.

She struggled against it and although her arms flailed about, she could not move anything else.

Following up his Impact, Dacian leapt out of the bed, coming to stand right in front of Judith. His dark eyes were alight with triumph.

"See, I am quite capable."

"Unhand me!" she said. "You ... you ... cad!"

His face fell. "I'm not touching you." Immediately, he released his hold. She stumbled a little and he put out a hand to steady her, grabbing her elbow.

"Sorry, Judith."

"I said, unhand me!"

Robert's voice came hollowly and nervously from the cupboard. "Is everything alright, Lady Avely?"

"I am fine," said Judith, impressed that Robert had the courage to speak out against his noble employer. "It is just the duke behaving like a small child."

Dacian let go of her arm. "I was trying to demonstrate my ability."

"You've always been a braggart."

"I was trying to show you that you can return to your room now!"

She folded her arms. "Get back into that bed. I'm not leaving."

He sighed. "That's the problem with widows: they ignore your requests to leave."

"Ha," she said. "As if you've ever told a widow to leave before."

A muffled snort came from the cupboard. Dacian frowned, then looked back to Judith, the line between his eyes deepening. He seemed to be about to say something, then Marigold hissed from the door.

"Shhh." She held up a tiny hand. "I hear footfalls."

"Who now?" muttered Dacian. But he did it under his breath

and clambered back into bed as Marigold disappeared behind the sewing basket.

Judith tucked Dacian in rapidly, arranging the shawls appropriately. Then she sat down and swallowed. She needed to keep her mind clear and not be distracted by memories from long ago, and pesky widows. She drew a deep breath and let it out slowly, closing her eyes, trying to relax with false sleep.

The room became deathly silent. The apparition of Mary's face drifted over Dacian's, even more wax-like than before. Dacian became as still as stone beneath the blankets.

Belatedly, Judith realised her hands were curled in tight fists. She placed them flat on her lap, heart beating fast. She felt vulnerable, unable to see, propped up like a doll next to a supposed corpse. The duke, at least, would be able to see through Robert's Illusion. She would have to rely on Dacian's quick reflexes should anything go wrong.

Suddenly, it all seemed like a terrible idea. What if he could not free his hands from all his blankets and bosoms in time?

In the heavy silence, a tap came at the door. It was a very soft tap. Almost as if it didn't really want to be heard.

Judith held her breath. The door slid open and a voice spoke, low and questioning.

"Mary?"

It was Lord John.

In which death is a waxen mask

Beware of reasoning too closely when one is under the influence of Bemusement.

    - from *Lady Avely's Guide to Truth and Magic*

"Mary, it is I."

Judith kept her face neutral, her thoughts chaotic. If John had tried to kill Mary, why would he talk as if she were still awake?

There was the sound of the door swinging open and shut. Then John's tone sharpened. "Lady Avely? What are you doing here?"

Judith's eyes shot open despite herself. Lord John's voice was loud with amazement and likely would have woken her anyway, she reasoned.

His lordship stood in the doorway, clothed in a lavish dressing gown of Chinese silk, coloured luridly in red and purple. His face was a parody of surprise and confusion as he stared at Judith. Behind him, Marigold peeped from her sewing basket, brown eyes wide.

"Lady Avely?" he repeated. "Why are you in my wife's room? Is something wrong?"

Judith was nonplussed. Was Lord John acting? Or did he really not know anything of the accident? She could hear no lie in his voice. Belatedly, she remembered that he had not witnessed the scene in the entrance hall, and Dacian had not yet had time to tell his brother what had happened. Perhaps John really *was* innocent.

Also, if he had known nothing of Mary's accident, then John was here for a very different reason.

"Ah, Lord John." Judith cleared her throat loudly, hoping that Robert and Dacian would keep to their parts. "I'm afraid that this, ah, is a bad time."

"What do you mean?" Suspicion coated John's voice. He pulled the Chinese silk round him tightly, the purple making his eyes seem more shadowed. "Is Mary ill? What's wrong? She looks awful."

"No, she fell," said Judith. "Down the stairs."

She hesitated. It was one thing to tell the household in general that Mary was dead; it was quite another to inform this sad fact to her husband. She prevaricated. "Indeed, I fear for her life. She was knocked out by the fall, so I thought I should wait by her side til she regains consciousness. She took a severe blow to the head."

Horror spread across John's pale face.

"Mary!" he whimpered and leapt toward his wife.

Judith cringed, knowing that John's touch would destroy the Illusion. Fortunately, however, the duke's hands were tucked well under the blankets, so John's attempt to grasp his wife's hands was foiled. He clutched at the covered lump anyway, staring hungrily at Mary's visage but not caressing it, thank goodness.

"Oh God," he said. "She will die! It is my fault. And I came here to apologise!"

Judith swallowed, hearing only truth. "Apologise for what, my lord?"

"We fought." He looked up fretfully. "She must have told Nottley of my suspicions. Or perhaps she withdrew her affections. No doubt he grew angry and pushed her. Or maybe she threw herself down the stairs, wracked with guilt."

No lie coated his words.

"Your suspicions?" said Judith slowly. "Of Nottley?" This was a two-way road, it seemed.

Lord John stroked 'Mary's' hand pitifully. "I knew she was having an affair. I've seen her walking into the village and making assignations at the Gryffin. And I've seen her lurking with Nottley in the house. They show no shame in flirting before my eyes!" He bowed his head over the bed. "I forgive her, I forgive everything, if she would just return to me. Even if she killed that footman to keep her secret, I forgive her!"

Judith could hear only truth in Lord John's wild ramblings. "You believe that Mary killed the footman?"

John's face drooped. "She was reading Polonetheus's commentary."

"Oh. Surely not conclusive?"

"Polonetheus is Nottley's interest! She betrays me even in her reading material!"

Judith examined the floral pattern on the bedspread, and wondered how to proceed.

"Lord John," she said carefully. "Mr Nottley was, er, not having an affair with Mary."

"How do you know?" A tentative hope infused his voice.

Judith hesitated. "Because Nottley is having an affair with someone else."

Lord John's eyes bulged. "With you?"

"No! Another female currently living in this house."

"Good God. Miss Atkinson?" He frowned. "I knew that woman had no taste. She's not fit to watch my children. She is probably instructing them on Polonetheus herself."

"Not Miss Atkinson," said Judith patiently.

Lord John stared and finally appeared to reach the right conclusion, his eyes widening in shock. "Mrs Bunn?"

"No!" Judith huffed in exasperation. "Your sister, Lady Agatha. I saw them myself, and she confirmed it. So you may renounce your suspicions of Mary."

"But I've seen Mary! I've seen her disappearing into the woods and Nottley following."

"Perhaps Agatha then followed Nottley," said Judith. "Maybe Mary was simply going for a walk." Even as she said it, she felt a flash of doubt. What had Mary been doing? Had she been pursuing another affair, maybe with the dead Gilbert? Judith remembered, suddenly, that Mary had lied at the lunch table that morning when she claimed she was going to rest in her room. What need did she have of lying, if she was innocent?

"You mean Aggie and Nottley...." Lord John seemed lost for words. He turned to look at Mary. "My poor darling Mary, to be so maligned. Will you ever forgive me?"

Seeing he was possibly going to shower kisses on the duke's face, Judith interposed herself by tucking the blankets carefully over Dacian's shoulders, being careful not to touch the Illusion of Mary's visage or, heaven forbid, destroy the duke's bosom. "Now, Lord John, if you wish to make amends, you should let your wife rest. She needs time to recover." John was still staring at Mary, so she added, "A silent sickroom is what she needs right now."

John drew back, his white face flushing. "Yes, yes. Of course." He gave a last convulsive clutch at the hand under the blanket, then stood. "Please send for me if there is any change. Has a doctor seen her? Her head looks rather swollen."

Judith cleared her throat. "Yes," she said, for if the doctor had not yet seen Mary, he would soon be shown via the back entrance to the Gold Room. "He advises rest. I will watch over her."

"Thank you," said Lord John. He seemed to realise suddenly

that he was clad only in silk, and tightened his belt as he backed away. "Thank you, Lady Avely." He cast a look round the room and nodded with approval at *The Extensive and Detailed Biography of Constantine the Great,* and gathered his composure. "I will return in the morning with some other suitable books to cheer my wife's spirits. Poor dear, loyal Mary. Some Ovid, perhaps, for some light reading."

He sent one more longing glance at the figure on the bed, then let himself out.

The door clicked shut behind him.

Marigold slipped out from her hiding place, grinning, but with a finger to her lips. After a long tense moment, she dropped it.

The Illusion of Mary slipped away and Dacian heaved a huge sigh. "The devil take it. That was dreadful."

"He almost kissed you." Judith couldn't help smiling in the alleviation of tension. "What a shock that would have given him."

"Poor fellow," said Dacian. "He seems to have his cravat in a tangle."

Wooten stuck his head out from under the bed. "Don't joke. That dressing gown was bad enough."

"You don't want one, Wooten?" asked Marigold. "I quite liked it."

"Of course you did," said Wooten.

Judith drew in a breath. "At least that explains why I saw John questioning the inn-keeper. And all his suspicions about Mary mean that he didn't kill Gilbert himself." She gave a sigh of relief. "I had feared that John did it, mistaking Gilbert for Lewis in the dark."

"I should hope not," said Dacian. "John is addle-pated, but he is not completely incompetent."

Judith looked round thoughtfully. "I can't help but think that perhaps Mary *was* up to something; that Lord John was right to be suspicious." She wondered over to the dressing table and opened the drawers. It was terribly distasteful to rifle through the injured woman's belongings, but Judith was curious. She had a feeling she was missing something. Had Nottley tried to point the finger at Mary, after all? But then why would Mary be pushed down the stairs?

She moved the mirror to look behind it and even bent to look beneath the table. As she put the mirror back in place, she lifted it slightly, revealing a gap between the mirror and the desk. Neatly slotted into this hiding place were two books.

"*A Sicilian Romance*," Judith read out the spines with surprise. "And *The Old English Baron*, by Clara Reeves. My goodness, it seems Mary doesn't just enjoy Ovid." She looked up. "Do you think *this* is what she has been hiding: a penchant for gothic novels? Maybe that is why she was disappearing into the woods."

"Is that a Radcliffe novel?" asked Dacian, his head popping up again, comical under the purple mobcap. "Then yes, she would keep it discreet. John despises Radcliffe. Far too lightweight to kill anyone."

"John thinks that Agatha reads them." Judith carefully returned the books to their hiding place. She felt relieved to have Mary's secret turn out to be so innocuous. Then she paused, her hand resting on *A Sicilian Romance*. "Could Mary be the source of our apparitions then? She most certainly would have perused *The Castle of Otranto*."

The duke shook his head, ribbons bobbing. "She wouldn't risk such foolery. If she's reading those novels, she is trying to hide her interest, not flaunt it."

"Hmm," said Judith. "Sometimes if you squash something out of sight, it can burst forth unbidden."

Dacian raised his eyebrows at her, and she blushed.

She straightened the mirror, covering the books, and wandered over to the window. The thick blue curtain was heavy in her hand as she parted it. Grey streaming clouds rent the dark sky, lit only by a waxing silver moon.

Being on the third floor of the house, Mary's window had a good view of the back gardens. Judith stared down. Had Mary stood by the window sill earlier this morning? Had she seen Judith following Agatha to the cemetery?

Judith cringed. What must Mary have thought, if she had seen Judith creeping after Agatha like a thief? And had she known of Agatha's assignations?

Robert cracked the cupboard door open. "Can I come out again?"

She sighed. "Very well. I don't think we will have anyone else visit for a while. That corridor is a veritable highway. Any villain will wait for the household to settle back into sleep."

Robert stepped out, cricked his neck and grinned. "Lord John didn't spot the difference. I'm starting to think I'm quite good at this."

Dacian frowned reprovingly. "You are starting to be quite Bemused."

"Yes, your grace." Robert wiped the smile off his face.

"I think you're doing a wonderful job," chirped Marigold. "The duke is garnering quite a few gentlemen admirers tonight."

Dacian scowled, but his attempt to be quelling was mitigated by the purple silk ribbons hanging round his face. Judith smiled reluctantly.

Wooten emerged from under the bed, peering down at his immaculate clothes. "I think there is *dust* on me."

Robert bent down to examine Wooten. "No, but I can see a cobweb."

"Where?" The vampiri twisted around frantically.

Robert chuckled. "Just pulling your leg, little fellow."

Judith smiled at Robert, seeing a trace of Nicholas's light spirits. Wooten, on the other hand, was not impressed. "Do *not* call me that."

Robert looked abashed. "My apologies, your gracel."

Wooten brushed an invisible speck of dust from his arm and stalked over to Marigold. "Miss Cultor, I think we should swap places for a while."

The two vampiri began bickering over this, while Robert retreated to the far corner to undertake a series of stretches against the wall.

Dacian twitched restlessly in the bed, moving his broad shoulders. It had the effect of quivering his bosom. Judith remained seated beside him, trying to maintain her countenance. She was starting to feel rather ... tipsy. She certainly ought not to stare at the duke's shoulders and remember how hard his chest was, or wonder what it would be like to lay her head on that shoulder. They had a murderer to catch, for goodness sake.

Besides, Dacian was an inconstant, lustful man. *That* had been established long ago. She was not one more widow for him to seduce....

Dacian pulled his hands out from under the blanket. She admired the strength in them, then tutted to herself. What was strength, or beauty, if one didn't know how to temper it?

He spoke quietly. "Please, won't you go, Judith?"

She shook her head. "Tomorrow, maybe. Once we've sorted this tangle out."

"That's not what I meant!" He frowned at her. "Don't leave tomorrow, I beg you. You've only just arrived."

"Fickle man." She raised a brow.

"At least you are not wearing a mobcap now." He cast a glance at Robert and lowered his voice. "All that remains is to rid you of that ridiculous matronly gown."

Judith's glare became icy. "Your grace, you must learn to

restrain your penchant for widows. Not that you ever have before."

Dacian's jaw hardened. "Unduly harsh, my dear."

"Not *unduly*."

"Perhaps you don't know everything, Judith, as much as you like to think so."

"I know enough," she said coldly. "I know that you will indulge your pleasures, regardless of the hurt to others." She glanced over to see that Robert was crouched down next to Marigold and Wooten, the three of them talking quietly, studiously ignoring her conversation with the duke.

Dacian's jaw worked. After a long pause, he spoke again. "There's something you should know, marchioness, from the last time you visited Sargenet."

She narrowed her eyes. "I don't wish to know any further details from that night."

He paused uncomfortably. "I am referring to Mrs Bleau's visit."

Judith gave him a repelling look. "So am I." She pulled her dignity round her, her mind suddenly sharp, her voice low and cross. "Whatever you did with Mrs Bleau, I want no part of it."

He winced and spoke quietly. "That's what I need to tell you, Judith. *I didn't do anything*."

She stared, uncomprehending. "What do you mean?"

"I didn't invite Mrs Bleau over that night. She invited herself."

"Oh, *really*?"

Dacian shifted on the bed. "Yes, really. Fitzroy let her in, because at one point we'd had that sort of arrangement."

"At one point," repeated Judith.

"Yes, but not at *that* point," said Dacian. "I was surprised to see her. I was drunk, I admit, and heartsore." He paused and took a deep breath. "I told her to leave but she didn't listen. She stayed in my bedchamber, trying to offer me some sort of consolation, but I refused. Then I heard you banging on the door below."

Judith frowned. "But she was in your bedchamber."

"Yes, in my bedchamber. Not in my bed."

She felt as if the room was spinning, as if she were in some odd sort of dream. The memories of the past returned and twisted into a new shape.

She latched onto the point that swam into clarity. "You *lied* to me."

"I didn't lie!" said Dacian. "I told you the truth. I told you she was in my bedchamber."

Judith's cheeks grew hot. "You misrepresented the truth! You lied to me, a Truth Discernor!"

Her voice had become loud. The others turned to look at them, Robert's ears red with embarrassment, Miss Cultor's face open with curiosity.

Dacian sat up in the bed, abandoning discretion and his bosoms. "I told you only the truth. You were the one who jumped to conclusions. *You* were the one who twisted it."

"What else was I supposed to believe?" she hissed. "That you were just having a little ... chat? In fact, I *still* don't believe it."

She did, though. She could hear the truth in his voice. It made her want to cry. How could he have lied to her about something so important?

What could have been different if she'd known the truth of that night? *Everything.* Everything could have been different.

"I thought it was for the best," he said. "I thought you belonged to Nicholas. I was giving you a way out."

"How *dare* you," she uttered. "How dare you say who I belonged to?"

In which there are tears of blood

Even those who appear to be the most innocent are capable of deceit.
  - from Lady Avely's Guide to Truth and Magic

THEY STARED AT EACH OTHER, both flushed and angry. Dacian's hand reached toward her. "Judith."

She ignored it. Her head was pounding. Tears threatened in her eyes.

"Um," said Marigold nervously. "I think I hear steps. Moving fast. On the stairs."

Judith struggled to compose herself, looking down and blinking furiously to keep her hot tears at bay. Robert leapt into the cupboard and Wooten vanished under the bed. Dacian slid back under the blankets, hiding his hands again, his expression wretched but soon overlaid.

Mary's face was slightly wonky.

Shakily, Judith adjusted the mobcap so that it hid the misalignment. Her fingers brushed Dacian's thick hair, and her head and heart ached. However, even she could hear the footsteps now. They were moving quickly along the corridor, thudding. Whoever this was had abandoned secrecy for speed.

The door flung open, hitting the wall with a bang.

Otho stood there, his blonde curls disheveled. His face was pale and his arm tightly wrapped in a bandage.

"Mother!" he wailed, and threw himself on the bed.

Judith stared in consternation at the young boy, all other thoughts pushed aside. Tears streamed down his face, and he clutched the figure on the bed with his free arm.

"Mother? Is she dead? She can't be dead!"

Before Judith could answer, something else caught her attention. Above the bedhead, the wall began to weep blood. Bright red trickles etched their way down the wallpaper: tears of lurid treacle, garish in the civilised femininity of Mary's room.

Judith looked sharply at Otho. "No, your mother is not dead. Calm yourself, Otho."

She went to the door, shut it, and turned back to the tableau. Otho gave a lurching sob and the blood on the wall thickened, threatening to pool on the bedhead.

"I heard Miss Atkinson talking to the maid," he wailed. "She said mother fell down the stairs. She looks dead."

"Well, she's not. Mary had a little tumble but she is still alive. You need not worry."

Otho sniffed and blinked back tears. "Truly?"

Still the wall wept ugly blood.

Judith returned to her seat. "Yes, truly. Your mother is just resting. Weren't you given a few drops of laudanum in your milk, too?"

"I pretended to drink it," confessed Otho, wiping his cheek. "I poured most of the foul stuff into the potted fern."

"Wouldn't Miss Atkinson notice? Or did you Illuse the cup so it appeared empty?"

Otho's eyes darted to Judith's face. "What?"

She raised her brows skeptically. "Can you cast Illusions, Otho?"

He shifted, holding his sprained arm as if suddenly aware how much it hurt. "No?"

This was a lie, the first she had heard with absolute certainty in this room. But she did not bother to curl her hands into fists. This lie came from a child, who would never have pushed his mother down the stairs, let alone killed Gilbert.

"You have a Gift," she said. "It is showing itself on the wall. Please desist, for I find it most disconcerting."

Otho glanced at the wall and flushed. Without a sound, the creeping blood vanished as if it had never been.

"Thank you," said Judith calmly. "I suppose you made the skull and the mouse in the woods. I can see a similar artistic flair at work."

The boy sniffed. "I made the skull. I was only trying to fetch some help. I thought if I floated Manfred up, someone would notice and investigate. But I never did a mouse."

"Manfred?" Judith was momentarily distracted.

"That's what I call him."

"You dreadful boy. From *The Castle of Otranto*? Did you despoil the books in the library too?"

Otho nodded sullenly. "I'm so sick of Mother and Father's boring books on Ancient Rome. And I don't like the way they treat Mr Lewis. He deserves better. I know the truth about him. He is my brother and he should be part of the family. He's like Theodore in *The Castle of Otranto*."

Judith felt her heart fracture a little. This boy was more open in his affection than Mary, John, or even herself. He knew how to welcome an outsider and extend the generosity of love.

She sighed. "*Otranto* is scarcely suitable for a child of ... how old are you? I thought you were only seven."

"I am eight and a half," said Otho sulkily.

"That is early for the Gift to show," muttered Judith. She was peeved with herself. Why hadn't she thought of Otho as the culprit? It was because he was so small, his blonde curls so charming, and his face so sweet. Dastardly little squirrel.

Then she frowned. "The bloody mouse, with its neck broken? You didn't do it?"

Otho shook his head. "Must have been a real one you saw."

Her frown deepened. Otho's words rang true, yet she had seen the creature vanish before her eyes. "And the skull in the drawing room? Was that you?"

"Oh yes, I sneaked down after Attikins put us to bed. Wish I could have seen everyone's faces," he said proudly. "It's better to have an audience. No one sees it in the ballroom except the bats."

Judith realised that the nursery in the west wing must *also* connect to the upper ballroom gallery. It would be a simple matter for the boy to slip away and find a hiding spot in one of the alcoves to practice his newly blossoming skill.

She sighed. "You should be in bed, you scamp."

"Yes, my lady," said Otho cheerfully. "So, will Mother be better by tomorrow? She doesn't look very good."

He stood up and peered at Mary's face. Then, before Judith could even think to stop him, he leaned forward. With his free hand, he brushed a ribbon from the deathly white cheek.

The Illusion crumbled at his touch. Under the fading wisps, the furious scowl of the duke was revealed.

Otho shrieked.

"You little monkey!" said Dacian. "*You* made the phantoms?"

Otho backed away, his eyes wide. "Uncle Dacian!"

"Little *mongrel*." Dacian sat abruptly, letting blankets fall. He maintained the attack, but Judith was relieved to see he wasn't actually employing any Impact. "Do you know the trouble you've caused with your tricks? Why didn't you tell me?"

Otho ignored the questions, frowning. "Why are you

pretending to be Mother? Where is she? What have you done with her?"

Judith spoke soothingly. "Your mother is safe in the west wing, tended to by a doctor. She will be fine, I hope."

"So why is Uncle Dacian here?" Otho glanced around. "And who cast the Illusion? Was it you, Lady Avely?"

Judith hesitated. "Er, yes."

Otho gave her a measuring look. "Mother's face was a little wonky. And it was a bit too waxen. I *thought* something was wrong."

A huff came from the cupboard.

"Yes, well, *your* skulls are too luminous," she retorted. "And you need to go back to bed, young man."

The boy sniffed. He still looked pale and he was holding his arm with his other hand. "You promise Mother is safe?"

"Yes," said Dacian. "But you can't tell anyone about this, understand? Just go quietly back to bed. Don't stop to speak to anyone."

Otho's forehead creased under his curls. "I don't understand."

"You don't need to understand." Dacian's voice grew sharp. "You just need to return to your room."

Judith sighed. "You are fond of issuing that instruction, your grace. However, you are right in this instance." She glared at him, suddenly remembering what he had confessed earlier. She needed time away from his presence; time to think, and for her head to stop aching. Perhaps she *should* retreat to the Gold Room. "Otho, I will escort you back. We can see if your mother has recovered her wits yet."

She stood, smoothing her skirts.

"Thank God," said Dacian devoutly.

Belated comprehension dawned on Otho's face. "You think someone pushed Mother!"

"Well, yes," admitted Dacian. "And I am lying in wait for whoever did it. *You* are getting in the way."

Otho stood straighter and nodded, determination pinching his lips.

Judith pointedly turned her back on Dacian, taking Otho's arm. However, before she could take another step, a knock came at the door.

Otho's eyes widened in fear. Everyone swivelled their heads to the door in surprise. Judith saw that Marigold was peering with a desperate expression from under her sewing basket: Otho's presence meant that she had been unable to warn them of the approach.

Judith glanced at the cupboard and the bed. Dacian was quickly settling back into his blankets. She could not escape this room just yet; there was one more visitor.

"Your bosoms!" she hissed at Dacian.

Dacian gave her a wry look and adjusted his padding.

Robert, having heard the knock, conjured the mask of Mary's face again. Otho, his eyes darting around, winced and stood closer. Mary's face suddenly became more life-like, if a bit younger in appearance.

Then Otho slid underneath the bed.

Frowning, Judith allowed it. Once the duke appeared to be a lovely corpse again (albeit with a large head), she went over to the door and opened it.

On the other side was Miss Atkinson, still in her mauve gown. Judith sighed. Would every single member of the household visit Mary's room tonight? Meanwhile her whole life had been turned upside down by two sentences from the duke, and she still had to deal with a murderer on the loose.

The governess's hands were clasped nervously and she peered into the room over Judith's shoulder.

Judith blocked her view callously. "Good evening, Miss Atkinson."

"Lady Avely." Miss Atkinson bobbed a perfunctory curtsy, looking flustered. "Have you seen Otho? He is missing from his bed. I thought he might have found his way here."

Judith stepped aside, lying easily. "No, I haven't seen him."

The room was still and empty except for the funereal figure on the bed. Miss Atkinson drew closer, her cheeks pink. "Oh Mary! So beautiful in death." She stood at the foot of the bed. "I feel terribly guilty."

Judith followed. "Why is that, Miss Atkinson?"

The governess turned sombrely. "Lady Avely, there is something you must know."

"Oh?"

"You are a Discernor, are you not? I saw your lapis lazuli pendant earlier."

Judith winced internally. "Indeed."

"You asked me about the apparitions." She paused, her face serious. "I feel I must tell you that Otho is the cause of them."

"Really?" Judith widened her eyes. Otho gasped with betrayal from under the bed - or perhaps he had just made the acquaintance of Wooten. Either way, Judith hoped that Miss Atkinson mistook the gasp for her own. She parted her lips in astonishment and sat down on her chair with a plop. "Otho?"

Miss Atkinson gripped the bedpost with one gloved hand and nodded. "He has the Gift of Illusion. It has shown early in him. I was going to tell Mary today - but I did not want to get him into trouble, especially when he has just hurt himself. Now I fear that he caused Mary's fall."

The governess's words fell clear and unencumbered. Carefully, Judith laid her hands flat, signalling to Dacian that there was no lie. The last thing they needed was for the duke to leap up and fling his power at Miss Atkinson.

"How so?" Judith asked, raising her brows.

"If Otho was running wild in the house, casting his awful images, it may have startled her and caused her to fall." Miss Atkinson gulped. "Oh, it would be terribly tragic, if he caused his own mother's death."

"Surely not," said Judith. She was listening carefully, relieved to hear Miss Atkinson's words still rang true. Miss Atkinson, at least, had not pushed Mary. One less suspect to worry about.

The governess continued. "I feel responsible. If I had only kept a closer eye on him tonight. I thought the laudanum would settle him! Yet he has vanished again. I feel so dreadful." She turned her gaze upon Mary's pallid face. "I promise to do better, dear Mary. And please forgive your own son, if he did this to you."

This was clearly too much for Otho, for he stuck his head out underneath Miss Atkinson's feet and said, "Atty! How dare you!"

Miss Atkinson screamed and fell back. "Otho!" She put a hand to her heart.

"You traitorous snake!" Otho scrambled out from under the bed, clutching his sore arm and looking very pale. "How can you say I caused Mother to die? I never did any Illusions tonight, I promise! Or at least, not until a moment ago. Not in front of Mother!"

Miss Atkinson blinked. "You didn't?"

"No! I would never frighten Mother on the stairs!"

"Just scare everyone else," snapped Miss Atkinson, with a return of her earlier spirit. "What are you doing here, you rascal?"

"Oh dear," said Judith, belatedly feigning surprise. "Yes, Otho, how did you get here?"

Otho bowed his head. "I came to see Mother." Tears began leaking down his cheek. Fortunately, they were not of blood, though Judith was fairly certain they were magically wrought. This boy would be an absolute terror to manage. She felt a flash of sympathy for Miss Atkinson.

Or perhaps they were tears of pain. Otho's arm must be very sore. Judith felt her heart contract again. "Dear boy, I am so sorry. Give your mother one last hug and then off you go to bed. Miss Atkinson, if you would be so good as to escort him back. We can discuss the other matter in the morning. Now is not the time."

Miss Atkinson nodded briskly. "Yes, of course. Come, Otho."

Otho threw himself on the bed, sobbed noisily, then allowed himself to be led from the room, shoulders hunched. Yet at the door he turned to look at Judith, and winked, a glint in his eye.

"Good night, Otho," said Judith firmly. "Thank you, Miss Atkinson."

She shut the door behind them and stood for a moment, listening. She could hear footsteps receding, Otho's young voice objecting about something, then fading away.

In the bedroom, Mary's face became less convincing, then fell away altogether.

After a long stretch of silence, Marigold emerged from behind her basket and nodded. Judith sighed and returned wearily to her seat. Now she didn't have an excuse to leave with Otho. She avoided Dacian's eyes, her wretched feelings returning once more, sweeping over her as she remembered what he had said.

Her whole life had been predicated on lies. Her choices had not been made while in full possession of the facts. Yet her path had given her her daughter and son - dear Elinor and Peregrine - and she could not bring herself to regret them, even as she mourned the life she might have had at Dacian's side.

Her chin sunk to her chest, and angry tears sprang into her eyes again. Fortunately, Wooten provided a distraction.

The vampiri emerged from under the bed, with his cravat in perfect order. "Now I *am* dusty. The little brat squished me against the floor."

"Oh, stop your whinging." Marigold stood with her hands on her hips. "It was Otho all along! A mere boy!"

"With vulgar tastes in reading," added Wooten.

Dacian grimaced. "He is lucky I didn't throttle him. However, it still leaves much unexplained. What was that about a mouse, Judith?"

Judith blinked away her tears. "Oh that," she said blankly. "I saw a mouse in the woods, in the middle of the path, with its neck broken. And one in the library."

"The library! How do you know they were Illusions?"

Judith sniffed. "I touched them and they disappeared."

"Dreadful," shuddered Wooten.

Dacian frowned. "Yet Otho denied the mouse. Truthfully?"

"Yes," admitted Judith. "So it seems we have two Illusors."

"That complicates things," Wooten began strutting to and fro along the carpet, his hands behind his back. "The murderer could have imitated Otho's tricks, to murky the water."

"Or maybe it was a thief, after all." Marigold came forward. "Maybe we were misled by the apparitions to think it was anything more. Perhaps Mary simply fell on the stairs."

"What of the vases?" Dacian was still frowning. "A thief wouldn't have left them in the well."

"The vases are crucial, somehow," allowed Judith, glad that they were able to talk rationally together. "It was only after they were discovered that Mary was pushed."

"Do you think Mary knew something about them?" asked Marigold. "Perhaps when she saw them, she realised something important."

"Mm," agreed Judith. "But what?"

Her mind was woozy from the effort of Discerning all evening and her emotions rent by the recent turbulence. Her capacity to reason logically was impaired. It felt as if the pieces of the puzzle were all before her, yet she couldn't see how they fit together. She was looking through a glass darkly; she must put away childish things, and see the view unobscured....

She frowned. Childish things. The unobscured view.

In the silence, she stood and made her way to the window. Pulling the heavy fabric aside, she looked down again over the grounds, to the rose arbour, the apple trees, and the pond.

Previously, she had been worried that if Mary had stood in this spot, she may have witnessed Judith trailing Agatha through the apple trees. Yet the view by the window also revealed something else.

The rose arbour, in autumn, was still awash with flowers: an abundance of pink, white, and red. In winter, however, the roses would be pruned and the leaves grown sparse. Mary, standing here, would have had an unobstructed view of her son's mortification on that winter day, so long ago.

Judith peered down, imagining the scene. Felix sparring up to Lewis, jeering arrogantly. Lewis throwing juvenile punches that nonetheless packed a formidable power. Lewis pummelling Felix to the ground.

Felix helpless, hurt, frightened.

What would a mother feel, watching that? Especially a mother who already resented and feared the presence of an illegitimate son. A mother who couldn't bear to see the evidence of Lord John's unfaithfulness, let alone have that same bastard boy attack her firstborn with effortless violence.

It had been Mary who pushed Lewis into the well. Judith was suddenly certain of it. Mr Nottley had hinted as much, when he referred to 'divine retribution'. Mary had seen her son's apparent victimisation and she had retaliated. Perhaps only on the spur of the moment, when she was walking in the woods, and saw Lewis sitting there so carelessly. Or perhaps she knew that he made a habit of perching dangerously above the dark drop.

She had pushed him in. Maybe she had even hoped that Lewis would die or be maimed.

Judith stiffened, her hand tightening on the fabric. She let it fall, turning abruptly.

"Mary," she said. "Mary is with Lewis."

Dacian peered from under his mobcap. "What do you mean?"

"I must see Mary."

"As I've been saying!"

Judith was already moving. She had no time to explain. Her stupidity had left Lewis alone with the very person who wished him harm. Had Mary been the one who had killed Gilbert, mistaking him for Lewis?

Judith grabbed the brass candlestick and ran out the door.

In which there is terrible guilt

Lies are usually told to advance selfish interests: pride, greed, envy, lust, vanity, laziness, and resentment. Sometimes they are told to protect another.

- from *Lady Avely's Guide to Truth and Magic*

THE EAST WING corridor was dark, the shadows dancing eerily in her lone candlelight. She had to slow her steps so that it would not blow out. The carpet muffled any footfalls, her feet cold in her slippers.

She tried to walk evenly, though she felt dizzy from Bemusement. She kept the important thing at the forefront of her mind: to reach Lewis before Mary regained consciousness.

Opening the door into the upper gallery of the ballroom, she stepped through. A sense of black space loomed, and she thrust the candle forward, her fingers clenched tightly around the brass holder. *Please let me be wrong.* All too vividly she could imagine Mary rising from the dead, while Lewis nodded off at his post.

Would Mary, stupefied and groggy with pain, take the opportunity that presented itself?

Judith made her way across the gallery, skin prickling as if someone was watching. Perhaps it was just the faces in the portraits, their eyes tracking her progress. Reflexively, she glanced across at the chandelier to look for a skull, even though she knew Otho was in bed now. The hanging crystals caught the reflected candlelight, unmoving above the dark pit of the dance floor.

No skull. At least Manfred was asleep.

Her eyes adjusted to the gloom, but she heard the click of the door opening before she saw it.

At the end of the gallery, the door swung open from the west wing.

Mary stood there like a ghost in the dim light. Her blonde hair was loose around her shoulders and she did not carry a candle. The pale blue sarcenet made a pallid shroud in the doorway.

Judith froze, tempted to blow out her own light. It was too late. Mary had seen her.

"Miss Atkinson? Is that you?" Mary's voice was fretful. She took a step into the gallery, hesitant, her face as pale as the false corpse that lay in the other room.

Judith cleared her throat. Gathering her courage, she strode forward. "No. It is I, Lady Avely. Where is Mr Lewis?"

Mary shivered, her eyes two sunken pools. "You mean the steward?"

"Yes."

"Why do you care?" Mary's hair was a mess, her feet bare, her hands clenched in her blue skirts.

"Just tell me." Judith raised the candle in a threatening manner, coming to stand a few feet away. "Did you hurt him?"

"Hurt him?" A sneer distorted Mary's face. "Of course I did not hurt him, that *furcifer*. Why would you say that?"

The lie was faint, confusing. Judith tried not to be distracted by Mary's use of Latin insults and to parse the truth. "I mean tonight, Lady Mary. I don't care what you did in the past, as long as he lives now."

"Do you take me for a fool?" She took a step forward. "He is fine. He has gone to escort the doctor out."

Judith sagged with relief at the truth in her voice. She lowered the candle slightly. The two women stared at one another.

"Who put me in the Gold Room?" Mary demanded peevishly.

"The duke. We wanted to keep you safe. Mr Lewis was watching over you. You should be grateful to him."

Mary's face contorted again. "I don't want that boy anywhere near me."

Judith felt a flash of terrible guilt that she had once felt the same thing about Robert. "He means you no harm. It is not his fault he was born."

"You seem to know rather a lot about it." Mary's lips were pinched. She walked forward, forcing Judith backwards. "What do you mean, what I did in the past? Has Nottley told you something?"

Judith swallowed. "Nottley? Ah, no. Not directly. What would Nottley know about it?"

"Nothing," said Mary quickly.

It was a lie. In the shifting darkness, the truth came to Judith. Nottley had seen Mary push Lewis into the well. He had tried to indicate Mary's guilt, but in doing so he had also revealed his own knowledge of it.

"Has he been blackmailing you?" Judith asked slowly.

"What? No!" said Mary, and it was another lie. She loomed in front of Judith, her face grim. "You go too far, Lady Avely."

Judith felt as if they were on a stage, two figures lit by the pool of candlelight, the vast pit of the audience below them. Except that there was no one in the ballroom to hear this confession except her, and only she knew the lies for what they were.

She took courage from the fact that there were no handy books for Mary to wield, and examined the bitter face close to her own. The final pieces were slipping into place.

"Is that why you met Nottley in the woods or at the inn? So you could pay him?" No doubt they shared a hiding place in the well, to conceal the payments she made.

Mary's eyes darted wildly to the gallery behind Judith. "I didn't meet Nottley in the woods."

Another lie.

"My mistake," said Judith carefully. "I thought, perhaps, that both of you knew the secret ledge in the well." She paused. "Nottley knew of it, didn't he?"

"No," said Mary. "Nottley never left anything in the well. I don't know what you are talking about."

Her words were coated with tin.

Nottley had left the vases in the well. Judith was sure of it, hearing the flat tremor in Mary's voice.

She lifted the candle high again, peering into the white face. "Why are you trying to protect him? He pushed you down the stairs, didn't he? He knew you had guessed the truth about Gilbert. You must put a stop to this now, Mary. Tell me the truth."

"Don't talk nonsense." Mary's voice was low, her hands clenching convulsively.

"It's not nonsense." Judith was certain she was right, despite the woolly edges of her mind. "Nottley killed Gilbert, didn't he? The footman must have figured out his little blackmail scheme and threatened to tell Agatha. So Nottley killed him with his book." She shook her head. "Tsk, tsk. Now Agatha will most certainly deny his suit."

Mary winced, cowering away, lowering her gaze as if Judith's words were a threat.

Judith stared, confused. Then a new voice came from behind her.

"On the contrary," said Mr Nottley's suave tones. "I think you are unduly pessimistic about my prospects, Lady Avely."

Judith swung around. The candle spluttered wildly, showing Mr Nottley standing a few yards away.

He was still clad in his evening waistcoat, the silver stripes gleaming. His right hand was aloft, his fist gripping the handle of the letter-opener from the study. The long, thin knife glinted.

He crept up on me, Judith thought distantly. *Marigold is never going to let me forget it.*

"Mary, off you go," he said. "I will see to this ... situation."

Behind Judith, Mary swallowed audibly. Then came the rapid thud of her footsteps as she retreated to the west wing. The door banged shut.

Judith was alone in the gallery with a killer.

She backed away slowly, her eyes fixed on the sharp blade.

Nottley advanced toward her. "You seem to know rather a lot, Lady Avely. How is it that you guessed so much?"

He must have heard everything, she realised, hiding in one of the alcoves. His eyes were narrowed on her in speculation, his lips pursed in his beard. The hand that held the letter-opener did not waver.

She weighed up her choices. Then she turned and ran.

He was prepared for it. Worse, her reflexes were slow from bemusement. Like a snake, he sprung forward and grabbed her, his left hand wrenching her arm backwards and seizing her close.

Cold steel pressed against her throat.

"Not so quick," he murmured in her ear.

The sudden gust of movement guttered the candle, leaving them in pitch black. Judith felt hot wax dripping onto her wrist. She hefted the weight of the candlestick in her hand, wondering if she could swing it at his head, if she dared risk it. Nottley's fingers dug into her shoulder, his arm across her chest, the blade sharp at her neck.

"Let me go," she said. "I won't tell anyone, I swear." The lie was patently false to her own ears.

"If I let you go," he hissed, "it will be as you topple over the railing. An unfortunate accident to have in the dark, marchioness."

He jerked Judith round so they both faced the direction of the railing that ran along the edge of the gallery. She shuddered, remembering the black pit before them, and the polished floor three stories down.

"Walk," said Nottley. "Forward."

He pushed her a step, feeling his way in the dark.

Judith tried to gather her thoughts, her pulse beating in her ears. Her effort was not helped by the fact that she could not see anything and her arm was burning with pain. Dared she risk applying the candlestick? The likelihood was that even as she swung it, Nottley would stab her in the throat with that sharp little blade.

Despair threatened to overcome her. Would someone come by and help? The house now seemed fatally quiet. Was Dacian still in bed, pretending to be dead? Damn useless duke.

At that moment, Judith felt a faint brush of air against her cheek.

It felt like a door opening nearby. Or, perhaps, the movement of bat wings.

She straightened, pushing against Nottley's forward motion. She had to gain time, and keep him from throwing her over the railing.

"What about Mary?" she asked. "You can't kill us both."

"Can't I?" Nottley chuckled, a grating sound. "Mary will keep her silence. She cannot expose me without exposing herself."

"Mutual blackmail," acknowledged Judith. She dug her heels in, straining against their inexorable progress. Nottley merely changed his tactic and shifted his weight so he could pull her instead.

"The book," she said, casting around for something else to distract him. "Why Constantine? Please satisfy my curiosity on that matter, at least."

As she had hoped, Nottley stopped. He gave a snort of amusement. "Ah, that was a ploy to divert you. I needed to shift the attention away from Polonetheus, seeing as the Odyssey is my particular interest. Who better to represent the Romans than Constantine, that old terror? I thought you might suspect Lord John with Constantine in play."

Judith was reluctant to admit this had worked, but she did so anyway, hoping to keep Nottley talking. "Very clever."

Nottley sighed. "All sorts of stratagems are required to make a good marriage these days. You must know that yourself, Lady Avely. Don't you have a son and daughter of marriageable ages? So difficult to find a match of wealth and breeding. You can forgive me for resorting to some subterfuge."

"I can see why you want to marry Agatha," said Judith placatingly. "It will connect you to the ducal line."

"Agatha is just a woman," sneered Nottley, pulling forward again. "She'd be lucky to marry me rather than be a spinster, for all that she thinks so highly of herself. Come now," he added. "The railing is here. Not long now before you plunge to your death."

She pulled against him but Nottley was stronger and imbued with ruthless determination. He wrenched her forward and the hard banister dug into her stomach. She froze, unwilling to struggle now, hoping that Nottley would lose his nerve. The steep drop echoed before her. Her eyes were stretched wide and she could see the glint of the chandelier in the gloom.

Strange, for one needed light to see and the candle had long blown out. It seemed that a new light now waveringly lit the vast space.

She turned her head, searching for the source.

In which there is a distorted embrace

DACIAN'S tall figure stood in the doorway of the east wing, his dark coat open, his throat bare. He held a three-pronged candelabra in his left hand. It threw a glow over the purple mobcap that still adorned his head.

His voice thundered across the ballroom. "Stop! Let her go, Nottley, or you die."

Nottley shifted away from the railing so he could see. He kept Judith tightly wedged against him, so she was jammed between him and the railing. Cold, thin metal still pressed against her neck.

"Your grace," said Nottley. "Nice cap."

"Let her go." Dacian ground the words out. He raised his right hand, with his fingers spread. It looked like a supplication, but Judith knew it was a threat.

Nottley seemed to know it too. He was stiff beside her, taut as a bowstring about to snap. She could smell the stench of his sweat and anger.

"As you see, I have this implement across Lady Avely's throat, your grace. If you fling your power at me, I cannot say how it might go for her."

Nottley tightened the hold at her neck. She expected to feel a sting and hot drip of blood, but she was only suffocated. The nightmarish grip on her made her limbs leaden with fear.

Dacian took in the glint of the sharp blade. His hand lowered slightly, his face like stone. Like Judith, he must realise that the letter-opener was enough to slice her open. Even if his Impact pushed Nottley away, the knife could tear into her throat.

The candlestick hung uselessly by her side, tempting her to use it, even though her arm was wedged against the railing.

"An impasse," said Nottley pleasantly. "You want to kill me and I want to kill her. What shall we do, I wonder?"

"Let her go," said Dacian, "and we will let you go. Come, Nottley, you have no choice. If you throw her over the railing, you will lose your bargaining chip. I can give you my word of honour that if Lady Avely is returned safely, I will let you leave Sargenet unharmed."

Judith did not move a muscle, hearing the lie in Dacian's words.

Nottley snorted. "And then what? You will send your hounds after me. I am not one to be fooled by a double-edged promise, duke." He paused. "However, your suggestion has merit. Perhaps I will return your marchioness - once I am safe."

"You will return her now."

"No, you are right in that she is my bargaining chip. Perhaps she is worth more." Nottley shifted his grip on Judith. "How about this, your grace: you call up a post chaise for me and I will take Lady Avely away with me. When I reach Exeter I will leave her there for your convenience, once I've boarded a ship leaving England."

Judith heard the lie in Nottley's voice. She fixed her eyes on Dacian, widening them meaningfully. He glowered back, impassive. Then she remembered the hand signals they had agreed on.

She dropped the candlestick. It landed with a thud on the thick carpet.

Nottley gave a small jerk, but fortunately he did not cut her neck open. Judith gave a gasping sob, as if she were frightened, and she clenched her fist by her side.

Dacian's eyes went down to the fallen candlestick and her curled fist. He looked back to her face. She sensed rather than saw his flash of understanding.

"Exeter?" he demanded. "You can't drive Lady Avely all the way to Exeter."

"I can if you lend me your post boy," said Nottley. "Lady Avely will stay by my side until I am safe, with this handy knife to play chaperone between us. You give me one whole day to arrange passage, then you may fetch her from Exeter." Judith kept her fist clenched. Nottley continued. "Though I add that if I hear anyone in pursuit, I will simply throw the lady out the window and leave it for you to tend to her injuries."

Judith flattened her hand by her side. Nottley was not bluffing on this matter. She swallowed against the pressure at her throat.

Dacian's face, already grim, became like granite. "You are mad."

"Maybe so, but I shall be mad in France. Oh, and there's one more thing. I want the Eye of Truth to take with me. Agatha told me about it and I rather fancy having it."

"That is a priceless heirloom," snapped Dacian. "You ask too much."

"Not at all. If I can't have Agatha as a wife, I need another way to seek my fortune. The Eye of Truth should guide me well. If all else fails, I can sell it to the highest bidder."

Judith drew a shaky breath. Nottley must not know that the Eye required Robert to wield it. The divination tool would be useless in Nottley's hand, but it would be a terrible loss to the Sargens.

"So do we have a deal?" Impatience sharpened his voice. "You'd best hurry, duke, or my hand might slip."

Dacian finally let his own hand drop, powerless, by his side. "Very well. I will call the steward; he is with Mary."

He bellowed for Lewis. The shout echoed in the vast space of the ballroom. Dacian bent and put the candelabra down slowly, so as to not startle Nottley. Then he stood, folding his arms across his chest. His face was lit from below now, stark and forbidding. It reminded Judith of another time when candlelight had lit his face, long ago, in the library. The time when he had lied to her face, out of some misguided sense of honour. Now he was lying again, this time to save her.

Lewis stumbled through from the west wing, beyond Judith's line of sight. He knocked the door back in a way that would earn him a reproving look from Fitzroy. Judith wondered where Robert was: probably collapsed in Bemusement in Mary's room.

"Yes, your grace?" Lewis's voice was nervous. He probably thought he was going to be chastised for losing Lady Mary.

Dacian didn't take his eyes off Nottley and Judith. "Run to the stables. Order Ned to ready the two greys for the post chaise at once, with William to drive. Mr Nottley and Lady Avely are leaving tonight for a journey to Exeter."

Lewis must have managed to gather himself, for he did not question this outrageous request. "Yes, your grace."

Nottley called over his shoulder. "Once you've done that, fetch my purse and valise from my room and put them in the chaise."

Lewis hesitated. "Yes, sir."

Dacian nodded his acquiescence. Judith heard the steward's feet move quickly down the southern gallery, at right angles to where she stood with Nottley. Out of the corner of her eye she saw Lewis descend the grand staircase down into the ballroom, bolt through the empty dance floor, and push through the large ballroom doors.

The duke spoke to Nottley. "You do realise that I am the only one who can fetch the *Lapis Veritatis*. I have put strong defences on the safe that only I can undo."

"Very well," snapped Nottley. "Then bring it to the ballroom and put it on the floor. I want you in my sight: by the wall but no further. If you come any closer, duke, this knife goes through her pretty little throat."

Judith twitched. Through the fear clogging her mind, she had just heard the clang of a lie in Nottley's voice.

Did this mean he lacked the resolution to kill her? She clenched her hand into a fist, uselessly. Dacian was already turning away, his shoulders set in a tense line. He strode along the western gallery, mirroring Lewis's path. Dacian still wore the purple mobcap; he must have forgotten all about it. Judith bit back a smile, feeling amusement well up in her despite the danger of her situation. The Bemusement was muffling her sense of preservation. Yet the blade still prodded into her neck and Nottley's grip on her arm was hard and unforgiving. The railing dug into her stomach and the dark drop threatened hollow beside her.

At the bottom of the grand staircase, Dacian paused and looked up from under his ribbons.

"I will look for you in Exeter tomorrow, Lady Avely."

She heard the lie but she dared not nod. He would look for her before that, she knew. He must have a plan to intercept them.

Dacian turned his implacable gaze to Nottley. "If you fail in our bargain, I will hunt you down and dismember you slowly. You know I am capable of it, Nottley."

Nottley sighed in Judith's ear, then raised his voice to speak into the void. "We are both on the same side, your grace. Let us work together now."

A grimace twisted Dacian's face. Then his expression flattened. He turned and pushed his way through the ballroom doors, leaving one propped open.

Judith felt a terrible aloneness, despite Nottley's presence breathing down her neck. The candelabra left behind gave only a dim light, leaving the huge room cornered in darkness. A moment's silence stretched while she and Nottley remained in their distorted embrace.

"You coward," she said coldly. "Using a woman to protect yourself."

"I prefer to call myself a strategist." Nottley pulled her roughly away from the railing. "To the stairs, my dear bargaining chip."

They lurched along the southern gallery in tandem, his hand like a vice on her upper arm. She wondered if she should try to twist out of his grasp, but a fight in close quarters with a knife was inadvisable. She had to be ready for when the intervention came, as surely it would.

Nottley pulled her to a halt at the top of the grand staircase. Judith almost tripped, her heart in her mouth, feeling the knife on her neck. The metal was warm now from resting on her skin for so long. She was only surprised that it had not yet nicked her flesh. Or perhaps it had and she did not know it, steeled into insensibility by the turmoil of the last hour. She imagined the blood dripping down her bodice, like one of Otho's awful spectres, then blinked rapidly. This was not the time to become overwrought. She must keep her wits about her, though they were already in tatters.

Nottley held her tight against him. "Time for a little chat, marchioness. How did you know it was I?"

Judith tried not to shudder at the scratch of his beard on her neck. "Mary told me."

"No, she didn't."

Belatedly, she remembered that it was her Discernment that had allowed her to parse the truth from Mary's lies. "She told me you blackmailed her. I guessed that Gilbert must have discovered you. However," she added, to distract him, "I thought you had left Sargenet the day he died. Why did you return?"

Nottley's voice was bitter. "Mary hadn't paid me. John, the jealous husband, kept following her round like a puppy dog. I had to pretend to leave, to allay his suspicions. Mary let me into the drawing room later."

With the spare key. "And Gilbert saw."

"Unfortunately for him. Luckily, Polonetheus was at hand. When he turned away, I grabbed the book and slammed it on his head."

Judith repressed a wince. "I'm surprised it was enough to kill him."

"Oh, it took a few whacks to be certain."

She said nothing. Her nerves were stretched beyond bearing. She needed this interval to rest and gather her resolve, but time seemed to extend out in a horrible suspense. What was Dacian doing? How could he leave her alone with this monster? She should be ready to flee if the opportunity arose but her feet were numb and her mind a desperate jumble.

At that moment, something swooped through the centre of the ballroom. It was a bat, flying in graceful arcs around the chandelier. Judith watched it in a daze, her heart quickening. Was it Marigold, or Wooten, or some Illusion?

The darting, quicksilver creature drew closer and flew around their heads. Nottley winced away from it, his grip tightening on Judith.

"What is that?" he snarled.

The bat landed, swinging from the railing. Before their eyes, it hauled itself up, and transformed into a small, naked figure with a halo of brown curls. Marigold.

"Damn it!" Nottley's grip relaxed slightly. "Miss Cultor."

The vampiri's eyes were fixed on Nottley. She was smiling. "Well met, Mr Nottley."

Judith drew a breath of astonishment, both real and pretend. Belatedly, she remembered that Nottley did indeed know Miss Cultor. They had been bonded blood companions before.

"Mind if I join you?" Marigold said sweetly, as if she were not standing stark naked and thirty feet above a dance floor.

"If you must," Nottley muttered. "What are you doing here? I thought I left you at the Gryffin."

Judith stayed very still, wondering what Marigold proposed to do.

The vampiri strutted along the railing, sublimely at ease. "I was in the Sargenet stables," she replied, "and I thought I'd pop into the house. I didn't realise you'd still be here."

Mr Nottley wrinkled his nose as he examined Marigold's bare limbs. "Got bored of stable-hands, did you?"

"The stable was interesting for a week," said Marigold airily, "then it became rather smelly. Are you still without a companion? I couldn't help but overhear that you are going to Exeter. I could be convinced to visit the seaside."

"I suppose you might be useful," allowed Nottley.

Marigold smiled happily, then she looked at Judith, raising a brow. "And who is this?"

"Lady Avely," sighed Nottley. "As you see, she is providing surety for my trip."

"Hmm." Marigold sat on the railing and swung her legs idly. "She is practicing some kind of magic. I can sense it."

Judith stared. "I am not," she said hoarsely.

"Yes, you are." Marigold kicked a bare leg. "I can sense Musing. I can't imagine that Mr Nottley is practicing Memory right now, so it must be you."

Judith furrowed her brows. What was Marigold trying to say? "I swear to you, I am not practicing magic," she snapped.

Nottley interposed. "In fact, I am trying to recall the local map - to determine the fastest route to Exeter. For God's sake, Miss Cultor," he added, "where are your clothes?"

It was transparently an attempt to change the subject. Judith felt his clammy breath on her neck. What was he hiding?

"Oh, my gown was dreadfully cumbersome," said Marigold airily.

"Well, don't hang round here," snapped Nottley. "Do you want to breach the Edicts?"

"You're breaking a lot more than the Edicts." Marigold gave a pointed look at the letter-opener across Judith's neck. "Do you expect to receive many letters in Exeter?"

"Ha," said Nottley. "Yes, when I let it be known about my latest acquisition."

"Where did you find the knife?" Marigold continued, with an odd, flat note in her voice. "It is pretty."

"In the study," he replied. "A neat little blade, is it not?"

Judith froze.

His words scraped like glass over stone. He was lying. He hadn't found it in the study. And it wasn't a neat little blade.

It took her a moment to realise the truth: the letter-opener was an Illusion. It was being cast with the magic that Marigold now sensed.

It was a small Illusion, enough to convince her - and the duke - that Nottley held a weapon all along.

Judith remembered, suddenly, the decapitated, bloody mice. Small Illusions, placed there to scare her. Just like this one. It must have been Nottley who had cast those particular horrors, watching her from the shadows of the trees and the hall. After Agatha had asked him to warn Judith away, he had tried to do it by frightening her. For of course a matron would be afraid of a mouse.

She drew a deep breath, feeling the pressure at her neck. *Something* was pressed against her skin. If not a knife, then what? It was something long, thin, and cold.

Marigold winked at her, quick as blink.

What could it be? Judith cast her mind about, searching for the answer. Whatever it was, Nottley had not found it in the study, for that had been a lie. He must have fetched it from his own room, or Agatha's.

The truth came to her in a flash. Before her mind's eyes, she saw Agatha's dresser with its set of steel knitting needles resting on the wood. Two long, metal rods with pointy ends. Long, thin, and cold.

Nottley was holding a knitting needle.

In which light is shed

If a lady finds herself confronting the criminal elements, she will be forgiven for using any tool available to apprehend them.
   - from *Lady Avely's Guide to Truth and Magic*

JUDITH WEIGHED HER CHANCES: they looked better now. She might be able to overcome Nottley. She might even stab the knitting needle through his eye. Marigold was also here, so between them they should manage a cowardly scholar who had no access to his books. Agatha's knitting needles, she remembered, were pointed at both ends; they were not in the new Continental fashion with knobs.

At that moment, the ballroom door swung open. Nottley's breathing hitched once more. Dacian stepped into the ballroom below them.

He was still wearing the mobcap which, combined with the huge scale of the ballroom, somehow diminished his figure. It did not, however, disguise his scowl. His black brows were lowered thunderously, his lips pressed in a grim line, his cheekbones slanted sharply.

Nottley took a step backwards, wrenching Judith with him. He was still half-afraid of Dacian's power.

"Stay there! Or I slice her open!"

This time the clanging lie made sense, but Judith's clenched fist was too late. Dacian stayed, glowering. He held a small wooden box in his hands. Even at this distance, she could see it was the same beautifully crafted receptacle that he had shown her before: containing the *Lapis Veritas*.

"Put it at the foot of the stairs." Nottley's voice rasped loudly in Judith's ear.

Wordlessly, Dacian strode forward and placed the box at the bottom step. He did not look at Judith. He retreated, fists clenched by his side, to stand in the far corner of the ballroom.

"Turn around," Nottley yelled, making Judith jump.

The duke glared. Yet he said nothing and turned to face the wall, putting his back to them both. It gave the ballroom a good view of his silken mobcap. His hands flexed helplessly, then clenched into fists once more.

Judith's chest was hot, her throat dry. She tried to think clearly. This was their chance, but they must act together. How could she gauge the right moment if Dacian was not even looking at her?

Her eyes dropped to his clenched fists. Was it a sign of his impotent rage, or was it a different type of signal? She remembered his expressionless mien, his grim silence. His face had been like a mask.

Like an Illusion.

Judith drew a ragged breath, eyes narrowing. The figure with his back to them was not Dacian. His shoulders were not broad enough. It was a likeness of him, framed by the ballroom and given extra visual emphasis by that ridiculous purple mobcap. Dacian would have looked at her, and given her the reassurance of his gaze. They must be his clothes only, on another: Robert or Lewis.

Robert had cast an admirable Illusion of the duke's scowl, but he hadn't dared risk imitating his voice.

Dacian was somewhere else.

"Come, marchioness," growled Nottley. "Down the stairs. Don't try anything."

They lurched down, step by step in a horrible dance. Judith heart was hammering, even though she knew it was only a knitting needle at her throat. Her heightened senses could feel the wisp of power gathering in the air and she only hoped that Nottley would not notice.

She cast a furtive glance round the upper gallery. A glimpse of shadow moved along the east side. She quickly averted her gaze, though Nottley could not see her face.

Fortunately, Nottley was focused on the difficulty of guiding them both down the steps. Marigold added her own mite of distraction, whizzing down the polished bannister on her bare bottom.

"Wheeee!" she shouted at the top of her voice.

"Must you, Miss Cultor?" snapped Nottley.

Marigold flew off the end of the bannister, somersaulted, and landed on her two feet. "Ouch. I think I got a splinter."

Nottley snarled. "This sort of conduct is why I bade you stay in my room."

"Spoilsport," said Marigold sulkily. "Can I borrow your handkerchief next time?"

Nottley ignored that indecent suggestion, and jerked Judith to a stop after the last stair. The wooden box lay at her feet.

"We bend together. You pick it up," Nottley hissed in her ear, keeping the steel rod pressed against her neck.

She nodded minutely. Nottley pushed her forward.

Marigold, hands on hips, tilted her head.

Judith braced herself, then grasped at the steel at her throat. Instead of the sharp blade she still half expected, her fingers met the familiar length of a knitting needle.

This was something she knew how to wield. Quickly, she wrenched it out of Nottley's grip. Taking him by surprise, she twisted violently, quick as a purl knit, and stabbed the needle in his shoulder.

She threw herself to the left, and he let out a high-pitched shriek.

A blast of power came from the gallery above. It whipped past Judith, fluttering her skirts. The force flattened Nottley on the stairs, knocking him over as if he had been hit by an invisible pile of rocks. Abruptly, his scream silenced.

Judith sank to the floor, shaking. The wooden floor had never felt so solid. She put her cheek against its comforting surface, disregarding any audience, and drawing deep breaths to fill her lungs.

"Serves you right!" shouted Marigold, dancing around Nottley's fallen form. "You crazy old ... scholar!"

Dacian appeared at the top of the grand staircase. He was dressed in Lewis's plain black coat and brown breeches. His hands were held out in front of him but he lowered them slowly. Nottley wasn't going anywhere: his bearded head lolled, oddly still.

"Judith." Dacian's voice was hoarse with anxiety. "Are you alright?"

She lifted her cheek from the floor. "I'm fine." She cleared her throat, seeing that he didn't believe her. "You've returned to your former masculine glory, I perceive."

Dacian smiled and patted his black locks. "The mobcap suits Lewis better."

She turned to see that Lewis had abandoned his post by the wall, his true face revealed. He was dressed in the duke's dark blue breeches, white waistcoat, and blue coat tails, which on closer inspection hung slightly on his smaller frame. His usually sullen expression was transformed by a boyish grin. He ripped the purple mobcap off his head and cast it on the ground.

"What a lark!" he exclaimed. "Is Nottley dead, do you think?"

"I hope not." Dacian came leisurely down the stairs, as if making an appearance at a ball. "I can't afford another dead body. I intend to stay in England this time."

At that moment, Nottley stirred and muttered something unintelligible. He opened his eyes to find Dacian looming over him.

"You're coming with me," said Dacian. He hauled Nottley up, grabbing him by both shoulders. He stalked out the room, Nottley shouting as he was carried with his feet hanging a yard above the ground.

Judith pulled herself to sit on the bottom step, still shivering a little with reaction. She had come close to death herself, even if Lewis thought it was all a great adventure. The dark, hollow drop from the gallery flashed before her eyes again, making her shudder.

"Wasn't I clever?" Marigold chirped from the floor. "I spotted his Illusion. There was no blood on that knife, which made me suspicious. And I could sense the Musing."

"Very clever." Wooten's voice came from the ballroom door. "You hussy, put that mobcap on at once."

Judith glanced over to see the male vampiri still immaculately dressed and trotting his way over, a scandalised look on his face. For a moment, she thought he was talking to her, then she saw Marigold flounce over to the purple silk.

"*You* should wear it," huffed Marigold. "I don't wear purple."

"You don't wear *anything*," retorted Wooten.

Marigold busied herself with tying the mobcap haphazardly around herself, while Wooten issued advice. After a while, Dacian returned and strode over to the stairs where Judith still sat in a daze. He sat down beside her and put an arm round her shoulders. "Lean on me. You're freezing."

She leaned into him thankfully. She was very Bemused, and so was he, from the night's trials. They might be forgiven for blurring decorum a little. Proper lines could be redrawn in the morning. Right now, she was in need of some warmth and strength to bolster her nerves.

"Did he hurt you?" Dacian asked roughly.

"No," she lied.

Dacian muttered under his breath and a pressure formed in the air. It dropped away just as suddenly. He sighed and drew her closer, his arm a strong bar round her. She melted against him, letting her eyes flutter closed.

"Admit it," he murmured in her ear. "I was manly even in the mobcap."

"I admit nothing."

"If you want me to put it back on again, I will."

She turned her head to smile up at him. "I am the one who wears mobcaps, not you."

"More's the pity." His lashes were so dark, his lips curving and sensuous. Judith's own lips parted slightly.

At that moment, Robert entered the ballroom, his face flushed, his hair disordered. His footman's livery was not in its usual neat condition.

His face was split in a huge grin. "Did I do good?" He was slightly unsteady on his feet as he approached and gave a little bow. "Your grashe, it was an honour to Illushe you."

Oh dear. Robert was thoroughly musedrunk. His pupils were dilated, his smile infectious.

"Hmm," said Dacian, his arm still round Judith. "You made my head too big."

"Not at all," said Robert anxiously. "It wash the mobcap."

Wooten tutted. "A gentleman should never have to contend with a mobcap."

Dacian rested his head against Judith's hair. "I quite agree."

"You did very well indeed, Robert," she said. "The head was well proportioned and the scowl most life-like."

Dacian murmured, "I *am* rather well-proportioned, I'll have you know."

Judith blushed.

Wooten said, "You were *well-proportioned* as Lady Mary."

Dacian lifted his head to glare. "I trust you will all refrain from mentioning it in the future."

Marigold now looked like a round, purple flower, but she was inspecting the knitting needle that had fallen to the ground. "Where did Nottley find this?"

Judith explained. "It's Agatha's."

"You have a vicious right hook, my love," said Dacian. A tingling warmth ran through Judith at his term of endearment.

"I can't say I feel sorry for him." Lewis cast a dispassionate glance to where Nottley had fallen. "Good job, Lady Avely."

"Ay," said Robert admiringly, weaving on his feet though he was standing in one spot. "A shtout heart."

He grinned at her and Judith smiled back, glad that their joint brush with danger had softened the edges between them. She only hoped that it would not fade with their Bemusement.

"I quite agree." However, Dacian finally pulled his arm away from Judith's shoulders. "But now it's time for sleep. To bed, everyone."

Judith found herself bereft. She stared owlishly at him. "Are you ordering me about?"

"If you want, certainly."

"I most certainly do not." On the other hand....

"Well, shall I provide something hot and comforting instead?"

She blinked, all sorts of things springing, unbidden, into her mind. "What would that be?"

"Spanish chocolate?"

Judith stared. Dacian raised an eyebrow, grinning. Was he trying to seduce her or distract her?

Robert coughed and clicked his heels together. "I can fetch shome at once, my lady," he said solemnly.

"Lewis had better do it." The duke turned his head to examine the inebriated Robert. "You're not in any fit state to carry boiling hot liquid."

"Happy to assist." Lewis flung an arm over Robert's shoulders. "I'm not an expert, however, so I might have to taste it to make sure it is correctly prepared."

Dacian sighed. "Make four cups then," he allowed. "You both deserve some. Bring them up to the Gold Room, and we can all partake before bed."

Marigold tutted disapprovingly. "You'll all go deaf."

Lewis grinned and escorted Robert out the ballroom, keeping his weaving to a fairly straight line.

"What do you say, my dear?" Dacian turned back to Judith. "Chocolate in the Gold Room?"

Judith pursed her lips, considering. "I suppose it will be timely." She let her voice drop an octave. "Just what I need: something warm and indulgent in my bed."

Dacian's eyes darkened. "I couldn't agree more."

DACIAN INSISTED on carrying Judith back to her bedroom. She didn't have the heart to protest and he had strength to spare. He swept her up, unresisting, into his arms, and she nestled against his chest, revelling in the smell of him. She was Bemused, that was all. Perfectly and utterly Bemused.

In the Gold Room, he laid her tenderly on the bed.

"I'll be back soon," he said, holding her hand. "I must check on Nottley, and put the lapis away. Save some of that warm indulgence for me."

Once he left, Judith sat up and lit as many candles as she could. She was sick of dim, dark spaces. Soon the whole room was bathed in golden light: the bedspread glowing, the wood gleaming, every inch and corner lit up.

The curtains were drawn against the night, but she wondered if dawn was close. She didn't feel tired yet, still wound up from the night's events. A delicious flush still permeated her body from the duke's embrace. What would happen when he returned? Could she - would she - take advantage of him?

Yet slowly, in dribs and drabs, her wits came back. The conversation in Mary's room returned to her: Dacian's confession of how he had misled her all those years ago. She sat down abruptly on the bed, biting her lip. How could he have lied to her? How could he have renounced her? An aching fondness stirred in her, mixed with a desire to throttle him. He had allowed her to believe that falsehood for decades, and she was not certain she was ready to forgive him. After all, whether or not he had bedded Mrs Bleau, the result had been the same: Judith had left Sargenet with a broken heart. The fissure still remained.

And even when Nicholas had died, and she had discovered the truth about Robert, Dacian had simply left the country for nine years. His feelings could not be very strong. Not like hers. Judith's shoulders sank.

A tiny tap at the door heralded Marigold, carrying her yellow gown in her claws. Judith let her in, and Marigold dropped onto the bed, transforming into a naked woman in a tumble of yellow silk.

"Can you believe that fop, Wooten?" demanded Marigold as

she pulled on her gown. "Too much of a namby-pamby to take off his clothes and fly to the rescue."

"I suppose he helped Lewis dress in the duke's clothes," said Judith mildly.

"Yes, so he didn't have to muss his cravat."

"You two seem to enjoy each other's company," said Judith ironically.

Marigold looked up from her ties. "We are not bickering to flirt, like you and the duke, if that's what you mean." Judith blushed and Marigold continued. "Besides, Wooten is not my style. I prefer lady-bats."

"Oh," said Judith. "Really?"

"And while Wooten is quite feminine, he is not womanly enough for me." Marigold gave her a defiant glare.

"Indeed."

"Anyway, I suppose there was no point in both of us flying into danger," she sniffed.

"You did very well. I would be honoured if you would consider remaining my companion for a little longer," said Judith tentatively. "You could come to Cornwall, you know. Lanyon Castle is to be exempt from the Edicts and you will be able to fly about as you like."

Marigold raised a brow and flounced down on the bed. "Intriguing. I suppose *you*, at least, are not boring. Do you promise not to read or wield Polonetheus?"

"I swear on my honour." Judith grimaced. She rather preferred *boring* to the clutches of a murderer. "Do you think there is any chance Robert will come to Cornwall too? What if I invited Lewis as well?"

"The duke might have something to say about *that*," replied Marigold, nodding toward the door.

Judith turned to see Dacian. Her heart thumped at the sight of him, his dark hair tousled, his frown lines marked, his eyes tired but warm. He was still in Lewis's clothes, the black coat tight across his chest.

"Are you trying to steal away my staff, Judith?"

"Just for a short while," she lied.

He came to sit next to her on the chaise, indecently close. She allowed it, even as his warm presence set her heart racing. He took her hand and she felt a fission of energy bolt through her. All her doubts seemed suddenly superfluous. Marigold pretended to busy herself with her ties.

"Is everything under lock and key?" Judith asked.

"Yes, all safe. Now," Dacian settled his shoulders against the chaise and gave her a quizzical look. "What were you saying earlier about my masculine glory?"

She blushed. "Oh, you know very well what I meant."

"I'd like to hear it again." The gleam in his eye made her quiver. "Especially from you."

"Well, as you know, you have a small dose of masculine vigor," she said airily, and untruthfully. It was a very large dose from where she was sitting.

He leaned closer. "Perhaps I can increase the measure. I wonder how."

Just then, however, Lewis kicked the door open with his foot, carrying in a tray with a large pot and four cups on it. Dacian gave her a private smile and squeezed her hand before turning to face Lewis.

"The divine brew," Lewis announced, smiling in an unsteward-like way. "As ordered."

"Oh, thank goodness," said Judith with feeling.

Dacian sighed. "Once again, I am outshone."

Lewis grinned. "You can't help it if you aren't frothy, your grace." He put the tray down on the rosewood table before Judith.

"It does smell good," admitted Marigold from the bed.

"What is the secret ingredient?" asked Judith, as she set about pouring a cup of the creamy beverage. "Will you tell me now?"

Dacian held her gaze. "Only if you promise not to leave tomorrow."

"Very well," she said with dignity, as if it did not accord with her own inclination.

"It is two ingredients, actually."

"Oh?"

"Saffron, and another golden flower called doradozón. It is reputed to have comforting properties."

"That explains the lovely colour." She handed him a cup, allowing their fingers to brush.

Just then, Robert came in. Judith was glad to see that his cheeks were less flushed and his gait more steady. Wooten was on his shoulder.

"Ah, chocolate!" he said. "Just what we need."

Marigold tutted.

Wooten looked around from his vantage point, and his gaze fixed on Lewis in the duke's clothes. "My dear sir, you *really* ought not be wearing that coat without a cravat."

"I wasn't given a cravat." Lewis defended himself. "If the duke wasn't wearing one, you can't expect *me* to wear one."

Dacian laughed and took a sip of chocolate. "My cravat was used for indecent purposes," he said. "Under Wooten's instructions, I might add."

Wooten ignored that. "In fact, you *really* oughtn't be wearing that coat at all."

"Take it off, Mr Lewis!" said Marigold, from the bed. "I concur that clothes are cursed uncomfortable."

Wooten turned to glare. Then his expression became one of outraged shock as Robert picked him up between thumb and forefinger and deposited him on the chaise armrest.

"There." Robert turned to Dacian. "What did you do with the rascally scholar? Do you need help restraining him?"

"Dear boy," said Dacian, taking another sip. "I'm quite capable. I've locked him in a room with some strong Defences. No one should be able to get in or out without my say-so. We'll haul him before a justice tomorrow."

Lewis looked worried. "Lady Agatha won't be happy."

Having poured the chocolate, Judith removed herself to a safe distance by sitting on the bed, but she kicked off her kid slippers and swung her legs up in an unladylike fashion. Her ankles were exposed but she was trying to seduce a duke. Wasn't she? "I think you will find Agatha will be glad to escape an engagement. She prefers illicit liaisons and Nottley wanted marriage."

The duke cast her a smouldering look under his brows but declined to comment, simply passing her a cup of chocolate.

Over sips of hot, aromatic cocoa, they all chattered. Lewis demanded an account of what had happened in Lady Mary's room, so Marigold and Wooten took over the tale, describing the various encounters. Lewis seemed to find it very amusing that Otho had named his skull Manfred.

The duke pulled the spindly chair close to the bed. Marigold, in a fit of uncharacteristic propriety, manoeuvred a blanket to cover Judith's feet and ankles. Judith sleepily allowed it. The warmth of the chocolate filled her stomach and the heat of Dacian's glances sent tingles across her skin.

Yet she was more tired than she knew, her mind vague and weary. As the others talked, she drifted off into sleep, the cup empty in her hands. She was only hazily aware of Dacian hustling everyone out, taking her cup, and pulling a claret-coloured blanket over her.

"Shouldn't we talk?" she murmured, putting out a hand. "Or ... something else?"

He took her hand, his eyes crinkling at the corners.

"Tomorrow, my love." He brushed a finger lightly down her cheek. Her eyes fluttered closed with pleasure. "We have plenty of time."

In which a question is left unanswered

A lie can last for many years before you stumble across it.
  - from *Lady Avely's Guide to Truth and Magic*

THE NEXT MORNING, Judith slept very late and awoke to a tapping on the door. A maid bore in a steaming cup of chocolate, the rich scent making Judith sit up. She was still tired, but in a comforting, restful sort of way, her limbs heavy beneath the blankets that Dacian had placed over her.

Late morning light streamed through the windows as the maid pulled the curtains open. "His grace wishes to see you below-stairs," she said. "When you are ready, that is, my lady."

Judith permitted his grace that request and took a thoughtful sip of chocolate. Her mind was much clearer now, and she certainly had a few things to say to Dacian. She had promised to linger one more day and she would make the most of it. She might even finally welcome his attentions - serious or not - if he could answer one question to her satisfaction.

After leisurely finishing the chocolate and a tray of breakfast, she dressed in a lilac gown and defiantly put on the matching mobcap. If Dacian took it as a challenge, so be it. The soft lilac rather suited her blonde colouring, and the long sleep had restored her countenance. Or perhaps it was anticipation flushing her cheeks.

Downstairs, she encountered Robert in the breakfast room. He bowed, looking rather wan but cheerful as he waited at his post. No one else was about.

"Are you feeling alright, my lady?" he murmured as she passed by.

"Better," she replied with a smile. "You? You're on duty early. I'll have a stern word with his grace."

"It's past midday." Robert grinned. "Though I've a bit of a headache, I'll admit. I think we both overtaxed ourselves last night."

Judith paused, considering. She was not above making the most of their new camaraderie. "Have you thought more on Cornwall? You could simply come for a visit, you know, and spend some time painting the landscapes. It need not be for long."

His grin wavered a little. "I'm not sure, my lady. I wouldn't want to ... impose."

She swallowed, feeling the weight and judgement of that sentence. "You would not be an imposition," she said firmly, and truly meant it for the first time. "I am certain my son and daughter would like to meet you."

He blinked nervously. "A strange proposition for us all. Yet I don't want to abandon Lewis. He is more a brother to me, if you don't mind me saying."

Suddenly, Judith was aware of an unexpected wish that Nicholas, too, could meet his son now, and see the man he had grown into. She realised that her anger toward her husband was fading, replaced with compassion. And she was not going to give up her quest easily.

She withdrew to the door, and paused, resting her fingers on the frame. "Lewis is thinking of leaving Sargenet. Why don't you invite him to Cornwall too?"

Robert was startled. "I doubt you have the resources for us both, my lady."

"I may certainly invite guests for a few weeks. Also, Lewis might be useful with his Gift. Not all is right at the castle, I've heard."

"The castle?"

"Yes, just a little castle. Apparently, it has its own ghosts. I might need some help, between your artistic endeavours."

"Oh." Robert's face was a picture of curiosity and wariness. "I could ask Lewis, I suppose...."

Judith accepted this gladly. "Now, do you know where the duke might be?"

Robert nodded. "He said to tell you that he is waiting for you in the rose arbour."

Judith turned away, repressing a smile. So Dacian was finally going to show her the roses, was he? Twenty-three years too late. Or perhaps now was just the right time.

She picked up her skirts and made her way sedately out of the house, her heart beating rather fast for a matron on a garden stroll.

The day held the lovely calm of autumn, clouds blanketing the sky. She approached the arbour, laden with white, pink, and deep red roses. The blooms were still extravagantly unfurled despite the receding summer, and she passed under their bowed curves.

Dacian was sitting on a wooden bench, near an archway covered entirely in tiny red roses. He stood, dressed in well-fitting tan breeches and coat. It set off his dark colouring, and his eyes lit up at the sight of her.

"Judith. How do you feel?"

"Much better, thank you." She coloured faintly, remembering

her behaviour last night: but why blush at that now, when she might do much worse?

"Come." He held out his hand. "I've wanted to show you this secret for a while now."

She put her hand in his, and he led her through the arch of tiny roses. The fragrance was heady: a sweet, delicate scent. The arch opened on a small arbour with a bubbling fountain at its centre, in a deep, round pool. Around them, the climbing roses completely shielded them from view.

A stone bench circled the pool. Dacian gestured for her to sit.

She did so, reluctantly disengaging her hand, and found that she did not know what to say.

"Feel the water," he grinned.

Raising her brows, she drew her gloves off and put her fingertips in the pool. It was warm. The heat was both surprising and sensuous.

"Goodness. A hot spring."

"It's been here for centuries, but we try to keep it quiet. Nice for bathing."

She was suddenly struck with an image of Dacian sliding, naked, into the warm water. She cleared her throat. "Certainly. A private spot."

"We could try it sometime. Tonight even, if you are brave enough."

Her cheeks warmed at his audacity. "Don't rush me, Dacian."

He looked abashed and pulled her bare hand to his lips. "I have waited so long, Judith."

Heat tingled from her skin all the way into the centre of her being.

"Have you?" She wanted to hear it, so she let him retain his grip. Besides them, the fountain bubbled harmoniously.

"Decades. You know it. Ever since I met you, I wanted you."

She squeezed his fingers to still the trembling in her own.

"Why did you give me away then? How could you let me choose Nicholas?"

Dacian's gaze darkened. "You had already chosen Nicholas, and he had chosen you. I did not want to come between you. He was my friend, and a good man, despite his sins."

"So are you," she said slowly, "and it was for me to decide."

"I see that now." He looked down. "If it is any consolation, I suffered agonies for it."

Her heart constricted and she brought her other hand up to finally trace her fingers along his face: the strong jaw, the sharp cheekbones, the full lips. Her whole body was quivering with the magnitude of it. Yet - did Dacian mean the agony of love or that of frustrated passion? Unbidden, she wondered if he had brought many other widows to this hot spring, in a practiced act of seduction. The thought plagued her even as she tried to dismiss it.

She met his eyes. "I have one more question for you."

"Anything."

"Why didn't you write to me? While you were abroad?" She dropped her hand. "Nine years is a long time to go without word."

He drew a breath. "It was difficult for me. What happened at Garvey House - what I saw."

This was unexpected and she raised her brows, confused. "What you saw? What do you mean?"

Beside them, the water gurgled and insects hummed among the roses. Dacian withdrew his hand from her lap, his brow creasing.

He said, "You and Lord Garvey alone, in the maze that night."

Judith thought she had misheard. She frowned. "What?"

"I saw you, Judith. In one of the alcoves. Half-clothed." Dacian's voice hardened a little. "I take full responsibility for my actions, but I was wild with jealousy. And I assumed you would not want to hear from *me*, either, after what happened."

Judith stared, uncomprehendingly. Then she began to grow

angry, as the import of his words sank in. "I was *not* alone with Lord Garvey."

"I saw you, Judith."

"You were mistaken," she said icily. "And I certainly was not *half-clothed*. How dare you suggest such a thing?"

Dacian's fists clenched in his lap. A faint pressure gathered in the air as his frown deepened to a scowl.

"I was not mistaken," he ground out. "You were wearing that black dress with the gold trimmings. It had fallen down to your waist."

Judith's eyes widened with horror and anger. "I swear to you, that never happened."

His angry gaze met hers, questioning and tense. Then the pressure faded and his hands loosened, as he saw the truth in her face.

"Then who, or *what*," he said, "did I see that night?"

"Another woman," she said coldly, "who you mistook for me. It sounds like you weren't looking at her *face*."

Dacian's jaw hardened again. "It was unmistakably you. Do you think I would kill a man simply on a hunch?"

"I don't know!" she snapped. "You must have been drunk!"

He stood and began pacing. "I *was* drunk, but I can't have mistaken that dress. I remember it too well, even now." He shot her a glance. "And I did see your face - clearly in the moonlight!"

Judith, too, could hear that he was telling the truth as he saw it. She gnawed on her lip. "Where did this all happen?"

A hint of discomfort flashed across his features. "I was walking in the hedge maze, and came across the Apollo alcove; you know the one, with the statue. You were leaning back against the stone, and I saw your profile. Your lips were parted, your eyes closed, but it was you. Your blonde hair spilled over your shoulders, undone, and the gold lace of your bodice was trailing over your hips."

Judith swallowed at this picture of abandon. "Are you certain you weren't so distracted by - er - what my bodice revealed, that you became confused?"

Dacian let out a sharp bark of laughter. "Lord, Judith, yes, I was distracted, and half mad with jealousy. But it was undeniably you. Which leaves me with an unsavoury conclusion."

"What?" Judith was still bamboozled by the fact that Dacian had, up until a minute ago, believed he had seen her exposed breasts. She did not know where to look, *even though it wasn't true*.

"I must have seen an Illusion," said Dacian grimly. "And Illusion expressly designed to enrage me so that I would kill Lord Garvey."

... To be continued in

*Lady Avely's **Guide to Lies and Charms***

Author's Note

Thank you for reading *Lady Avely's Guide to Truth and Magic*. If you enjoyed it, please say so in a review. Reviews are essential to any book's success, and I appreciate any time you take to write one.

Lady Avely's Guide to Lies and Charms is out now if you want to hasten back to that rose garden. Or you could subscribe to my Patreon - and read an earlier scene from the duke's point of view that I rewrote just for fun.

To keep up with my new releases, book recs, and recipes, you can simply join my mailing list at rosalieoaks.com/newsletter. Subscribers also receive a free e-book, *A Pendant for Trouble*, which provides the low-down on what exactly happened to plunge Miss Elinor Avely (Judith's daughter) into scandal in London.

Much love to my readers. You make this whole authorly endeavour even possible.

Happy reading and chocolate drinking!

Rosalie

Thank you to Patrons

A huge thank you to my Patrons who have supported me throughout the long year that it took to write this book.

Your generosity and encouragement are very much appreciated.

Annelise Bauer
Julie Margaret Collins
Tania Clucas
Anna Fridlund
Myra Galland
Sarah Hamblin
Ginny Harris
Linda Hawkins
Justin Kennedy
Shane Kennedy
Mary Lee Vacca
Susan Mason
Kristin Rafe
Karen Slater

Much love to you, and my eternal gratitude!

Deep thanks also to my proof-readers, *Xenia Tashlitsky* and *Carmen Rutter-Hedley*, who graciously gave their time to polish this manuscript.

With love,
Rosalie

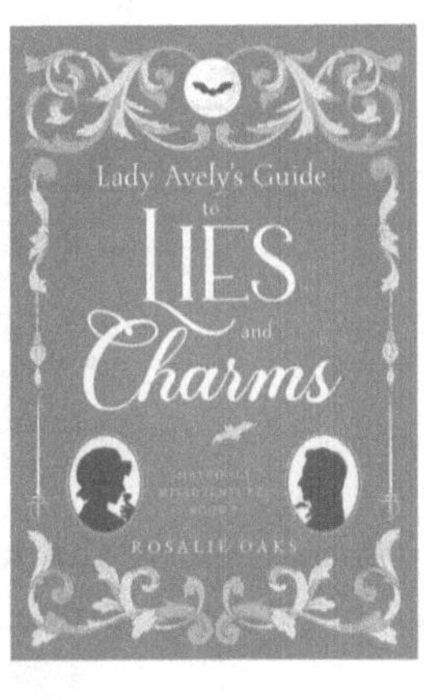

Lady Avely's Guide to Lies and Charms

(Matronly Misadventures 2)

A lady shouldn't be seen to incite a duel... but Judith wasn't even there when it happened.

Lady Avely doesn't know what infuriates her more: that someone used her image to provoke the Duke of Sargen into killing a man, or that the duke actually believed it was *her* trysting in the maze that night.

Now she and the duke must concoct their own subterfuge to shake out the culprit. Otherwise, Dacian might be arrested for murder, or worse, the shadowy guardians of the Musing might inflict their own cruel punishment for the misuse of his Gift. Judith will need her most respectable mobcap, and unfortunately, the duke will need a false moustache.

With Judith's ability to detect lies and Dacian's now carefully contained power, they set out to uncover the truth - but their own hearts make them easy to manipulate. Facing a master of deception, as well as the duke's renewed determination to win her, Judith will need a stiff drink of chocolate and the help of her cheerful, tiny vampiri companion before she can find her way out of the deadly tangle...

Can Judith and Dacian unmask the killer before more blood is shed? And how many different ways can one disguise a duke?

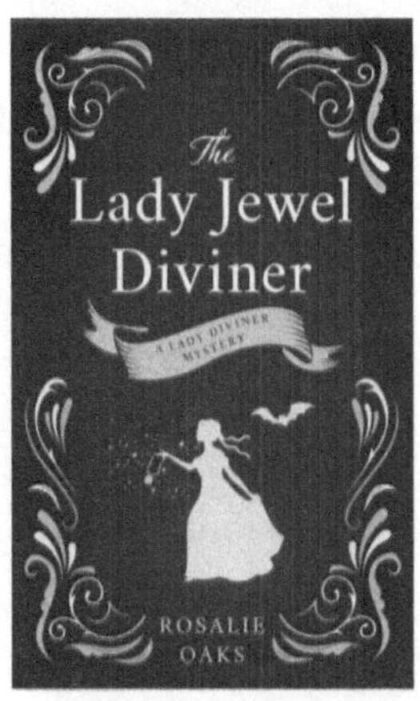

The Lady Jewel Diviner

(Lady Diviner 1)

Diamonds, Death, and Devonshire tea... in a magical Regency England

Miss Elinor Avely's proper upbringing cannot prepare her for the tiny, spinster vampire who crashes into her sitting room and demands to be fed with a sheep.

Elinor already has enough troubles without having to catch ruminants.

First, her gift for divining jewels has landed her in scandal and exiled her from London society.

Second, a nobleman of dubious repute has asked her to find a cache of smuggled jewels, hidden somewhere along the Devon coastline.

Last – and worst – Elinor has been invited to cream tea at the local manor. And while the autocratic and magnificent Earl of Beresford might be there (and perhaps the jewels themselves too), Beresford is the last person Elinor wants to meet over cream tea.

When a dead body is discovered along the cliffs, of course, such delicate considerations become secondary. Fortunately, Elinor now has a small vampiric chaperone – even if said spinster has a habit of appearing stark naked – and together they are ready to risk the hard questions.

Where are the jewels hidden? Who killed the smuggler? And just when *is* the cream tea being served?

The Lady Jewel Diviner is the first book in a cosy mystery series set in Regency England, with generous servings of magic, manners, and romance.

About the Author

Rosalie Oaks writes novels set in a magical Regency England full of manners, mystery, and soothing beverages. As a child, she loved conducting home-made theatre productions with her three younger brothers. Now she directs her characters instead, but like her brothers, they don't always do what she says.

While writing, Rosalie consumes vast quantities of tea and chocolate, and steadfastly ignores the housework.

Further intimate details, such as her favourite books and recipes, can be found in her Private Tea Parlour on Patreon.

Books by Rosalie Oaks

Lady Diviner

A Pendant for Trouble (prequel novella)

The Lady Jewel Diviner

The Moria Pearls

The Sapphire Library

The Golden Flute

The Selkie Scandal (an internovella)

Matronly Misadventures

Lady Avely's Guide to Truth and Magic

Lady Avely's Guide to Lies and Charms

Lady Avely's Guide to Guile and Peril

(releasing 2025)

rosalieoaks.com